The Red Chill

The Red Chill

Sandman

iUniverse, Inc.
New York Bloomington

The Red Chill

iUniverse books may be ordered through booksellers or by contacting:

iUniverse
1663 Liberty Drive
Bloomington, IN 47403
www.iuniverse.com
1-800-Authors (1-800-288-4677)

ISBN- 978-1-4401-9476-4 (sc)
ISBN- 978-1-4401-9477-1 (ebk)

Printed in the United States of America

iUniverse rev. date: 11/25/2009

It's a cold summer morning Dannie just awake to a cold chill. The window she hadn't closed was letting in a cold icy wind. Slipping out of bed still in the nude she walked to the window to close it. Looking out over the corn field that made a wall around her yard. The sounds of an animal crying in the woods beyond the fields of corn, chills run up her back her nibbles harden as if she was hearing a long loss lover. It had a sound for something being hurt or killed, she was cold and sleepy still so she returns to her warm bed.

Dannie was a model in the small town of East Millinocket.East Millinocket was a town like any other in the USA, sleepy with a mill making up one side of town and Main street down the center. The town as you came in had a grave yard at one end and a Morgue at the other side of town. You could say the town was surrounded with death. Dannie could remember what the town was like in her younger days. The mills were fill with people and everyone had a job the school had lots of kids. The main street stores were all filled with locals and flatlanders. Now it's only a shell of its old day charms. Almost a house on every block was for sale dirt cheap.

Dannie had Long blonde hair and a body that would stop a tree from falling to the ground. She loved the quiet county and it's warm charm. Work was enjoyable but sometimes hard. She lived in a small log home with and beautiful view of a corn field and a mountain in the far center of her back yard. Like something out of a Norman Rockwell painting. She loved spending time on her deck sunning herself and making her body tan. In the local town not a mile away a group of people meeting about the death of a kid last night. The child was pulled apart and half eaten. The locals feared it maybe a large cat or some type of wild dog. Fred said it would have been really big to eat as much of the kid as it did. Fred was a local hunter. He was a cross between a big hairy bear and smelly hillbilly.

The town manager Al said big or not it has to be hunted down and killed. Al was a tall man with gold hair in his middle 40th.He got the job as manager because he was about the smartest one in town and he was in movies awhile back, will if you can call porn movies. The local doctor and coroner Mike said maybe this was a one time thing. Mike was an ugly man 5'3" hairy than an ape and scary as hell itself.

Fred said most animal hunts within a small area where they can find loses for food. The town manager Al said lets put on a few more cops on tonight here, keep moving around the town to see if they could see anything. What about the FBI think we should call them in on the case. Mike said maybe we should wait until the local cops get done with the case before we do anymore.

The local cops Fred said they can't find their ass if it wasn't apart of them. Al said now Fred Adam the chief is a good cop and his policeman Chase was also a great man. Fred said if they're so great where are they now. Al said working the crime scene with the state cop. Fred said yup getting coffee and donuts for the state cop. Mike said they sure got your ass a few years back with the illegal hunter thing. Al said ok guys where here to do something about the kid's death not to open old wounds.

Fred said ok then when do you want me to hunt down the animal for you. Al said we are going to let the state cop tell you when. Fred said great another kid may die before then and then what? Al said I don't know Fred maybe next week we will get you to do it and pay you. The price will go up for everyone killed after today Fred said. Al said we'll have to take that change.

Dannie was getting out of the shower setting in the kitchen cutting some fruit. She loved fresh fruit and coffee to start the day. Today was going to be and great day she said to herself. I've got a shoot at 10:00 a.m. then lunch at Max's place. Max's was a little bar outside of town that make the best chilli ever. Max was a big man with a soft heart. Loved cooking and seeing Dannie enjoy his chilli so much.

Dannie got to the office and began to read the morning paper. She was saddening to read about the kid in the local paper. She returned to her desk. It was a cool one it was make all of glass and with blue light place under it to gave it a life of its own. On the wall were pictures of her in different layouts. The rug was black fur. She liked the rug it makes her feel great when she walked on it without shoes. The computer on her desk was chrome, some how chrome turned her on.

Good morning Crissy said Dannie's boss. Did you read the paper this morning? Yes and it was depressing Dannie said. Crissy was an older model who's looks were going. She was hoping that she could make Dannie into the next best thing to slice bread. Dannie asks did anyone know the kid. Crissy said yes but no one is speaking until the parents know. That morning when

Adam and Chase got to the scene they just stop at Annette's place and had a large breakfast. Will, that didn't last long? Shortly after looking at the kid ripped into parts the meal came up. It was a bad scene never had they seen so much blood and parts all over the place. Arms and legs 20 feet from each other and the head ripped from the body. The eyes of the kid were still open as if still watching himself bring Eaten.

All that was left was a legs one arm half his chest and the head. Whatever had done this did eat a lot of the kid. Chase asked if Adam know how it was and Adam

said yes. It was his paperboy a good kid that got the paper there first so he could read it before work. The state police show up. Shortly after the two got there.

Office Peter of the state police closed off the scene to help protect any clues. Peter was a thin man gray hair man with and straight shooting cop look about him. Peter asked if the boy parent had been called. Chase said no they just got here. Pete said who found the body. Adam said a girl that couldn't sleep and was out for a walk. Pete said a hell of a way to try to sleep. She may not sleep again.

Yup Adam said her name was Sandy from a farm down the road. We just got back from dropping her off she was really shaking up over this. Sandy was a young framer kids who had bonnie hair and loved life. Peter said hurt to have any kid see some thing like this, hell for that fact it not my funniest time. This animal or whatever it was surly big to make a mess like this here. Adam and Chase both said yes and animal we hope. Pete said what else could it be, a man wouldn't eat the kid like this would he. Adam said yes it has to be an animal no one was this sick he hoped.

Dannie when to bar at Max's Place she parked her jeep outside under a tree for shade. Max's Place was an old time white and red bar looked like a throw back from the 50ths.She walked throw the double doors the inside it was fine, make her feel like she was in a movie. Max and about ten other people were there all eyes turned as she walks by even married eyes. Max looked up and saw her like a big old cat with a mouse in its teeth he smiled and said hi. Dannie liked Max and he could cook to for a big man and nice to the eyes. Dannie said hi and sat at the bar. Max waked over and smiled would you like a beer? Dannie smiled back and said yes and a bowl of chilli with cheese bread. Max said the chilli is real hot today you sure? Yup the hotter the better Dannie said. You should know said Max with and big smile.

Max got her a beer and her chilli with cheese bread hope your hunger. Dannie said yup could eat a horse. Got one of those out back if you want me to throw it on the grill for you haha. Dannie smiles and laughs she really wishes he would ask her out some time. She broke the bread in half put it in her bowl. Dannie Ate the first bit of chilli. It was almost better then sex. She enjoyed the chilli and then, Max came back and said did you like it Dannie.Dannie said any better I would have to get a smoke haha. Max's big face turned red and he smiles at her. Dannie said I think your chilli gets better each time. Max said it much be the old shoe I put in it this time. She payed her bill and went back to her jeep the day was warm maybe I can get a little sun after I get home.

Adam, Chase and officer Peter went back to the station so they could clean up and get ready to go see the parents of the boy. This was the part of the job that Adam didn't like. The bad thing about it was he know Tommy and his Mon and Dad will, that's the way it is in a small town. The station was a small build that was set up in town after the donut shop closed, it still has the sign on front between the first and second stories. It read Dicky's donuts the old sign with no lights and had seen it's better days. If you tried really hard, you could smell grease from the old shop. After cleaning up the cops got into the state cop's car and went to Tommy's house.

It was a small country farm house with white on blue trim and a big red barn out back. The drive way was dirt like most farms around here. Rolling up the drive way, Mr Miller Tommy's Dad meet him out front. Adam got out and said hi to Sam Tommy's dad. Sam was and older man with worn out cloths on and you could see the years of farming in his face. Sam looked at Adam and said you couldn't be here with any good news I would say. Adam said no it about Tommy can we go inside and speak. Sam said yes and you could see the water forming in his eyes.

The four of them went in and Kaci's Tommy's mom hears them come in she came to meet Sam. She looked at Sam and know something bad had happen. She grad Sam and started to cry. They went into the living room and sat down. Adam said I don't know where to start other than saying we found Tommy and it wasn't good. I'm sorry but Tommy is dead. Kaci started crying hard Sam break down to and cried with her. How did it happen Sam said? Peter said we think it was a large cat or a big wild dog.

Sam said why don't you know didn't leave tracks. Peter said yes but I haven't ever seen anything like them before. Kaci said can we see your son. Adam said yes, but I'm going to tell it isn't nice. Sam said did you check with Fred he Knows every thing that is in these woods. We did and he said he'd never seen one like it. What are you doing to find this thing Sam said?

Adam said were going to follow the tracks tomorrow morning with dogs that are coming up from Bath. Sam said hope no one gets hurt before then. Chase said were going to put more people on tonight so we can watch the town. Kaci said when can we see Tommy. Adam said as soon as Mike gets done with him he will call you in tomorrow. Peter said is there anything we can do for you people until then?

Sam said find what killed them. Adam said we will do our better Sam. Sam and Kaci said thanks Adam. The three cops got up to go and went back to the station. Will I going to find a room for the night Peter Said? Chase said I have a room at my place your welcome to it. Peter said ok is there a small bar around to get something to drink and eat. Adam said yes Max's place down the road. Good care if we join you. No said Peter if you do mind if I drink a few. No said Chase think we all need a drink tonight. Great lets go and maybe we can speak about tomorrow.

Dannie got home around three that day. She was happy the sun was still out. She was still full from the chili at Max's Place. She got a few bears and a little cheese and put it on the porch. She went up stairs to undress and get into her see throw nighty. She loved the feel again her skin. She makes it back out to the porch to find her friend from next door setting at the table on the porch.

Pat how are you today? He said fine and I see you are to. Thanks Dannie said so what brings you by Pat. I saw your jeep and the sun was out and said you my be on the back porch. Yup your right was going to get some sun. Dannie said like a beer and some cheese Pat. Yes sounds good Pat said. Will set in the chair there and I'll go get me other beer Dannie said. Pat set in the chair and had a peace of cheese and a drink of the beer.

Dannie came back out and set her beer on the other side of the little table in between them. She took out her nighty and lay it in the chair and lay down on it. Pat was speechless and his face turn red. Dannie said I'm sorry Pat but aren't you gay. Pat said yes but even a gay can see you get one hell of a body.

Dannie said if it upsets you I will put the nighty back on. No Pat said you just got me off guard. Pat said will the reason I stop was to tell you to lock up around tonight because of what happen to the Miller boy last night. It wasn't little Tommy was it Dannie said? Pat said yes It was Tommy. She put her hand to her mouth and start to form tears in her eyes. Dannie asked how did you know this Pat?

Pat said my brother Chase is a cop. What happen to him Dannie said? My brother Chase said the boy was ripped apart like a rug doll. Oh my God said Dannie how did that happen? Pat said they think it was a large cat or a wild dog. Dam Dannie said this morning I hear an animal far away being hurt or killed hope it wasn't Tommy. Chill run down Dannie back as her set there.

Pat said no it was about three or four miles away. Dannie said thanks Pat and she would lock up the first floor tonight. Pat said good wouldn't want any one else getting hurt. Pat got up and drank the last of his beer and said thanks of the beer and cheese Dannie.Dannie said no trouble anytime. Pat start to leave when he looked back at Dannie's nude body he said to her if anyone was going to make a gay man straight it would be you. Dannie smiled and her face turned red. She said thank Pat she like people saying she was nice looking. Dannie told Pat to has a nice night and see you around soon.

Pat said ok and walked back to the road. Dannie set and enjoyed the sun it was warn again her skin. Thinking of what Pat told her she started to cry some more for Tommy and his Mom and Dadoed shouldn't happen to nice parent like them. Will for that fact no one should have to Barry they're kids.

She turned over in the chair so the sun would hit her back. She looked up to the window in her up stairs bed room. It was about 25 to 30 feet out the porch. It would be safe to leave open. She spent an hours in the sun and went up stairs to take a bath. She made sure everything was lock up down stairs because some times she fell asleep in the tub. Dannie filled the tub with warm water felt cool again her warm skin. She started a few candles around the tub rails.

She washed up than lay back to chill out for a while. She had a book to read but don't get ready into it tonight. The bath was nice. You could see the outline of her body in the tub. The phone ring good thing she had a cordless phones around it seems every time she got in the tub someone would call. Dannie said hello in a ruff sounding voice.

Hello it's Mom sorry did I cut in on something. Dannie said hi Mom no I was just in the bath and about to fall asleep. Oh I can call you later if you want Mom said. No it ok now. Dannie asked who's Dad and you? Mom said great. Me and your Dad was going to stop by tomorrow if you going to be home. Dannie said she would be right home after work tomorrow around three. Great see you then oh make sure you're dressed this time don't want Dad to get mad again. Yes Mom Dannie said I'll will be in my sweats. Good Mom said you know what your Dad is like, an old time man. Yup Dannie said wish sometime he would come to the 20'th century .

Mom laugh and said will it's funny. He doesn't seem to mean when I walk around here nude. Mom Dannie said you don't do that did you. Like mother you are hun, but Dad still see your as his little red fire ball not a grow up woman. I guess Mom Dannie said it nice when he thinks of me that way makes me feel special. You are hun your our little girl Mom said. Will ok see you tomorrow Mom kiss Dad for me I will Mom said see you tomorrow.

Dannie hanged up the phone and set back down in the tub. She felt all warm inside. She loved her parents a lot. Mom was an older view of Dannie and it makes her happy to think she would look that good when she got older. Dad was a big man but as soft as a teddy bear. She smiled thinking for all the times she and Dad lies on the bed. He read to her before she went to sleep.

Dad was a great story teller he would make up a new one every night and most of the time Dannie was the star. It makes her smile a little harder and laugh to thinking how someone could make a story up out of thin air.

Dannie got out of the tub and dried off she went to her room that was right off the bathroom. She open the bedroom window and let the cool air blow over her nude body. She pulls back the covers on her bed. She wasn't in bed long before she got sleepy. She rolled over to set the clock and curl up in the covers.

Adam called the two men he hand picked for the night watch. They were two young men who needed a job. Kevin and Steve both best friends and brothers. They where good old boys. You know both red heads with long hair and blue Jean's white T shirts. The two were fine as long as they wasn't together in the same car.

Adam asks Kevin if the night watch was going ok. Kevin said yes quiet and the town is locked up still no one out at all tonight. Adam ask if Kevin had he seen Steve. Yup Kevin said ran into each other about an hour or so ago. Good Adam said it going will. Kevin said if you call having to fill in dent and repaint my car ok. Adam said what do you mean Kevin? Kevin said we run into each other every hour. Adam laughs and said I don't know what I'm going to do with you two your not drinking.

Kevin said hell no it would be a lot more hitting if we were. Adam said will keep them on the road and I will call you in the morning, but if you see anything don't be a dumb ass a try to get it, call me and we'll go in as a team. Ok Adam Kevin said call if anything goes down.

Adam returns to the two cops setting at the bar. Peter said every thing ok Adam? Yup if Joey Chitwood and friend can keep it together. Chase laughs Kevin and Steve up too there games again. Adam said yup same old shit with no beer. Chase at less that's good new they get drinking and the town would be in for a fun time tonight.

Peter said a few good old boys. Adam said yup two that don't want to grow up, but good man just wild. Peter, Adam and Chase order a meal and had a few drinks. After dinner the three went over to Chase's house for a few drinks. Peter walked into the house and looked around looked like a nice house if it wasn't for the house keeper doing her job.

Adam looked around and laughs see your girlfriend is cleaning house for you again. Chase said yes the only thing she does is clean out the food and my wallet. Peter said haha I've had a few of those women myself. Adam said I've got to run, but will see you two when the state tracking team comes up from Bath tomorrow. Peter said well have a good night Adam. You to Peter and Chase.

Adam went back to his car and headed home it was around 8:00 p.m. or so. He lived in town over the station house. It was a small place, but didn't need a big place anyway. Adam grads a beer and set in the chair to watch some tv. He keeps a blanket near the chair just in case he was sleepy and didn't want to get up.9.30 pm no word from Kevin and Steve hope they aren't running into anything but each other.

Good Adam said a football game is on the Pat's and Bills. Adam enjoys football he had been a pat's fan for a long time back when they went to their first super bowl game. They got their assess handed to them by the Bears but didn't give up the fight. The game was seven to 14-pat's ahead good looks like a good game. Adam liked a good game where the teams were even.

Drinking down the last of his beer Adam grads the blanket and kicked his shoes off. Setting there thinks about tomorrow and if they could find this thing, his eye grow heavy and he slowly fell to sleep.

It was about 2:00 a.m. Dannie wakes with a jump. Her heart was beating like a drum in her chest. She was covered with sweat her hands felt clammy. She recalls the dream she was having. She was running throw the woods at a speed more like the wind then she would run. She saw an old chain gate it was about 8 feet in all, she didn't stop just jumped and landed on the other side.

She ran up a road to a big burned out mill of some type and a house in one corner and some small builds around it. She stops running an smelled the air like she could pick up a smell, she could hear dogs and some people, but also something else a large thing moving closer to the sound of the dogs.

She stated to move in the same area. It was when she looked down and saw she was a long ways from the ground she was tall not just tall but really tall. Her feet and hands were different hairy and not human. She looked again to see the other large animal in front of her, but it didn't see her it was still moving to the sound of the dogs. She followed behind him and they came to a group of men and one woman and two dogs.

It seems the group was hunters for something, but only one had a gun out and it looked as if he was holding it on the others. The animal came closer. It was going to kill the group. She knows she had to do something and fast. She ran at the animal jumped and landed on the other animals back. It was clear she was big then the first one by two to 3 feet. She put her hands on both side the animals head and broke it necks. It wasn't all she pulled up and ripped the head off the animal.

She dropped to the ground as the group stated to draw their guns on her. She turned an ran like the wind again. The group open fire and they didn't hit her she looked back and found the other animal still some what standing making a clear shot at her too hard. She went back the way she came over the gates.

She hit the field outside her home as she was running she looked down at her hands and stopped. She was still holding the animal head in her hands she turns the head around to see its face and was so afraid she drops it. The face was a half dog and some man like parts. That's when it ended and she wakes up her heart slow down and she remembers it was a bad dream.

She gets up and went to the kitchen to get a drink for something to carm her down so she could sleep. She got a glass of red wine and sat in the living room chair and drink it. She said to herself that it must have been the chilli she eat for lunch that gave her the night mare. Dam she said it's still as clear as if it just happen for real. She drank the wine and returns to her bed she was still sleepy, but didn't really want to sleep so that she may not have that dream again.

Adam rolls over to look at the clock it was 6.30 a.m., will got to get up . He looked out the window that over looked main street it was quiet for this town. He looked at the sky it looks if it would be a good day. Adam jumped in the shower the water felt nice he started to wake up. After about ten minute Adam got out and dried off. He put on some blue geans and a blue East Millinocket police shirt.

He knew the walk was going to be ruff. So he wanted to dress light. It was a little after seven now the sun was coming over the hills. It was cool put would soon warm up to be a nice day. Adam walks down stair to Annette's coffee shop on the corner next to the station. She away was open at seven or shortly after. Adam looks at the coffee shop and the lights were on, good Annette was open.

Adam walks in and said hi to Annette that was behind the corner, she was making a pot of coffee. Annette was about 45 short but good looking lady with a nice ass. Adam set down at the counter and reach over the bar and grad Annette's ass. Annette turned around and smiled at Adam your looking for morning hash brown today. Adam laughs you know me to will don't you Annette. Annette smiled at him again and said too many men around here like that, but I don't mind it makes me feel young.

Annette older bother Bob pulled up to the shop and came in Hi Sis Bob said. Adam and Annette both said hi. Bob was in his 50th tall and good looking also.

Annette loved having he bother show up ever day it would make her morning. Bob set beside Adam and said to Annette I'll have a big breakfast with bacon and hash brown's two eggs and that great coffee of your. Adam said dam sounds' good. I'll have the same. Annette said two grab ass special coming right up. Bob wasn't in on the joke so Adam filled him in.

Bob asked Adam any clues on Tommy's killer. Adam said I'm going to follow the trail of the animal today to see if we can see it. I'm just waiting for

Chase and Peter from the state police and two dog trackers from Bath should be here soon. Good Said Bob hope you get the thing. Annette said me too was a little scared coming into town today.

Make it more so when Kevin and Steve shot pass looked like they were in a race. Adam just put his hands to his head and said dam those to guys. Bob said thing never dell around with those guys. Adam said yup sure isn't. Just than two cars came down the main street. One pulls up in front of the station the other runs in the back of the other. Looks like Kevin and Steve are here Adam said.

Bob said or hell's angels are in town. Adam and Annette laugh. Kevin and Steve walked throw the door and said hi to everyone. Everyone said hi back. Boss the night was quiet other than seeing Fred this morning about six no one else on the road. Adam said Steve where was Fred going. Steve said looks like he was going hunting for something today. Dam I hope he doesn't get hurt out there Steve said. Adam said I'm more afraid for the animal then him.

Kevin said by the way Annette sorry about this morning I was sure you were Steve coming at me. Annette said that's ok just glad you didn't hit me. Adam said I will call you two about four tonight if we run the night watch. Kevin said ok and the two went home in and cloud of smoke and spinning tires. Adam looked at Annette and said it's a wonder those two aren't dead.

Annette said someone is watching over those two. Adam said yup he must have a going time watching over them. Adam said what do I owe you Annette. She said ten and a good tip for the ass grab she smiled. Adam gave her 15. bucks and a hug, see you and your ass in the morning. Adam went and open the station up and make a pot of coffee. Peter and Chase showed up around at eight the two trackers around 8.30.

Dannie's clock rang it was time to get up still with the memory of last night's dreams. She got up and turns on the shower and stood there and let the water run down her back. She washed up and got out and went to the bedroom windows. Looking down at the field she could see an old ford truck moving along the corn field roads. She though that's funny that it was moving slow and it seemed to be looking for something.

She got her robe and went down stairs to put a pot for coffee on. Then went out to see how sunny of a day it was on the porch. The sun was warm and it felt great it was going to be a good day at work. She went back into the kitchen shutting the porch door and locking it. She made a cup of coffee and some fruit and some left over cheese. She went into the living room to watch the local news. Maybe they found more on Tommy's killer, but no just local weather and farm reports. She ate her breakfast and washes the cup out in the sink. She went back to her room to get dressed. She got on a nice red shirt on and it was almost see throws and a short blue jean dress. She looked in her full length mirror and said dam your hot girl. It was 8.30 had to run, got to be at work at 9.00.

Crissy her boss can be a bitch about that sometimes. She went down stair turned off the coffee pot and tv grads her bag and truck keys. She had a 2006 jeep wrangler was blue and had mag rimes. She walks up to her jeep and was piss out. A Dog had pissed all over the rear tire. She wouldn't had been so mad but she didn't had a dog and she wash it the other day. Will she said got to run she got in her jeep and headed to work.

She got there just two minutes before she was to check in. Crissy was set at her desk looking at her watch. Dannie said good morning to her and sat at her desk. Good morning Dannie Crissy said. Dannie you got two young girls coming in to interview you and the office around ten. Hope you make use look good. I will Dannie said but under her breath she said only if you could have a drive throw face left.

I will show them the ropes around here do a photo shoot with one and show them some of mind and your work around town. Crissy said ok but don't go nuts and put use in the poor house. Dannie said ok it will be cheap but fun. Crissy did we get the photos from my shoot back from yesterday Dannie said. Oh yes and the man that took them said he loved working with you Crissy said. I looked at them and your were hot in them kido. Thanks Dannie said Crissy didn't make that type of comment often.

Adam, Chase and Peter set down with Mary and Devvan from the Bath tracking team. Mary was about in her 20's Devvan the same. Mary had browns' hair and was a nice girl to look at Devvan was a soft-spoken man but very strong looked like a wood's man. The two had been on the same team for about ten years now. They worked 911 when the twin towels came down.

The two had two black lads that were the best in the business at tracking. Adam showed the crime scene's photo to them and told them what he know about the case so far. Both Mary and Devvan were shocked by the mess and blood at the scene. Mary said this is not going to be a small animal. Devvan said no its maybe around 8 feet tall or better. Adam said how can you tell this by looking at picture.

Mary said see this one here is where the animal was eating and in the others are how far the other parts are away. Devvan said yes most animals don't throw there food around like that. Adam said so you know it's an animal. Devvan said yes no man I know could throw parts this far and eat so much of the body. Mary asked did you get any foot prints. Adam said yes we make a cast of them I will go get them.

Adam returned with two casts and gave one to Mary and the other to Devvan. Devvan turned it over and said to Adam is this a joke. Adam said not this is the track. Mary said I've never seen anything like it. Devvan was sure he saw prints like this in an old case it was out of Worcester Mass, but this case was 50 years old and the animal that make them was killed. Adam said maybe we can look it up on the computer. Devvan said yup I've got my laptop here. Devvan open the laptop and turns it on he got to the file and opened it.

Devvan said shit as his face looked as if he was a dear in a set of headlight. Mary ask what is it, she know Devvan will and it took a lot to scare them. The pictures of the animal and with all the detail to Devvan said. Devvan said I'll read the faxes first and then show the picture. Devvan began reading it, it was about 1952 Worcester Mass. the local report a dog like man was loss from a research place in the city.

The paper said this animal was part of a cross breeding program the government was doing. Trying to make a better man to fight war with. The program was cross breeding man with wolfs and apes. The animal were very unsalable and very strong. One of the wolfman crosses was so strong it ripped three metal doors to the outside off the wall. It makes its way into the city and killed 20 people and hurt one really badly. The animal was run into a corner in an old build, there 20 cops open fire and was reports about 70 rolls pumped into the animal before it went down.

The cops returned to the research place to find it empty and not clues around but one doctor with a broken back hidden in a case in one room. The doctor told every thing he know about the animal and how many were left. Seems two ape like man were taking and all the records. The doctor said the wolfman animal was one of a kind. The government funded the research it was going good until the wolfman got too big to handle it brock his back as it throws the three doors across the floor. He said he crawled in to case to hide and pass out. The doctor was in the local hospital one night, the next morning someone had taking him he was gone without a trace.

The government denied anything to do with the program. Devvan said the animal was 8 feet tall and was around 700 lbs. Adam said dam that's big and I hope it not what was tracking today. Mary said how could it be the one was killed. Mary's face turn white as she looked closer at the pictures of the animal. Chase said what wrong Mary? Mary said look at the picture with the feet in it, as she held the case up to the laptop screen. The feet look real close to the ones they had. It seems the hold room said dam at the same time.

Mary said again how could it be the dam thing was dead. Peter said maybe someone is making more of them. Adam said but where and why 50 years ago they could control it why now. Mary said it could be more then ten or more miles away because most animals only hunts in small area. Adam said the only place around here is the old mill up in the hills. Chase said but that burn down all but the main house and a few small builds .Beside Doctor

Mike bought that about ten years ago to rebuild the old house and rewire it.

Peter said there power all the way back there. Adam said no the mill run from power that it got from the river, but that place burn down. Mike told me it would cost too much to rebuild so it been up for sale about two years now. Adam said Mike will be here soon to drop off the report on Tommy.

Will Adam said it looks like we are going to have to bring some large guns. Peter said we could go to the army down the road. Adam said no need I've got just the guns we will need here, Adam open up the gum case and pull out two AK 47s . Here Mary and Devvan these two are for you and here same spare clip belts. What are you going to use Mary said to Adam? Adam pulled two bolts from the back of the case.

The case came away from the wall there was three very large guns. Chase said dam you told me you sold them. Adam said I told you that so you wouldn't be looking around for them. Peter said what in the hell are they? Adam said me and my Dad made the three of them two years back. They are 50 caliber six round shot rifles. Dam Peter said as Adam handed the gun to him what did you make these for? Adam said his father and him wanted to see if it could be done and fired from a standing shot. Peter said can they? Adam said yes but more better from a kneeing shot.

Chase said you would shit to see how hard the gun ripped thing apart. Adam and I shot two large maple trees about 50 tall. One shot ripped throw the base and the tree fell. Peter said dam this sound stop anything. Adam said you better hope it does because if it doesn't we are in deep shit. Adam handed them three more clips and rounds of the guns.

Peter said ready for a war now. Just then Mike walked throw the door hay Adam going to war with the Medway boys tonight? Chase said hunting a wolfman. Mike said a wolfman where you see this thing? Adam said we think it's something like that but haven't seen it. Oh Mike said glad I'm staying in town. Adam said Mike did you do anything with the old mill up in the hills. Mike said no I'm Tring to dumb it, The place would cost 200 thundered to rebuild and get the power on.

I hadn't been there in two years or so. Adam said are the gates locked. Mike said no got tried of the kids cutting them off. Adam said how did you know it was kid? Mike said because when I did go up there I saw some of them running away and hiding. Adam said ok if we get up there we will check the place. Yup said Mike you can tell me how the place is looking up there. Ok Adam said but we may not get up there for days. Mike said yup and headed out the door. Adam went to get food for the group at Annette's coffee shop.

Mike called Sam and Kaci. Sam pick up the phone and said hi. Mike here you can come to see Tommy now if you care. Sam said we will be right over. Sam and Kaci went to Mike's place. It was a small but nice looking place. Mike meets them at the door Sam said hi to Mike, but Kaci was still in shock and didn't say anything. Mike said I want you to know it not going to be good Tommy was in bad sharp. Kaci grad Sam and there went to the table where Tommy was. He was cover with a cloth that you could see some blood had made it red. Mike looked at them and said your sure you want to see. Sam and Kaci said yes. Mike pulls back the cloth to show Tommy's face and chest, not the lower because he know it wasn't good.

Kaci screamed and grad Sam hard and began to cry. Sam was Crying with hurt in his eyes. Mike put the cover back on and moved the two out to the other room. Sam said do you know what happen mike? Mike said I don't but Adam and a group of tracker are going to try to find the thing today. Sam said thanks and Kaci and Sam went back home to cry and miss their beloved Tommy.

Dannie was looking over her picture from the shoot the other day. She enjoyed looking at them and she was happy with them all but one. She though its funny her eyes were almost black and no real color at all. Dannie said Crissy did you see this one. Crissy said the one with your eye's black almost gone. Yup that's the one Dannie said isn't that funny. Crissy said no that happen to her once when she was at a shoot the camera must had gotten a shot of you when you were looking that the back ground.

Oh Dannie said will we can change it with the computer to show my eyes. Yup said Crissy a good thing to we can cover up mistakes. Ok Dannie said, but she was thinking wish it could work that way in real life not for her but for Crissy. Will two young girls walked throw the door Dannie looked at the clock 10.02 a.m.. The girl came up to Crissy desk and said hi, Crissy looked up at him. The girls said we from the high school and we are here to do an interview with your bunnies.

Will Crissy said your fine looking young ladies, but is the hooker look back and your not on time you're fired. The girls looked at each other than at her and said we not here to work, but as a school program. Crissy looks at him and smiled then they know she was kidding with them. Crissy said just a joke girls, but maybe Dannie can show you same make up tips.

Oh and if Dannie was just a few minutes slow to a shoot she could stand to loss ten grand and she couldn't afford that. The girls looked at each other again and looked at Dannie, hell is that what you make? Dannie said yes on a good day you could make that but you work hard at keeping in sharp and looking good. Will girls lets going back and show you the ropes. Great the two girls said by the way my name is June and she April. Will welcome June and April my name is Dannie.

The girls said we know you're all over the football team's picture a few years back when you did the cheerleader thing for them. Yup your right it was fun and the boys were nice in a jock type of way. The girls laughed and most of the boys still have Dannie pictures in their lockers. Dannie laughs with them. Will lets make you that hotly and do a picture shoot and a little video to boot.

Cool the girls said where do we start. Will here in make up is the first thing, got to make you look hot not trashy. So Dannie got the girl's make up done and put them both in a hot looking outfits. Now lets going to the photo lab and start shooting. The girls follow Dannie down the hall to the lab it was set up to look like the main street of any New England town. Cool the girls said. Dannie said now the hard work start.

Dannie put on the video cam and put some dance music on. Ok girls start at one end and walk slowly and look at me and make love to the camera. The girls got up on the set and started walking and looking at the cam. Doing a great job with the shoot, this went on for an hour it seen, then Dannie said take a brake girls and came here. The girl looked like they could get some rest. Dannie said so did you like it, Yes the girls said but is it this hard all the time. Dannie said well it was a small shoot it could go on all day like this.

The girls said wow didn't know it was so hard the look good. Dannie laughs that's why we get the big money. Will lets go to the computer lab and see what we have. The girls went with Dannie and make the picture into and video. After watching the film Dannie said bet your girls get a few boys numbers with this. The girl laughed and said just a few phone number would be nice. Dannie said bet at less ten for both of you. The girls has a shit eaten smile on their faces.

Dannie said oh by the way you two can keep yourself fit and do your makeup as I showed you, you got a good change as models. The girls said thanks for making use pretty and sexy. No trouble I love to show women how to dress and look they best, oh by the way if you two would like the dresses you can have them . The Girls said are you sure? Yes Dannie said there some of mind. Thanks the girls said. Dannie said ok I will give you a bag that the models around here use to put your cloths in.

The time came to a close and the Mom of one of the girl's stopped to get the two, thanks for every thing the girls said and said thanks to Crissy. Crissy said your welcome and you look much better. The girls got in the car and the Mom set there for a few minutes and then came into the office.

How Dannie she said and Dannie got up and came to her. I'm the mother of one of the girls who was here. Thanks you for everything the girls look like girls now not hookers and they can't stop tacking about how cool you and Crissy were. The Mom hugged Dannie and thanks again. I should have tried this sooner. Will see you and the Mom went back to the car. Dannie turned around and Crissy said good job kid. Will not anything to do now you can go home if you want. Great Mom and Dad are coming today I will. Good Crissy said say hi to your Mom and Dad for me. I will Dannie said see your later she went out to her jeep a went home.

Adam walks into Annette's coffee shop again only one person setting there it was Vicki. Vicki was Annette best friend she was a short woman with good looks. Hi Vicki said to Adam and Annette yelled hi from the kitchen. Adam said hi and said to Annette need about six sandwiches and some chips to go. Any type of sandwiches hun you want. Make any thing that can stand a warm day in the woods. I'm making some right now to sale in the cooler got about 5,will make one more and bring them out. Vicki said you going hunt today with Fred.

No Adam said why did he said that. No but he was at Max's last night and he said he was going out to kill some type of animal in the morning . He didn't really say much because he was drinking pretty heavy last night. Vicki was a bar keep at Max's place she didn't have a man but always was looking. No I hope he still home sleeping it off Adam said. Annette came from out back and set the sandwiches on the counter and got a hand full of small bags of chips.

Annnette said you keep this up I'm going to had to going on a trip. Vicki laughs and said yup she smoked her breakfast again this morning. Adam and Annette laughs, will how much do I owe you.40 dollars and a threesome tonight with me and Vicki. Sounds fun see you later sweat checks. Vicki smiles and throws the salt at Annette.

Adam loaded up the car and Peter and Chase road with him. The others had a truck with to two dog and follow them down the road to where Tommy was killed. They got there around 11:00 a.m. the heat for the day wasn't bad. A nice cold south wind was blowing. As they turned the corner they saw and red truck rolled over just in front of where Tommy was killed.

It was Fred's truck Adam said dam hope Fred's ok. They pulled up beside the truck Chase jumps out and runs over to see if he was ok. He stood up from the other side of the truck and said no one here Adam. As he was standing up Chase saw two large hand marks on the driver's door. Peter and Adam you got to see this Chase said ! The two men walked around with the other two behind them. Peter looked shit it looks like something run them off the road.

Adam said no you see the road where he stopped and where the truck was pulled sideways for a few feet than rounded over here. No blood said Peter the truck is locked to he said. But as Peter started to stand he could see some thing in the oak tree across the road about 20 feet up in the tree looked like a bike. Peter said did you find a bike with Tommy's body? Adam said no but his father said he had one. Peter said look up in that oak tree across the road.

Chase said its Tommy's bike all right, but how did it end up there? Peter said it was throw there from the way it landed. Ok can we going home now Chase said this is getting a little scary. Adam said carm down the dogs would be going nuts if there was anything around here now. Mary said yes your right Adam and the truck has a ladder hocked on the driving side rail. Good Adam said Chase help Devvan gets the ladder and me and Peter will grab the guns.

Ok Chase said and put the ladder up to the tree he climbed the ladder and stated pulling the bike wheel to them. The bike came loss and almost pull chase off the ladder, the bike hit the ladder than the ground. The bike was bent to and that's not all and hand was still holding the handle bar. As everyone looked at the bike Mary said is that Tommy's hand? Adam said it got to be. Devvan said he was still on the bike when the attack happened. Looks like that Peter said, fuck I'm getting scared now.

The ladder was put away and everyone got ready to move. The two tracker got the AK's and the dogs and got to work. Mary said the dog's name are Maxy and Pad. Adam laughs and said who gave them that name. Devvan said seem to fit at the time for two female dogs. Chase smiled at Mary and said whatever. Mary said don't look at me he named them before I joined the team.

The tracks run throw the trees to the left and down throw the woods Adam said. As they got to the tracks Adam saw foot prints from boots running along the track to the woods. Adam said Fred maybe still alive. Those are his boot print going off after the tracks.

Dannie enjoyed the ride home the sun was out and the air was cool. She got home to find that her parents haded got there, but that was good she could go get a shower in before they got there. She got out and got her bag and went in, she put the bag down by the door and went upstairs. She got into the shower dam the warm water felt good. She cleaned up and washed her hair and cleaned her makeup off for Dady.

Dad like to see her with no makeup on because he said she was to pretty, like her Mom to cover up. She put a towel on and started down the stairs to get some food and some ice water or a beer. She open the door to the ice box. It was fulled she though Mom and Dad must have been by and went back to town to do Mom best thing in life spend Dads money. Good she saw a bottle of cran berry juice her and Dad loved it, but she always forgot to get some.

She got a grass and got some juice and a few small peace of fruit. She returns to her bed room and got on her sweats, short blue fur, she loved them because it felt little a warm hug. Dannie made sure everything was ready for supper tonight she got some nice t-bones steaks and fresh Maine corn. She was making a salad in the kitchen and had got all farm fresh things . She was thinking to her self Dad got the cran berry juice, she had grinnerale and some Allen's Vodka good she would mix up a drink for Mom and Dad and her. She places the Vodka in to chill.

She hears a car pull up and she was happy because it was Mon and Dad. She went to the door and open it Dad was standing there outside with Mom. Mom had to have a smoke, Dad look sick a smile came on her face Mom must have got a lot for new things because that was the only time she smoked and Dad look so sick.

She came down the steps and run over to her Dad grad him and hugged him hard. Hi hun Dad said and gave her a big hug. She felt like a kid again Dad's little girl. Mom said hi and kiss her on the four head. Dannie said see you been shopping Mom because your smoking. Yup Dad said they had to close the town because they ran out of thing. Dannie laughs because she knows the women in the family like to shop. Came on in. I'll make use a drink. Dad said I'm going to need more than one.

Dannie smiled at him and said feel like barbarQ tonight. Dad said yes I love to grill because you know who cooks at home. Dannie said I was hoping you would I love watching you cook and have fun. Maybe you can make chilli some night to for use. Mom said for you two the last time he made some the dog wouldn't eat it. Dam the dog eats anything it must have been really hot then Dannie said.

Dad said the hotter the best for the heart. They went in and out to the back porch. Dad said I'll get the steaks ready and Dannie can make the drinks. Dannie said good while I'm doing that Mom can help me with the corn. Got it fresh from Sam's farm down the road. Mom said sad thing about little Tommy did they find anything out about it? Dannie said no but they had a night watch running every night. I hope they get the killer I wouldn't want someone else to get hurt. Makes going back a forward from work a like more scarier Dannie said. Dad said will lets get to the cooking.

Dannie said good she was going to make a different drink tonight. She got out the bender and some ice, she puts about eight ice cubes in it and two cups for vodka, two cups of grinnerale, and the rest was cranny berry juice . She turns the blender on until the ice was chopped up fine. She poured it into large glasses she had in the ice box. Here Mom Dannie said try this drink. Mom said I'm not a cran berry person like you and Dad are But this is really good. Dad here's your, Wow at is good and it hit the shot on a day like today what is it called Dannie Dad said. It my own drink it's called a Maine cold red chill.

Good name it fit the drink red and chilli Mom said. Will out to the porch and some cooking we go. Dad went first Mon stops Dannie and said thanks hun you make your Dads day by letting him cook. Dannie said I know I love it, makes me feel good to see you two smile. The two hugs and went to the porch. Dad said the steaks are cooking and the drinks are great could this be any better day.

Dannie tapped her feet on the porch as she had one hand on her side looking at Dad. Dad smiled and said you know I mean you two girls to. Mom looked at Dannie and said will we are as good as steak now. The three them had a good laugh and Dannie said I know what you mean, love you to Dad.

Dannie and her Mom went into get the corn and other food and some more drinks returned to the porch and set at the panic table. Mom said hay there cook those steaks done. Dad said another five minutes and it will be dinner. Dannie said good. I'm getting hungry. Dad gave the steaks to Dannie and she set them on the table. Looks good hun Mom said lets eat.

Mom said grace that's what all good people do. Dannie took the first steak and got some salad and corn. She cut into the steak and took a bit dam Dad this is just right. See Mom I told you Daddy could still cook. Mom said well your going to barbarQ more at home now, nice steak.

After dinner was done Mom and Dannie cleaned up. As there were washing the dishes her Dad came up behind them and gave both of them a big hug and kiss, love you girls. Dannie put some soap from the sink on here hand a put it on his nose love you to Dad.

Adam and the other had been tracking for two hours and then stopped a mile from the old sand pit to eat. Chase a said dam wish we had seen it by now. Peter said the tracks are a day old so it would be really remote of a charge. Devvan said some animal are know to made tracks and keep to them.

Mary said it could be walking right at use now. Devvan said stop that kind of took your giving me chills. Adam said I hear that will the pits is close maybe we can get a view of it from on top. Adam said I got some water here Devvan if you want it for the dog's there look like there could use some. Sure Devvan said thanks they do need some. After the animals drank and the food was done they got back to the job at hand. The dogs started to get funny Devvan said guys think were on to some thing. Adam said me and Chase will take the front Peter cover the back.

Devvan and Mary keep the dogs in between use and cover the sides. Chase said don't you think the dog should go first? Adam said if it wasn't for the dogs the thing would have getting a jump on use. Chase said I see your point. Chase and Adam started for the sand pit. Moving slowly to be able to get a shot if anything moved. The pit was about a mile just over the top of the hill. At the top for the hill Adam saw some thing standing at the side of the trail.

He stopped Chase and pointed it out. He could see it to about a 1/4 of a mile ahead at the top of the hill. Chase knees down and was ready too shot but Adam said no it my be Fred. Everyone in the group was now aiming at the thing waiting for it to move to give them some type of tip of what it was. Just then two shots rang out from the other side of the hill by the old sand pit.

The thing broke cover and headed to the pit. To fast to get a good shot. Adam jumped up and started run for the top. Chase said are you nuts? Adam yelled back and said Fred on the other side and the thing is going for him. The group started on a dead run the top after Adam. Adam hit the top first just in time to see the thing hit Fred and they looked as if there both went over the side.

Adam started running down the hill. Chase yelled what's wrong as the others and him hit the top. Adam looked back and yelled they went over the side. Chase said dam, Peter said what up? Chase said at a dead run its about 150 feet down to the bottom. Mary said shit and they all pick up their pace. Adam reaches the cliff first he looked down and saw the thing laying at the bottom of the pit face down. He looked around for Fred put didn't see him. The others got there and started to look for Fred to, where the fuck is he Adam asked.

Maybe under that thing Peter said look at the size of the thing. Is it dead Devvan said, it got to be Adam said it's not moving. Adam was close to the edge went a hand grad his foot. Fuck he yells and drew on the hand. Its Fred Chase said the men grad t his hands and pulled Fred up the side. Shit man Adam said we though you were dead.

Fred said yes me to for a second that thing came at me down the hill like a speeding train. I try to get a shot off but it was to fast. I turned and was ready to jump when I saw the tree roots at the edge there. I turned back to see where it was and it was I middle air just about to hit me. When I dropped over the side as it flu over me.

He was so close that I could make his or its face out. Fred said I think I shit myself. Adam said I think I would have to, to see that running at me. Devvan looked for the thing over the side where did it land. Adam said right there and Adam looked down, it can't be no thing could have make and landing like that and walked away. Chase said you can see where it was but where is it now ?

The group looked around to see where it may had move. Peter said looking over to the river is that it in the water. Fred said shit that two miles around the pit. Adam knee down and looked throw the scoop on his gun it the thing. He set to take a shot Fred laughs your not going to hit it from here. Adam shot the bullet landed two feet from the thing to the right. Chase started to try to take a shot and Adam said no, Chase looked at Adam and said why. He under the power line that run across you hit it and the hold town we are out for a week. It looks like it's heading for the island any way.

Mary asked does anyone live there. Not for as long as I been around Adam said. Chase said it because locals call it dead river drivers island. Adam said we get to head back it going to be dark in and hour. Mary said it took use three to get here. Adam said yes but we can hit the road over there out off the pit and it we take use 45 minutes to get back to trucks. Ok let move then Chase said If I'm going to fight that thing I want to see it coming. Fred said I see it and I didn't get a charge to fight dam lucky I'm alive.

Adam said ok lets get rolling can you make it Fred, Fred said ok I'm fine just got to get my gun I throw over there. Fred got his gun and they headed to the road. On the way to the road Devvan said why do there call the island dead Rivers' driver's island. Adam said shit don't get Fred started on that old story. Fred said it's a true story Adam my older bother was killed by the river drivers ghost. Mary said ghost how did that happen. Chase said here we go the tail of killer ghost now as if I'm not scared now with the wolfman.

Fred said what did you say Chase. Adam said I will show you every thing back at the station. Fred said ok does that mean I'm hunting with you next time? Adam said surely we could use other gun. Do I get one of those play toys what is that thing? Adam said it's a 50 caber rife. Shit 50 cal. dam you must be sore. Not ready it a soft shooting gun.

Mary said what about the island Fred? Ok Adam said tell them Fred but make it the true story. Fred said I only say the trust any ways. Chase said right and I'm a good loving to. Fred said don't be down on yourself Chase not everyone in town can make you girlfriend happy oh sorry they can. Adam laughs and said ok guys stop before it gets out of hand. Fred said ok I sorry Chase.

Fred told the story now. It was in the summer for 1940 or so, seven river drivers running logs down the river. One of the man when under a log and the others came to help get him out. They could have saved him but the logs hit the top of the island and stopped dead throwing the others in front of the moving logs. They all went under and were found a mile down river floating face down. But the funny thing was, they were all locked together arm in arm. The locals where afraid after they found them like that they beady them on the island as not to bring bad luck on the town.

Devvan said ok I can see way they do that but what about killer ghost. Adam said you ask for it. Fred said the next summer four young kids went to the island to see the graves. The four were not see until a boater see the four bodies floating face down arm in arm with pick polls run throw them. Right Mary said as if that would happen. Fred said its true one of them was my brother and I saw the poll in him myself.

Mary said sorry to hear that Fred. Chase said can I tell him about his truck now? Adam said shit I almost .forgot about it. Chase said Fred the wolfman did a number to your truck. Fred said I know I should for set there for a while. Adam ask why. Fred said I felt something watching me when I was there. Peter said and you got out, dam you are nuts. Was trying to draw it out in the open. I didn't know it was that big or I would have waited for you to show up. If you did you may have been dead now Fred Adam said. Maybe good luck Fred said maybe I should get a lottery ticket. Chase said a bath would help. The group made it back to the trucks and help Fred upright his truck. Adam pulled him behind the car until he got to the station in town.

Dannie and her Mom came into the living room and Dad was set in the recliner. Dad said I know what I want for father's day this year. Dannie said a good chair isn't it, I fall to sleep in it a lot. Dad said I Know I've been falling to sleep time to time. Good food and good friends does it everything. Mom said yes hun that was a great meal. Dannie said it was wasn't it, it makes a different when everything is fresh from the farm. Dad said sure does hun thank God for the farmers. Mom said same here we should thank God for good food and great friends.

Mom said Dannie your haven't said anything about boys in your life. Dannie said not anyone at this second but I'm trying to get Max to ask me out. Who's Max Dad said is it someone we meet before. No Dannie said the only one you meet here was Pat and he's gay. See hun I told you he was gay Dad said. Mom said your Dad keep seeing him check out his ass. Dannie said your right Dad he said he though you were a stud for an older man. Mon said there you go hun a man that thinks your hot.

Mom Dannie said Dad is good looking for a man. Dad said now who feels like steak. They laughed and Dannie's Mom said your hot old man why do you think I got you. Will back to Max Mom said who is this man? Dannie said he owns Max's Place outside town as your came in he a big tall teddy bear of a man and he really nice. He hasn't asked me out, but I can tell he wants to by the way he jokes around.

Your Dad was like that Mom said I had to set in his lap one day and ask him out. Dannie said what did he say. Your Dad was speechless couldn't get the words out, but I know he mean yes Mom said. Dad said it wasn't I couldn't speak but your Mom was breathtaking. Mom smiled at him and Dannie could see they were still Maddy in love still today.

Will it six now what you say we going to see this Max and have a few drinks before we going to bed Dad said? Dannie said cool I would loved to go there with you two that's if Mom don't say anything to Max, OK hun I will keep quiet. Dannie said if we go soon we can see the live band playing tonight. Mom said any band we know. Dannie said yup do you remember the young boy who came over to learn me how the play a set of drums. Mom said Ray, I think. He could really song good. Dannie said he did a lot for CDS and got this band that plays all over.

Good sounds fun Dad said it's a date. Will Dannie said I'll go put some thing nice on. Mom said me and Dad will just spruce up a little to so we look ok for Max. Dannie went up stair and put on a light blue dress and some makeup. She came back down and Dad look at the both of them and said will Max is in for it tonight. The two of you look nice and you got your war paint on to.

Dad Dannie said you know you're the number one man in this group. Dad smiled and said love you. The three of them went in Dannie's jeep to Max's place on the way in town they pass Adam pulling Fred truck. Dad said at less the cops are good to the people around here you wouldn't see that in the city. Dannie said yup Adam and Chase are two local kids and hell of a good set of cops. Dad said Adam still get shit for the car crash at the bar. Yup people still pull his leg about hitting ice and run into two state police cars and one shief car at the bar two years ago. Mom said I see that in the local time someone painted hazzard county on Adams car. Yup that was funny but made Adam look dumb.

They when throw town on main street to Max's place Dannie pull up to the front of the bar. The band was unloading things and setting up for the night. Mom said is that Ray over there, yup Dannie said he still good looking. They went inside and sat down at the table across from the bar. The band was almost set to play and Vicki was behind the bar right now.

Max was over by the band and Dannie said there Max he's the tall one next the band speaking to them. Dad said dam now I know that big foot had youngings. I mean he a good looking for a man but tall. Mon said he is nice on the eyes. Dannie said he coming this way don't say anything Mom ok. Ok Mom said but you better ask him out or I will have to do it for you.

Max came over to the table and said Dannie you looking really nice tonight hope I can get a dance. Dannie turned red and said I'm all your big boy. Max couldn't say a thing too came back with, but said I see you have friends tonight. Dannie said yes this is my Mom and Dad. Max said hi and said I see where the good looks came from. Dad said in his smart ass came back not to fast boy I'm married. They all laughed and Max said what can I get you.

Mom said a Maine cold red chill. Dannie looked at Mom and gave her a dirty look. Max said can't say I've ever heard of it, do you know what's in it I can make it for you. Mom said no but Dannie made them for use today for dinner she could show you. Max looked at Dannie ok sounds' good. Max and Dannie went to the bar and Dannie looked back at her Mom as to say thank or I'll get you back Mom .

Dad said Max seems like a nice man, Mom said yup a big old teddybear like you. Dad said you know she going to get you back for that, Mom smiles and said what did I do, I didn't say anything just pulled a little. Dannie was at the bar with Max. Max said come back here and I can try your drink and write it down. So Dannie told Max how to make the drink.

Max took a little drink because he was working tonight. Dam he said looks like the house has a new drink. Vicki Max said try this drink. She did and said dam that good. Vicki gave it to some of the local boys and they liked it to. Max said looks like you got a winner. What did you call it again, Dannie said a Maine cold red chill. Good I will add it to the sign tomorrow.

Dannie smile and said thanks. Vicki hit Max in the side and said will shit head go ahead. Max looked at Vicki in a funny way as to say sorry? Vicki said you dumb ass ask her out. Max looked like he been pepper sprayed and couldn't speak. Vciki said the big guy is afraid to ask you out. Dannie smiled at him and said yes Max. Max was still stun at what Vicki said still couldn't speak. Dannie said would you like my number.

Max said In a half out of it looked yes sure. She wrote it on the peace for paper he wrote the drink on. So you call me then. Max was still in the clouds yes. Dannie came up and kissed him on the chin. Vicki said now the big man isn't going to be any good to work tonight. They smiled and laughed. Max made up some more drinks and helped Dannie back to the table. Dannie gave Mom her drink and kissed her on the chin and in a low voice said thanks.

Mom tried the drink and said it was just the same as Dannie. Good said Max and I'm going to add it to the bar sign tomorrow. Max said I've got to work, but I will be around from time to time. Mom and Dad said good loved to have you. Max went back to the bar and started working .The band started play the first song was Man Eater. Dad said looks like their play your song hun.

Mom said and you like it old boy. Dannie said you two are bad. Oh buy the way Max is going to call me sometime. Mom said great me and your Dad like him. They set back and had a few drinks and learned to the band play. Dannie looked at Max. Every once in a while he looked at her and smile like a big kid.

Adam got Fred's truck back to the station and told Fred too come inside and he would show him the old news report from Worcester Mass. Adam told

Chase to unpack the guns and the others come inside. Fred set at the laptop reading the newspaper recap. When he came to the picture, he turned as white as a ghost. Devvan said what's wrong Fred? Fred was looking at Adam he said that's the same thing that fell into the pit. That dam nearly killed me. Fred said but they killed it back then how can this be the same animal.

Al the town manager came in so what happens today Adam? Adam told him every thing and that the animal swam to the island. Good Al said the thing will did dead by morning. Adam said you really don't believe the stories of the island do you. Al said when I was young me and Patrick was fishing down at the top of the river and we saw a man with a long poll came out to the top of the island and throw the poll in the water. We sat there for a minute and then looked back to see the man and he was gone me and Patrick ran all the way home.

I told my Mom and that's when she told me about the river drivers and the kids that were killed on the island. Adam said will killer ghosts or not we're going to the island to hunt the animal. Al said your nuts man if you go there I wouldn't for a million. Adam said Patrick runs the rental boat place down on the rest area near the island right. Al said yes but your not going to get him on the island for not sums of money. Adam said we'll see tomorrow.

Fred was done the report and said I not crazy about the island but I will going with you tomorrow. Adam said good I will meet you at Annette's coffee shop in the morning. Good I've got to get some sleep Chase can you drop me at the house on your way home. Chase said sure if you ride in the trunk Fred. Fred said I don't care as long as I can get home and charge my shorts. Al said a bath wouldn't hurt to Fred. The team went home for the night.

Adam was going to get some thing to eat but was to run down from the day. About nine that night a knock came on Adam's door it was Annette and she was carrying some food and a bottle of something. Adam open the door and said hi to Annette .Can I help you Annette ? She said yes you can let me in and eat some food I see you don't stop tonight and I couldn't let my best costumer go hungry. Thanks Annette Adam said you're an angel with big tits.

She laughs at him and said you keep at up you my get lucky tonight. Annette came in and set the food out for him. I got a little slow grin here if you like to have some. Adam said yes slow grins would be great tonight. Adam set at the table and told Annette about everything that when on tonight. She said I can see why you didn't stop now. So what you going to do tomorrow. Adam said going to the island. Annette said please don't go there that island is evil.

Adam said just an old time story that everyone adds to, to make it scary. Annette said I don't know that but the island hasn't had anyone on it in 75 year or better. They drank and Adam was done his meal, Annette got up and kissed his chin and said I've got to run Adam. Adam graded her and hugged her with both hands on her ass.

Annette said slow big boy you moving to fast for me. So Adam let her go and watch out the window as she got in her car. Annette was really warm and her pants were wet, she said to herself dumb ass you should have made love to him. Adam locked the door as Annette drive off thinking dam needed a peace of ass tonight. Adam set in his chair than started to fall asleep.

Dannie was enjoying the music and thinking of Max. Mom and Dad were up dancing to look at them she said you think there were two young kids in love for the first time. They had dance almost all the songs. The song stops and Mom and Dad come over to the table hun you got to get Max to dances with you once. Dannie looked at the bar and Max was setting at the far end with a far away look on his face. Max looked up to see Dannie looking back at him he face lit up like a boy at Christmas. He got up and came over to the table and sat down.

You guys having fun Max said the band is great tonight. Dannie said I've been having a great night. Hear Mom and Dad said best band I've seen in a long time. Max said great will have to get them to play here more often. Vicki was over speaking with Ray she wanted him to play a nice slow dance for her. Ray said sure the next song is for you Vicki. Vicki returned to the bar and service a few more people. The band had ended the song and Ray said here's a slow one for you lovers out there.

Vicki throws a bar towel at Max and it hit him in the head. Max looked at Vicki and she said dance you big fool. Max looked at Dannie and started to ask but she got up and said yes before he could get it out. Max looked at Vicki and throws the towel back at her, he said think you can handle the bar. Vicki said I've been doing it most the night space case.

Dannie's Mom and Dad got up to and danced. Max put his hand on Dannie's side and handle her like she was a china doll. She looked up at him and said you can hold me I wouldn't break. She put her head on his chest and her arm around him. See she only came up too just under his chin. Max was ready to pass out but put his big arms around her and held her. She could hear only the bet for Max's heart as it got faster. She was in heaven she feels warm and safe in his big arms.

Dannie's Mom looked at Dad and said think our little girl is in love. Dad looked at them and said think your right hun as he pulled her closer. Mom said you big softy. She could hear him laughs when she grads his ass. Dad said remember women we're staying it Dannie's tonight. Mom smiles at Dad he said your bad woman. The song ended but both Max and Dannie didn't want it to. They went back to the table it was 11 now and Mom and Dad looked sleepy. Dannie looked at Max and said We're going to hit the road for tonight call me. Max said yes I will.

Max went over to the bar and Vicki looked at him you shit head you didn't kiss her. He turns to go back and kiss her good night and as he turned she was stand right behind him. Dannie said you left something at the table she grads his face and gave a big kiss. Max was so surprise at his legs started too give out he sat on one of the bar seats. Max was speechless and glassy eyed. Dannie said good night and turned to walk away. Max felt a hand hit him on the back of the hand it was Vicki again say good stupid. Max without think came out with good night stupid. Dannie looked back and smile same to you Max. Than Max said sorry I mean Dannie.

Dannie said I know and they left the bar. Dad said out side he's a nice man. Mom said yup he as bad as your Dad when I first meet him. Dad said but you still got me. They got in the jeep and went home. They got in the house and Dannie said you two can have my bed tonight and I will sleep down here on the pull out. Mom said no we will sleep down here and you keep your bed. Dannie said ok I sleepy I'm going to bed now she said there some bedding in the side closet and some blanket there to good night. Dad give her a hug and kiss and she went up stairs.

Dannie got into to her night cloths and clawed in bed she was still thinking for Max and started to smile. The window was open and she could her Mom and Dad outside and they weren't sleeping. Dannie put a pillow over her head so as too not hear anything else. She slowly falls into a deep sleep. She started to dream about Max and her dancing. But it turned into another night mare real fast.

This time she was running in the woods near Tommy's house. She saw a wolf like man in the middle of the field. She stops and the two of them saw each others. The wolfman started to run away as if he didn't want anything to do with her. She started after him she said to herself what the hell I'm I doing . Then the two run throw town down to the boat rental place and the wolfman jumps in and started swinging for a island out in between the two rivers. It was the dead river driver's island.

She stops at the shore and wasn't going the follow, but like all good night mares she could help it. She jumped in and began to swim after the wolfman. He Hit the shore of the island stops to see if she was behind him. He turned and runs as if she was going to kill him. She was about to hit the shore when she hears something hit the water on the other shore. It was a bright white she wolf and it was following hear. Great she though I'm chasing a wolfman and his wife chasing me. She hit the shore and started running up the hill after the wolfman. She came to and opening just before she saw the wolfman hitting the other side.

She runs hard after him but as she hit the middle of the field she saw what looked like and old rusty gate with seven head stone behind it. Seven ghost like man point to the woods as if to telling her where to go. Her heart was beating faster than before. She hit the other side and looked to see if the white wolf was still coming. She turns and headed to find the wolfman she didn't have to go long he was just jumping into to the river again. She jumped and landed on top of them again.

She grads his head again and broke his neck. She let him go under as she swam to the other shore. The white she wolf was standing on the other side looked at her as to say good job. Then she wakes up with a jump. Dam she said to herself that was scary but fun as her hands shock .It was 12:00 a.m an she didn't want to wake Mom and Dad or going down stairs and see them doing it. She rolls up in her blankets and went slowly back to sleep.

Adam's clock went off it was time to get up .He walks over to the shower and turned on the water .It got warm pretty fast he likes getting up this way it make him think better the first thing in the morning .It was around 7:00 am he got dressed and was going to meet Chase and Peter over to Annette's coffee shop for breakfast. Mary and Devvan would be there about 8:00 am because Patrick's boat rental place open around nine.

Adam went down and stood in front of the build he looked around the town, it was still quiet but for a few locals showing up for work that day. Adam looked up at the sky it was another good day on a tap. He looked back to see the old sign just above his head. Thinking to himself, I've got to do something about that sign some day. It was the old sign from Dicky's donuts. Adam walks to Annette's shop that's funny she here most of the time by now.

Adam turned around as Annette came from the side of the build the two jumped each other and Annette screams and said dam Adam you scared me so bad that I almost shit myself. Adam laughs and Annette unlocks the door. Adam said thanks for the drink and lunch last night. Annette said no trouble you looked a little run down last night. The two move into the dinner as Adam help Annette with an grad on the ass.

Annette said my now I won't have to have coffee today. Adam set down at the counter and watched as Annette turns on the lights. Annette brother Bob pulled up out front and comes in. Bob said hi to Adam and He yelled back to Annette. Annette came out with a big smile for Bod said hi brother. Bob said to Annette I will have the same as the other day.

Adam said that's sounds good same here. Chase and Peter came in Peter said hi to Adam .Good morning to you two didn't think you be in so early Adam said. Chase and Peter sat at the counter with Adam. Annette came out front and said hi boys can I get you anything. Chase said two coffee and whatever Adams having. Peters ask what's Adam was eating? Annette told him. Peter said the same for me to.

She got them coffee and went to the kitchen to cook. Peter said to Adam Me and Chase looked up the island last night and found out not much about it only about the dead river drivers. Bob stopped drinking his coffee, Bob was a man that keep to himself. He said to the guys your not planning to go out on the island are you. Chase said yup why ? You know the stories of the place that island is evil even the Indians wouldn't live on it.

There called it death island and that was before the river drivers got killed. Peter said the internet said it was not even own by anyone even the state doesn't know who own it. Will Adam said were have to go to it because the thing swam over their yesterday . Bob said what thing? Before Adam could stop Chase from say anything. Chase said the wolfman.

Wolfman Annette said from the kitchen. She came out with the food and gave the guys there plates. What is this wolfman I hear back there? Adam said we have only seen it far away. Chase said but Fred saw it up close. Adam looked at Chase and said why don't you call the paper and tell them. Chase said what wrong Adam said by the end of today Fred will have the town speaking about it.

Adam said I wanted to be the one who spoke to the town you know how small towns work. By tonight the wolfman will have killed 50 people and all the cows in town. Chase said sorry your right but I can't stop Fred from saying any thing. Fred pulls up in a black car it was Kevin's. Fred said good morning guys I ready for today I've already got a ride from hell this morning. Adam and the others laughed. Kevin said what I was only doing around a 105.That was slow for me and Steve.

The car will do a lot faster than that. Chase said that was fast for an old chev. Nova .Kevin said a chev nova yes but dodge vipers under the hood. Adam said it's a viper motor in that thing. Kevin smiled and said yup Steve has the same motor to in his carmro . Adam said you guys are real works of art aren't you. Chase said by the way where is Steve, just then a crash came from out side.

Adam said I think he's here. Steve walked in and said sorry I did it again. Peter looked at them both and just shock his head. Kevin said to Steve we got to get home soon to help Dad and then sleep for tonight. Steve said I'll race you Kevin said you're on. Adam said no racing in town guys. The boys left the coffee shop and burned rubber as they left. Adam said will we should get over to the station before Mary and Devvan show up. The guys payed and went to the station.

Dannie got up around 7.30am the sun was up and it was going to be nice day. Dannie said I've got the day off today maybe we can go to the Springfield fair. The Springfield happens once a year like all the other fairs around it was a fun time for people. Truck and tracker pulls. Horses pulling music from local kids and group. The best thing was the cotton candy and fried doe. They had rides and games to play. It would be a fun time and Mom and Dad loved thing like that.

She started down stair and saw that the fold out wasn't open. She said maybe they got up and went for breakfast. She went into the kitchen and no note someone was going to get hell for not writing a note for her. She started a pot of coffee and went to see how the weather was on the porch. She got to the door and found it funny that it was unlocked. She knows that she locked it last night before bed. She open the door and walked out on the porch she found the reason for the unlocked door.

Mom and Dad were sounds asleep roll up in blankets in the back yard. Dam she though the cat or animal could had killed them out here last night. She knows they were alright because Dad was snoring like a motorbike without a muffler. She was mad and was going to wake him up and gave him a peace of her mind, but standing there she though I'll get those two fools.

She stepped back into the house and on one side of the door was the control for the lawn sprinklers. I think the lawn is a little dry this morning as she had that devil look in her eyes. She turned on the system and went into the kitchen too got a cup of coffee and set at the counter as if she didn't have anything to do with the water.

Dannie set down and she heard Mom and Dad hit the porch they came throw the back door and saw Dannie setting drinking a coffee. Dannie said I think there a change of rain today. Mom and Dad looked at her and they all started laughing. Dannie said you two have fun last night. Mom said as she hugs Dad sorry but yup. Dad Dannie said don't give me hell for walk around in the nude and she smiled.

Buy the way didn't you remember about the cat or animal that's was running around here. Dad said sorry hun but I had your Mom to protect me. What's she going to do take his credit cards. Mom and Dad laughed and said there were sorry again. You two I don't think you ever grow up sometimes, but I still love you. If you two could keep off the back lawn for a while we could go to the Springfield fair. Mom said great do they have rides at this fair. Dannie said yes but not the kind your can take your cloths off on.

Dannie said go take a cold shower and I'll cut some fruit and cheese up for breakfast I have bagels to. Great Dad said looks like a good day after the rains stop. Dannie said you two get out of here and get some cloths on. Dannie set there thinking to her self if me and Max get together hope it like Mom and Dad life is. She though about Max and a big smile and warm feeling came over her.

Adam ,Chase, Peter and Fred were setting in the office. Chase looked at Fred and said what with the new jeans a shirt. Fred said a man can't look good for a charge. Chase said but it not like you to dress up nice unless you were going to a wedding. Fred said maybe yesterday charge me a little. Adam said now Chase don't get him going this morning. Chase said I wasn't just want to say he looked good for a charge.

Fred said thanks and then Adam looked funny at Fred to, Thanks Adam said how are you and what you do with Fred. Now don't you starts said Fred. Fred said life is just a little bit sweeter tonight. Mary and Devvan came in and got some coffee hi guys. So when do we head for the island Devvan said. Adam said we can pack and head down to Patrick's boat rental. It was 8.30am now and he opens in a half hour Chase said. Good lets roll Adam said.

Fred said can I get the 308 bolt action out of the case, my 30\30 didn't seem to stop the wolfman any yesterday. Adam said you sure you hit them. Yup Fred said he moved a little each time a shot landed. I don't remember seeing any blood Adam said. Wasn't any Fred Said not a drop. Adam said ok and throw the keys to the case to Fred there two boxes for shell in the case to.

Fred pulls the 308 out of the case and said, see you stand up to this wolfman. The team loaded up every thing and headed to the boat rental. Adam and Peter took Adam's truck and Chase and Fred took the police car. Mary and Devvan follow in there truck. Peter said this doesn't sound like a ford ranger I've ever heard. Will I had a little fun rebuilt this girl Adam said? I got it off a young man

That loss his home to the bank and sold it to me for 2000 dollars. You could see it killed him to part with her, but he got a new one when he got back on his feet.

It has and motor from a ford gt the new sports car and tran. I made the pipe myself and the hood vent and put a hard cover on the back with wing. I put about 20 grand in all together in it. She will fly like the wind. Peter said why would anyone need a fast truck like that around here?

Ask Steve and Kevin one day they though they would loss me by hitting the interstate. I came up on them at around a 105 miles an hour and then smoke them both with the cars they had today. I hit almost 172 miles an hour when I back out because the truck was coming off the road. I pull over and Steve and Kevin were nowhere to be seen. I set there a few second and you could hear the two of them flying trying to get me.

I set my blue light on the roof and make a sign for them to pull over, there did and they were fit to be tied. Will needless to say they never try that again. Dam Peter said faster then I want to run. Will I only use her around town and for auto shows. Peter said she sure a good looking ride.

Adam said thanks. The group got to the boat rental and Patrick was there and setting up two people and kids in a boat. Patrick yelled hi to Adam and that I'll be right with you. Patrick was a young man with a new baby and wife to take care of. He open this rental place and he was doing great.

Adam was Glad because he knows how hard Patrick tried. Patrick came up to Adam and said need a fishing boat. Adam said no we need you and a boat to go down to the island. Patrick face turned pale white he said are your nuts. Patrick said you not getting me on that place. Adam said ok we need you to drop use on the north side and then back off to the middle and set.

Patrick said ok but you'll have too turned your radios to my CB channel. You sure you want to go there. Adam said yes. Ok it's your life. We'll take the party boat it's big and has a powerful motor to keep it in place in fast moving water. The team loaded on Patrick's boat and he called his wife to come and run things. Patrick's wife showed up and the team set off.

The water was carm the sun warm. The party boat cut throw the water like a knife. As they moved down the shore line to the island under the new bridge that was built a few years back to replace the old one. Peter said what are the rock in the center of the river for. They were old boom log holder. Mary said what's a boom

log? .It and old river drivers say Chase said, the river drivers would hock large tree to each other to form a pen for the logs.

They could see the old sand pit to there right and just ahead the island. Patrick said dam she looks the same as it did all those years ago, still gives me the chills. Patrick pulled up to the north side of the island. Chase throws a rope with a hock on it at one of the big pine so as to pull them in. The hook went around the tree and lock in Chase slowly pull the boat to the shore watching all the time for anything moving.

Adam got off first with Peter and Fred there made there way up to the top of the bank. Mary and Devvan started to the front to get off, but the dogs didn't want anything to do with the island. Adam said what's wrong? Devvan said the dogs won't get off on the Island. Mary said we can leave them and do the tracking our self. Patrick said ok with me. I can watch them for you. Chase said I can stay here to watch him. Adam said get up here you chicken shit. Chase and the other two got off and joined the others on the bank.

Patrick was happy they were off the sooner he could leave the better. Patrick and the dogs move the boat to the middle of the river and turn on the CB. Adam said can you hear me Patrick. Patrick said back loud and clear happy hunting. Patrick looked at the dogs and said glad I'm not out here. Adam and the group move down the shore to find where the wolfman had came to shore. They found the spot and Mary and Devvan leaded the way.

The island was a far size island with pine tree on it, not hard going. Devvan stop at the edge of a field. The group moved up to help look over the field. The grass was short not like the main land. Fred said you can see were the wolfman went throw. The team started into the field a cold chill came throw the air. Fred said you feel that? Adam and the others all felt it. The team form a circle. Devvan and Mary up front, Adam and Chase on the sides, Fred and Peter cover the back.

The group moved slowly and watched for anything that moved. About half way Mary said she could see a gate and what looked like a grave yard ahead. The air was still and everyone was on edge. As they came to the small grave yard they could see seven small head stones in it. Fred said this must be the river driver's graves. Peter looked at the graves from one side of the old fence and said that's funny. Adam said what's Peter? The graves are set foot the foot to each other the stones are around the out side of the graves not side to side to each other.

It was true the grave's seven in all with five out side and that form a pentagram the others were set to form an upside down cross. Chase said lets move on I don't like this. The group seen the think the same. As they started back up Chase falls over some thing and cut his legs. Chase said dam what the fuck was that looking at the blood on his leg. Fred kneed down and got the thing that cut Chase's leg as Fred pulls it up his eyes open wide it was an old pick poll. Chase was just about to stand up and loss it when an icy wind filled the air.

Mary said can you hear that? Devvan said yes. On the wind was a soft but cold voice leave our island the voice said, it did it for a few minutes then carm. Chase was all ready to run back the way he came when Fred grads him, carm down Chase were almost to the other side see you can see the edge of the river. The group came back together and follow the tracks to the shore he went in there Mary said. Adam called Patrick on the radio to came around to the other side. Patrick called back said ok be there shortly.

Patrick came around to the other side and Chase grads the boat and held it for the team to get on. Chase jumps on and looking back at the island and said lets get the fuck out of here. Patrick said fine with me he pulled the boat out in the middle. Patrick said where too now? Adam said to the other shore to see if we can spot the track of the wolfman. Patrick said good he didn't like the island.

As the boat went up stream to the top of the island and the open water. Your could see the old singing bridge and a work crew under it. Adam said that's funny I don't remember the bridge being posted for repair. Patrick pulls the boat up to the crow and Adam said hi. Adam said didn't know anyone was working on the old girl.

The boss of the group said yes we going to close it soon and replace it. The boss had on a hard hat that read Reed and Reed .Adam asked did they see any strange animals around. The boss said no hadn't been here long. Ok will have a good day and Patrick started the boat down river. As the group started to pull away Patrick said that's funny. Adam said what funny Patrick? Patrick said for workers we were really clean and there all had radio and sneakers on.

Adam looked back at the crow as they pulled away. The group went down the shore line for about a mile under the interstate bridge. Adam told Patrick to hit the other shore and head up stream. No signs of where the wolfman got out. Maybe the wolfman went under a flooded down stream Chase said. Patrick said maybe the river drivers killed him with a pick poll. The hold team looked at Patrick. Patrick said what wrong did I say some bad? Fred told Patrick what went down on the island. Patrick said glad I didn't go on I would have dropped everything and hit the water and not stop until I was safe in town.

Chase smiled I almost did, as he showed Patrick the cut on his leg. The group returned to the rental landing and payed Patrick for his time. The group headed back to the town and the station. Fred said what's next Adam. Adam said I've got a town meeting here shortly to tell everyone what's going on. The group unpacked at the station and made some coffee and set around to recap the day.

Dannie and her Parent got ready to go to the Springfield fair. The trip down there was nice. It was all back roads that when throw small town. The road were ok for summer running but really bad in the snow and cold of winter. They were some funny little town with one store and few homes. Most for them had short names like Win , Lee and Medway. All the same but different from each other.

Springfield was one of the smaller one if the fair wasn't there you would going right pass the town in a seconds. Dannie turned the last corner to the fair grounds. The cars were all over the place they stop in a field that a local church own. Where they got out and walked down the road to the fair. It was ten dollars to get in but a great deal in all.

Mon and Dad saw the truck pulls were going to start. So Dannie got a cotton candy and they went to the grand stands. The trucks were fun to watch and the locals cheer on everyone. One team was local to Medway Dannie know the drivers. The power pulling team was a father and sons team. After that came the tailor's pulls. Old farm tailors from all over.

Dad and Mom were having a great time so was Dannie. When the pulls were over Dannie and her Mom and Dad went to the check the thing around the fair. Dannie said Mom look ears rings made from morse shit. It takes a

Mainer with a twisted mind to come up with that. Dad here's a black fly trap guess you have to be from Maine to get the joke. Dannie got everyone a fry doe it wouldn't be a fair without it.

Dannie was walking down throw the fair and saw the petting zoo. She went in the animal seem to come to her like she was there Mom. Mom and Dad laughs just like when you were young you always came home with a cat or dog behind you Mom said. They went over to the horses and the same thing all he animals seem to be drawn to her. Mom and Dannie went on some rides and Dad stayed on the ground he wasn't must for trill rides.

The day was going fast the locals started the music part of the show. It was local country and rock bands and kids singing and playing drums. But the funny part was just about to started car crashing. Kevin and Steve the two on night watch were in they seems they could win with the running into things they did. The show was fun and the fire works were going to start soon.

Dannie was thinking how Steve and Kevin would get back in time for there watch tonight, but they didn't stay for the fire works. Dannie loves the color of the fire works and the noise they made. The show was small but real fun. It had been a long day and they started for home. Mom and Dad said we had a great time kid. Dannie said so did I.

Getting back to the truck Dannie looked up at night sky and the stars, they were bight and the sky was clear. Mon said it almost too good to go home. Dannie said you two keep your cloths on. Mon and Dad laughed at each other. It was a cool ride home the night air was fresh and made you want to sleep. Mom and Dad said we're going to stay one more night. Dannie said in the house this time you to. Yes hun Dad said.

They got back home and Dannie was sleepy. Mom and Dad sat on the love seat. Will I'm going to bed Dannie said. Mom and Dad said good night we are to. See you in the morning Dannie said love you two. Love you to hun they both said.

Back in town just about noon time that same day Adam was Making himself ready for the town meeting in a few minutes. Adam also looked up the work bring done on the old singing bridge. The report said Reed and Reed were going to do the work on replacing the bridge, but weren't going to start until next month. Adam said to himself they must have wanted to get started sooner.

Adam and the team headed to the town office just down the road. The town office a large white building with and old bank on one side and a Drug's store on the other. You walked throw two sets for double door to the hall. The hall was lager with a full kitchen down stair. The hall its self had see better days and old stage at the far end and over head setting as you came in.

Adam and the group set up down front next to the stage. There was already some people in the hall. Al came in and went to see Adam. Al said so do we know what killed Tommy. Adam said we have a very good idea. Al said we should started the meeting it looks as if everyone in the town is here.

Ok Adam said lets do this thing. Al walks up to the mike and said can we all start this meeting please be seated . Al said I know that most of you heard that Tommy was killed the other day. Adam and his team have been tracking this thing that killed them for the last few days. Now Al said I will turns this meeting over to Adam.

Adam stepped up to the mike and started by saying people I'm sorry that we have to meet this way. The people were on edge. Adam said the other day young Tommy was kill by some type of animal. Adam said we track it to the island where this morning we looked for it and it was no where to be found, but it seems that it left the island and swim ashore. We looked up and down the river but couldn't find where it may have been getting out.

Someone in the group said so what kind of animal are we tacking about ? Adam said a wolf like man. Everyone looked at Adam as to say you're crazy. Old lady May stood up and said you mean we got a werewolf running around town killer people. The group became upset and everyone started yelling out from all over the room. You mean someone in this room could be a werewolf and killer his friends. Adam said no in a loud voice.

Someone said I heard it kill all Sam's cows to. Adam said quiet down I will tell you everything we know. The group grow even more upset looking around at each other to see if they could tell how the werewolf was. Adam said came on people carms down here let me speak, but you could see the group wasn't learning. Someone said do we need silver bullets to kill it. The meeting was clearly getting out of hand.

From over head in the seats above the group a loud wesiel sounded it was Fred. Fred stood up and yelled shot up and let the man speak. The group started to came back around. Adam said thanks Fred and he began to tell everyone the facts. The animal is not a werewolf as far as we know. It some type of man like wolf cross. Someone said isn't that a werewolf .Adam said yes, but a werewolf in the movies can charge from man to wolf, but this animal as far as we know is only a wolfman. Adam said that is he stays a wolfman all the time.

Adam said unlike the movies to the wolfman can be kill with just lead bullets. Someone said so how do you know it's a wolfman did you see it. Adam said from far out, but Fred saw it from close up. Everyone looked back at Fred still standing in the over head seats. Adam said I will let Fred tell you what it looks like, but first we have a few things to do.

Adam said I've got some printouts on an old case in Worcester Mass. where the first animal was made. Someone said someone made this thing. Adam said it appears this is what happen. Adam said there also a picture with it and Fred said it looks the same as the thing he saw. Adam said as you read you'll see what in 1940 some government place in Worcester played with the idea of crossing apes with man and wolfs with man. The wolf man cross broke out and after kill 20 or more people was killed by the local cop after shooting it 70 times.

Now back then the guns were shot guns and small hand guns, but even so 70 rounds is a lot of fire power. Adam said also when the cops went back to the lab they found it cleaned out and everything gone. They're was one doctor pass out in a case that told them that two apes like man and the others got away. So is this and ape-man someone said.

Adam said no it looks like the picture and we think that someone maybe trying to start the lab up again and this time the animal got loss also. Someone said what kind of sick son of a bitch would do this and where. Someone else said what about the old mill in the hills. Adam said we are going up there tomorrow to look around, but Mike said most the mill was burned down and just a few buildings an the houses are there.

Adam said besides someone work need power to run the place. Someone said what about the old power station up there. Adam said the station was burned to the ground to, just the base is there from what Mike said. Adam said I will let Fred speak some and than I'll let you ask some more question.

Fred came up to the mike will the picture your looking at is an old photo, but the animal there is a lot like the one that almost killed me. Fred said it was shit luck or someone watching over me that keep me safe. Fred said I shot the thing two time with my 30/30 and it run at me as if it didn't feel it.

Fred said if it wasn't for the two of use falling over the side of the pit it would have had me to. Someone said the pit isn't that a long drop and how did it get away. Fred said the wolfman landed at the bottom about 150 feet down, but some how it got up and made it way to the island. Old May said you don't mean that thing went to the dead rivers drivers island. Fred said yes May that island, we just got back from it this morning that's how we told it's not there still. May said you guys nuts that island is bad news. Fred said after this morning some of use think so.

Will I'm going to let Adam finish this meeting. Adam returned to the mike will thanks Fred. Adam said so you got an idea at what we're facing now. Adam said I know we depend on the outer states to run things around here, but maybe we should think of closing down hunting season in the town this year. The group started to came unglued again. Someone said you, don't have a business that depends on that money, you close the hunting down you could kill the town. Adam said it would be a lot better than killing a shit load of people out there. May said maybe we can give a reward for the killing of this wolfman.

Adam said bad idea we would have 600 money hungry nuts running in and out of here shutting at ever thing with two legs. Adam said we got two days before the season starts we may get lucky an kill it before then. Adam said that he had a cast of the animal's prints on the table please look at it on you way out and report to me if you see any tracks, don't try to kill this thing alone.

The meeting slowly let out as people came up to Adam to see the print and ask some more things about the wolfman. Adam looked at the group and said will its now 6.30 time to call it a day. We will meet in the morning to go to the old mill and look around. Mary said can we drive all the way there? Adam said yes the road is a little grown over but derivable .

The road Adam said is about seven miles in before you get to the gates. Well see you all tomorrow then around 8am.Peter said you going to Annette's for supper? Adam said sure its sounds good. Adam said I've got to stop and see how Chase is doing first, but after that I'm going over. Peter said good mind if I go with you to see Chase? Adam said sure lets hit the road.

As Adam and Peter was walking out the door Al stopped Adam and said we can't afford to shot down hunting season. Adam said you think we can afford not to. Adam and Peter turned and walked to the station. Think I will get the ranger out for a ride. Cool said Peter. Adam and Peter went over to Chase's house. Chase was sitting in the livingroom watching TV and drinking and beer.

Adam and Peter came in and Adam said what the doctor say Chase. Chase said Mike told me I should be ok in the morning and not to do any log runs in the mean time. Good Adam said we going back to the island in the morning. Chase spit his beer out and said are you nuts I didn't sleep all night because of that. Peter said then it must have been your girlfriend cutting the wood last night.

Adam laughed and said no Chase were going to the old mill. Chase said good Fred can ride with you and tell the story of the old mill. Peter said don't tell me another ghost story. Adam said no ghost but 70 people burned to death up there. Peter said remind me not two get a job in this town. Adam said this all happen a long time going in the old days of the town. Peter said still the same that's 77 dead people in one town. Chase said 79 two murders to. Peter said two murders to. Adam said yes one young lady about 25 years ago and a cop about 100 years ago.

Peter said dam it's not safe to be a cop here. Will Adam said me and Peter are going to Annette's for supper care to join use? Chase said yes but we all can't fit in that truck. Adam said take the town cop car in. Chase said I could but you know who gets pissed when we use them when we're not on duty. Adam said we can say that Peter was picking you up form doctor Mikes. Peter said it sounds good to me. The three started back to town Adam was in front in his truck. Peter and Chase in the rear in the car.

Chase called Adam on the radio. Adam said ok what do you want Chase. Chase radio back the two mile flats is coming up seeing if the truck still got the nuts in it. Adam said ok I will hit it, but back off a little. Peter looked at Chase why back out? Chase laughed you see. Adam hit the top of the hill and hit the gas the rear tire broke loss and put down 20 feet of rubber before the truck hooked up and shot off.

Peter and Chase hit the top as the truck got going, dam Peter said that truck is flying. About one mile Adam flu by two cars on the side it was Steve and Kevin the two gave them the finger as he shot by. Adam said shit they're not going to let me live this down. Peter radio Adam see how at was on the side. Adam came back laughing yup went by them at about 150.

Chase called back see you at the dinner. Adam said ok going to put the truck away and walk over. Peter and Chase meet Adam out in front of Annette's shop. The three started in and Steve and Kevin came down the street. They stopped out front and yelled at Adam. Steve said you see where Darrell Ernheart went. Adam smiled and said get to work you to. The boys shot off and went to watch the town.

Adam walked in and Annette and one other people was setting at the counter. Hi there boy's Annette said come to make me rich. Adam said were going to get supper and some of your cheesecake. Peter said cheesecake love it hope it's good. Annette said the best in Maine. The guys sat down at the counter and had they're supper and chesses cake. Adam said woman best chesses cake I've ever had going to have to marry you.

Annette laughs your going to have to wait in line with the rest of them. The cops sat there until the sun went down and Peter and Chase went back to Chases. Adam said will Annette going to call it a night. He paid her and grads her ass on the way out. She turned to see her and she smiled. Adam went home and kicked back with a soda and watched TV.

Dannie got undress and ready for bed. She tried not to think of the last two night's dreams. She sat on the edge of the bed and could see the phone machine flashing. She was hoping it was Max. She play to messenger and he said if it wasn't to later call me would like to have lunch tomorrow at the bar. She looks at the clock a little after 9.00.She called the number that he left the phone rang she could feel her heart jump as he picked up the phone. Max said hi can I help you. Dannie said yes you already did by calling me.

Max said hi I was wondering if you like to eat lunch with me here tomorrow. She said yes love to. Max said great I'm making something good for use tomorrow. She said I can't wait. She ask Max how his day went so far. Max said it was good but now it's great. He told her that he was afeard to call until Vicki hit him and dialed the phone. She told him that she like him and he shouldn't be afraid of her she's just a little thing. Max said I know but you're so beautiful and not stuck up. He said you know the type of girl I'm speaking about to pretty for there own good. Dannie said yes I do and I not like that.

Max said I still don't know why you chose me I'm not a looker and I'm not good with the words. Dannie said it was you heart I could see you're a kind and sweet man. Max said thanks I needed that, so around noon tomorrow. Ok Dannie said I'll be there with bells on. She kissed to phone and said see you late sweety . Max, Max, Max, Max are you there. Vicki said hi Who's this? Dannie said it me Dannie Vicki is there something wrong with Max. She laughs the big fool passed out what did you say to them. I just kiss the phone and said good night sweety. Dannie started to laugh is he ok. Vicki said just a minute. Dannie could hear some water spelling on the floor.

Vicki said here he is a little wet but alive. Max got back on the phone and said I'm sorry for that you just made me so happy I pass out. Dannie was laughing she said sorry didn't mean to do that. Max said ok I'll see you in around noon. Yes good night oh I'm going to kiss you again and she kissed the phone. Max, Max oh dear not again she said. Max laughs no I'm here this time good night beautiful.

She put the phone down and curled up in bed. Dannie said he could be the one and a big smile came on her face and warm feeling run throw her body. She still had a big smile on her face as she slowly slips to sleep. Her dreams were going great she was walking down the main street. She Stopped at the cross walk in the center of town. She waited for the light to charge then as she started across some thing was moving in the old bank on the cover it was a bight white light.

She had too hold her hand up to cross the road. The light felt warm and safe. She came to the front of the bank. It still had the rent sign outside and the lawn was high because no one had cut it. She felt the light pull her to it. She moved to the front door and pulled on it, it was unlocked she moved inside there was a second door she open it. She was standing there and the light was warmer , but still felt safe.

She hears a voice she couldn't tell were it was form it seems to be everywhere and even inside her. The voice said will you fight for me ? Dannie said how are you? The voice said I'm your father. Dad why can't I see you. The voice said again will you fight for me. Dannie said Dad you know I would fight for you but why?

Good my child then a bean came at her and she put up her hand to block it. The bean burn her hand then the light disappeared. It was gone the bank was all that was left she turned to move out the door. Her hand was still warm she came out the last door and turned her hand around. She could see five stars in the form of a pentagram and a dove with a rose in its mouth in the middle. She set down on the steps and tried to get some air.

When a loud noise like a really big dog cut throw the air from both sides of town, but the noise was as if the dog was in real pain. She stood up and stated back down the street. She got to the corner by Davis's drug store. She could see far away someone moving to her. She didn't know who it was, but as the person got closer she could see it was Max.

She though great he's here to save the day. She ran to him and jumped in his big arms. Max said did you say yes to your father? She looks at him and said yes, but what fight? Max said your father fight. Max hugs her and they both kiss. She wakes up with a jump this time but one of love and safety. She looked at her hand the mark was gone. She looked at the clock it was 3am. She could feel her heart beating fast as she laid back and slowly went back to sleep. The night watch was going ok for a change the boys we're not running into thing as much anymore. The two had CB in there cars and could speak to each other. Steve said to Kevin where are you now. Kevin said right behind you and Kevin turned on his lights. Steve called him, ok you got me that time but I still got more hours in the night to get you back, the two went pass Mary's Ann Market and turned a left.

Steve pulled over to speak to Kevin. Kevin Said, I'll race you to the other end of the street. Steve said you Know what Adam said about racing in town. Kevin said you chicken. Steve said no because we do need the money were getting from this job. Kevin said yup your right. Hay there no houses from here to the top of the hill Kevin said. Steve said ok you're on, but only to the top of the hill. Ok Kevin said your on.

The two lined up and looked at each other ready go. The two left side by side and the tire were making a hell of a noise. They stayed right even with each other as they came to the thrip way mark. Steve looked up and pointed to the road ahead some thing was in the middle about the half way mark. They both stopped. Kevin said that's a morse isn't it. Steve said morse have four legs that standing on two. Steve turned on his high beams.

Kevin said shit is that the wolfman thing. The wolfman was mad that it couldn't see so it started move to the lights. Kevin said shit it coming at use. Steve yelled hit the gas and run it down. The two put down on the gas and started heading at the wolfman. Steve yelled out it's not getting out of the road. Kevin said were got to hit it. The two pulled their cars closer to each other as the two hit the animal at the same time.

The wolfman hit Steve's car first than went in the air and rolled off the back of Kevin. The two could see it roll down the center of the road and stop, laying still on the hot top. There stop in the middle of the road. Steve got out to look back at the wolfman. Kevin said Steve did we kill it. Steve said I think we did. Steve said give Adam a call. Kevin handed the phone to Steve as Adam said hi. Adam said you guys ok did something happen ? Steve said we're just outside of town and we ran over your wolfman I think it's dead. Adam said ok I on my way don't get near it.

Before Adam could finish saying things He could hear Steve says shit. Adam said what's wrong Steve? The thing is moving. Adam yelled into the phone get your assess out of there now. Steve jumps back in his car and pull it into drive and the two burned tires and started to leave. Kevin looked back and could see the animal it was up and on a dead run for the two. Adam said what going on Steve? Steve said the dam it's coming for use. Adam said stand on the gas you two and get out for there meet you up to the church by the school.

Steve and Kevin were driving for all they're worth this time it was for their lives. Steve looked back to see where the wolfman was as his car hooked up and got moving away. The dam thing was almost on top of them. The cars started to pull away from the wolfman and the animal seemed to not be giving up, but as the two hit the top of the hill there could see it slowing then stops. The wolfman let out a blood chilling howl.

Kevin could feel the hair on the back of his neck stand up and a cold chills run down his back. The two make it to the church parking lot out front. Adam pulled in right behind them. The two boys got out of the cars and were as white as sheep . Adam said you to ok as he jumps out of the car. Steve and Kevin could just beady speak. Guys slow down and tell me what when on. Kevin said we were on the wildness driver road side by side when the wolfman came out in front of use we couldn't do anything but step on it and run it down.

Steve said we hit so hard that it should have been dead. Adam said it fell a 150 feet to the ground in the old pit and walk away. The two showed Adam where the wolfman hit the two cars. Adam said it looks like you hit a morse. Steve said it felt like it. Adam was running his flash light up the car and saw something in the molding of Steve's window shield. Adam walks over to the thing and got his knife out to remove it. Steve said what is that Adam?

Adam said think it's a part of the wolfman. Adam looked at it close, it was about one inch by three inches long black almost looked like a lager fish scale. Adam said dam if this thing is cover in this that would be the reason

Fred's 30/30 didn't stop it. Steve said you think the dam thing is got amer. Adam said sure looks like it. You get in the car and show me were you hit it. The boys looked at each other and said do we have to?

Adam said I've got two of my guns with me. Kevin said hope they're big ones this thing can stand a beating. Adam said yup I got the 50 caber ones. The three got in the car Steve in the front with Adam and Kevin in the back. Steve said dam this gun should kill it. Adam said I really hope so to guys. The three got back to the spot where the wolfman was last seen.

The sun was about to came up and they could see good now. Adam said is this the place. Steve said yes just after the black marks. Adam slow down the rolled down his windows. Using his flash light and the cars spot light he began looking over the woods and the side of the road. They turned around and started back up the road moving at a very slow speed. Steve and Kevin both ready to shot anything that broke wind. Almost at the end of the road Steve said stop.

Adam said that's the wolfman's track they are going up the old road to the mill. Adam said good it's heading back out of town then. Adam said I'll bring you two back to your cars and you can call it a night. Steve said were not going to follow it. Adam said no me and the others are going up their around nine this morning. We will have more fire power and dogs to track with in the moving.

Adam said you two are welcome to come with use. The two boys looked at each other a said no thanks. Ok Adam said here your cars I will see you tonight right. Kevin said can we carry these gun with use. Adam said yes as long as you make dam sure of what your shooting before you pull the tiger. Steve said yup we're not flatlanders. Ok then stop tonight and pick them up. Ok the boys said there both got in their car and headed home. Adam looked funny at them no spinning tires and black smoke. Adam returns to his place.

Dannie wakes up she was happy and feeling great. She remembers the dream and the phone call she made to Max. She put on her sweats and went down stairs. She was hoping Mom and Dad were sleeping still not anything else. She came down the stairs and the two of them were asleep on the pull out. She runs over and jumped in the middle of them. They both wake up what is going on Dannie Mon said. She got in between them I call him last night.

Dad said Max why did he do something? She said yes he call me and left a messenger on the machine in my room. Mom said and what did he say? Dannie told them all about the phone call and Max passing out. Dad and Mom laughed Dad said he's a real shortly isn't he. Mom hit Dad with her pillow she said I remember a man who pass out when a pretty girl kissed him on the chin. Mom and Dad hugged her and said were happy for you kid.

Dannie said I've also got a date with him this noon time. Mom kissed her and said great. They laid there for a while and laugh at her. Dad said she grow up isn't she Mom, and Mom said she a big girl now but still my Dady. Dannie said I've loved having you two over this week end it's been a really fun time. Mom and Dad said we've had a fun time with you to hun.

Dannie said I know my lawn will never be the same. They all laughed and hugged. Dannie set up in the middle of them and said I got to find a nice dress and get ready for work. But I need to eat and take a shower to. Dannie grad her Dad by the shirt help me I can't think. Dad pulled her back down in the bed and hugged her and her Mom said it called love Dannie.

Dad said you go make yourself beautiful and me and Mom will cook breakfast. Dannie said thanks and ran up stairs like a school kid. Dad Grad Mom's Butt and said it nice to see her so happy. Mom rolled over and looked at Dad I know she said as she hugs him and gave him a big kiss. Dad said looks like we started cooking already their woman, hear a lawn calling use. She hit him and said you're bad as she pulls the cover over them. Dannie was in her room looking for a good dress, she though I've got a new blue dress that I haven't put on. She pulled it out and held it up to her full length mirror. She said this is the one.

She put the dress on the bed and went for a shower. She was so filed with life she could almost blow up. She washed and stood in the shower and let the water run down her front and back. She got out and set in front for her makeup stand and dried her hair and put on her make up. She took her time to look good for Max. She went down stairs and her Mom and Dad were in the kitchen cooking breakfast.

She stopped in the door way to watch him both, she though hope me and Max are this loving if we get together. She walks in the room and Dad turned around and said dam hun you're as beautiful as your Mom. Mom looked backs you look great Dannie.Dannie said what we having I'm hungry. Mom said Dacron, egg, cheese, and fruit.

Dannie sat down and began to eat and tacking with her Mom and Dad. Dannie said maybe we could go to Baxter park next week end. Max's loves the out doors to. Mom and Dad said sounds like a plan see what happens. Dannie said got to run and she kissed them and said I love you two see you later.

Mom said maybe we will stop and see you on the way home today. Dannie said ok and headed out the door to work. Dannie came out of the house got in her jeep and headed to town as she road she was still on cloud nine. She got to town and make it to work on time. Crissy was there at her deck she looked up as Dannie walks throw the door, will don't we look nice today. Dannie said thanks I feel great today.

Crissy said well a good night's sleep or a hot date last night. Dannie said a really good night's sleep and a hot date for lunch. Crissy ask is it anyone I know? Dannie said you my know him, its Max who runs Max's place. Max said Crissy he's and big old sweet heart of a man. Dannie spun around and set down at her desk. Crissy said it sound like someone in love. Dannie said I sure hope he the one.

Dannie told her about the call last night and everything that happen. Crissy smiled and laughs she said sounds like he's in love. Crissy said the school call the teacher said thanks the girls got A+'s on their programs, and ask me if you my did willing two do a class or two on makeup tips. Dannie said love to is it after school hours. Crissy said yup it would be from 4to5pm.

Crissy said I've got to run to Bangor today so this after noon after your hot date your can head home if you want. Dannie said ok I've got some computer lab work to do and my work should be finish of the day. Crissy said great then I'm going to go now when you leave lock up and have fun this noon time. Dannie said I'm sure going to try.

Adam was at the station after his breakfast at Annette this morning. He was really getting into the peace of the wolfman that was left behind. Peter and Chase walked throw the door and Fred right behind him. Adam said hi their guys. Peter looked at Adam though some thing was wrong he asked Adam did something go down last night? Adam said yes I'll tell everyone when Mary and Devvan shows. Fred ask what that you got their Adam? Adam handed to Fred and said part of owner wolfman. Fred said it black and looks like hard bone.

Adam said hand it around and have a look guys. Chase looked at it and He said looks like a peace of body arm. Adam looked at him and said why would you say that Chase? Chase said the new body amer. that came in last month I told you about and you said to put it on the shelf out back. Oh I though it was something else said Adam. Chase said I'll go grad one and be right back. Peter said you're not say this thing is armored are you? Adam said it sure looks like that. Chase returned from the store room with one of the vest and set it on the table in front of Adam. Adam said dam the two do look a lot a like but this vest is man made and this peace looks as it was living ones.

Mary and Devvan came in hi there what going on? Adam sat them all down and told them what went on last night. Devvan looked at the vest and said isn't that what they call dragon scale? .Chase said yup and show him the peace of the wolfman Adam got this morning. Mary said shit we got a wolf tank running around out there. Adam said it sure looks as if we may have.

Adam said ok. You guys want the bad new? Chase said what could be worst than this? The wolfman was headed to the old mill last night and that is where we're heading today Adam said. Adam said lets load up and get rolling. Fred, Peter, Chase you ride with me and Mary and Davven you bring up the rear Adam said. Chase said is the road ok to run a car on? Adam said Mike said the last time he was up there it was in good shape. The group left town and turned on wildness drive they when to the end and turned right onto the old mill road.

The road was ok a little over grown with grass. Peter said why would they put a mill so far back in the wood? Fred said it was own by a man who didn't like the city and wanted to be able to control the works. Peter said what kind of a mill was it? Adam looked at Chase then looked back at Peter. Fred didn't say a thing he was watch for the wolfman. Pete said what did I said anything wrong? Than Fred said in a low voice it was a dry beef and dry fish plant.

Peter said ok beef jerky and smoke fish so why the long faces? Fred said Adam you going to tell him? Peter said tell me it's not another ghost story? Fred said no ghost just a very evil man and his meat. Adam said go ahead Fred and tell the story it was before my time.

Fred said the year was 1890 and a man name Jack came to the USA from England. He open a small shop in town for dry meets and thing. Back then no ice boxes and the people had to dry meat to keep it. Jack was about the best meat dryer the town ever had. The local wanted too now who he did it. Jack wasn't telling anyone about how he made or dried his meat.

So one night and few people broke into Jack's store they tried to find how he did it, but only ended up with a load of buckshot in their ass. The three men lived but Jack was so mad that the cop in that time wouldn't put them in jail he locked up the shop and move it out in the wood where no one would bug him.

He came back to town about two years later and reopen his shop and he had all his drying things at the mill. The business got so big that he put someone in change of the store and went back to work at the mill full time. The locals couldn't under stand how he was making so much meat and how it was so good. So people started to try to see why he could make it so fast. Most of the time he know they were coming and ran them off.

One local boy got up the mountain on the back side of his mill and sat there for a few days watching him work. The boy said he had some how gotten about 100 Chinese workers in to work the mill. The people only came and went throw one door no windows in the place. The boy came back to town and report what he saw. The locals were mad that he didn't use them as workers in the mill. One day when Jack came out to drop off meat one local came up to him and said they were going to close his store if he didn't hire works from town.

Will Jack told the man no trouble he would close the store and sale meat in other towns. The local was so mad that he bet Jack until the local cop showed up and stop it. Jack got on his feet and looked at the cop and said you going to do anything. The cop said no you started it by hiring those people. Jack didn't say a thing and left town to returned to his mill.

That night Jack came back into town and burned down the store with all the locals meat in it. The town was so mad that they wanted to go to the mill to bet or kill him. As they got close to the mill, they could smell smoke and burning meat but not meat from any animal, a sweet sicking smell of human flesh. Jack had locked the door with all the works and him inside and set it on fire.

The local got as close as they could to the place but the heat was too hot to fight the fire. People said you could hear the people inside yelling and burning alive. After the fire whet out the locals looked around the place and found a safe in the old mill that didn't burn. They opened it to find the thing they had been asking Jack of years inside. The reason his meat was so good it was mixed with human meat to make it sweeter.

But that wasn't all they found a book with old England news papers in it. The stories were about the killer Jack the riper. Peter said you full of shit Fred Jack the riper was near found. Adam and Chase started laughing. Fred looked at Peter and said that the way my great grand father told it to his son then it was passed down to my Dad who told me. Peter said did they smoke more than just meat back then. Fred laughs and said could be but that's the way I heard it.

Peter just put his head in his hands and said I had to ask. The ride was good and Adam could see the gates. They were open and they road throw to the mill, just a little ways more Adam said. They came around the corner and saw two trucks setting in front for the old house. Adam said we got someone here. Peter said didn't Mike say theirs was no one up here. Adam said yes, one truck looks like Crissy's the other one I don't know. They pull up to the house and Crissy said hi to Adam and the others. Adam said Mike said no one was up here. Crissy said I didn't want everyone to know I was looking at the place.

Chase said thinking of buying it. Crissy said yes I was and I got Allen up here to look over the place to see if it was worth the price he wanted. Allen came out and said hi there to all the guys. Crissy said Allen is my husband. Adam said you're married you never told anyone in town that. She said and no one will know right Adam and you to Fred. Adam said why? Because we just got married and we want to tell Dannie our self ok. Adam said sure. but did you know the wolfman was headed this way last night. Crissy said yes we saw it this morning around 7:30 am.

Did you see where it went Adam said? Crissy said it was going up to the old power station over the hill there, but we when down stairs to the old boom shelter here. Chase this place had a boom shelter. Crissy said just about everyone did back a few years ago. Adam said none the less the wolfman is really strong.

Allen said he would have to be supper man to get into this two-foot thin doors with four feet thin steal reiforced cement. Dam Adam said that's a hell of a big one. Will were going to look around to see if its still around if you want you can follow use back to town. Crissy said ok yell to use when you get ready to leave. Adam said ok we will, but you may want to stay inside until we get back. Adam said I will leave Chase here to guard you two. Crissy said that's ok we will go back down stair to the shelter and stay until you get done, all you have to do is push the third red bottom inside the door it will ring the shelter and we will come back up . Adam said ok that sounds like a plan.

The group got together and started to look around the grounds they went over to the place where the old builds were and the old mill was standing. They walked throw what was left of the old burned out mill. Peter said looks as if the fire was hot. Adam said yes the floor is soft and brooked up. The dogs stopped pad was digging at something in the grass that was sticking out. Devvan said what is it girl as he bent down to free the thing from the grass. Devvan stood up and turned to show the others what it was is a human skull.

Adam said dam Fred you think that's Jack. Peter started laughing. Devvan and Mary said what the joke? Peter said Fred can ride with you on the way back and tell you. Devvan said not another story. Devvan set the skull back down and headed to look at the builds. The team didn't find a thing in the builds and started up to the old power station. Adam said look tracks it's been here all right.

They got to the power station and saw the burned out shell of a build that was the plant. They walked to the floor of the old station. Fred said the wolfman was here today. Chase said how do you know that? Fred said there a small spot of blood and some hair right here. Adam said good the thing is hurt. Devvan said not good. Fred said why did you said that Devvan? Fred you of all people should know the worst animal is one that been hurt Devvan said.

Chase looked over the side of the dam floor to the ground below hay guys theirs a door at the base of the plant. The group move down the side of the wall of the dam. Adam said the door is not locked because it's open a little.

Chase said that's good. Adam said how can that be good Chase we got to see if the wolfman is in there. Chase said shit I forgot.

Adam said Chase and Peter take your safety off and set your self in a spot to shot anything that comes out the door. Chase said what you going to do Adam? I'm going to open the door. Fred said Adam you should get ready to and let me open the door. Adam said you're sure you want to Fred? The group set up for the door. Adam said ok Fred does it. Fred open the door and set him self to the side to shot anything that moved. Adam said can you see anything Fred.

Fred said no but throw me your light. Adam gave Fred the light and Fred held the gun with one hand and the other he used the light. Fred started to look the door way over, he could see it was a very long one as he hit the back wall of the hall he saw a set of eyes he fired. The other set with hearts racing for some thing to come out of the door. Adam said Fred what was it?

Fred said I think I killed a mirror. Chase said great more bad luck. Fred moves up to the door way and he could see the hall was clear. Adam its ok Fred said. The two men move slowly in the door way. Chase came up to the door and looked in he could see a switch on the wall inside the door he switches it up the over head light came on. Adam and Fred both aim at them because the lights had jumped them.

Chase said I think the lights work. Adam said do that again and someone may get shot. Chase said sorry. Adam moves down to the end of the hall and stayed low and Fred aimed high. They came around the corner to see two small water tubbing and power panels on the back wall. Adam could see it was a small room and there was no room to hide. Adam said to Chase its all clear.

The group move into the room to look around. Devvan looked around he said this must be a sub station for the power plant. Adam said why didn't it open when the other mains failed. Devvan said it my be manual. Look there the main's switch for the cross over. There are still on primary side. Devvan pulled the set of switches to the sub side for the controls. The meter came to life and the light flashed. Seem the power back on Chase said see when we get back down to the house.

The team left the built and shot the door. They headed down to the house to get Crissy and Allen. Adam walked in the house and pushed the red button and Crissy came up from the basement. Crissy said what the lights are on. Adam said there a sub station under the main power station. Crissy said great now the place is worth the price Mike asking for it. The group left the old mill and headed back to town.

Dannie was setting at the computer watching the clock. She doesn't want to miss the date she had with Max at noon. It was now about 11am just 15 minutes and she could lock up and go. She finished up her work with the photos she had to do and went to check her self she still looked great. She shot down the computer and went up front to lock up. She looked out the windows to see the local shops getting ready for the hunting season.

The locals could hunt tomorrow than the flatlanders could started the next day. Dannie though to herself it was sad to kill something so pretty and soft. She turned out the overhead lights and locked the door.

She got in her jeep and headed out to Max's place. She was happy more than happy she felt like she could step out of her truck and just float along beside it. She turned into the parking lot of Max's Place and parked her jeep out front. She walks throw the door and Max was just coming out from behind the bar with a beer for someone.

He looked at her and drops the beer on the floor and his mouth was wide open and all he could do is looks at her.

She walks up to Max and with a small soft hand shot his mouth. She said I take it I put on the right dress. Max said you look great Dannie.Dannie looks down at the beer on the floor and said you got a drinking problem. The man said that was setting at the table behind Max no that's my beer I got to problem. Vicki yelled to the guy too come set at the bar and she would gave him a free one.

Max said will follow me and I will take you to the office where I set up lunch for use. She walks around the corner and down the hall to the office. Max open the door and setting in the middle of the floor was a table with candles and wine setting out with flower on the table. It was her first time back here the office was big and had a love seat and a desk in front of a double see throw mirrors that he could watch the floor as he worked on the book.

Max pulls out the chair and took her hand and sets her at the table. The rug under her feet was a thin shag rug. Max said I will be right back with lunch. He left the room and in a few returns with two plates with fry chicken and hash brown and fruits on the side. She said to her self how did he know that was her most loved meal. Than she stops Mom had told him the other night when they were here.

She smiled at Max that looks great. He turned down the light so the candles could fill the room with their soft light. Max pours them both some wine. Dannie cut into the chicken and began to eat she felt the chicken melt in her mouth. Dannie said how did you learn to cook so good? Max said my Mom was a great cook and she showed me how to cook. Dannie said she sound like a nice woman. Max said her and Dad were great parent's wish they were here to meet you. Max said they were both killed in a car crash ten years ago hit and morse and both die on the scene.

Dannie said sorry to hear that would have loved to meet them. Max said they would have enjoyed you to. They finish the meal and Max took the plates and said be right back. He returned with two sundays with cherries and nuts, they eat it and set the bowls on the table. Dannie said why don't we set on the love seat and shot the shit for a while. Max said you don't have to be back at work soon. Dannie said no I've got the rest of the day off.

Max said great I'm not working until seven tonight. So the both of them got up and Max set down first. Dannie started to set down and then set on Max lap and put her arms around his neck and gave him a kiss. Max as shocked to say the less and he passed out again to boot. Dannie looked at him and said you big marshmallow. She gets up and was going to get some water to wake him when see show a foot stools and a blanket on the back of the love seat. Dannie had and idea. She put Max's feet up and set back down on his lap and put his big arm around her and the blanket on them both.

She curled up and lies on his chest she could hear the sound of his heart beating. Max came to in a few minutes and felt Dannie laying on him. She looked up at him and said I see you living again. Max laughs and said sorry. Dannie said I know how to get you over this slowly just lay there hold me and we can take a nap together. Max didn't say a thing And held her and close his eyes. The two felt as if they were in heaven soon the two were a sleep and dreaming of each other.

Adam and the other got back to wilderness Drive Devvan, Mary and Fred pulled over. Adam, Chase and Peter pull in behind. Adam said wonder what's wrong? Crissy and Allen drove by. Adam got out and went up to the truck. Devvan rolled down the window . Him and Mary were laughing so hard there couldn't get air so they had to pull on. Devvan looked at Adam laughing and water running down his face he said Jack the riper and he started laughing harder.

Adam just turns and said see you guy back at the station. He headed back to the car just shacking his head. Adam got in and Peter said is everything ok with them? Adam just smiled and said yup jack the riper hit again. Peter just shock his head. Adam pulled out and started back to town as he turns the corner to rt. 157 he saw his worst night mare coming true the town had pull up a big bander and it read welcome hunter.

Dam Adam said that son of a bitch is going to kill people for money. Adam was pissed. He turns on the lights and headed for the town managers' office. Chase said Adam carm down we don't need you to kick Al ass again like in high school . I'm not I'm going to try to knock some sense into shit head Adam said.

Adam pulls up in front of the town office. He put the car in park and gets out Chase and Peter tried to carm him down and he started up the stair to the office he run into a sign of a wolfman and the sign said bag a wolfman and make ten grand. Adam

grads the sign and pushes throw the front doors. He looked at the people standing at the window were is the asshole. There said he in his office.

Adam tried the door it was locked he stepped back and kicked the door in. Al was setting behind his desk Adam throw the wolfman sign at him. Al said let carm down Adam and lets speak about this like two humans. Chase and peter came throw the door and grad Adam and held him back from hitting Al. Adam said you don't know what your doing you dumb ass. Al said trying to make the town some money off this trouble. Money for the town Adam yelled what kind of town will be left when ever one is dead asshole.

Al said I'm going to take care of two problems one who to kill the wolfman and getting out for it cheap. Peter and Chase looked at each other Peter said he really is a dumb ass isn't he. Chase said it sure looks like it. Adam said the wolfman can take two 30/30 shot at close range and a150 feet drop off and cliff you think some asshole with and shot gun with buck shot is going to bring them down your fucking nuts. Al said I think this is our best plan of getting the job done. Adam said the only thing your going to get done is make the town a ghost town and kill all my family and friends. If you think I'm going to set here and let you do it your nuts.

Adam took out his I D and throws it on the deck. Al said Adam you don't know what your doing. Adam said I'm going to try to save my people from you asshole. Al looked at Chase Guess this mean you're the new chief. Chase said guess your dumber than you look he throws his ID on the desk to. Both Peter and Chase let go

of Adam. Al said you guys you don't know what your doing. Adam said at less I won't have the blood of my friend and family on my hands.

The three turned and walked out the door. Adam walks over to the car and shot it off and turned the light off and got his rifles. By that time a group of people were out side. Adam what's going on? Adam said ask your new chief of police Al. When someone said Adam we need you and Chase we can afford to loss you two. Adam said it out of my hands now.

Al walked out the door of the town office and the group turned and boo him and throw trash at him. Adam laughs and look at Chase maybe he should run for trash man. Chase said lets get out of here .The three walked over to the station so they could tell the others what was up. They walked in and Devvan, Mary and Fred were setting there. Fred said what's up? Adam said we are off the case and Al is running the show now.

Mary said what you going to do Adam? Adam said I'm going to kill this wolfman on my own. The group said the fuck you are Adam. Adam said this is my fight now you guys don't have to come with me. Chase and Fred said we live here to it owner fight to. Adam said thanks I could sure use you guys. Peter, Mary and Devvan said count use in to. Adam said this isn't your fight and I can pay you.

The three said were cops' first and it our duty to protect the people. Adam said great let get out of here and going up stairs to set up a plan in my house. The group started out the door and the people out side said Adam please, you got to help use. Adam said it all Al plan from here out. The group went up to Adam place.

At around four that day Dannie wakes to find Max watching her sleep. Dannie said to Max who long have you been awake? Max said about 20 minutes and I was enjoying watching you sleep. Dannie gave him a big hug and kissed him again. Max was helpless under her spell. Dannie looks up and smiled your not pass out this time see I told you it would work. Max didn't care about the passing out but how lucky he was to have a beautiful woman that care so much for them. Max hugs her and they kiss and set there until about five.

The two went to see how the bar was doing Max held her hand and walks with her around the bar. Vicki saw them and said see you two love birds are doing good. Max smile and kiss Dannie. Vicki said will that much better your still up right. Dannie laughs and look at Max. Will we got a few hours to kill Max said who about a short ride in my truck. Vicki said I hope Dannie driving? Max laughs and said I'll be ok maybe as he looked at Dannie. Max and Dannie went out the back door to the car port in the back dooryard. Max pulls the cover off the truck and it was a ford lighten.

Dannie eyes open wide she love the red paint and the sharp looks for the truck. Max went around to the passage side and Max open the door and helped her in. Max got in and started the truck Dannie was in love with Max and his truck. Max said where to Dannie? Dannie said lets go to the swinging hole in Medway and set on the sand. Max said ok were off. Max though to himself man I've got the hottest lady and she riding with me. Max was in heaven he blow the horn at every one he know as to say looks I just won the lottery of love At the swim hole in Medway Max gone out and help Dannie out her side and walks over to the edge of the water and sat down. The wind was soft and Dannie could feel the coldness of the sand but girl was floating about all that setting there at Max's side. Dannie put her head under Max's arms and hug him. Max held her and they sat there watching the river flow by and the kids play in the cool water. The time went by to fast and Max had to get back to the bar and get ready of work.

Max stood up and said I wish this day didn't have to end. Dannie said me to and hugs them. Max pick her up and carry her back to the truck. Some of the wife setting watch their children hit their husbands and said why can't you be like that? The husband said I didn't bring a forklift. His wife dumped her water on his head.

Max and Dannie returned to the bar and Max got ready for work. He walks out to Dannie's jeep with her and hugs and kissed her then watched as she drove off. Dannie went back home and still couldn't believe the hold thing wasn't a dream. The sun was warm and she though she lay out for a while. She went up a stair and got her see a throw nighty on and went down the stairs to the kitchen.

She cut up some fruit and cheese and grads two beers and head out to the porch. She got out and set everything down on the table than set on the chair to get some rays and recap the day's fun. Dannie was so happy with the way the day whet she smiled. Dannie was done with her snack . Dannie felt warm and loved she got up to go back in and take a shower before bed that night. She close everything down stairs and locked all the door.

Steve and Kevin called Adam. Steve said Adam what's going on the office is close and the sign read call town manager Al. Adam told the boys about everything that went on and how they walked off the job. Steve said Al isn't good to run night watch anymore. Adam said hope everyone is ok tonight. Adam and the others set back and drank a few beers and made plans to hunt down the wolfman.

Fred said tracking it in the wood with everyone shutting at anything with two legs would just be too hard. The others said yes and real dumb. Chase said we could use scanner and CBS in our cars and truck and run the roads in the day hoping that the people run the wolfman out to the road. That could work said Fred at less it's a change they could take. Adam said will we can all meet tomorrow morning around 8am at Annette's place and start the hunt.

The group broke up for the night and Adam went down to the truck to put the CB in it. It only takes about five minute and he turned it on to here what my be going on. The radio was quiet thank God of that he said. Adam turned the radio off and went over to Annette's for something to eat. The place had one man in there he was setting near the windows. Adam walks in and Annette was behind to counter she said hi and Adam said hi back.

Adam said I see that you don't have wolfman sign up. Annette said you're right I think its dumb and Al is an asshole. Adam said you hear about me and Chase. Annette said yes and was some of the reason she didn't do anything. The other customer got up and pay her and left.

Annette said can you use a little pick me up? Adam said sure can. She turns to go out back to get the LDT and Adam reach over the counter and grad her ass. Adam said feel better already. Annette turned and smile at him she went out back and returns with a jag for LTD she put two shot in two grasses with ice and coke, she set a cherry on top for Adam drink. Adam said no cherry of you Annette .Annette smiles no I lost that long ago.

Adam laughs and said you know just what to say all the time don't you. Annette said I try my best there kid. Adam said I thing I will have a grilled cheese with ham and hold my pickle. Annette smiles coming right up there stud. Annette returned with the sandwich and set it down in front of him she said will down with them pants so I can hold at pickle. Adam laughs and said your bad Annette.

Annette smiled and said but I really good at it. Annette said so what going to go on with the wolfman thing? Adam said will me and my team are going to keep watching on the road in town in hopes it run out for the woods by the hunter. Annette said you be care then you guys wouldn't want to see you hurt. Adam said it should be really fun when the flatlanders came to hunt. Annette said I know last year my brother had to paint cows with big letters so they wouldn't kill them like the year before.

Adam said it did work I don't remember going out there to fine anyone. Good thing flatlanders can read. Adam said what do I owe their Annette? Oh yes and some of your cheese cake to go. She said ten will cover it. He got up and grads her ass on the way out the door. He went back to his place and sat back in his chair to watch TV and enjoy his cheese cake. It didn't take long of the stress of the day to hit him and he fell to sleep. Dannie went up stair to the tub. She put on some candles and fill the tub with bubble bath. She slipped into the warm water and began to wash. When she finished she lay back to enjoy the warm water and candle light. She was real getting into her though of today with Max when the phone rang. Dannie picked up the phone and said Hi. Max said hi back to her. A big smile came over her face. Hi Max how everything at the bar today Dannie said. Max said everything is great but I miss you really enjoyed the day today. Dannie said so be I and she miss him. Max said so what you been up to tonight? She said just think about the day and getting some sun. Max said oh sounds' fun. Dannie said I taking a bath right now oh maybe I shouldn't have said that. Max, Max Dannie said. Max said I'm ok just thinking. Dannie said see you're getting better all the time big guy. Max laughs and said I guess your right Dannie. Max said I wanted to call before you with to bed. Dannie said I'm glad you did I was going to call you when I jumped into bed. Max said I've got to run but, will call you at work in the morning if that's ok. Love you Max said. Dannie was at a loss for words for the first time in a long time. Max said Dannie you didn't pass out did you? Dannie laughs and said no and I love you to Max.

Max said good night have sweet dreams I know I will. Dannie said good night and hope she did to. Dannie hung up the phone and got out of the tub and dried off. She was so happy she started singing. But all she could sing was

Tears in heaven it was a heart braking song. The songs make her happy and sad at the same time to hear a Dad love for his son. She got into bed and set the clock. She set up and looked out the window she could see lighten and dark clouds.

So she got up to close the window the cold rain hit her body and she jumps a little but it felt nice again her bear skin. She put the window down and returned to bed. She was getting sleepy and she curled up in bed and fell to sleep. The Strom grows in size the flashes were close together and the rain fell hard. Dannie was asleep but some how could still hear the roar of the thunder. In her dreams she got up and went out side to her back porch.

The Strom was wild and she didn't feel afraid. She could feel some thing in the dark as the lighting flash she could see it. It was the wolfman but she didn't run back inside to hide. She moved out to the stairs and headed for the wolfman. This time the wolfman wasn't running away he started to move to her. The lighten hit hard all around them as if an big battle was about to began. The two move in a circle at each other.

The lighten flashed again and she could see why the wolfman didn't run this time he was in between her and two other white wolf like animals that keep him from running away. Dannie could clearly see that she was the larger of the two of them but was she the better. The lighten hit again and the thunder roared the wolfman man came at her and she locks horns with the animal. She throws the wolfman down to the ground and he rounded and returns to the fight.

She was also clearly the more powerful of the two. She hit the wolfman and he flipped over and landed face down. The other two wolf thing came up and graded the wolfman by the arms. The wolfman was kneeing between the other two wolf things. She moved up and grads the wolfman head and broke his neck then pulled his head off his neck. She stood there with the head in her hands and felt the rain run down her face. A lighten bolt came down next to her and she could hear a voice in the lighten say will you fight for me. She held the head up and said I did. And wake up with a jump. She lay down and watch the lighten and listened to the Strom. Slowly she went back to sleep.

Adam wakes up and it is7:00 am he said to himself seems funny not to be getting up for work. He's been the chief now for seven years. Adam got into the shower and stood in the water for a while the water run down his back and he started to wash up. He steps out of the shower and got dressed he went to window over looking main street he could see the street was buzzing with hunters and flatlanders coming in for tomorrow. Adam though to himself Dam Al doesn't know what he's facing looked like orange covered lunching meat out there.

Adam went down the stair to the front of the build it must have been a Strom last night the roads were still wet and tree branches were laying down in the street. He makes his way over to Annette's place seemed she was doing good this morning. Adam went in and sat at the far end of the corner. Annette said hi and got him some coffee what will you have there Adam? Adam said hi and a big breakfast please.

Annette said good be right up kid. Adam looked around the shop he was wondering how many would make it back home tonight to their family. Annette returns with Adam food here you are Adam. Adam looked around again and said where Bob this morning? Annette said with a long face he's home he know that the morning was going to be full around here so he's coming in for dinner today.

Is he going hunting today Adam said? Annette said thank God no he didn't want anything to do with this madden. Annette said beside if he did he would have something more wilder than a wolfman on his ass. Adam laughs and said some how I believe that. Adam pays Annette and grads her ass. Annette said at less something around here is still the same.

Adam started back home he could see a half dozen hunters looking at something on the station's door. One man said ten grand looks like I going wolfman hunting today. Adam looked at the sign and tore it down he looked at them and said the only thing your going to do is get kill. The hunter said what makes you sure of that? Than Fred came up and said because I shot the wolfman twice with and 30/30 and he dam never killed me and your going after it with shot gun.

The hunters looked at their guns and said maybe we should stop and get bigger gun at home. Adam said you should stay at home. Adam and Fred went up stairs and Adam put on a pot of coffee. The others should be here soon Adam said. Chase, Mary, Davven and Peter showed up a little before nine. Peter said I not sure how long today I'm going to be with the group today Because I'm the only law man around for miles.

Adam said I though of that so. If you get Called for the wolfman we'll join you and start tracking him from there. Peter said sounds like a plan. Adam said also I would like each car to have one for the big guns in it. Davven and Mary think you could handle the gun Adam said. The two said like to think we could but it would be a safer shot if someone else was using them.

Adam said ok how about Peter and Davven, Chase and Mary, Me and Fred. Mary said Sounds good to me with a smile. Chase said cool here to. Fred said Adam you've heard all my stories.

Adam said yes we don't need Jack the riper killing anyone today. The group laughs and started down stair to the cars. Mary said can Pad ride with use Chase? Good idea Chase said fine with me and Chase smiles at her. Ok lets run one thrip of the town each. Davven and Peter take wildness drive two the hardware store Mary and Chase the center up to the Schenk high school Me and Fred will take from the station out to the town line. Ok everyone lets do this thing and kill a wolfman.

The group loaded up and started to working the street. Chase was driving pass the town office when he saw a group of people out front holding sign that said Hirer Adam and Chase back and fire Al. Chase blow his horn as he and Mary drove by the group. Mary said looks like you two have a fan club. Chase said yes and I didn't have to pay them.

Mary said what do you mean about that? Chase said my girlfriend packed up and left. Mary said sorry to hear that, but she wouldn't because she like Chase. Chase said it's for the best now I'm free and she can do anyone she wants now. Mary said she was a slut?

Chase said will lets put it this way she gave more free rides than the pony at the local fair. Dam Mary said that's bad. Adam called to see if everyone was ok. Peter said all quiet here. Chase said same here ,but you my want to swing in front of the town office on the way back throw. Adam said why? Chase said we got a fan club out front. Adam said ok we will thanks. The radio was quiet and the scanners to thank God of that but it wouldn't last long.

Dannie wakes up she was still a little sleepy after last night's dream. She set up and tried to make sense of it all. Why did her Dad keep asking her to fight for him and what did the other two wolves have to do with the dream? She put the hold thing aside and started to think good thinks like Max.

She got up it was around 7:00 am she got ready for work and Crissy twenty questions . Will Dannie got up and went down stair for coffee and fruit. She stopped at the door for the back porch she could hear something hitting the door. She came up to the door and her heart was pounding fast. It hit the door again and she jumps back a little.

She moves to the window to look out she couldn't see any thing so she got closer to the door. All at one a lawn chair hit the door she jumps and her heart skidded a bet. She said dam the thing most had set there after the Strom last night. Her heart came back down in her chest and she open the door and moved the chair back to the center of the deck.

Then she moves the rest of them back in place to. She went back inside a got some fruit and she would stop at Lennie's for some of Peggy coffee. Lennie's was a store that started up when the mill came to town Jim's father started it as a little store. Dannie could remember the fun she had walking to the store

Now Lennie's is the biggest little store north of Bangor. Dannie headed out the door and she got into her jeep. Dannie could see that the hunting season had stated truck were setting on the side of the road locals looking like pumpkins. She had hope that the hunting wouldn't take place this year. She didn't want anyone killed by the wolfman or each other. Dannie pulls into Lennie's the dooryard was full.

She walked in and Jim and Peggy were filling out paper work for the hunters. Jim said hi Dannie can I get you something this morning. Dannie said a coffee one cream and sugar. The men were looking at her and wishing there were home with their wives. One local said I wish you were in season sweet thing.

Peggy said hay that's not called of. Dannie looked back and said that's ok Peggy. Dannie looked back at the local that said it she said from what your wife tells everyone your gun is too small and you shot blanks. The hold store broke out and laughed at the man. Jim said she must really know your wife and the group laughed the harder. She walked out the door and gets in her jeep.

The hunting with the red face said dam she good and put his head down and felt like a dog at the end of his rope. Dannie got to work and Crissy looked as if she was on a three day coffee hi. Dannie said hi what's up with you Crissy? Dannie went to set down at her desk. Crissy said remember I told you I was going to Bangor the other day. Dannie said yes. Crissy said I signed paper for a house and me and my husband is going to move in.

Dannie said stop the train you're marred. Crissy said yes we got married yesterday. Dannie got up and gave Crissy a big hug I'm happy for you. Crissy said so how did your hot date going the other day with Max. Dannie said it was great he's a great man and as kind as a baby kitten. Crissy said it looks like will both had a good day then. Crissy said I've got some more news tomorrow we are going on our honey moon for two weeks and I'm giving you two weeks off with pay. Dannie was so happy for Crissy. She hugs her again.

Dannie said what's his name and were did you meet mister wonderful? Crissy said we meet in and house buyers training group. She sat next to him and all the two could do is looks at each other and smile. After the meeting I ask them out for lunch Crissy said. We been in love now for six months oh and his name is Allen.

Dannie said I hope me and Max hit it off like that to. Crissy said I think you will Because you look just like I did after the next day. Dannie smiles and said it shows that bad. Crissy said yup I see love in your eye's girlfriend. The two laugh and hugged again. So Dannie said when do I get to meet this Allen person? Crissy said he should be here shortly and pick me up. Dannie said running away so soon. Crissy said yes and you can close at noon if you want. Dannie said ok I will and then run over to see Max.

Adam called on the radio to check in with the others. Everyone was ok, but Peter didn't call back right off. Peter came on the radio and said Adam head over to the Millers farm and I'll meet you there. Adam said ok what's up? The wolfman it looks like Peter said. The group all meant over at the farm.

As they came up the drive a man waving his arm flag them over to the barn. It Was Jim, Jim was a friend for Sam and Kaci. Adam got out and said Hi to Jim, Jim was pale and very sick. Adam said what up Jim? Jim said I didn't see Sam and Kaci in town the last few days so I came out to look for them. They weren't in the house and I came out to the barn to see if they were out here. Jim said I make it to the door and that was as far as I could make it.

Adam it's bad really bad the thing kill them and all the animals I couldn't tell where Sam and Kaci started from the animals. Jim set down with his face in his hands and started to cry. Jim said why them didn't they lose their son and now this? Adam said Chase take Jim over to his car and stay with him. Adam and Peter open the barn door as the light from the open door hit the floor the two men became very ill.

Mary came around the door with Devvan. Mary turned and throws up. Adam said your two don't need to be here if you don't want to. The two said that's ok its just my God what happen here. Adam said God didn't have anything to do with this. Devvan looked down at what was left of Kaci's body he said get the gun now, get the guns ! Adam and Peter looked at him and said why? He pointed to Kaci's body there was still some stream came from the body.

Devvan said the dam thing my still be in there. The group turned and ran for the guns. Chase looked up to see what was going on he looked at Jim and said get the hell out of here. Jim started the car and spun out for the drive to the main road to watching from a safe spot just in case he had to go for help. The group got the guns and got together to go back to the barn. They made it back to the barn. Adam said Chase and Peter move around to the rear of the barn. Peter said ok I'll yell when were set.

Mary and Devvan back off about 100 feet and lay down to cover the front. Devvan said why lay down? Adam said it will make you a smaller target. Devvan said good thinking Adam. Peter yell we're set. Adam looked back at Devvan and Mary they were ok to. Adam open the door all the way as to gave Davven and Mary a good shot at anything that my came out.

Adam looked at Fred and said are you ready. Fred said feel like I back fight a war. The two slowly move in the door opening both covering each side. Adam said the light switch is on the pole just ahead. Adam reached out to turns the lights on as the light came to life. Adam and Fred stopped in their tracks the barn was covered from top to bottom with blood and human and animal parts.

Fred put his arm out to stop Adam from moving another step. He points to the far left side of the barn some thing was moving. The two aimed at the thing in the back corner and was ready to shot. The thing start too came at them and Adam shoots as the animal noise comes out of the dark. Fred shoots the second shot, But it wasn't needed Adam's shot hit the animal between the eyes and it blows up like a can in a fire place.

Adam looks at the animal and said dam I think it was a cow. Fred said I think you're right. It was a cow the only thing the wolfman didn't kill. Adam and Fred looked the barn over and it was clear. They returned to the front and Devvan and Mary were ready for war. Adam said stand down it's clear. Peter and Chase came back from the rear of the barn. Chase said you kill it? Fred said yup and that cow well never gave milk again.

Adam said lets call Mike too came clear up the bodies. Peter said me and Adam will work on the report. Chase Adam said get a statement from Jim and then take him home. Chase said ok I will then come back. Adam said don't hurry its going to be a long time before this is done. Mike showed up he walks in the barn and couldn't believe his eyes. Mike said you know this didn't need to happen if Al would have close the hunting down and you two were after the dam thing Sam and Kaci would maybe still here.

The group got all the body parts that they could find and loaded it into Mike car. Peter said what you going to do about all the animal part. Fred said we could pile them in the center and set in the hay lofts and hope it came back to feed soon. The team looked at each other and said you know Fred that's not a half bad idea. Adam said you guys in for a all nighter we can leave one light in the middle on so we can see.

The team looked at each other and said lets do this thing. Adam said Mike can we use some of your suits to move the animal? Mike said sure I have two more in the car. The team got to work moving the dead animals to the center of the build and setting up the hay lofts of best look out of the pile. Adam said to Devvan and Mary go in town and stop at Annette's for some coffee and donuts and tell her I'll pay he in the morning.

Devvan and Mary went into town. The Other three got to work moving the dead animals it take them the better parts for two hours to move all them and set up the lofts. Adam said lets get their suit's wash off and in the car. The three got to suit clean up and Adam said I don't see how Mike can do this for a living. Peter said it not always this bad.

Adam said I guess your right Peter. Devvan and Mary returned from town. Annettte said to say hi to everyone and be dam careful. Adam said

Chase, Mary and Fred on that lofts and me Peter and Devvan on this one. Keep your radios down low and use the ear and head sets.

Devvan said what about the rest of the team I'm not leave my dogs out side for the wolfman to kill. Adam said sorry we can put one in each loft that way they can tell use when the wolfman is near. Dam good Idea Fred said. The team set up for what could be a long night. Adam said work in two hour shafts two on and one sleeping every one was set.

Dannie left the office shortly after noon time and headed over to see Max. She stops at Mary Ann store on the way out a get a thing of flower for Max. Dannies cell phone rings it was Mom, hi Mom Dannie said whats up? Mom said me and your Dad had a great week end with you. Dannie said so did I Mom. Mom said me and Dad would like to have a barbarQ with you and Max this week end that's if you two are seeing each other.

Dannie said I'm going to see Max right Now. I can ask him to see if he has some time off this week end for it . Mom said great your Dad and I like Max he seems really nice. Dannie said thanks Mom I like him a lot to and it's nice you and Dad like him to it means a lot to me. Ok hun see you this week end love you. Dannie said love you to Mom and kiss Dad for me and tell them I love him to.

Mom said oh I will. Dannie said Mom you two are bad, love you. Dannie payed for the flowers and headed out to see her man. She pulls in the parking lot and gets out. She walks throw the door and all man looked at her. She walks up to Max and kisses him and gives him the flower. All the men that know Max said looks like someone got a girlfriend and Max started to turn red in the face.

Vicki said don't make me get the hose out for you two. Max said you off for your lunch. Dannie said no I'm off for two weeks with pay. Max looked at her and said why did Crissy get married? Dannie said yes and how did you know? Max said I didn't just a lucky guess oh by the way Dannie I got some thing for you to Max pulls out from under the counter one dozen roses. Dannie said their beautiful.

Max said but not as beautiful as you. Dannie turned red your sweet she said and kissed him. The man in the bar said oh your sweet Max where's our flowers. They hugged and went to the office to find some thing to put the flowers in. After that Dannie sat down on the love seat and she said come here big man. Max walks over and set down. The two kissed and hug for a while. Dannie said Mom and Dad would love to have a barbarQ this week end with use if you can get the time off.

He said I have Saturday off and would love it, should I bring some thing? No Dannie said just you, so what's for the lunch special today. Max Said my best baked fish and baked spuds with brown Gary and corn. Dannie said I can almost see it, sounds great when do we eat. Max said right now we can go out and set on the back porch. Max stood up and takes Dannie's hand and pulls her up and put a big kiss and hug on her.

Dannie said dam and she makes it look like she passed out. She smiled and opens her eyes and kissed him back. Dannie and Max went out to get their meals and headed to the back porch. Max said be right back and went in to get and beer for the both of them he returned and sat down. Dannie said thanks that just what I needed.

Dannie said what time do you work today Max. Max said in about and hours. Dannie said ok we can set here and enjoy the sun . Max said it's a great end to other fine day. Dannie looked at the sun as it hit the lower part of the field she though to herself it's a sham that people today don't slow down to see the beauty that is all around them. They finished their food and set and kissed for a few minutes. Dannie said thanks Max for the meal it was get.

Max said thanks back for the flower and making the day brighter for him. Dannie smiles and kissed him they got up and went back inside. Max said I will walk with you to your jeep. Dannie said that would be nice. The man at the bar said ooohhh can you walk me to my car. Max grads a hand full of popcorn out of the bowl and throw it at them. The two walked out and Dannie gets into the jeep. Max puts his head in the door and kissed her and said I love you.

Dannie set back in the seat and said I love you to Max. Max gave her another kiss. Dannie said by and call me later as she back up to go. Max yelled I will and watched as she drives off. Max walks back in the door and was meet with a white cloud of popcorn. The man at the bar said ok lover boy we need beer. Dannie head to town as she got closer to the town office she could see a group of people walking around with signs.

The same group that was asking of Al to step down from his office . Dannie blows her horn as she drove by, in support of the people. Dannie wasn't much for town office things but she know the people were right in this case. Dannie gets back home and went up stairs to change.

She puts on her sweats and got a book to read it was by her flavor writer the sandman. She liked his tales and he keeps you on the edge until the end. She looks at the cover and the title was Meat your maker it was about the old mill and how it make dry beef out of people. Just reading the back cover with the writers picture on it sent chills up her back. See knew not to much was known about him only he was from Maine and the picture was of a man with a hood on and you couldn't see his face. She sat on the love seat and began to read.

Adam and the group got set up to work the night. The Light out side grow darker and the cool smell for dead animals filled the air. Devvan said to

Fred over the headset it's going to be long night got anyone good story Fred. Mary said no stories about Jack the riper. Fred said I have one story about gold coins hiding in Maine. Adam said you don't mean the Baxter stories do you? Fred said yes that would be the one.

Adam said I guess that's ok of this group the last time he told it was at Max 's Place to a group of drunk flatlanders. Devvan said so what's wrong with that? Chase said we had a call from the Baxter state park rangers that a group of flatlanders where digger hole all throw the park and made a hell of a mess. Fred said I couldn't help that but the story came from and old book my grandmother had.

Adam said ok Fred I guess it couldn't hurt at less it would pass the time. Will this happen back when I was in my teens I was helping my grand father at the time clean out the up stair. We had boxes on boxes of old newspaper. I ask him why grandma keep all there up here. He said it was paper from her Dads house filled with old news stories. I said could we bring them to my tree house so I can read them. Grandpa said I can't see where it would hurt sure Fred. So we both took the boxes to my tree house grandpa got the old farm tracker too left the boxes up to the deck and I move them in the tree house.

We went back to his place and I helped clean the up stairs out. It was night then so I went home to sleep. The next morning I got up and my Mom packed me a lunch and I went to the tree house to read. I found a box fill with old ghost stories I sat there for hour reading the old stories. I went throw four boxes of old stories and then, I came on a book that said on the cover the lost Baxter gold coins. The Baxter were every rich people and owned lots of land in the area. Mr Baxter himself left the state park lands to the state in his will. Will it was about three years before Baxter had passed away that the stories started.

Baxter had about 200 hundred gold coins with his family shield put on it. The coin were said to be wroth one million at that time, but today would maybe be more like 100 millions in today market. Devvan said dam go on Fred. Ok Fred said will Baxter wrote a clue in one of his book on the Park that told where the 199 coins could be found.

Mary said didn't you say there was 200 coins. Fred said yes Baxter keep one with him as a way to show people the stories was true. Will he dead and the gold went unclaim up to this day. Ok Mary said where did the book said the coins were hiding. Fred said ok as I read this book on the Baxter I came on a page with the story in it. The story said that the coins were hiding so some day Baxters could have the tail to tell and pass it down throw his family.

Baxter had hidden the book in the local library here in town were it set until my grandma came and check it out. She both the book home and started reading the stories. She had dead that years and the book never made it back. The years went by and me and grandpa clean the room out. I read the book from cover to cover to find the clues of the coins.

It said that the one coin hid the clues to the others. Peter said did anyone find this coin? I read a saying in the book at I tough was a clue to the one coins. It read under my coat the one I keep and a clue. I looked the pictures over from top the bottom when I was just about too gave up the back cover had a picture of Mr Baxter in it holding the one coin.

I was so mad to think to story was all bullshit I throw the book hard. It hit the wall and something shiny fell out. I walked over to the spot where it fell and pick it up it was the one coin from the story. I picked the book back up and looked it over, the coin had come from under the picture of Mr Baxter in the back of the book.

I moved the paper back to see where the coin had rested all these years. In the bottom for the hole it had something written on it. I said could this be the clue to the others. It read it in the middle where two limbs meet the other's lay at their feet. I spent years trying to under stand the clue and looking at the pictures in the book but I haven't got a clue.

Mary said good story too bad it isn't true. Chase said Fred show her. Fred pulls and coin of gold out for his pocket and showed it to Mary. Devvan said is it true Mary? Mary said it sure looks like the gold coin. Peter said maybe after this shit is over we can all set down and look at the clue with Fred.

Fred said it sounds good love to find it. It was closing in on moving no sign of the wolfman. Adam said it doesn't look like the wolfman will show. Just as Adam was going to sat up the dog came to life. Adam said hold it everyone the dog heard something. Mary said my dog is doing the same. Adam said set yourself and keeps the dogs down. The dog looked behind Adam to the wall. Adam could hear something moving alone the out side wall. Than a set of finger nails ran across the side of the build to the front.

Peter could see the door move than it stopped. Adam said take good aim we may only get one good shot each. Fred said come on you ugly son of a bitch. Chase said he could hear the animal smelling the air. Then a blood chilling howl came from the animal. Adam said shit he knows we're here open fire at the side of the door. The team open fire and cut the right side and the door off the front. Adam and Chase turned on there flash light to see if they could see anything laying on the ground.

Adam said shit we missed it. Fred said should we get down and going after it. The sun was almost up and they can see good. Adam said one down the ladder at a time and the other cover. Devvan said me and Mary will get down first and you can hand the dogs down. Ok Adam said Devvan and Mary got up and went down the ladders there got the dogs down and set them self facing the door. Adam said Peter and Fred next. The two started down the ladder when a loud crash came from the back of the barn the big door ripe off the wall and fell in, but the wolfman was no where to be seen.

Fred said the thing is playing game with use now. The others move down onto the floor and form a circle to protect all sides. They all hear other howl this time from out front and far away. On the other side of the farm house it seemed as if the wolfman was moving away. The Team made it out side the sun was up and they started to move to the sound. They got to the front of the farm house to see the wolfman on the other side of the long field heading for the old mill area.

They went to get in their cars and the wolfman had run his nails around the hood of Peters car. Peter said as he looked at Fred I think you're right he's play some type of game with use. Adam said game or not I plan on winning. The group headed back into town.

Dannie was reading and fell to sleep on the love seat. She was dream about the book she was reading Meat your maker. She was back when the town was still new. The mill was full of trees and workers. Times were good the paper mill were running night and day. She was walking the main street in town it was fulled with all types of people and all type of food.

She walked into a small dry meat store the owner was an old England man. His name was Jack. Jack said hi there would you care to try my dry meat? Dannie said sure. He cut her off a peace. She tried the meat it was sweet and had a good flavor. Dannie said who in the world do you make it? Jack said come back and I will show you how it was made.

Dannie and Jack went back into the rear for the store. The man said this way and she walks throw a door and she was hit from behind. Dannie wakes up she was hanging from a hock that went throw her back and came out her chest. She was still alive and the blood runs down her. Her hands were nailed to the beam over her head. Jack came in the room with a knife and said you wanted to know how I made my meat.

Will I only use the best cuts of meat and today it's you. Jack turned to her and as he began to cut into her she wakes up. Dannie jumps out off the love seat and scearmed she ran around the room as if she was still in the dream. She sat on the steps and her hands were shacking like leaves she put her hand on her chest and she was all right.

She than remember it was only a dream. After her heart got back in her chest she went back over to the love seat to pick things up. She grads the book she was reading when she fell asleep, the back cover had an orange label warnings don't read before going to bed. She said as she throw the door on the table now he tells me. She made her way to the kitchen. She put some cool water on her face and started to laugh at how she got so scared.

She said to herself dam he real can make you feel like I was there. The phone ring and she jumps again. Dannie said hi and sat on the counter. Max said hi their beautiful sound like you been running. Dannie said you could call it more like hanging around and she told Max her dream. Max said no wonder you sound so out of wind. Max said you're not going to read the book any more tonight I hope.

Dannie said I may not read it until I'm really drunk. Max laughs and said other then going the hell and back How your day? Dannie said it was great and how is your going hun? Max said fine I wanted to call and see if you want to going to Bangor with me tomorrow. Dannie said yes if you don't mind me shopping a little? Max said no and will can and go to a movie and dinner to if you want.

Dannie said at what time? Max said around ten maybe. Dannie said do you know where I live? Max said no but you could meet me here and on the way out you could show me. Dannie said great it a date. Well see you tomorrow Max said I love you. Dannie said I love you to Max see you in the morning. Max hung up the phone. Dannie was now in heaven another date and Bangor she loved going down there.

She got a beer and headed up to the room she looked at the book on the table and said you're a bad book as if the book could hear her. She stopped on the stair case and said I should lock up around here before going up stairs. She made sure every thing was locked and closed. She went up stairs and got undress to take a shower she let the warm water run down her and she felt much better.

Now she was thinking of tomorrow and Max she couldn't wait. She felt like a kid going to the mall with Mom and Dad. She finch the shower and went to look out the windows the sun was down and she felt sleepy so she drank the last of her beer and sled into bed. She rolls up in the covers and went to sleep. Dannie's dreams tonight were nice. She feels her self and Max floating in the air like super Man.

There landed on a sandy island were they ate sea food and had fruit drink. The best part was swimming in the clear blue water and her and Max hugs and kissing as there floating in the water. There got out of the water and went to lie on a blanket on the beach. Max said look at the sunset it as beautiful as you. Dannie looked at the sun as it was already half down on the clear blue water the rays of light dance off the water to the sandy shore she said it is nice.

She rolled over to kiss Max and wake up. Dannie though dam when she woke up it was only a dream, but she soon started laughs when see saw she was hold her pillow and there was a big kiss mark in the center of it. Then she said what the hell she hugs the pillow and kissed it again laying back in back smiling and laughing out loud.

This day was going to be a great day she could see the sun was coming up. It as now around 8:00 am she jumps in the shower a washes herself. She got out and dried off and went down stairs to get some fruit and check the weather on the back porch. She made a pot of coffee and got some fruit then went out on the porch. The sun was warm and the air had a little chill in it. She sat down on the edge of one of the chair it was wet from the morning drew.

She watches the birds fly over and remember her dream last night about her and Max. She finshed her fruit and started back in the house as she got up she could see about three trucks moving along the corn field it must be hunting time again. She went back inside and washed out her cup and went up stairs to get dress for Max today. She sat on the edge of the bed thinking should I ware a dress and heals or my jeans and a body shirt. She said to herself Max has seen me in dress but not jeans so jeans it is. She put on her best fitting jean and a blue silky body shirt.

She looked at her self in the mirror and said ok but she was going to have to put a bar on Because she didn't want Max to pass out before there even lift. She went down stairs and got her bag and shot the coffee pot off and went into town to see Misch got in her jeep and headed to town. But as she drove she could see a lot more hunters this year than any she could remember she though to her self that this couldn't be good with the wolfman on the lose.

She drove throw town and pass the town office the group seen to be getting bigger than before. She drove throw town and the hunters were everywhere it was good for the local stores but at what cost. She got to Max's place got out and walked in. You could have hear a pen drop as she walked across the floor. Max was behind the bar because Vicki was still on brake.

Max was making a drink and when he saw here her drop the grass and it hit the floor. She came around the bar and gave Max a big kiss. Max looks at her like a deer stuck in the head lights of an on coming car. She said so Max I look ok today. Max said with a puppy dog smile better then ok.

Dannie said good thing I wear a bar and Max almost when down. She grads him and said breath their big guy. Vicki came out from her brake and said I sure have guessed it was you out here. Vicki said hi to Dannie you bring the big guy back from Bangor in one peace.

Dannie said with a smile he'll be ok after he comes back around I hope. She got Max back to the office and set him down on the love seat. She sat on his lap and kissed him he seen to be coming out of the spell she had over him. Max said wow I never saw you in jean and my God your beautiful. Dannie face turned red thanks you hun Love to hear that from my man. The two hugged and kissed until Max could stand on his own two feet.

The group returned to town to find the town filled with hunters and the shops doing good. Adam was almost sick all he could see was body bag and a lot of them. Peter said dam as the group stopped out back of McLaughlin's auto repair across from Adam's house. Adam said I haven't seen this many hunters in a long time. Chase said this could only spell trouble.

Mary said some are drinking right on the streets, beer and guns not a good mix. Adam said will guys I'm going to take nap until noon got plenty of room for all you guys to crash if you want. Everyone said sounds great need some down time. Adam and the others went up stairs to his room. It was a two-bed room place with two big beds and lots of chairs to kick back in.

Adam set his gun with the other near the door. Adam grads a chair their a bed in that room and a love seat to. Adam said anyone use a beer? Just about everyone but Fred said yes. The group head to the chairs and Peter and Fred and Devvan hit the living room. Fred and Adam went into his room Fred took the love seat.

Chase and Mary headed for the second bed room they looked at each other and smiled as their walked in the room. The bed and love seat looked nice and Chase hit the bed and said their more room then I need here if you want a soft bed to lie on. Mary looked and then set on the bed with Chase they finch their beers and lay back on the bed. Chase turned and looked at Mary she knows he wanted to kiss her.

Mary said its ok kiss me if you want to the two kissed and hugged each other and lay their arm in arm. The group was all out cold the night had been a stressful and long night. The town out side was just getting started. Al the town manager was in his office and didn't want anything to do with the group out front. Al though to himself the group would thank him after the wolfman was dead in a few days he hoped maybe even hung him if it went wrong.

Al set their rubbing his neck thinking of the rope. Al knows he would have to get Adam and Chase back on somehow. The only way they would come back was that Al would have to step down. Al though it would be for the better of the town, but the people would love him again after the wolf was gone.

Dannie was hugging Max and he slowly came back around. Dannie said so big man you ready to hit the road. Max said ok as he got off the love seat and looked at her again. Dannie took Max's hand and lead him out back to his truck. You going be ok the drive Dannie said. Max said yes I'm doing much better now. Max watch as he open the door and she got in dam he though to himself.

Max went around and got in, off to Bangor we go. The two went throw town and it was the first time in a while Max had came to town. Max said my God why are all their people around for? Dannie said most are hunting and the one in front of the town hall are there until Al steps down. Max said Al really stepped in it this time. Will it a good thing we are go to Bangor to get away from the mess.

Dannie said yes and it would gave use time to spend together. Max said I like that idea. Dannie smiled and gave him a kiss. Dannie said Max why did you have to go to Bangor today? Max said I get some of my beer throw a discount place down there and it looks like I'm going to have to get more than I though. As they were leaving town Dannie said, my house is just on the right pass that corn field.

Max slowed down to look he was very unpressed. I like that place nice big yard and I love log homes. Max said it a lot better then the old room I living in. Dannie said thanks on the way back we can stop and I will show you around the place. Max said I can't while it must be nice. Max said as he pulls into the big apple store in Medway to fill up do you want some thing to drinking or eat on the way down Dannie?

Dannie said yes a green tea would be nice. Max top off the truck and said be right back. This time Dannie watches out the back windows as Max walk away, her mind went blind as she looked at his butt and smiled nice form behind to she said. Max.

returned to the truck with two ice teas he handed one to her and said here you are hun.

Dannie looks at the bottle and said this is the best type of tea to love this band. Max said wouldn't drink anything else myself. Max got back in and he headed throw the town of Medway to the interstate. The ride to Bangor can be a long one the only thing about Maine Max didn't like, but today with Dannie setting beside him under his arm the ride didn't seem bad but even fun.

They didn't say much on the way down but she looked up and kissed him every once In a while. They got to Bangor and got off the hogan road exit to the mall. Dannie said up as they came closer to the mall. They're one thing this girl loved was a good shopping day. Her and Max went in the sears auto side of the mall. Dannie's eyes came to life as she walks throw the door.

Max said where to first? Dannie said I'm following you we can hit them all one by one. Max said ok you sure I don't mind shopping with others. Dannie said no I will let you know if I want to look at some thing. The two went to almost every store in the mall Max wouldn't let her spend her money he pay of every thing. Dannie and Max came to one store that she made him set on the bench outside the store as she went in, she kisses him and said I will be right.

Max set their look up at the sign as he started to feel warmer it was Victory's secret. Dannie was in there of ten minute and came out with a little bag. Max said

what did you get Dannie? Dannie smiled and said you'll see later. It was a good thing Max was setting down Because he would have been as ham to pass out in the mall. She sat down beside him and hugged him. Dannie said so were to for dinner hun? Max said what are you in the move for Dannie? Dannie said I think the olive garden is a get place.

Max said cool he loved the food there and we could look and see what we want to see for a movie after. Dannie said it's a deal and the two went back to the truck and went to olive garden. They parked and went inside the smells as you walk throw the door were great. Max went up and said a booth for two. They didn't have to wait to long.

The two were setting in a corner booth Dannie liked the idea that she could set close to Max and eat with him. Dannie and Max slide in the booth. The waiter came up and said would you like something to drink while you look at the menu. Dannie said I will have the house wine and Max said that sounds good me to. Dannie said what you going to get Max?

Max said the three dish plate looks good. Dannie said I was thinking the same thing and Max smiled at her and kissed her. The waiter came back and set the wine down on the table. The waiter said are you really to order. Max said yes and looked at Dannie are you ok with this dish. She said yes it looked great. The waiter said that's one of ours best dinners the cook really know what he was doing with this plate.

Max said great we will have two of them. The waiter said this comes with a soup or salads. Dannie said salads for me and Max said same for me. Dannie said the salads is great here isn't it Max. Max said yes it the best he ever had. They tock a drink for wine and smiled at each other. Dannie took her shoes off and moved closer to Max. Max was thinking man I'm the luckiest man alive.

The waiter returned with the salads and said would you like some cheese on it Dannie and Max said yes at the same time. The waiter also both out some bread sticks. The two started to eat, the salads was great. The waiter returned shortly with their meals. The waiter said enjoy your meals. The two said thanks to him.

They began eating the meal it was great the food just melts in your mouth. Dannie took a fork of food and feed it to Max. Max did the same with a big smile, then he kissed her. After the meal had ended the waiter returned and cleared the table. Dannie said I would love a cheese cake but I'm full. Max said lets get two to go and eat them at your place. Dannie said sound like a plan.

The waiter returned will that be all. Max said no two cheese cakes to go and the check please. The waiter went and got the check and cheese cakes. He returned and said you two have a nice day and come back soon. Dannie said we will this is a great place. The two went out and headed over to the movies. Max said look transformers are playing. Dannie laughs and said that was my most loved cartoon when I was young I love bumble bee. Max laughs and said I loved prime.

Dannie said so that the one then that's If you want to see it Max. Max said yes loved to, he though to himself I've got to marry this one she likes everything I like. What was funny Dannie was thinking the same thing. The two went into the movies and sat up in the top seat .Not many in here Dannie said. Max said its noon time and not many kids out on a school day. Dannie set down near Max and pull up the center arm rest so she could hug and hold Max throw the movies. The movie started and it was better than there though it would be, the writters be a great job without change the transformers Looks.

When the movie was over and Max got up and graded Dannie's hand as they left the movie hall. Dannie said that was a great movie wasn't it Max. Max said it made me want to go out and buy a big truck just little prime. Dannie said bumble bee was cool to. Max said what next? Dannie said to the discount place then home for cheese cake. Sounds good to me Max said. So Max and Dannie headed over two Sam's club. Max fill the back of his truck with all types of beer and the two headed home.

The ride back was more enjoyable then the ride down they both had a great date. They pull out the ramp to Medway and turned to go to East Millinocket. Dannie said don't forget to stop at the house so I can show you around. Max said I've been looking forward to that all day. He went throw Medway and turned into Dannie yard. Dannie and Max got out and Max helped Dannie in with her things.

Dannie open the door and Max walks in and stops, wow Max said this is a really nice place. Dannie said thanks set the thing on the kitchen table and I'll show you around. Max went into the Kitchen and said man I could really enjoy cooking in this kitchen. Dannie show Max the back porch and her bathrooms up stair and the bathroom then she came to her best room the den .

Max walks in and couldn't believe his eyes a big scream tv with a surround sound and big soft couch in the middle. Max said wow did you do all this yourself. Dannie said yup most of it but Mom and Dad help me set up things.

Dannie said go have a seat and I will get the cheese cake. Max said ok and gave her a kiss before she left the room.

Max went over and sat down on the couch it was great he could fall a sleep on it. Dannie went to the kitchen and got the bag from Victory secret and went up stair to put it on. She came back down and got the cheese cake and went back to the den, She walked in and Max's back was to her. He turned around and his eyes open wide. Max said dam is that what you got in Bangor? Dannie said yes as she spins around to let Max see the outfit.

Dannie was wearing a full size body suit that hugged every crave and looked like a tiger with a tail in the back. Max was speckless he didn't know what the say as she sat down beside him. She handed him the cheese cake and said so I see you like it. Max took a bit for the cheese cake and said do I ever. Max's face was turning red.

The two finch the cheese cake and Dannie said find something on TV and we can lay on the couch and cuddle. Max said ok and started to look for a movie. Dannie set the dishes on the coffee table and got the blanket from the back of the couch. She Make Max lay back on the pillow and she lay down beside him and rap herself around him. Max held her and kisses her and he could feel the warm skin throw the suit.

Max said I have something to say hope you don't get mad. Dannie said I couldn't get mad at you less you were going to later me. Max said no it's I a little old school and I don't want to you know to man how do I say it? Dannie said just come out with it and say it I'm thinking the same thing I bet. Ok Max said I don't want to have and his face turned beet red to have ooohhh. Dannie put her hand on his mouth I feel the same way Max.

Max said you did good I didn't want to make you mad by not having sex with you. Dannie said me to I'm sorry if this suit is getting you all hot you want me to change. Max said no it just I want to wait until I'm marred you know. Dannie said with and big smile good I didn't want you to think I was bring to forward, it was you were bring so sweet today I though I would give you something good in return.

Max said you did you did Dannie. To two hugs and rapped up in the blanket. Max said I love you and Dannie said I love you to Max. The two lay there and Dannie fell asleep in his arm Max said it sounds like a great idea and slowly went to sleep with her warm body on them.

The group was sleeping when Peter was awake by his cell phone. It was his chief the chief said Peter what's going on up there I read your report from the Millers case your not trying to kill that thing on your own. Peter said no chief I got two state tracking dogs and handlers and four other in the teams helping. The chief said good will keep me up on the work that your doing and be careful. Peter said ok chief I will and he hung up the phone.

He looked at the clock it was around one that day dam he said I sleep like a rock. Adam came out of his room and said Peter every thing ok? Peter said yup just the chief checking in. Adam said where Devvan and the dogs? Peter said I think he took them out to let them going to the bathroom. Devvan returned to the room with the dogs. Devvan said did you look out the window? Adam said why is the wolfman dead and hanging on main street.

Devvan said no the hunters there all over the place must be two thousand or so. Adam said dam this thing is really getting out of hand isn't it. Peter said seems that way to me. Fred came out of the room and said we starting up tonight or we going to set back until tomorrow morning. Adam said we could run night watch if the wolfman hasn't been spotted today maybe laying low Because of all the hunters in the woods tonight.

Adam said you guy came over here of a second but be quiet. The group walks over to the spair room and looked in. Chase and Mary were under the covers and holding each other. Devvan said watch this Maxy come here, Devvan knees down go get Mary go. The dog jumps on the bed and both Mary and Chase wake up. There look at each other and was going to kiss until they could feel they were bring watched.

Mary pulls down the covers and looks you guys got anything else to do. Chase throw his pillow at them. Adam said its about noon time me and the others are heading over to Annette's for lunch. You two coming or you want me to bing you some thing back. Mary said be right out in a few she started to get up and remember that the both of them were nude she lay back down and said can you shot the door please.

Adam pulls the door shot and laughs. Mary round over to Chase and give them a big kiss good moving. Chase hugs her and kissed her back guess we got to get up. Mary said yup. The two smiled at each other and got dress they went out and everyone said you sleep good? Mary smiles really good. Will lets go down to Annette's and get some food. The dog can stay here if you don't mind Adam said.

Devvan said we can feed them and put them on the truck case in back. Adam said ok let roll then. Mary and Devvan put the dogs in the truck and feed them. The group went over to the dinner to eat. Walking though the door Bob was setting there, he said dam about time my sister been pacing the floor. Adam said is she out back? Bob said yup. Adam went out back and Annette's back was to him he came up to her and grad her ass. She turned around with a jump and dropped the knife she was holding and grads Adam and started to cry.

Adam said what's wrong Annette did I scare you. In a crying voice she said someone came in last night and told everyone here about the Miller farm. Then you sent Mary and Devvan down they said it was the worst thing they ever saw. Adam put her head up and said I sorry didn't mean the scare you like that. Adam said I'll tell you what I will give you my cell phone number and you can call me when you feel scared.

Annette held Adam again and said what would help some. Adam held Annette and walked out to see if the others wanted coffee. Bob said you look better sis now can I go home. She came around the corner and gave Bob a big hug and a kiss on the chin yes brother I'm going to be all right now thanks of bringing here. Bob said no trouble that's what a big brother is for. Bob said bye to everyone and Annette said will what's everyone want to eat. Adam said want the special for today? Annette said meat ball sandwiches with cheese cake for after.

The group looked at each other and said cool sounds' great. Adam said go get the meals and I will service coffee for you. Annette said great as she started for the back room Adam move to the coffee machine she grads his ass and said there's a big tip if you do a good job. Adam service up the coffee and Annette returns with the sandwiches. Annette said so what's the plan tonight?

Adam said think will run night watch and if we don't see anything then cut off at midnight and call it a night. Annette said that sound good hope everything goes good. Adam said well it's 3:00 pm now if we'll go until midnight we should be ok. Adam said what do I owe you for last night and today. Annette said 35 in all should do it. The group got up and went out to the cars. Annette said you guys be care ok. Adam said I will as he grads her ass on the way out the door.

Max wakes up and looked down at Dannie and she had round over with her back to them. He than found that his hand had a hand full of Dannie's chest. He squeeze shortly and she said oh see your awake Max. Max said he was sorry and pulls his hand down to her side. She said that's ok you been doing it in your sleep for the last hour and she moves his hand back to her chest. Max said its ok with you? She turned over said kiss him and said you're my men aren't you?

Max said but we aren't marred. Dannie said it only show you like me and it makes me happy that you like my chest. Max said like what's not to like? She hugged him and said I could lay here a night. Max said me to I'm having a great time as he put his hand down on her chest. Dannie said me to as she could feel his soft hand on her. Max said I got to stop this, is turning me on. Dannie said I can feel that Max sorry about that. Max said it ok that what cold water is for isn't it.

She laughs and paces his arm around him and she kisses him. Will what we going to do now Dannie said? Max said just hug and watch TV or whatever you want to do. Dannie said I just as happy to kiss and hug right now. Max said good I didn't want this day to end. So the two hugged and kiss then held each other and watch some TV. Max hugs her and said I love you. Dannie grads his arm and pull him closer love you to hun.

About and hour whet by and Dannie round back over to hug Max he still had a big smile on his face. Dannie said are you getting hungry Max? Max said a little but he didn't want to let her go. Dannie kiss him and started to get up. Max saw her tail and graded it and pulled her back down to him. He rapped his arms around her and ed and kissed her. They hugged and kissed for about and half hour before she said will I better go get out of this thing or we will never get anywhere.

Max said one more big kiss then I'll let you go. Dannie said ok and hugs him and kisses him again. She got up to go change she looked back to see Max smiling and watching go. Dannie was happy that Max love her so much. Max put his head back on the couch and said dam she nice how can I be so lucky to have her. Dannie went up stairs and put on her sweats. She came down stair and back in the den Max was still on the couch. Dannie walks up and climbs over the back for the couch and landed on Max. Max smile and hugs her. So what you want to do Max Dannie said?

Max said I" got to drop the beer off some time, we could stop at the Country Dinner and eat there they have good food. Then maybe after I unload the beer we can go up stair and I can show you my place. Dannie said sounds good Do you have to work tonight? Max said no so you got me all night if you want me. Dannie said you bet big guy and she kiss them. They got up off the couch and went out to Max' s truck. Max and Dannie drove back to Medway to the country Dinner it was a nice place to eat it was part of the big apple store but it was own buy a lady in Medway.

Dannie and Max sat down never a window and the waiter came over here some menus and would you like some thing to drink first. Dannie said I will have a tea and Max said sounds good gave me the same. Max said to Dannie I've had some meals here the turkey dinner is great. Dannie said ok that would hit the spot today. The waiters returns with the tea and ask if they where ready to order. Dannie said we going to have two turkey dinners. The waiter said great the turkey was just cook and few minutes ago.

Max and Dannie held hand across the table and looked at each other. Max said this is a nice looking place isn't it. Dannie looked around and said it's clean not like those big city places. Max said it has a homey feel the it. Dannie said yes it does. The waiters returns with the meals and they looked great more than Dannie though she could eat. Max took a bit and he said the turkey is really good. Dannie tried it and love it to.

The two finished their meal and went to the bar. Max pulls up out back and said if you want I'm going to be a few minutes you can go up to the room and check it out and I'll be up shortly. Dannie said ok I will and Max gave her the key. Max kissed her and said I'll only be a few. Dannie hugs him and went up the back stairs to his room. She got to the top for the stairs and it came out into a big deck. She looks around up there and said to herself would be a nice place to sun. She looked down and could see Max unloading the beer she said this is nice Max.

Max looked up and smiles at her thanks I like it to Max said. She turns and unlocks Max's door. It was A small place but really homey. She looks around the house was very clean for a man living alone in it. He had a nice kitchen that overlooked the main parking lots. She went into the bed room she liked it, there was a flatscrene TV with DVD on a rack and a nice looking warm bed.

She looked over the rest for the place and it was just right for one person to live in. She kicks her shoe out and turns the TV on in the bed room and lay on the bed. She love the bed it was just like and big soft pillow. Max came in the door and took him shoes off. He could hear the TV running in the bedroom. Max walks over and saw her on the Bed do you like the place Max said. Dannie smiles it nice and warm here. Max said it's a nice small place more then he would nice until later.

Dannie said will don't stand there come and get in the bed with me. Max said I though you never ask a make his way to the bed and kiss Dannie. Max lay down behind her and the both of them lay down and watch some TV. Max grads the blanket that was on the foot of the bed and cover them up and they move in close to each other. Max said there a good movie on in a few. Dannie round over and hugs him and kiss him. Dannie said anything you want to watch is fine. She was just happy with bring here with him. Max said ok and put the tv on a channel and lay they with her in his arms.

Adam said will I think we should split up like yesterday and keep in town and moving around. The group said yup that sounds like a plan. Adam said we will meet back here at midnight if everything goes ok. The group got in their cars a headed to their parts of town. It was around 6:00 pm now and everyone was closing down for the night all but the local bars. Adam always wounded how a small town like East Millinocket needed with four bars. There was Max's place out side of town and three little ones in town.

Adam though just maybe drinking was the only thing the town had left. Adam called the other car to see if every thing was going good. Chase and Mary said not a thing move around the center of town. Devvan and Peter said they just got done the grave yard everything quiet on this end. Adam said same on this end town to. Fred said for some reason he didn't feel it was going to be a quiet one tonight. Adam ask him why? Fred said the way the wolfman was playing game with use last night.

Adam said will if he tries that shit tonight at less we will be in the open to try to get a good shot at them. Fred said I sure hope so. The time was a little after 8:00 p.m. now and the sun had gone down. Adam said to Fred I'm going to stop at Annette's on the way throw want a coffee? Fred said sure I could use a new cup this one is cold and old.

Adam pulled up to the front for Annette's and went in Fred stayed in the truck to keep an ear on the radio. Annette came out from the back and said hi their stub what's up? Adam said not a thing quiet. Adam said could I get two coffees to go. Annette said sure she was just going to shot it off and go home. Adam said great just in time then. Annette said surely don't like going home at night with the wolfman still on the run. Adam said why don't you go over to my place a crash there. Annette said you sure you wouldn't mind. Adam said hell no I'm not going to be there until around midnight away.

Annette said you know I think I will can I take a shower? Adam said a yup just make sure to bring your LTD and some coke over I may need it later. Annette said ok I will and Adam handed her the spear key see you around midnight then. Adam grads her ass as he walks out. Annette said see you later then .

Adam returns to the truck and said here you are Fred hot and fresh. Fred said thanks and took a drink oh that's much better. Adam and Fred drove back out to the far side of town. Peter came over the radio Adam I think we just spot the wolfman. Adam said where are you now? Peter said in the grave yard he just went in the woods headed to town. Adam said ok I headed back for town now keep me up to date on where it is.

Peter said ok were headed over to the hardware store right now. Adam looked at Fred and said hold on this going to be a fast ride. Adam stepped on the gas and the little truck came to life. Peter said I see the wolfman I'm on park street heading into town Peter said dam that thing can move.

Chase said me and Mary will set up at the old church the try to get a shot at it. Adam said good Idea me and Fred will come in from the school side of the park maybe we can get him in the open. Fred said dam do we need to be going this fast Adam look down and he was around 120 and going. Adam said just close your eyes and we'll be there in a second. Fred said I got them close.

Adam hit the fire station and let off the gas. Peter said it almost at the old church can you see it Chase. Chase said yup it headed right at use. Chase was set to take a shot when Mary spotted something on the other side of the park it was other larger wolfman but white. Chase took his eyes off the first just a second to see what was going on and the first wolfman ran up over the font for the car and into the park.

Peter and Devvan pulled up and got out to and set to take a shot when there saw the second white wolf. Peter said Adam gets up here we got two of them now ! Adam said two and pulls the brake on too slow for the corner. Adam said hold on it going to be ruff maybe. Adam truck came into the corner by Davis's drug and the bar. Adam was hoping that he wouldn't run into anyone or anything the truck came throw the corner like a racing truck should.

They got to the park to see the first wolfman standing in the middle on one side for the grand stand. The other was coming right at the first wolfman on a dead run. The two hit each other and that's when the first wolf know he was in trouble. The white wolf seen to be a lot big and stronger. The first wolf turned an headed at Fred and Adam .Adam aimed at the first wolf and try to pull the tiger, the gun wouldn't fire Adam said shot Fred dam it shot it, Fred gun wouldn't work.

Shit Adam said as to two got back in the truck and the first wolf went by down park street than the white one was right on the first ones back side. Adam starts the truck and hit the gas and headed after them. Adam said Fred try to get your gun working. Fred said I'm trying its jammed. The wolfs where heading to main street. The first wolf hit the second wolf and there both went rounding across the street. The white one went throw the front window of Linscott's auto body shop. And the first one hit the car out front and got up and ran for the outside of town.

Adam came down the street with the others right behind them. Adam said were going after the first one the white one is in Linscott auto. Peter said ok we'll handle that one. Adam rounded the corner and the first wolf was almost at the end of town. As Adam came by the end for Linscott's the white wolf came out throw the end doors like a bullet out of a gun. The white wolf was right beside Adam and Fred going up the road.

Adam looked at the white wolf and it seemed to be bigger than the other one. Adam tries the hit the white wolf but it bent down and cut his tire with its claw. The truck went into a spin and came to stop a foot from Rick's front door. Adam and Fred jumped out. And got in with Devvan and Peter. They headed out of town after the white wolf that had a long lead on them now.

Adam said why didn't you guys shot the two in the park Peter? Peter said we tried but to guns jammed. Adam said same here but they seem to be all right now. Peter said same here.

The group saw the two hit the woods on the mill side of the road. Adam told Devvan to turn left on the road ahead. Devvan turned the corner and headed down the road. Adam could see the two were headed to the river he told Devvan to stop on the tracks and he would try to get a shot off. Devvan put the brakes on and the group jumped out, but the two wolves were long gone. Adam said dam what the shit just happen.

Chase pulls up behind them and got out dam that all went by to fast. They Set they're for a while to ran back the things that just went down. Chase said we couldn't get a shot off because our guns were locked. Adam said the same here but how could all the guns jam at the same time. Adam said will lets get back in it's 11:00 pm now I don't think were going to see them again tonight.

Peter said the two seem to be hunting each other not on the same side. Adam said that what it looked like to him. Fred said hope they meet up and kill each other then. Adam said that would be nice but he didn't think it would happen. The group went back to Rick's and help Adam change the tire on the truck. Adam said will we can all go home for the night and get some rest I guess we can pick this up in the morning.

Chase said to Mary that you And Devvan could stay at his place he has lots of rooms. Mary looked at Devvan and Devvan said sure and Mary had a smile on her face. Pete said to Adam call Linscott's owner and I will get the paper work he needs tomorrow morning. Fred ask Adam if he could gave him a ride to Stanley's Auto care center to get his slow truck. Adam said ok and laughs.

Adam and the group left the parking lot of Rick's and went home as Adam went by his room he could see Annette in the windows. He said shit I got to make A call. Adam calls the house and Annette was breathing heavy and almost crying. Annette said is everything ok I see the action from the window did I see two wolfman? Adam said yes and he would tell her about it when he got back from dropping Fred at Stanley's. She said ok she was feel better now that she heard his voice. Adam drop Fred off and head back home.

Fred said see you in the morning Adam. Adam drove back to his place and with up stairs. He came in and Annette was doing ok still a little scared. Annette meet Adam with a drink and said I made you some food if you're hungry. Adam said thanks and he was hungry. Annette said it looked like you guys had some action tonight. Adam said yes and told her all about it. Annette said that sounded ruff. Adam said for a minute it was ruff. Annette said I got some ham, peas and hash browns for you. She set the meal down in front of Adam and set down at the table with him.

Annette said I see the white wolfman seemed to cut your truck tire I was going to run down to see if you were all right but I see you jump in the other car. Adam said I don't think the other wolfman was male it looks more female that male. Annette said how could you tell you looking at her ass? Adam laughs and said no but it look female. They finch up there drinks and went to bed.

It was about nine that night and Dannie and Max was getting sleepy. Dannie said its time for me to go. Max said you could sleep here the night if you want I will be good. Dannie though and said ok and turned to him to hug him. Max said I got to change into my night cloths so I'll be right back. Max went into the bath room and came back out in a pear of short and a t shirt. He pulled back the covers and him and Dannie crawled in she lay on his chest and hugged and kissed him the two went to sleep with the TV running. Vicki came outside to have a smoke and saw Max's truck she remember that Dannie was out front.

She though to herself one day I hope to find someone who love me like that. Vicki said Max and Dannie were a great couple and she was happy for Max. Vicki with back inside the bar and it was filled tonight with horny drunk hunters. The bad thing is she was the only woman there right now. Vicki didn't mind it but some night her ass would be sore from all the flatlanders slapping it, but she though they did tip good.

Dannie was sleeping good in Max's arms. She could see herself running across a big open field. The night air was warm and had a bad smell to it as if meat left out three days to long. She got to the center of the field and found what was making the smell it was three half eaten bodies. One of the bodies had no head but the others where looking at her. There looked to be the bodies for Sam and Kaci, then she though the small chest must be that of Tommy.

Sam and Kaci eyes open and there started clawing to Dannie. She could hear a soft death like voice coming from the two help uses save the boy. Then the headless chest started to move and claw it's way to her also. The bodies were about six feet away form hear when their eyes saw some thing that made him round over and start to claw away in fear. Still she could hear them say save the boy save use. Then a thrip voice came from behind her it was Tommy voice save me.

She turned around to see the wolfman standing there with Tommy's head in his hand. The eyes were open and blood was coming from the base of the head as Tommy spoke save me. The wolfman looked at her and said you couldn't save their three what makes you think you can save the rest? The wolfman said this is my killing field you're not welcome. He drops Tommy's head as he charged Dannie but Dannie move and flipped the wolfman and he round over on top of Kaci's still moving body.

The wolfman could see the fear in Kaci's eyes as he picked her body up and bit into her again. Kaci screamed in pain. The wolfman looked at Dannie and said she's a sweet girl here have said the wolfman throwing the body at Dannie and it landed at her feet. The hand of Kaci Graded Dannie foot and

Kaci looked up and said save use. The wolfman laughs with an evil hiss save use save use.

The wolfman said you can't save the dead and I going to make you one of them honey. The wolfman charge again and Dannie hit the wolfman with a hard right hand. The wolfman round and then stood up. Dannie said as she looked at the wolfman and said is this your best man ! She throw her head back and howled come so I can finch this for you man.

The wolfman stood there a second then spun and run. Dannie said I though so. Just as she said that two white wolfwoman ran by her after the wolfman. Dannie ran with them as there ran down the wolfman. The two jumps and hit the wolfman bring him to the ground. The two wolfs stood there with him on his knee in between them. The wolfman looked at Dannie and said please don't kill me. Dannie said did. You gave Sam, Kaci and Tommy that choice?

She grads the head for the wolfman and broke his neck and ripped his head off his body. She looked at the head and the wolfman said this isn't over not by a long shot. Dannie wakes with a jump. She wakes Max up to Max said Dannie are you ok hun? Dannie said yes it was just a dream and lay back down on Max's chest. She felt save and loved in his arms. Max hugs and kisses her on the head then the two slowly fell back to sleep.

Adam wakes up and Annettte was already up and in the kitchen. Adam came into the kitchen and said dam Annette that a different look for you. Annette said hope you didn't mind I got one of your shirt on until I took a shower? Adam said hell no my shirt hasn't looked that sexy every and grad her ass that when he know that she wasn't wearing anything under the shirt.

Adam pick up the back of the shirt up and saw her ass dam girl that's a lot better to wake up too then a hot coffee and a good shower .Annette turned and smile have a set and I've get breakfast for you. What for breakfast their Annette Adam said? Some thing just for you Wild Maine Blueberry pans cakes . Adam said sounds great but where you get the Blueberry from?

Annette said I run over to the coffee shop I had some I was going too made you and Bob some pancakes with them. Adam said great Maine Blueberry are the best. Annette said so what's up for today? Will Adam said I going to get the group together and see if we can find a way for trapping this wolfman in and killing it one and for all. Annette said what about the female wolf? Adam said she seems to be different don't ask me who I know I just feel it.

Annette said different who? Adam said she seems to be trying to kill the other one and help use but it seems we getting in her way. Annette said ok then stop hunting it and hopefully she would kill him, but she said I know you can't do that Because you love the people of this town to right? Adam said as he eats a peace of his pancake you'll got me down to a tea don't you

Annette. Annette said it comes from servicing the people all those years and she got up and kissed them and went in the shower.

Adam was thinking man I should get up and take a shower with her but he was to affair of losing her as a friend. Adam came out the watch the local news and the report of Linscot's auto repair was on Peter was on the news telling what had happen that night. The reporter stopped them and said so you have two wolfman now is that what your saying. Adam also coud see a Reed and Reed truck set with someone in the truck watching the news reporter and Peter. Adam jumped up and went to the window to see what was going on. The man was setting there with the window open right across the road from the two.

Adam said to himself that's really funny what would a Constantin company want with a report on wolfs. Just than Annette came out of the bathroom in her birthday suit and smile at Adam and went into the room. Adam went over to the room and stood in the door way nice suit going to ware that to work today. Annette said no but I was hoping you could help me with my dressing with a big smile on her face.

Adam walks in and shot the door and got into bed with her. Needless say a lot of stress was worked out between them. After and hour was up Adam walks Annette to work her brother Bob was waiting in his car. Hi a sis under house arrest today Bob said? Annette said no but I sure was checked over good and they laughs. Adam said I'll see you later and kissed her and grad her ass.

Annette said see you later hope. Bob and Annette went into the shop. Adam went across the road to Linscott to see if things were ok with Peter. Peter and the owner were walking around inside. Adam came throw the door and look around, looks like a small Mack truck run throw the shop. Adam said hi to Peter and said see you on the news this morning. Peter said yup I know didn't want to tell everyone on TV about the two wolfs.

Peter said come see this back door Adam. Adam went to the door it looks as if a rocket went throw it. Adam said all I see was a wolf came throw not even stop cut my tire and run up the road. Clint the owner of Linscot said this is going to be hard to tell the insure company after last year's morse attack. Peter said morse attack.

Adam said I read that in the paper it was the funniest thing I ever heard. Peter said why don't you tell me about it. Clint said I'll tell you about it lets go and have a coffee at Rick's place and I can tell you on the way over. Peter said ok Adam said sure lets go. Clint started the story on the walk to the store he said last year around morse meeting seasons he got a call to pick up a wreck car in lee it was in the owners drive way. So Clint went there to the man's house the car was bended and the hood and roof fell in Clint said to the owner how this happen?

He looked at Clint and said and morse did it he was try to have sex with the car. Clint looks at the owner. I believe you said a morse did this? Clint laughs your shitting me. The owner said you want to see the vedio tape of it? Clint said sure I got to see this. Clint watched the movie and couldn't believe what he was seeing the morse was real try the do it with the car he fell down and laughing so hard his sides hurt.

That not the only funny thing that happen the cop that came was laughs so hard he couldn't stand as he sat on the floor, he said well the good new is in nine months you could look for baby Volvo in the yard. Peter and Adam couldn't stop laughing at the story only in Maine only in Maine Peter said. Peter said he would have the report set of tomorrow and would drop it off to Linscott in the morning. Clint said thanks and went back to his shop.

Peter said so what's on the menu today Adam? Adam said the first time is the set down and go over every thing. Then brake down all guns and gave them a good cleaning and oiling. Peter said that sounds good the other should be along shortly away. Peter laughs a morse that's almost as funny as Jack the ripper.

Adam laughs yup but the morse was real. Peter and Adam went up to his room the wait for the others. Dannie wakes up and remember she was with Max she could hear his heart bet in his chest. He was warm and she felt safe even after last night's dream. Max was still sleeping she though to herself this feels like when she was little and her Dad came home from a hard days work. He would lay on the couch and she bring so small then went and lay on his chest. Most of time Mom would wake use both up for supper.

Max was different he also made he feel safe. Dannie lay their looking out at the fog covered yard and woods behind the bar. Fog is a sign of a cold morning, but that was Maine the weather could go from 80 degree to-1 in a few hours hell she remember a snow Strom in the middle of summer once it was just for a day but was a fun summer break.

Max was moving he wakes up to see her looking at him. Max said good morning did I die and go to heaven. Dannie said no but it sure feels like it doesn't it. Max said you been awake long? Dannie said no just a few minutes. Max looked at her and kisses her and pulled her close and hugged her. Dannie said you keep this up I'm not going to want to get out of bed. Dannie ask what time do you have to open the bar up? Max said I should open around 10.30 but I go down to sweep and stock the bar around 9:00 .am.

Dannie said good I can help you and you can get done sooner then we can set at the bar until it opens. So Max went in to took a shower, then Dannie went in after to do her shower. The two with down to the bar and

Dannie swept the floors and Max fill the bar up and set the table up for people that day. After the bar was ready for the day they sat at the bar kissing and hugging.

Max was very happy that he had Dannie and She him. Max ask so what you going to do tonight Dannie? Dannie said she was going home to clean the house and wait for a big man to call her. How said Max got a man on the side? Dannie said no got one right in front of me. Max went to open the doors for business and Dannie ran and jumped on Max's back. Max just carries her to the doors an unlock them and carry her down to her jeep.

Were he grads her and spin her around and kiss and hug her. Max said it sucks to have this day end so soon. Dannie said I know I'm feeling the same going to miss you at home. The sun so warm it was going to be a good day for sunning. Will she kiss Max and hugged him as she got in her jeep to leave. Max said love you and will call you later. Dannie said I love you to Max as she drove out. She could see that Max was watching as she drove off.

She round down the window to let the air run throw the cap it was a great day. Max returned back inside where he began to turn on the lights. Dannie went throw town and the group in front of the town office was getting bigger and they seemed to be a little madder. Dannie said to herself that if this went on much longer that someone could really got hurt.

She headed out of town and pulled in her drive. She got out and went inside the house seemed cold without Max around. She went up stairs to change into some thing to clean house in. She knows it would take most of the day.

Chase, Devvan, Mary, and Fred showed up at Adam. The group set down and began braking down guns and cleaning and oiling them. Chase said what's the changes that all the guns miss fire at the same time? Peter said very little charge and how do you explain the guns are all working now? Adam said I don't know but we got a few things we all need to took over.

Mary said why it seems the white wolf only seem to want to kill the other wolfman and have nothing to do with use? Adam said right that's who I saw it to it seems to wanted me to stop when it cut my tire and keep on after the wolfman. Fred said or was she trying to protect the other wolfman from getting killed. If that was the case than why didn't she just turn and kill use right their Because Linscott door didn't stop her my little truck wasn't going to do the job.

Fred said that's true. She had the time to do it and run away still. Has anyone else seen a lot of Reed and Reed trucks around Adam said. I saw one this morning outside watching the news report. Chase said so there been all around town Because there are getting ready to remove the old bridge in Medway. Peter said last night when me and Devvan were chasing the wolfman in town one was setting by the hardware store. He left as we pulled in to watch for the wolfman too came out of the woods.

Adam said they seem there more than just building something. You think they my have something to do with the wolfman Chase said? Adam said I don't know but its worth looking closer at don't you think. Peter said I can see what the state has on the company. Adam said good anything can help at this point. Adam said now the real question where the wolfman hiding in the day and why he show up In the same area every time.

Fred said it could be like a human best hunting trail, why mess with a good thing if its working for you. Adam said right so if we find where he's going and where he been we could set a trap on him and box him in and kill him. Peter said sounds like a good plan when do we start? Adam said we can start anytime. Peter see what you can dig up on Reed and Reed company? The rest of use we see where the wolfman been hiding.

Fred said how we going to do that? Well here comes the fun part we are all going to map the spot on the road side that we saw the wolfman's tracks then set down and see if we can make some type of scene of all it. Adam said Devvan, Mary and Chase in one car with a dog and me and Fred with the other dog in a car. We can start at each end of town and hit every dirt road from here to the center of town we find. It's going to take a few days to do it but after it done, we can find the spots where he's been and set a trap.

Will lets get this thing on the road. Adam and Fred wanted to start up by the old mill and work their way in, Devvan, Mary and Chase went down by the dead rivers drivers island and started there. Mary Devvan and Chase weren't long before their found tracks. The hold shore line for a half mile was tracks, but the worst thing of all was there all seemed to be going the same place to the island it sent chills up their backs to think of having to go back and look the island over more for clues.

They keep marking on the map the spots the wolfman tracks were. Adam and Fred went up to the old mill to look around Crissy and her husband Allen were up there. Crissy said that the wolfman has been up here a lot in the last few days. Adam said you're not scare of it? Crissy said sure we are but we have trip light all over the yard about a mile wide so we have wounding when it's near.

Crissy said come on in and I will show you. Crissy said it was put in by the old man that had the place that's how he know the locals where around. Crissy shows Adam and Peter the room the room had a map for the land and all the light trips. See that one they it was at the main gate when you came throw it that's how we know someone was coming. Adam said that old man was some smart to make a system like this.

Crissy said he was really smart we found in the old boom shelter book he wrote showing how to make planes and car even before they came out years later. Fred said would love to see them they would made some great stories I bet. Adam said that's all you need is more stories. Crissy said come on down and I will show you the boom shelter. Adam and Fred with down stairs with Allen and Crissy. Adam said holly shit I though it was just a small three man place it looks as if you could fit 200 or more in it.

Crissy said the walls are four feet thin concrete with four inch plate steal on the inside the door is three feet thin steal. Fresh air and water and power it was made withstand and Adam boom. Allen said we spending the night down here until we hear that you have killed the wolfman. The wall over there had the same setup as the up stair so we know if there anything moving around before we get out.

Fred said hell why would anyone build this in the first place. Adam said look the lights up by the dam just came on. Crissy said it could be your wolfman coming throw on his way to town maybe. It looks like he moving at use right now. Fred said where the guns , up stairs in the hall. Crissy said you don't have time too get them now let close the door Allen said and see where he goes from here. The big door closed and locked. The lights just beside Adams truck when off. Crissy said I think your friend knows you're up here. Allen said you want to see something funny watch the lights the animal if it the wolfman when he starts for town he will howl then run down the road throw the gates.

Adam said you can hear it howl in this place Allen said yup there's and outside mike set in the hall up stair so you can try to hear who the person is. Crissy turns on the mike and it came to life sounds if it's your wolfman. Adam how can you tell that? Crissy said can't you hear him running his claw across some thing? Fred said it sounds like your hood Adam.

Adam said dam that cost me same good money to paint. Crissy said he done it to both our cars to. Just then a howl came cutting throw the room sending chills up everyone back. Crissy said watch the lights this is the funny part. The animal will taking off on a death run for the gate and town. Adam said dam that thing can move I think it about a mile to the gate isn't it? Crissy said yes and he can cover it in less than two minutes. Allen go ahead an unlock the doors we should be safe now. The light by the gate when off see he there that fast Crissy said.

Adam said we need a system like this for the town. The group went back up stair to get their guns and head back to town in hopes the see the wolfman. Adam said thanks for the show of the house. Maybe when you have time I can show you the other things the old man made. Fred said I would like to be here to. Crissy open the front door will Adam he made a mess of your hood.

Adam was pissed dam he said he cut right into the metal. Allen said he ripped my hood right off mind last week. I think he just saying I know you're around. Adam said he going to know I'm around if I get a good shot at that son of a bitch. Will thanks again Crissy we got to head back. Fred and Adam started back to town to see if there could follow the wolfman trail. The trail went to the end of the road and then on the other side headed to the river.

Dannie cleaned all the house she didn't mind cleaning but it was a big place for one person to clean. She got done and was going to cook a steak out on the grill and get some sun. Dannie went up stairs to get on her nighty and got out some steak and went out to the grill and put them on. She came back in to get a beer and set out in the sun. She watches the car ran back a forward down the old dirt road around the corn field. Every now and then she could hear a gun shot in the distance.

She didn't like hunting season Because of all the killing that went on. She lay there in the sun and could see Pat out back getting some sun to she yelled hi to him and he got up to came over but his boyfriend stopped them and he went into the house. Dannie turned the steak and put some barbarQ spices on it. She went in to throw a potato in the microwave to bake and got another beer and went back out to her steak on the grill. She sat down and looked at the sky it was a pretty blue with some clouds in it.

Her steak was done and she went in and ate her lunch. After lunch she returned to the porch and her chair she and was watching the sky and the cloud's again one looked like it may rain. The cloud move nearer and she could feel rain on her body it feel cold but she was enjoying it. Then it came down harder and harder it seemed to last ten minutes but she stays out in the rain the water was making her feel fresh and clean. The sun returned and the porch looked like a hot parking lot after a cold rain.

About two hours went by and she heard like ten or fifteen shot in a roll. She said the hunters must be getting some fire protect in the old pit. Dannie knows every inch of the town when she was young she spend a lot of time waking in the woods. She had a money cat that was her best friend. The cat would walk with her all the time. If Dannie was going to somewhere like school, she had too make sure the cat was in the house or it would walk to school with her.

She still has tears in her eyes for her spotty and it also makes her happy to think for the years they had together. Will Dannie got up and went inside to took her shower. The water was nice and she washes up and let the water run down her and now she felt alive again. She got out and went down stairs the get a beer and set an watch TV until Max called. The phone rang she looked at the clock it couldn't be Max he don't call until around nine. Dannie picked up the phone it was her Mom and Dannie said hello. Mom said I not keeping you from something am I. Dannie said no she was just thinking for Max.

Mom said so everything with Max is running good? Dannie said I think more than good I think he could be the one. Mom said she was happy for her. Dannie ask how Dad was and if he was cooking at the house. Mom said Dad ok but he only really likes cooking at your place. Dannie said he did a great job here. Mom said he had lot of fun that week end to. Mom said you want me to bring anything to go with the meals this week end. Dannie said no I have everything we need here. Going to hit the farmers market on Friday Dannie said that way the food will be fresh.

Will Mom said I love you and Dad said he loved you to I got to get some thing done around here see you this week end. Dannie said love you to Mom and give Dad a hug and kiss for me. Mom said I will see you. See you later Mom. Dannie set down on the couch and grads the blanket off the back she could still smell Max on the blanket and she smiled as she rapped herself up in it. She watches some TV she liked game show and the history channel. She slowly drifted off to see.

Adam and Fred marked the map and was just about to move went the scanner came to life. The local alert system went off Adam stopped and turned it up. The town Manager was calling the state police in to cover for a shooting that just happen three are dead and the shooters are still there waiting for cop to show up. Adam headed to the scene Fred said you're not a cop any more Adam. Adam said I know but doesn't mean we couldn't help the state police with they crime scene.

Peter should be there anyway. The manager didn't say where it was Fred said. Just roll down your window and you can hear the cop car coming for miles. Fred said he could hear the cars coming. Adam set at the end of wildness drive. The cops went by and slowed down in front of the grave yard. Adam and Fred headed to the grave yard and sure the shooting was at the back where the trail came across the grass. Adam saw Peter he walked up to the crime scene and said hi to Peter what happen here?

Seems the wolfman came pass this group of drinking hunters and headed down the hill at those three. The hunters open fire with automatic rife by the time the smoke cleared the three were death. Adam ask did the hunters have automatic gun license ? Peter said not a one for them. Dam Adam said hurts to see good man go down for something dumb like this. Was any of the dead locals Adam said. Peter said don't know we didn't get there Ids. Peter said came and look to see if you know anyone.

Adam went over to the body bags an open the first one no, the second one no ,then the three one no. Adam said there not from town. Just then Fred got out of the car with Adams rife and headed over to the group on a run.

Adam looked at Fred and could tell something was wrong. Fred said we still got someone watching use. Adam and Peter said where? Fred said look up the trail to your right see the big standing grave stone.

Adam and Peter said yes watch and see if something doesn't look around it in a few. Peter told the other two offices what was going on and they move the others into the car for safety. Adam said dam it is setting up their looking at use but why? Fred said maybe its playing with use. Adam said Fred can you shot at the stone on the right side but don't hit it and I will set to take a shot if he brakes cover.

Fred said sure can I shot the thing's hand if you want me to the next time he looks around the corner. Adam said sure they both set and was real for the shot. The wolfman put his hand out to look again Fred shot the wolfman he jumps up but was still behind the stone. Adam was ready to shoot if the wolfman came out. The group heard a loud howl and the wolfman went for the wood stranger behind the stone Adam couldn't get a clear shot.

Adam got up and stayed up the hill slowly with Fred next to them. The two got to where the stone was and found a half a finger that Fred shot off. Adam said man that wolfman is going to be mad the next time we meet. The two make sure the hill on the other side was clear and then came back to the finger and pick it up. Adam said now we can find out from the lab just what we are dealing with. Fred said good I like to know what it is to.

Adam handed the finger to Peter and said you think the crime lab can rush this throw to see what type of animal this really is. Peter said sure can we start working on the crime scene again? Adam said yup me and Fred will stand here looking for anything moving. Peter yelled to the other two cops and the three of them started to clear up the scene. Adam said to Fred thanks if that wolfman would have rushed use we all would be dead now maybe.

Fred said I don't think he was thinking of rushing use I think he was just hope to see what was going on. Fred said you know the way people slow down at a crime scene to see if they could see any blood or dead bodies. Will we sure be moving soon anyway it around five now it not long before the sun starts to set. Adam said Peter did you had a change to look Reed and Reed on the state profile? Peter said no but he would when he turn the finger into the lab.

Dannie was having a good dream it was with her and Max walking down the side for the road to the old sand pit. But that's when the dream got out for hand. Max disappeared and she was standing there alone. She could see wolfman by the hundreds lining the outer wall of the pit. She wasn't scare but did wounded how she was going to kill them all before there killed her. She got to the center of the pit and looked around she know it was going to be a losing battle. Just then from behind the old dump truck two more white wolfs appeared.

They looked at Dannie and said did you think your father was going let you stand alone? Dannie said how are you two? The two wolves said we are your sisters why? Dannie said my sisters. I'm an only child. Not sisters but sister in the fight. The three stood back to back as the first ten came at them their kill half the first round then the rest the second round . The other to she wolf look at the other wolfman and said is that the best you can do? Then the rest of the wolfman came charging. The battle seems to going on for hours until Dannie stuck the last of the wolfman down with a hard blow to the face nearly ripping the head off the wolfman.

The three stood and looked at each other. The two looked and said I think she ready father. The shy was bright and he said I will let you know when the time is right until then go in peace. The wolf's walked up the road out of the pit then the two females were replaced by Max .She hugs Him then they walked over to the rest area to watch the moon on the river.

She wakes up she hear the phone ringing. Max said hi how you doing their Dannie.Dannie said I'm doing great now that you called. Dannie said she was missing his warm hug and strong arms. Max said how your day go did you get anything done today? Dannie said got the hold house clean and looking good. Dannie said so how's your day going Max did you do anything fun today? Max said no the bar was pretty quiet all night, but it should pick up here shortly.

Max said if you want you could come over and have a few beers and then maybe set at the bar and shoot the shit until 1:00 am. Dannie said you know that sounds like a good ideal Max be their shortly. Ok Max said park out next to my truck that way your's wouldn't get scratch in the front parking lot. Ok Dannie said see you in a half hour or so love you Max. Max said love you to Dannie.Dannie got up and went up stairs to get some cloths on.

She came back down and headed over to the bar. As she was driving throw town, she could see it was quiet for a night like this no kids out. She pulls into Max's bar and went around two the back an went in. Max was at the bar and saw hear walks in his face turn on like a Christmas tree. Dannie walks behind the bar and hugs him and kissed him the guys at the bar said oooohhhhhh Maxy poo.

Max said I love you and she sat at the end for the bar an watched Max service drinks. She loves to watch him work he made it look so easy. She sat there and looked around the room Vicki was there with a man she said hi to her. Vicki said hi and started to speak to her friend again. Max came over with a beer for Dannie and a kiss. Max said if you get bored you can go up to the apartment and watch TV. Dannie said she was having fun just bring here with him. He said ok and kisses her again and went back to service more drinks.

Adam dropped Fred at the corner where his truck was, will see you in the morning Fred Adam said. Fred said sure about 8:00 a.m. maybe. Adam said ok with me good night. Adam parked his truck out back in his parking lot. He took his guns up stairs in his room. Then went back out and headed to Annette's shop. He got there and a few people were setting their eating their food. Adam said hi as he walks over to Annette and grad her ass then kisses her. Annette said I'm glad to see your ok tonight. Adam didn't tell her about the wolfman he didn't want her to get up set. He set down and said I think I will have a cheese burger and some onion ring with your good coke and he smiles. Annette said ok their men be right out with a coke. She went out back with a grass and ice and came back with LTD in it and some coke here you go try this and I will get your meals. Adam takes a drink and said just right.

Annette returns to the kitchen and made Adam some food. Annette came out with Adams food and said here you are I made you a few more onion rings Because I know you like them. Annette said did You have any luck with hunting down the wolfman Adam? Adam said Fred shot off the animal finger at the grave yard a while back. Annette said didn't get any good shots off. No but the finger will tell use if it human or wolf or both . Peter took the finger back to the crime lab Adam said.

Peter is also looking up some leads on the Reed Adam started to say. Annette grads his hand and said in a low voice don't say anything I will tell you later. Adam looked at her and said ok. Adam said so has Chase and Devvan and Mary been by. Chase left you this note to call them when you got here Annette said. Can I use the phone in the kitchen Adam ask? Annette said surely I'll be there in a minute. Adam got up and went to the kitchen to call Chase.

The phone rang at Chase's house and Chase pick it up. Adam said you wanted me to call when I got in? Chase said yup got some funny clues to look at tomorrow morning before we head back to the roads. Adam said oh like what? Chase said like no foot prints left by the second wolf and it seems the trail is going back to the island. Adam said dam I though we were done with that place. Adam said ok we will meet at my place and run this over with all of use in the morning around 8:00 am.

Chase said ok will see you later then. Adam hung up the phone and returned to the front the two men that were setting in the back got up too left. Annette rang them out and came around the corner to set with Adam. Adam said so what this about the Reed and Reed men. Annette said there been coming in for lunch and supper for the last few nights. Don't know if they're trying to hear about the wolfman thing or just bored at work. Adam said I don't know they were out side the other day watching the news cast to.

Annette said they didn't look like construction workers that she every seen. Adam said why do you say that Annette? Annette said because they to clean and they were wearing sneaker not boots. Adam said you know Patrick said the same thing to. Its nine o'clock now time the shot down for the night Annette said. Adam said you coming over or going home tonight. Annette said like too come over that's if you haven't got anything to do tonight. Adam said good I can help you shot down what you want me to do. Feel like seeping the floor. Adam said gave me a broom and stand back. Adam help Annette clean up and shot down the shop.

Annette turns off the light and shot down the grill and coffee maker. She and Adam walked out and locked the store for the night. Adam and Annette went up to his place and set down and kicked their feet back. Annette takes her shoes off dam she said my feet are killing me. Adam said lay back and give them to me. Annette lay down and Adam rubbed her feet she was in heaven Adam had nice strong hand, but as soft and kitten fur. Adam rub her feet until she felt better than Annette turned around and lay her head on Adam lap.

Adam runs his finger throw her long black hair. Adam said to Annette would you like a beer? Annette said I sure could use one right now. Adam got up a got two beers for them and Annette sat up on the love set so she could hug her man. Annette said are you getting sleepy Adam? Maybe Adam said with a Smile .Annette said you better stop reading my mind you may get horny you know. Adam said sorry pass that time already. So the two got up and went into the other room.

It was now 12:00 pm Max was getting sleepy behind the bar. Dannie ask Max to come down to the other end of the bar and she would help him with his sleepiness. Dannie jumped on the bar and sled her leg over the side and graded Max and gave him and kiss that would make him come back to live. Max stood back after the kiss and said dam I needed that thanks. Dannie just smiled and hops down behind the bar. She started to help Max service the customers.

Dannie was doing good and Max love the help and hot looking woman that was his. The Men on the other side of the bar was yelling for other round so Max got them their beer and returned to the back of the bar. Dannie was waiting with a kiss. Then the time for last round was going to be yelled Max looked at Dannie you want to call last round. Dannie said can I Max? Max said sure and he grads her and set her on top of the bar. She stood up and yelled last round and ever one in the place looked at her and orders other beer.

After Max had service ever body their drinks he got behind the bar and started to close the bar down. Max was sleepy and she could see it in his face.

The last of the people walked out of the bar and Max locks the doors. Dannie said now you're all mind. Dannie ask what time he had to work tomorrow? Max said from four pm to one a.m.. Dannie said great we can send some time together. Max smiles and said that would be nice.

They went out the back way after Max grads the tip jar and the cash drawer and took it back to the office safe. They locked the office door and went up stair to Max's room. The two stood on the porch and look at the moon in the shy it was nice again the stars in the sky. Max hug Dannie and the two went in. Dannie said maybe I should go so you can sleep. Max said I was hoping you would spend the night. Dannie said I would but all I have is this not a thing to sleep in. Max said ok but I don't like you driving you had a few drinks.

Dannie said I know how we can fit this Max get into something to sleep in and you can drive my jeep home and spend the night with me. Max said that sounds cool I be right back out. Max went into his room and charge into his sweats. Ok Max said ready to go. Dannie said ok then lets hit the road. Max got in Dannie jeep and set behind the wheel Max said I always wanted to drive one of there. Dannie said good I don't let just anyone drive my truck. Max pulls out of the parking lot and headed to Dannie's place. Dannie had the widows down and the fresh air was filling the cab.

She said to Max a good night to lie on the beach and watch stars Max said it would be if there wasn't a wolfman on the loss. Dannie said yes I almost forgot about it, but she didn't really she still could hear the voice of the wolfman in her head it's not over She set back in the seat and round up her window Max turned into the drive way and park the truck. Dannie and Max went in and Dannie said why don't you head up stair and I will make sure everything is lock up here.

Max looks out the back door and could see some lighten looks like we may get some rain. Dannie eyes bighting and Max looks at her funny Did I say some thing wrong? Dannie said no I will tell you up stairs. Max went up and Dannie locked the windows and the back and front doors. She went up stair and Max was setting at the edge of the bed almost asleep. Dannie said don't wait for me get in bed I got to put some thing else on first.

Max moves the covers back and got in bed. Dannie came out with her pink sweats on she got in bed and hugged Max and Kiss him and pulls the blanket over her. Max said this bed is great I'm going to sleep good tonight. Max said to Dannie ok what about this rain thing. Dannie looked at Max like should I saying anything, he going to think I'm nuts. Ok Dannie said in the summer when it hot out I little stand on the back porch in the rain nude. Max started to laugh I though it was some thing bad. I like it to myself but would never had told you that because you would think I was crazy.

Dannie laughs that's why I was hoping you forget it by the time we got up here. Max said when we get marred some day we can try it together. Dannie said Max stops your turning me on. Max's face turned red and he held her and they laugh together. Max was slipping off to a deep sleep and Dannie could hear his heart beating in his chest. She put her arm around him and lay down to sleep.

Dannie dreams would not be sweet ones tonight. Dannie got out of bed she looked and Max seen to be still holding her. She went down stairs and out the back door to her porch. Stand at the end for the field was the wolfman with the head of Tommy still in his hand. Tommy's eyes were open and you could hear a low voice saying save use. Dannie was mad and started to the other end of the porch. The wolfman said yes come to me with your anger. She was stopped at the last stair out the porch by the two white wolfs.

The old of the two said don't fight with anger in you heart. The other said it's is love that make you strong and he fairs that. She looked at the wolfman and he seems to be pushing her buttons come to me you little chicken. The wolfman turns and headed to the woods. She stopped for and second looking at the other wolfs. She could hear Tommy's voice save me, save me. Dannie turns and runs to the sound she seems a little slower than the other nights, as she got to the other end of the field and looked back the white wolf were standing there not come with her.

Then she head the voice again save me, save me. She turned and heads for the voice again. As she ran she know the trial, it was the one that went to the island. She could just see the wolfman up ahead. He jumps off the side of the pit and landed at the bottom on his feet. Dannie came to the edge and looked down at him. The wolfman said don't you care for Tommy's and his friend anymore.

As Tommy face looked at her with tears in his eyes' you can't save me, the head said. Dannie started to cry and the wolfman turned and ran for the island. Dannie could feel she was stronger somehow. She jumped out the edge and landed at the floor of the pit she got up and ran after the wolfman. The wolfman hit the water and swam to the island. Dannie was hot on his trail she hit the water and got to island and follow the wolfman to the grave yard and the big open field. The wolfman was standing there and turned to face her. She could see the bodies of all that was killed setting around the wolf.

Dannie could hear a low death like voice coming form he bodies save use. Dannie said I will do my best to help. The wolfman man laughs Because he could feel her fair. The wolfman said as he picked up one of the flatlanders and bit into him yum the flatlanders are good this year sweet and juicy want some. Dannie ran at the wolfman and he stood there as she hit him and she fell to the ground on the other side of him. The wolfman laughs again you're in my hell now little wolf.

The wolfman hit her and she hits up again a tree the wolfman grads her around the throat and pen her to the tree. Now Who's stronger girly. Dannie close her eyes and though what is wrong with me and why his he so strong tonight. She could hear the two white wolfs words don't fight with anger but with love. She started to think of Max and how he loved her so much. See open her eyes and the wolfman could see she was charging he tries to drop her and get away but she grads him by the arm and said so that how you did it you use my fair to make you stronger.

Well not anymore she could feel the full strong of he love come back and she grads the wolfman's head and broke his neck. As she stood there with the wolfman on his knee, the bodies of the dead seem to fade away in a soft light. She looked down at the wolfman and ripped his head off. The wolfman head said I still have time to win. Then she wakes up. She could feel Max and gave him and hug and slowly try to sleep again. She felt safe.

Adam wakes up Annette was still in bed with him. He kisses her and said it's almost 6:30am .She said dam I slept good last night I'm going to have to get up to get you some thing and get to work. Adam said don't get me any thing just get a shower and I will eat at your Place after I shower. Annette said you sure about that? Adam said yes now get yourself in the shower so you don't make Bob come looking for use. Annette laughs yup my Brother loves me.

She got up and headed of the bath room. Adam got up and turned the local news on. The report said it was going to be a nice day. Adam though it must be Indian summer this week Because of the warn readings for the rest of the week. Annette came out of the shower and sat in Adam lap nude. Annette said do I smell good with a smile? Adam said nice suit to. She laughs and gets up and put her cloths on. Adam walked her down to the coffee shop and kiss her and said he would be back in a few going to hit the shower.

Annette said ok see you in a few. Just then her Brother Bob pulled up and got out. Annette said hi to Bob and they went inside the shop. Adam returns to his room and got washes up and went back to get some thing to eat. Adam went down stairs and headed to Annette's coffee shop. Annette was just said good bye to her customer. Annette saw Adam coming throw the door and Annette said well sailor what can I do for you? Bob just shock his head as he walks by and said hi to Adam.

Adam said leaving so soon? Bob said yup got to go to my friend's house this morning. Adam said ok have a good day. Bob said same to you. Then Adam sat down at the corner and said to Annette how about a ham steak with home fries and a coffee. Annette said here you coffee and I will be right back with the food. It's almost 8:00am and I haven't seen and signs of Fred. Annette said that does seen funny he's always in town by 7:00 am or so. Adam gave him a call the phone lines were busy.

Adam said to Annette must be tacking to someone. His line is busy will if he was in any trouble we would know about it by now. Annette said yes he would do something to get use. Annette came out with the food and she set in a chair she keeps behind the corner. Annette said so what you want for supper tonight Adam? Adam said anything would do but he hasn't had stuff green pepper for a while. Annette said your in luck then I will start them here and we can eat together tonight at your place.

Adam said great I haven't had a good green pepper in a long time. Adam said your sure it isn't going to be any trouble. Annette said hell no stuffing green pepper is a tit job to do. Chase and Devvan and Mary walks in they said we though we find you here. Adam said good mornings have any you guys seen Fred? No everyone said we though he be in town by now. Adam tried too give him other call the line was still busy. Adam said he been on the phone for a half an hour now. Chase said that doesn't sound like them he doesn't stay on the phone that much.

Adam said I think I should take a ride out and see if he all right. Chase said we will grad a coffee and go with you. Adam said Devvan your can ride with me if you want. Devvan said great And they left the coffee shop. Annette said see you later Adam. Adam said yup see you tonight. Adam and Devvan got in Adams truck and started for Fred house. Devvan said what happen to the hood Adam? Adam said the wolfman clawed it at the old mill yesterday. Fred place was on a small dirt road if you didn't see it you would drive by it. Adam turned on the road and went to where Fred house was. Fred truck was upside down and the front part for the door way was missing.

Adam said grad the guns something went on last night here. Devvan said where Fred's house? Adam said I think it under his truck. Devvan looks at Adam and said what there's no build here. Sorry Adam said I didn't tell you Fred lives underground. Devvan looks even more funny then before Underground what is he and mole. No he just likes the place to be hiding that's the way he is.

The two got out and looked around Adam could see that the truck was laying on what was left of his front enters. Adam said to Chase grads the chain out of my truck can get the truck back on its wheels and off here. The truck rounded over good and they pulled it off the door way. Adam looked around and moves some of the wood off so they could go down and see if Fred was ok. Adam said Devvan, Chase stay up here and guard use. Me and Mary will go down and look for Fred. Adam started down the stair to the first landing Mary went down behind him. Adam came the first wood door it was ripped open and lay on the floor in peace. Mary said is that the only door between use and Fred? Adam said no this place is like fort knocks.

Adam came to the last door. It was a metal door about four inches thin. The door was still in place and it looked as if it was in a war. Adam tried the door it was locked. Adam hit the door and yelled for Fred .Someone came to the door and unlocked it but didn't open it. Mary said this isn't good is it Adam? Adam said stay low and I will stay high but don't shot unless you know it the wolfman. Adam slowly pulls the door open he got it about four inches open and he yelled to Fred. Fred are you in there it Adam.

Fred yelled back hit the dirt and cover your ears. Adam went down to the ground and cover over Mary with his body as to protect her from what every was going to happen. Just then a loud boom and something fly over there heads and down the hall. Fred came running out and said dam you guys ok. Mary and Adam set up what the fuck was that? My cannon I thought the wolfman was come throw the door sorry. Adam said good thing we got down. Fred said dam yes. Chase radio down from the top side what the fuck was that Adam.

Adam said we ok carm down it was just the cannon going off. Chase said ok but how in shooting a cannon at use. Just Fred Adam said. Well you can tell Buck Rogers he just killed his ranger truck. Fred said shit dam what else is going to happen. Devvan and Chase came down and walked into the house. Adam and Mary were cleaning the dirt off them self. Devvan looked up and said dam this is some house here Fred. Fred laughs it been cleaner.

Chase looked at the cannon and said shit is this what when off. Fred said yup it an old Maine war cannon. Adam looked at the size of the cannon ball and said that's what flue by me. Fred said sorry again I was all set for the wolfman to come throw the door the son for a bitch has been here for about three hours banging on the door. Then just as I got the cannon set to go he stopped. Close the door Chase an lock it and we go down to the living room.

Fred's house was something out of a story book. The place was unreal it had stone work all around the place with large lights hanging from the ceiling. They walked down a stair case with a water fall running down both sides for the rail. At the bottom was a glass floor where the fish could be seen and fed. Mary said did you build this place Fred? Fred said no my grandfather build it a long time ago.

He left the place and land to me when he dead. Devvan said it must had taking years the build it. Fred said every room had a date when it was started and when it was finished from what I can make of it. It took him 20 or more years to do all this work. Mary said it must had been fun down here as a kid.

Fred said we didn't know about the place until one night the old house burn down. Devvan said you mean he keep this place from everyone.

Yup Fred said we didn't find the trap door until we clean up the old build and we wouldn't have found it if the tractor hadn't broke throw the door. Dam Mary said sounds like a good story. Fred said when I tell people they just laugh like the Jack the ripper story. They went to the live room and sat down. Adam said we tried to call you but the line was busy. Fred said yes the line must have getting ripped out when the door way was kicked in. Fred said dam I just got the main door shot when he hit it I'm lucky I got it locked.

Fred were just glad your ok. Fred said glad someone came looking for me. Chase how bad is the truck Fred said? Chase said if you take the spear tire off and put it on a new truck it would be looking pretty good. Dam Fred said going to have to get grandpas' corvette out and run it. Adam looked at Fred and said you got a corvette? Yup Granddad left them to me there in the old mill house in town. A voice from the back corner of the room said honey is everything ok?

The group jumps all but Fred. Fred said carm down it just my wife. Adam said wife you never told use you were married. Fred said yes and Jean wanted that way. Adam by your right hand there's a yellow handle pull it out. The lights in the house when out for a second then were replace with soft almost cold light to the feel.

Ok Jean you can come out now the lights are turned. A 5'5" woman in white came out from the back. Fred said it ok hum there my friends. She came and stood next to Fred she hugs him and said after the boom I though you were hurt but you told me to stay in the back. Fred said sorry hum I should have run back and told you every thing was ok. Oh Jean by the way this is the group that help me when the wolfman attack in the pit. Jean said in a soft voice thanks I don't know what I do without my Fred.

Chase said thanks Fred you could have told the wolfman a story and when he was laughing he could have run. Jean laughs and kissed Fred on the chin I see your friends have head your stories to. Oh Fred said that smart ass is Chase he the was one of the cops in town. Mary and Devvan are from the state police tracking team from Bath. The one who turned the lights over is Adam. The group said Hi to Jean. Jean looked at Adam said I told you Fred I know Adam .Fred said so it was Adam you see all that time ago.

Adam said sorry Jean but don't remember ever seeing you. Jean laughed did you ever see a ghost as a child? Adam face turned white yes but how did you know that. Because Jean said it was me. Jean pull back her hood and her face hair and eyes were as white as snow. She was all white hand to. Adam looks like he was in shock. Jean said you ok Adam? Adam said my Mom said

I was just a dreaming when I saw you. The group said can we get in on this joke to.

Jean said ok I was about 12 years old I live in the old farm house at the end of the wildness drive road. Chase you my remember it as the ghost house with the blacked out windows. Chase said yes men were we all scared to walk by that place it seemed like someone was watching use. Jean said may it was me I wanted to go off so bad to play like a real kid. Jean said see I was a kid I had a sicknesses that keep me out of the light it would kill me if I got out in it for an hour.

Jean said every once in a while some kids would get close to the house and try to look in I remember one little boy with a red sox hat on put his face to the window and I bent down to look him in the face. He pulls back and ran for home I think. Adam said I did I though you were a ghost And I ran all the way home and tried to tell Mom. Jean laughs I never did see him again, but another kid started to come around and Dad ask him to come in his kid would like to meet him. The boy was Fred and he also though he was seeing a ghost to.

But we because good friends and then husband and wife, But no one knows of me but Fred and you few now. Adam said wow all this time and I wasn't dreaming. Jean said no but I have some thing for you. Adam couldn't think for what it would be. Jean went into the other room and came back with a red sox hat and handed it to Adam. Adam said I dropped it when I was there. Jean said I know that's why that night I went out to get it. Adam said if you like you can keep it as a remind of me. Jean said your right Fred he is a nice caring man.

Chase said now. Fred this is what I call a real story. Fred said thanks now maybe she let me tell it. Jean hugged Fred and said my man always looking of a good story to tell. Jean said isn't there one messing from your group. Adam said yes Peter he looking up some thing for use in the crime lab. Jean said my be your all can stop by some day and have tea or coffee with me and Fred. Adam said that would be nice then maybe we can look at the rest for this place then.

Jean said that would be nice I've never had any real friends before. Will Fred you never stop me wounding about you Adam said. But we got to go now and see if Peter is in town and see what he found out. Fred said ok but help me hock the phone lines up so Jean can call me if she needs me. Adam said your sure she going to be safe here. Fred said yes after we go she will shot the second amer. door that is one foot thin chrome steal. There isn't any other way in or out of here. Adam said good I wouldn't want to lose a new friend.

Jean smiled and said thanks. Chase said me and the other we run down the phone lines and see where it's broken and Fred can get ready if he wants too came with use. Jean said if that's all he took about is your guys. So Adam, Chase, Devvan and Mary went back up to the door and went throw it they walked alone the hall looking at the wires. Adam said it was were Fred said it would be broken at the door the wolfman kicked in.

Mary got out her knife and started to put the wires together she ask does anyone have tape. Adam said yup here some election tape I carry on me. They hocked the wire up and Adam called to see if the lines worked Fred picks up good he said now Jean can get me thank's Adam. Fred said I'll be out shortly. Adam said ok we will be at the trucks. Adam and the group came out of the path way to the sun light it was bright and hurt their eyes.

Adam looked in front of them and saw a ford ranger hot dog bun. The cannon ripped right up the center of the truck. Adam said as he looked at the truck of Fred's all their years and you think you know someone. Mary said his house is amazing. Chase said dam and he's marred too never would had though that.

Fred came out of the hallway up the stairs looked at his truck dam he said wish the wolfman was standing there. Adam and Chase looked at Fred and Fred said what is there something wrong? Adam said I never know you were living like this and marred. Your wife by the way seems really nice Adam said. Fred said she likes you guys to, she wants you to come back after this is over to set at the pond and have a barbarQ. Chase said what pond she can't come out until dark she said.

Oh Fred said I have an under pond that's feed by the river that run throw the room. Chase said I need a drink or I'm drunk. Adam said tell her we all will come and see she her after this is over. Thanks Fred said she always wanted people to come over it will make she very happy. Adam said will lets get in town and see what Peter can come up with. Fred said ok then I can go get the car out and get it going. The team headed back to Adam's place and set down and waited for Peter to call.

Dannie wakes up it was 8:00 am and Max still sleeping. She slipped out of bed but Max wakes up she kneed on the bed and kisses him and said go back to sleep I'll be right back in and few. Dannie went down stair and make some coffee and cut up some fruit and put it on a tray and went up to feed Misch got on the bed and Max opened his eyes with a smile. Max said will I've never had breakfast in bed before. Dannie said you can eat and we can go back to sleep for a while until you feel like getting back up.

Max said sounds like a plan to me. Max said this bed is unreal it's like sleeping on clouds. Dannie said I know I love it for that reason. Dannie said I hope you like fruit for breakfast? Max said I could live on fruit most of the time, but I like a good steak to. Dannie said we going to get alone great Because we like the same things. Max said now only if you like the pat's football team you're in the Max women's hall of records. Dannie said how many women are in this hall? Will if you like that Pat's only you and he laughs.

Dannie said it may shock you but I loved the Pat's from the first time they went to the super bowl and the Bear handed them and ass kicking. Max said dam you're a real fan not an arm chair cheerleader. Dannie said yes and put a peace for fruit in Max's mouth and kissed him. Max pick up a peace and put it in her mouth and kissed her back. Dannie said so did you sleep good last night. Max said I felt like I was flying. Dannie said great I love it when I dream of flying. Max was done his food and his coffee. So Dannie took the tray and went back down stairs with it.

She wanted to go out and set on the porch and let Max sleep, but she could use the sleep to. She went back up and Max was just coming out of the bath room. Max grads her and picked her up and put he on the bed. Max got back in bed and curled up with Dannie. They set there in each others arm and kissed for a while. Max said have you though about use where we my end up in a few years?

Dannie said yes and it makes me smile when I think of you and me. Max said great then I was hoping that it was going good between use. Dannie said why would you think it wasn't Max.? Because you're so beautiful and I'm so plan. Max Dannie said I don't look at the out side I look at what a man is made of.

Max said great Because my insides love you with all my heart. Dannie said I feel the same way now lay back and get some more sleep and clear your mind for all this nonsense . Dannie curl up under Max arm and put her arms around them. Max hugs

her and they slowly went back to sleep, but this time he was more than just happy he was Maddy in love with her. Dannie fell into a deep sleep. She was hoping her dreams would be good and fun not like last night. That wasn't to be .

It was a warm fall day Max and Dannie was going up the Grindstone road to do some boating. Max pulls in at the rest area about ten miles up the road. It was a nice rest area with tables and a nice view of the river. Max set the boat in the water and Dannie got in then Max push away from the shore. The day was going great there floated by the Pine Grove camp ground and could see people pulling in the camp ground. The river was carm but it started to move faster and faster Max looked into the water and it had a bloody red look to it.

Dannie could see it to the shy was getting dark and the water was getting ruff. Then something came out of the water and pulled the boat over. Max went under and Dannie was yelling for him. She took a deep breath a dove under to find him she could see Max with the wolfman pulling him under by his leg. She swam to Max and kick at the wolfman hand and he let go, she got Max to the top of the water.

He was still breathing and they were headed down stream as if the river was running wild. Then bodies started come to the top of the water pale white and half eaten. The eyes and hands were moving and swim to Dannie and Max. The bodys hands keep pulling at them as if to get out of the water or from something in the water. Dannie could see the rest area ahead she started swimming for it with Max in toe.

The bodies pulled them both under again but Dannie wasn't let go of Max of anything. Then Dannie kicked free from the body a hit the water top again this time the sun was out and the water was slowly down. Dannie pull Max up on the shore out of the water and put them on his side to get the water out of his lungs. Just then

hand came out of the water and graded Dannie by the legs and tried to pull her back in the water. It was the wolfman again.

She kicked the wolfman in the face and he fell back into the water an disappeared. Dannie came back to Max and he was coming back around she hugged him and kissed him then she wakes up and looked around she was safe in bed with Max. Max was awake to and said good moving beautiful she hug him and said love you.

Adam and the group were back at Adam home putting down every where the wolfman was spotted and he attacked. Fred was right it seem to be a trail that the wolfman like to hunt from. It went back and forward between the island and town. Chase said you know we've got a big problem now don't you. Devvan said what that Chase? Chase pointed at the map between the woods and Medway Middle School the trial run no more then 50 to 100 feet from the back of the school. Adam said shit your right Chase we have to go and Show Al this maybe he will do sometime now. Chase said right he hasn't done anything as of now.

Peter called Adam picked up the phone hay their Peter how things on your end. Peter said its getting real weald here the finger I both in is from some type of man c.

Adam said that didn't surprise me. Peter said you remember the report of the wolfman in Mass? Adam said yes. Guess who was working on the build the time the wolfman got out. Adam said don't tell me Reed and Reed. Yup the same ones that are work on the bridge, but the state log has them starting next month not now.

Adam said we got to go over to the town office and see if we can't speak to Al and show him what we found so far. Peter said ok see you soon then. Lets get the guns and trucks ready and head over to the town office. Chase said it only a block from here we could walk. Fred said the wolfman was only 100 feet from use yesterday to. Chase said yes your right. Fred said better safe than sorry.

The group head down stairs to the trucks and went to the town office as they pulled up the group up front was getting bigger. Adam pulls in across the road and got out. The people were holding sign and yelling at the town office. There wants Al hanging from a tree and Adam and Chase put back on the streets. The crowd move aside to let Adam and the others move throw. Adam said surely glad there on my side.

The group went up the stairs to the office. Adam walks throw the door first and looked at the woman behind the window she was pointing up stair in the chicken coop . Adam laughed and headed into the hall and up the back stairs to the upper seats. The town manager was setting in the Middle of the seats.

Al saw Adam and said so you're here to help the crowd? Adam laughs and said yes there needed someone who knew how to hang a person. Al sallow deep and tried to speak so why you here? Adam said we got a big problem on our hands and you have the power to stop more children from being killed. Al said what are you tacking about Adam?

We been tracking the wolfman for the last week and we know were he coming form and what trails he been using. The main trail that he uses is running right behind the Medway Middle school. Adam showed Al the map they been working on. Al eyes saw the School and he said my kid goes there what can I do I don't run the Medway school system. Adam said I know but you know all the town board and they will learn to you.

Al said you're right but until I get the school close can you and your group go watch over the kids. Adam said were heading there next. Al said ok I'm going down stairs to make the calls now. Adam said you can help the town by closing hunting season. Al said I know that now but we going to have to call a town meaning to do it.

Adam said good then lets do it. Adam and the team headed out and the town manager looked down at Adam as he walks across the floor. Al said Adam it would help the town if you and Chase took their thing back. Al throws the ids to the guys. Adam looked at Chase and said ok it your call this time Chase. Chase looked at the ID then at Adam I guess the boys are back in town. Adam said ok then lets get to the school. Adam and Chase walked out and the crowd could see that there were back to work and the crowd cheered.

Chase looked at Adam and said you're right I glad there on own side. The group load up and started to the school it was just on the out side of town after wildness drive. Adam pulled into the school and went into the office.

No one was around the class rooms that he could see that they were empty. Adam walks back to the main hallway and look in the Jim. Miss White was walking across the floor at him. Miss White said Adam can I help you? Adam said were, is everyone?

Miss white said in the back play ground get ready for a picnic why? Adam said dam that's were the trail runs by. Miss White said I don't understand Adam what's the trial got to do with the kids. Adam said does a panic for a wolfman ring a bell. Miss White said oh my God you mean that thing could be out their right now in the woods? Yes Adam took his gun and went with the others to the back for the build the kids were there.

The group came out the back door with guns in hand and the kids started to get worried they started to get scared. Miss White yelled for the kids the get back in the school house now. The teachers all knew Adam and started too round up the kids. Adam said to Miss White get the children in the Jim near the center would be better. The teachers and the kids with into the Jim and Adam and the group followed after. Miss White was trying her best the do a head count.

She said John one of the teachers is missing. Adam yelled did anyone see John one of the kids said he went in the woods with three kids to get leaf from the trees that were turning. Adam said shit Fred came with me, Chase, Mary and Devvan lock the Jim doors and wait for the buses. Fred and Adam ran out the doors across the courts and started looking for foot print going in the woods.

Fred said over here where they went in. It was a small trail that the locals use to walk to the main trail, Adam and Fred started on a dead run down the trail and it was about a mile in when they saw John and the others. Adam ran up to John and said is this all the kids that are with you. John looked around yup the three of them are here why?

This trail is the one the wolfman been using. John turned white and got the kids together. John said Adam what do we do now? Adam said Fred take the front and I'll stay back here. Move fast but not loud and if we say get down hit the ground and stay there. John and the kids said yes. Adam said ok let get back to the school now then.

The group moved fast but not to fast as too not make a sound. Adam could feel the hairs on the back of his neck stand up but he couldn't hear or see anything. Adam could see the schools and the courts. Fred stops the group and told everyone to get down the kids and John lay on the ground. Adam said you see something Fred? Fred said came here and see if you see the same thing.

Adam moved to the front of the group. Fred points to a black thing off to the right about 1/4 a mile away. Fred said it's been moving with use for the last few minutes. Adam said what do we do now. Fred said we could open fire in front of it maybe it will turned back and run or came right at use.

Adam said to the kids and John when we take the first shot I want you and the kids to get up and run for the jim ok. Adam said Fred ready to fire. Adam looked at John and said go. Adam and Fred started to shoot at the dark thing it moves back and started to run away then drop behind a big tree. Adam shot the tree it blows up little a hand full of power in a strong wind. The tree came to the ground with a crash. Fred said where the thing? Adam said I don't know can't see it.

Adam looked down the trail and saw the kids and teacher made it to the school house. Adam stood up to see if he could see better I can't see a thing. Fred said lets move to the school slowly and get the kids to safety first then came back to see. If we can see anything. Adam said yes as they moved with back to each other and they made it out of the wood. They hear the wolfman howl it was chilling to say the less. Will we know he not around use now.

Adam and Fred took a breath and headed to the school house. Adam stood out side and get some air then call Al to see if the buses were on the way. Al said is everything ok? Adam said yes but really close this time. Al said the town meeting is set of tomorrow noon. Adam said good it a start. Adam and Fred came into the Jim and the kids cheered them. John walks up said thanks for everything. The buses show up about ten minute after Al had called them. The kids were safe now and the school was lock up. The teach all said thanks to the team and got ready to go home.

Dannie got up and said to Max do you want to have dinner here or go out. Max said you know I think I would like to eat here and kick back on the porch if it's good out that's if you don't mind Dannie? Dannie said no I like setting on the back porch. She got up and kisses Max and went to the shower. She got out and put on some short and a white t shirt. Max hops in the shower and got him self washed up.

Dannie went down stairs to look to see what they could eat for dinner. She found two T-bone steaks that she got at Maryann markets she loved the meats there the fresh she ever had. Good she said I can make a salad to. Max came into the room and kissed her, man he said I never had a good nights sleep like that in a long time. Max said that's for dinner hum. Dannie smiles do you like t-bones steaks. Max said love them are we going to barbarQ them.

Dannie said you know that sounds like a good idea. It was now 11.30 a.m. and Dannie said lets go out on the porch and I can slow cook the steaks on low heat. Max said got any beer in there. Dannie said yes think I'll have one. She handed Max the steaks and his beer and they went out to the porch.

The two went out and started the grill and put the steaks on low. Max said this is a great place quiet and out of town. Dannie said that's why I like it out here I did live in town but the people next door keep bugging me so I moved out here and never with back.

It looks like a nice warm day on tap to sky is clear and theirs a soft cool wind blowing. The two sat down in the lawn chair and drank there beers. Max round on his side and looked at Dannie enjoying the day. Dannie looked over at Max smiles and blew him a kiss. Dannie said to Max a penny for you're though. Max said sure he looked at her and said married me?

This time it was Dannie who pass out and Max got up to see if she was ok. Dannie eyes slowly open and she looked at Max setting on the deck next to her. Max said you ok Dannie she looked at him with a big smile and said yes. Max said well I though I was the only one who did that. Dannie said no I mean yes to you're though Max. Then Max turned white and passed out. Dannie got up and sat down next the Misch rubber his four head and he started to came back around.

Dannie lay on Max's chest and the two began to laugh. Going to had to put crash suit on for the wedding. Max started laughing harder and said we're bad aren't we. They got up and hugged and Dannie went over to check the steaks. Dannie said the steaks are almost done how about a salad and some fruit to go with it. Max said yes that does sounds good. Dannie and Max went into the kitchen.

Max got out plates and fork and knifes and some paper napkins, Max said would you want other beer to Dannie? Dannie said yes and they went back out and sat at the table. Max got the steaks off the grill and put one on his plate and the other on Dannie plate he sat down and said the food looks great. Dannie said try the meat bet you going to love it. Max cut into the steak and started to chow it.

Max said you're right Dannie Maryann's has the best cut of meat. Dannie said I always buy my meats there. Max said they got me hocked I'm going to started to get meats there. Max said to Dannie after were finch this we can go in and curl up on the couch if you want. Dannie said sounds great to me.

It was now noon time the two within and put their dishes in the sink and went into the live room and got on the couch. Max kissed her and got the blanket off the back and rapped them both up in it. Dannie said what you want to watch their big guy. Max said anyone thing you want. Dannie turned the TV on and headed to the discory channel. Max is this ok Dannie said? Max said great I love this channel. The two curled up and watched the TV.

Adam and the other return to the station. Chase said it nice to be back at home isn't it Adam? Adam said will I did miss the place. Will lets use the map and see what we have as a team. Chase said yes and we got something wrong with the second wolf. Fred said what's that? Chase said it doesn't leave tracks. Fred said it had to left some type for track. Mary said we looked all over the shore line and the trails of the wolfman is all we could find.

Fred said she didn't run in the same trails did she. Devvan said there would have been some funny tracks if he did. Fred said yes but how could that be this shit is getting Weider by the minute. Adam said now we can add the school to the map. Al walks throw the door and he was white as a ghost.

Adam said they let you out of the office Al. Al said I had two came down and thanks you in person. Adam said it's all in a days work. Al said my kid told me what you did today see she was one of the once you broth out of the woods today. She said she was really scared but you two save her and her friends. Fred I didn't know the words to say thanks for this Al said.

Fred said it ok anyone of use would have done the same thing. You could see that Al was upset with what went on and he started to cry. Mary hugs him and said let it go your feel better after. Devvan said you keep this up and I'm going to cry. Al charmed back down and set on the chair to learning the team set up a plan. Adam said that Peter has some things to tell use to, but I'll just tell you some of it now and he can fill use in tomorrow morning. Adam said Peter got the finger back from the lab and it had some type of man DNA.

Devvan said so this is like the wolfman from fifty year ago in Mass. Adam said I'm afraid so. Al said what's the wolfman and Mass. got to do with it? Devvan said go ahead Adam and I'll show Al the report. Devvan and Al got up and Devvan showed Al the report on the laptop. Adam said and Peter was looking up Reed and Reed for use he found that they worked on the Mass. Lab just before the first wolfman got out.

Chase said should we go raid the place? Adam said no we don't have the hold true as of now. Fred said I had and old tree house about a mile up stream that looked down on the place. Adam said we could post someone up there to keep an eye up on them. Al shot the laptop cover down and said My God how could this be why would someone so sick and twisted makes this thing. Devvan said it someone how thinks he God maybe.

Al said even God wouldn't do this type for thing to use. Adam said you're right we need to try to stop as much for this killing as we can and hunt down this wolfman. Al said I will do my part to help you close the season. Adam said we going to need a lot of people to vote to close the season. Adam did you forget to tell Al something Chase said? Adam said ok I think will told him about the wolfs and the finger, Just then Al said did you say wolfs as in more the one? Adam said yes but the other wolfwoman seems to be trying to kill the wolfman.

Al said great male and female ok soon we will have wolfchildren the deal with. Adam said I don't think that's the case here they got into a good fight the other night in the park. Al said you don't know for sure it can have been same type of foreplay. Chase said good now we can file assault changes on the female. The group started to laugh. Adam said I'm going to call Kevin and Steve back in to run night watch again. Al said ok only if you keep those two on a short rope.

Max and Dannie lay on the couch until about three. Max looked at the clock oh Dannie I've got to get up and get to work. Dannie said let me run up and put some cloths on and we can head to town. Dannie went up stair to put her jeans on and a light top. She came back down and her and Max went out the door to the dooryard. Dannie said you can drive Max and he got behind the wheel and they with to Max's place. Max said if your hungry Dannie you can come in and I will make you some fish and chips for supper before you go home.

Dannie said sounds great you got a deal. Max and Dannie went up stair so Max could get into work cloths. Max came out and the two went down stairs to the bar. Vicki was behind the bar and she saw Max and Dannie walk in hi their kids. Dannie said hi and sat at the bar and Max went in behind it. Max said hi to Vicki and said you have a good time tonight Vicki. Vicki said I always try to have a good time. Max said I'll run back and get your supper ready. Dannie said ok. I'll keep and eyes on thing out here. Max went back and got Dannie her meal. Dannie was thinking that fish would really be good tonight. Dannie serviced a few beers to the men and they said hope you going to be around for a while.

Dannie smiled and said I'm just here until Max comes back out. Dannie just laughs to herself she knows man well, that the more they drank the more the other head did their thinking. Max returned with the fish and chips. Dannie kiss him and said it smell great hun. She went back to the end of the bar and sat down to eat. Dannie tried the fish. It was a melt in your mouth good.

Max said would you like a drink Dannie? Dannie said a Maine red chill if it isn't too much. Max said this is a bar isn't it? Dannie smiled and said yes a great bar sweety . Max made her the drink and said How the fish? Dannie said it was out of this world good. Max said glad you like it I charged fish dealers and everyone like the fish better. Dannie said it's good and it very fresh.

Max said the guy said if I didn't like the fish he would buy it back when he came into town this week. Dannie said you can go wrong that way can you now. Max returned to the bar and service more drinks. Dannie was real enjoying her fish when someone sat down beside her and said can I buy you a round pretty. She looked up at the guys and he got off the bar stool and said sorry Dannie didn't know it was you. Dannie said ok just say hi to your wife for me. See it was the same dumb hunter from Lennis the other day.

Dannie just laughs at the way he tripped over his feet as he tries to get away. Max looked at her and laughs that's my girl he said. Dannie finch her meal and her drink and when behind the bar and kiss Max good night. Dannie said I got to do some shopping for steaks and things for when Mom and Dad come over this week end. Max said ok get some of those steaks from Maryann's they were good. Dannie said you bet I'm hitting that on the way home.

Dannie said Max call me around nine if you can tonight. Max said no trouble and hugs and kisses her before she went out. Dannie went out back and got in her jeep it was about six Because the sun was going down in the top of the trees. She headed to the store to get some things. She stopped at Maryann's market and got some steaks and things to have this week end with Mom, Dad and Max, but she also wanted one of Maryann's sandwiches.

Maryann made some of the best sandwich she had and if you got there before noon there were always nice and fresh. Maryann's was a nice store always clean and nice people to service you. It was your corner Mom and Pop store set up to a hometown charm. Dannie pay of the food and on the corners were some of Maryann's bake beans Dannie's mouth watered just looking at them. The only beans better than this were bean hole beans. Dannie got some and went to put every thing he hear jeep. Dannie drove home and unloaded the food and put it away.

She took her sandwich and a beer to the back porch to check out the sun. The day was over cast but nice and warm. Dannie lived all over Maine at one time but love the quiet of the country and the smell of the air. Oh she said though it would be a good time to read the book she started. Dannie went inside and got the book out the table were it lay from the last time. Dannie picked it up and flip the book over and read the warning again she laughs to herself at how afraid she was when she went to sleep in the love seat.

She went back out to the porch to read some and eat the rest of the meal. The story was builds around a young girl name Kaci and her life In the old days. She wrote down her live story as she saw it and her night mare as close as she could remember. Dannie though man if I had night mare like this I would be Insane .Dannie stopped and though well my dreams of the last few weeks have been crazy. She set in her lawn chair and began to read.

Adam said will it seems that all we have to do is find a spot where we can get this wolfman in the open and bring him down. Chase said he seems to move throw the old sand pit a lot may be we could watch the rim and box them in from they're. Adam said it sounds like a good idea, but we are not going in the woods until the hunters are out. Fred said yes I understand that. Peter called Adam on the phone and said I got the printouts and I will see you in the morning at your place. Adam said we are set up in the station house now.

Peter said oh why down there? Adam said me and Chase are back on the force. Peter said great its good Because my chief was getting on my back for working with plan street poeple. Well good Peter said I shall meet you at the station around 8:00 a.m. then. Adam said they're not much we can do around here but call the night crew and set them lose. Al said I wish you wouldn't put it like that I almost feel safer with the wolfman on the street then those two.

Adam laughs some times I wounded myself about them. Adam call Steve and Kevin and ask them if they wanted the do night watch again? The boys were happy to but wanted the use the Aks if there could. Adam said ok but remember call for back up and don't do anything dumb ok. Kevin said after the last run in with the thing that wasn't going to happen. Adam said that they should stay in town and move around stay off the dirt road until morning. Kevin said sure will Adam.

Adam said stop by the station and get the guns. Kevin said we are coming in the door right now. Adam hung up the phone as the two came in. Chase said we didn't even her you two pulls up. Steve said couldn't wreck all the work we did on the cars. Will here are the guns and some more rounds but don't be a dumb ok. Get out of there and call me. Kevin said you got it. The two boys went out and left for night watch. The two pulled away from the side walk like two will trained, drivers should.

Al said maybe we should cage this wolfman and train him to teach drivers ed. Adam and the others laugh looks like it happy those to. Will I don't see why we have to stick around anymore. Fred didn't you want to get a car in the old mill house in town. Chase said what car last year when we run the kids off there wasn't anything in there. Fred said Because there are under the floor of the building. Chase said I see other stories coming on. Fred said not a story the real thing. Adam said I've got to see this. Ever one else looks at each other and said counts' use in to. After Fred house I think I've seen everything said Devvan. Adam and Fred went out to the end of town to a house and barn. Adam and Fred got out and the others pulled in behind them. Chase ask so why is this call to old mill house. Fred said because when the mill was first built in town there wasn't a lot of places for people just coming in to live. So my Grandpa built this place for people to stay in than when they got their home's built they could move in them.

Chase said but you only can fit three maybe four at a time in there. Yup Fred said that's why the barn is part of the main house. My Grandpa said he had 12 to 16 families in here at one time. Chase said that must have been some fun in the winter. The group walk together into the barn. The barn was huge about twice the size as a New England barn would be.

Adam said so where the car you told me about. Fred said your standing on it just about now. Adam said it in the ground. Fred said yes and no it underground but not beared. Fred said come over here and you can help me open the doors. Fred went to the center of the room where two old hand brakes were mounted in the floor. Fred told everyone to stand behind him and Adam. Fred said ok Adam we got to move there at the same time Fred said.

Adam said why not just pull one then the other. Fred said it was set up that way so it couldn't be open by less than two people. So you ready click to the first stop now. The two men pull the handle back to them one click. The floor started to move some. Ok one more click now, again the floor moved. Fred said Now Adam we need to move back to the first spot and do it now. Puffs of air and dirt rose from the center of the room. Dam Adam said what that? Fred said the landed is unsealing from the main floor.

Now Adam we have to move two back at the same time ok ready go Fred said. The two clicks the last to stops and the center for the room started to go down. Fred said follow me and I show you the way down. Fred said the doors haven't been open in a few years now so we may have to pull on them. Fred went over to the far side wall and took out a key and put it in a hole in the wall. The wall looked to be sold steal panels. Fred turns the key and a handle drop out of the wall. Then Fred went over and pulled the handle to him two doors move slow and open a little hard but not too hard.

Fred said come this way. The door open to a set for stairs running down under the barn floor. Fred turned on a switch at the bottom of the stairs and the underground was full of light. The group said Fred You said there was one car here I see that less ten. Fred said I said I had one corvette but didn't say what the other 15 were. Adam said I can tell from here that the one over there under the cover is a vet.

Fred said yes but not a stingray it's back at the far end. Chase said they're only made a few different models of the corvette. Fred said I think that one is a Monterrey. Adam said your shitting me they are the most rair of the corvettes. Adam went over and pulls off the cover it was the Monterrey and it had the plate still on the seats. Adam said we it run? Fred said this is a vacuum sealed room after it shot it we suck the air out and sealed the room. Fred said go ahead and see if it will turn over. Adam opens the door and sat behind the wheel he was in love. He turned the key and the car came to life, just as if it wasn't ever made until today. Adam got out and said now I guess your going to tell me you have a gray ghost down here.

Fred said their only four of them around but only two know of to be in the world today. Devvan said then you got one of them here? Fred said no I got the other two over there in the center on that side. Devvan and Chase went over and pulled the covers off. The hold groups mouths' drop when there saw the two cars. Fred said that first one is number three and four beside it. Adam ask Fred do you know how much there three cars go for? Fred said they're so old I didn't think they were worth much. Adam laughs your nuts the two ghosts would go for around one million a peace. Fred sat on the floor dam !

I was Go to put them up stair next year for a 1000 a peace. Chase said what is the other ones and it looks like you got a motor bike here? Fred said yes but I wouldn't ride it be afraid of scratching the gold. My grandpa said it belong to some guy who play rock music I think he said it was Elvis or some name like that. Adam looked at Chase, Devvan, and Mary and said no it can't be that bike. Fred said on the bottom of the seat it read to my wife Priscilla.

Adam went over and pulled the covers off, it shines like it was new. It was a gold-plated hog and the seat did have the writing on it. Fred Adam said this is the long lose Elvis bike that been missing for years. Fred said Elvis who his Grandpa said he both it off some rock music guy and I've got the bill of sales back home. Adam said I bet it stills run to. Fred said yes I rode it around down here two years ago. Adam said if your grandpa did buy that's bike its worth maybe around ten to fifteen million.

Fred said grandpa did say it was going to be worth something one day but not that much. Adam said do I dare ask what under the rest? Fred said that one is a road runner the other four are picks up form ford Grandes like his fords. Will lets cover them back up and I got two get back home to my wife Fred said. Adam said you going to take the corvette out. Fred said no I'm a truck man myself. Fred said this one is the truck I love the most he pull the cover back and it was a first year ford ranger pick up.

Fred went over and got in and started it up the truck run like it was new. Fred moves the truck on the center ramp and said ok you guys ready to go home now. Adam said the man give use a heart attack and wants use to go home. Fred said after we are done I will let you have the vet. if you want it. Adam said for real dam thanks. Fred said if you guys need a car or truck your welcome to one. Dam the others were speckless.

Will we got to get back up stair or we going to be locked in here. The truck in the center started to going up. Fred said come on we got to move now the group ran back up the steps to the main floor. As soon as the truck came up the door shot and the floor locked back in place and you could hear the air bring pulled out of the floor from below. Adam and the group headed back to town still stun at what they saw. Adam said I will see you guy back at the station tomorrow.

Dannie was still read so she though when she could feel some thing weird happing again. She set up in her chair and could see around the field someone in a dark long coat coming across the field. It looked like the man from the back of the book. She turned the book over and it was the sandman from the book. She tried to get up and move but she was glue to her seat and she couldn't yelled for help.

The dark man came onto the porch, see your reading my book? Dannie said yes in a low voice. The dark man said how do you like it so far? Dannie said will I

Can't understand there you come up with the things you write about. The dark man said it easy the night mares are mind. Dannie said who are you and what are you some nut. The dark man said no hun I'm just dead as his pull back his hood and showed his skill to her. Dannie scearmed and jump up.

The dark man grads her with a boney hand and said don't you dead to and his eyes were red as flame. Dannie wakes up at that very minute and jumps out of the lawn chair a throw the book, shit she said he got me again. Dannie went in the house and throw some water on her face and tried to cool down. Dannie said dam that just a book how can it make me jump so.

Dannie looked out the back door at the book she started to laugh and went out to pick it up. Dannie said I should put your ass on the grill and be done with you, But it was the type for book that keep making you come back for more. Dannie said will I'm getting hungry and I'm going to make some tuna sandwich and have other beer. Dannie looked at the book and said one more time and your going to be a cooked book.

Dannie came in the doors and set the book on the counter in the kitchen. Dannie made her self some sandwiches and got a beer and went back out to the back porch and set to eat. The shy was getting darker and the day was growing cold. Dannie was thinking about Max and what he may be doing right now. She got done her sandwich and finch off her beer and went in to take a nice shower and get ready for bed.

Dannie went up stairs to the bed room and got undress she got into the shower and let the water run down her back and front to get good and wet. Dannie washed up and got out and dried off. Dannie went to her bed and turned on her over head tv to watch the news or something else. The news had a local story saying that the town of East Millinocket was trying to shot down the hunting season because of the wolfman troubles.

It also reported that more than seven people had lose their life so far and that the local cops saving a few lives at the school yesterday. Dannie didn't know how bad it really was Because she had been with Max the last few days. The phone ring it was Max, Dannie said hi their Max is everything ok your caller a little before I though you would.

Max said great but he had some down time right now and had been thinking of her all night. Dannie said Max your sweet I was laying in bed just think of you. Dannie ask how the night going so far? Max said I keep getting man coming up to me ask where the pretty bar keep was? Dannie said they didn't mean me did they. Max said will there weren't tacking about him.

Dannie said you never know what beer and men will come out with. Max laughs and said you're right on that the more beer they drink the dumber there get. Will Max said I don't have to work until four tomorrow think you want to go to Millinocket and look at some rings. Dannie was quiet and didn't speak for a second, but did get the words out yes, yes, sure Max.

Max said good will come and get you around say ten tomorrow? Dannie said sure can't wait. Max said good if you find something you like maybe we can tell your Mom and Dad over the cook out this week end. Dannie said we better make sure they are setting when we do ,its Dad he can be as bad as you with passing out from good news. Max said that's good I like your Mom and Dad they seem like nice parents.

Dannie said that great my parents like you. Max said will it's a date then see you tomorrow around ten love you. Dannie said love you to Max see you tomorrow. Max hung up the phone and had a smile about a mile long on his face all night. Dannie was still hanging on the phone and kicking her feet and hands yelling he loves me he really loves me. Dannie put the phone down the got out of bed and dances around the room.

Dannie though of calling her Mom and Dad and telling them, but that would spoil the week end for Max. Dannie floated down stairs and into the kitchen said got herself a beer and said to Max the man of my dreams. She went around making sure the door and windows were lock. She went out on the back porch the cold night wind felt great. She could see the stairs in the shy and a few clouds over head.

The night was so quiet that you could hear big truck running the interstate over ten miles down the road. Dannie could see the town light in the night shy, she was so happy that she yelled he loves me. She went back in and locked the door behind her. Dannie went up stairs to go to bed but she knows it wouldn't going to be a cake walk to fall asleep now. Dannie got in bed but wish that Max was here to hold her in his warm big arms. Dannie curled up an lay there looking at the night shy throw the open window, she though she was so high on life that she could float out the window and fly around the town.

Adam returned to the town and parked his truck and walked over to Annette's coffee shop. He walks in an Annette was the only one in the shop he said hi there sweet thing. Annette turned around and said will just in time for my nighty pick me up care to join me? Adam said yes if there was a cheese bugler and same onion ring to go with that. Annette said there sure is big man. Adam said How your day going here in town? Annette said a lot of hunters are pissed at Al for trying to shut down the hunting season but I think it about time.

Adam said the same thing it's the brake we need to trap this wolfman and take him down. Annette said they a news cast a while ago and said what happen at the school the other day. You and Fred are some kind of man to lay down your life of others. Adam said all in a day's work for me. Annette said that's the only thing about your work that scare me. Adam said it shouldn't it doesn't happen like that every day. Annette said yes but when it does it scares me. Adam said I'm sorry that you are scared but I have to face that fear on a daily bases.

Annette came out with his supper and said as she kissed him here your are Adam. Adam said it looks great Annette, Adam ask Annette how much do you know about Fred and his wife? Annette said not much his wife keeps inside because she can't came out in the sun at all. Annettte said I hear Fred is pretty will off and he had some money that his Grandpa left them. Adam said see you know everything about the town don't you.

Annette said can't help it when the locals come into speaking of thing that happen around town. Adam said it helps to have someone like you around to fill me in. Adam said did you know about the cars and bike he had at the old mill house outside of town. Annette said I've heard people speak of it but everyone said their Notting out there. Adam said oh there something out there all right he has Elvis's long lose gold-plated bike is out there.

Annette said your shitting me aren't you? Adam said no I sat on it and looked at the bottom of the seat. Annette said I though a long time ago when I was young Fred Grandpa rode a gold colored bike around town. Well you don't dream it Annette it was they're with about 15 other cars and trucks Adam said. Annette said were in the old barn? Adam said no under the old barn in an air sealed room. Annette said dam that man gets weirder the more you know about him.

Annette said so would you like anything else before I shut up for the night. Adam said no but did the Reed and Reed men show up today? Annette said same time every day like clock work, she said they sure don't speak much but they sure like to learning to every thing began said. Adam said Peter is bringing some paper work tomorrow on them and I see what he could dig up.

Annette said you think they have something to do with the wolfman? Adam said don't know going to check all my clues and see if they line up. Will Annette said its time to close shop for the night. Adam said you need help doing anything? Annette said no you set there and enjoy your food and I will turn thing off and close it up. Adam said the hamburger is great and your going to have to tell me how you made those onion ring so good.

Annette said I use beer not water to mixes my batter it makes to ring's cook better. Adam said is that all it seemed like it was an old family tip. Annette said no just good old beer and that's is all. Adam finch off the last for his burger and set and watched as Annette got ready to close. Adam and Annette went out and locked the doors and headed over to Adams place. Adam said let take a small wake in town just down to Lounsbury's Food center and back.

Annette said that seems like a good walk but will we need your gun. Adam said it wouldn't hurt to carry it along with use. Annette said I sure would feel a lot safely with it. Annette said we going to have to go and get some of my cloths later to, that's if I'm going to send anytime here with you I like my work suits but I'm running short of them. I going to have to work in the nude soon. Adam said I bet your tip jar would fill up fast that way as he graded her ass.

Adam stopped and got his gun out of the his room and the two went for a walk down the old part of a main street the night was cool but the air was fresh and made the night seem good. Annette said you see how many home are for sale around here? Adam said you see more and more each week the young people are moving out for a better life never the city. Annette said even the town in slow became just another small ghost town.

Adam said if it wasn't for the flatlanders and the hunters the town would be dead. Annette said can you remember when the mill was new the people would fill the parking lot now it has only about half the car it once did. Adam said it sure is sad a good little town just fading away. Adam saw Kevin coming and said maybe you should walk on the side walk Kevin coming. Annette said you think that's safe with the two of them driving.

Adam laughs and said no but it would give use a change to run. Adam watches as Kevin drove by and the car he was driving look good the boy really were doing work on their cars. Annette said you sure that was Kevin sure didn't drive like he did. Adam said it's him the boys had a run in with the wolfman the other night and it some how charge them. Well that was a short walk here we are at Lounsbury.

Lounsbury was an old store with a lot of years on it. The parking lot looked as if the state was growing their potholes there. Lounsbury is a nice little store the locals work in it and they are all nice people. Annette and Adam headed back to the other side of town. The night shy was fill with stars and there was a full moon. Annette said look it's a full moon tonight Adam. Adam laughs don't think this wolfman is like the movies at all.

Annette said I sure hope not. Adam said it sure is a nice night out isn't it. Annette said sure is I'm not looking forward to the winter at all. Adam said don't worry I've keep you warm at night. Annette smiles at Adam and said I bet you will. They made it back to Adam's place and went to bed.

Dannie fell to sleep she was at the back porch of her house. The night sky was clear but it had a cold chill in the air. A chill of death was running throw her mind. She could see that she was at full power she felt like a house of bricks. She could hear to sound of a wolf crying in the distance. She jumps off the porch and headed to the sound.

She though what type of fight would she be in for tonight. She could hear the voice of the wolfman say came to me little wolf and I will gave you something to fight about. She ran down the trail along her back field. The sound of the wolfman wasn't getting any closer. She ran down the road to the pit.

She stopped at the top of the hill and she could see the wolfman standing there with something in his head. It was Tommy's head the wolfman turned around and said I still can kill you I have the time to do it. Dannie said you didn't kill me all the other times I don't think your going to do it this time. He looked at Tommy and said do you thinks she right and took a bit out of his head. Tommy cried out why do you not save me please stop this wolfman?

Dannie could feel the pain in Tommy's heart and the wolfman was afraid of this. He dropped Tommy's head over the side and said come and helps the others to if you can. The wolfman jumps down into the pit and you could hear them howl. Dannie moves to the edge of the pit and stops in shock. The pit was filled half way up with death people. The wolfman sat in the center and said are you able to stop the killing and save the people to?

Dannie said all I have to do is to kill you, you son of a bitch. The wolfman said good get mad. It makes me stronger. Dannie said not this time I know how to defeat you. The wolfman looked scared and started to run for the shore. Dannie jumps down and landed in the piles of dead people she started to run of the wolfman, but the hands of the dead slowed her down. She said I'm trying to help you and she push on.

She came across Tommy's head he looked as if he was crying. Dannie said don't worry this will be over before you know and you and your Mom and Dad can go to heaven together. Dannie got to the shore and drove in and swam after the wolfman he was headed to the island. She could see him get out and start to run inland to the grave yard. Dannie hit the shore and went after him. The two got to the grave yard and the wolfman turned and look at her.

The wolfman said you think you can kill me on my island do you. Dannie I did before and I will kill you again. The two came at each other Dannie hit the first blow. The wolfman round over and said is that your best as to make her mad. Dannie said you're not going to get in my head this time. The wolfman knew that he was going to have to try harder to make her mad.

The wolfman said is Mom and Dad safe from me I don't think so. Dannie said they are fair away and you can't get them. The wolfman said maybe I will barbarQ them this week end. Dannie was pissed. The wolfman said did I hit a soft spot girly. Dannie said I will kill you before you even get close to my parents. The wolfman said you come and do it then if you can.

Dannie charges the wolfman this time he hit her and she rounded out of the way. The wolfman howl and laughs at her, he said getting slower Dannie. Dannie was going to change them again. Then Dannie stopped and though of how much she loved her parents and Max. The wolfman said you are scared aren't you Dannie? Dannie opened her eyes and said no I'm in love. The wolfman turned to run and Dannie jumps on his back and broke his neck again. She turned the head to her and said you feel pulled apart again then she ripped his head off.

The wolfman said dam and she wakes up. Dannie's heart was racing and she felt as if she had gone a round with and boxer. Dannie lay back down and tries to get back to sleep. Dannie looked at the clock it was about six a.m..

She knows that she was going to look at rings today, that made her a little happier.Adam and Annette got up. Annette said I going to take a shower and she round over and kissed Adam. Adam got up and put on a pot of coffee he was thinking for what was going to happen today and where they could trap the wolfman. Annette came out of the bathroom and went to see what Adam was doing. Annette saw Adam setting they're with a far away look in his eyes. Annette came in the room and Adam looked at her and she said not thinking of the wolfman so soon are you.

Annette dropped her towel and said maybe this will help you this moving. Adam face turn red and he said dam woman I couldn't think of anything better than you in the morning. And the two went to the bedroom. After that Adam walked Annette to the coffee shop and kiss her and said see you in a few. Annette went in the shop and Adam went back to take a shower. Adam got in and the water felt good he still had a smile from what happen a few minutes ago.

Adam got wash up and went back out to Annette for breakfast. Adam started out the door and said shit I made coffee and he went in and shot off the coffee maker. Adam went down and looked around the main street it was still quiet, but would be alive with hunters soon. Adam though well maybe today. Town meeting would going good and they could close the season and get to business of hunting the wolfman down.

Adam went into Annette's and she and Bob were speaking to each other. Bob said hi and so did Annette, Adam said hi to the both of them and sat down at the counter. Annette said can I get some thing for you Adam? Adam smiled and said I already got that, but some coffee and French toast sounds good this moving. Bob said guys I'm trying to eat here. The two laugh and Annette said ok French toasts it is.

Bob ask Adam are you going to just shut down hunting in the town or you trying for the towns of Millinocket, East Millinocket and Medway? Adam said would like all three towns but I'm only going of East Millinocket right now. Bob said good I like hunting but don't care for the wolfman hope you bag it soon. Adam said so do I Bob. Annette returned with Adam's meal and give him some more coffee.

Annette said what time is the meeting today? Adam said it should be around noon time or so. Annette said I hope it goes all right this time. Adam said I hope so to Annette said. Adam got up to pay and head over to the station to open for the morning. Adam grads Annette on the ass and gave her a big kiss. Annette said see you later then. Adam said sure will. I will be over after the meeting to tell you how it went.

Adam walks out the door an over to the station. Peter was standing out front with Fred. Adam said hi and they went into the station. Adam made a pot of coffee and sat down at the table. Chase, Devvan and Mary came in hi guys. Adam and the others said hi. Adam said Peter what type of news do you have for use on the wolfman and the Reed and Reed company? Peter said some good and bad news.

The bad news is that the wolfman can grow back parts that it loses. Adam said like a snake. Fred said how do you know this can happen from just the finger of the wolfman? Peter said as he pulled the finger out of his shirt. The finger was starting to grow just bring cut out from the wolfman. Devvan said dam so every time we shoot the dam thing could be starting other wolfman from the parts dropped off.

Peter said it would seem to be that way. Peter said that's not all the finger is still alive like some from of plant life. Mary said alive how then do we kill it? Peter said after the wolfman is killed we will have to burn it and make sure there's not any of it left. Chase said I hope the good news is better. Peter said Reed and Reed seems to get a lot of government jobs. Adam said this seems to make them part of the trouble then. Peter said I don't know they could be trying to set the wolfman up to kill it to maybe I couldn't say.

Adam said or they could be just doing the government a job by keeping tabbed on the wolfman works. Peter said that could be true to we don't have the clues to tie them in. Fred said that's true we can just jump on someone with no reason.

Dannie got up it was around 8.30 am she jumped in the shower and got ready to go with Max. Dannie wasn't sure she would get a ring in Millinocket or not, but she knew that Max really cared for her. Dannie got wet and washed up and stood there for a while to let the water wake her up. She began to smile thinking for Max and his warm big arms. She got out of the shower and dried off.

Dannie went down stairs to look and see how the weather was on the back porch. Dannie opens the back door to see the weather. The sun was out and it was going to be a good day. She went into the house to make a pot of coffee and cut up some fruit. Dannie didn't want Max to send a lot on her ring because she could feel the love for her that Max had.

Dannie got her coffee and got some fruit and went back to the porch. Dannie sat down to watched to summer birds' fling south for the winter. She could see that Pat was out in his back yard and she yelled hi to him. Pat yelled back, good morning Dannie. Pat's boy friend came out and the two headed over to see Dannie.Dannie was thinking that she should go back in and put something on, but they were there already.

Dannie said hi and Pat boy friend said oh I see what you mean now Pat she is and great looking female isn't she. Sorry Dannie Pat said but he been riding my ass because I told him how you looked in the nude. Dannie said thanks but she though he was mad at her the other day when Max was out here. Pat said no he saw Max and though I was hitting on him. Pat said so you and Max are you to going to be man and wife? Dannie said yes we are going out to look at rings today. Pat said that's great Max is a nice man. Dannie said thanks I think so to.

Dannie got up and said it was nice to meant you but I've got to get ready for my date today. Pat's boy friend said dam your right she looks hot when she stands up. Dannie's face turned red thank you. Pat said you have a good day and I will see you later some time. Pat and his boy friend left and went home. Dannie went inside and went up stairs to got a nice dress on for Max today. She looked in she room for the right dress. Dannie said here it was a red dress with white trim. Dannie put it on and got ready of Max to show up. It was about 9.30 a.m. now and she head Max's truck pull up out front. She got up and ran to the door and watched him come to the house. Dam Max look nice he was in a set of dress pants and a white shirt her heart jumped a bet.

Max came to the door and she opened it and said my God you look hot today their Max. Max looked at her and said so do you there sweet thing. Max said I love you as he came in and graded her and picked her up and kissed her. Dannie was helpless to Max's power full arms she didn't mind she was in love to. Max said I started sooner than I wanted but I couldn't sleep good. Dannie said the same here I could only think of you all night and today.

Max said will would you like to go to town and check out rings. Dannie said I'm all yours their big guy. Dannie and Max headed to town of Millinocket the store up there were ok but not as good as the Bangor area. That wasn't all ways that way it was. When Dannie was young, the main street in Millinocket was the place to be. Just like East Millinocket the young people headed to better paying jobs down south.

Dannie and Max went to Farland store to look at rings. The younger Mr Farland was running the store that was started by his dad. Dannie looked at the first ring and it was ok. Dannie was looking for something more her. Max said he liked it 'but it wasn't what he wanted for her. Dannie looked at everything that Mr Farland had, but couldn't seen to find the right one.

Max said good by to the owner and the two went back to the truck. Max said we could run down to Linclon if you wanted to, they have a better store down there. Dannie said it's ok with me and they went on there way to Linclon .Now Linclon was a small mill town to that have seen same better times, but the thing about Linclon was you could smell it a mile away.

The ride to Linclon was ok they went the interstate down. Dannie and Max stopped down town at the jewel's store and went in. Max saw right away that this was a much better store and Dannie said yes she though so to. A woman came up to them and asked if she could help? Dannie said yes we are looks for rings. The woman said she though so by the way the two looked at each other.

She showed Dannie and Max to a chair and both out some rings for them to look at. Dannie said this is more like it. Max said yes some people know how to sale. The woman said try them all and if that wasn't what she like they would being out some more for her and Max to look at. Dannie looked over the sets and one ring cried out her name. Max eyes came to life when she picks the ring. Max said do you like that one hun. Dannie said yes and no because she looked at the cost. Max said do you really like it? Dannie said yes and she showed Max the price Max said to the woman this is the one she wanted. Dannie said you sure about that? Max said I was happy with that ring last week when I saw it I was pleased that you pick it to. Dannie said you were looking at the same ring last week?

Max said yes for some reason the ring said it was for you. Dannie had tears coming to hear eyes and hug Max and kiss him. Dannie said you and I seen to be on the same page. Max said yes and kneed on the floor and said would you marry me Dannie and make me the happiest man on earth? Dannie started to cry and said yes, yes, yes I will Max !

Dannie was so happy that she wanted to call Mom and Dad to tell them the good new. Dannie said to Max Mom and Dad are going to be so happy tomorrow when you show them. Max said but I bet they be even more happier if they come out and said it to you. Dannie said what you mean my parents are here. Mom and Dad came in from out back and said surprise we were hoping you pick the ring.

Dannie was so happy she hugged everyone and started to cry harder. Dad said to Max I'm glad and happy to call you son and shook Max's hand. Mom hugged Max And said welcome to the family. Dannie was so happy she couldn't stop crying and hugging Max. Max said to the woman thanks and put the ring on Dannie's finger. Max, Dannie and Mom and Dad went out for lunch.

Dad looked at Max and said so when you to going to make use Grandparent. Dannie looked at Dad and Mom and they both looked back at her. Dannie said we not going to have kids until we are marred, But if you want one right now me and Max could start right before the meal gets here. Mom and Dad laughs we didn't mean right now. Mon said but you are going to have kids right? Dannie looked at Max and said so hun how many kids we want? Max said I was thinking 40 is a good number to shot for.

Dannie looked at Mom how's face started to turn red, and said so that going to be all right with you two. Max looked at Dannie with a big smile we could start tonight on your back lawn. Mom coked on her water and Dad face turned red. Mom said Dannie you didn't tell Max about last week end did you? Dannie said sorry but I though it was funny. The hold group started laughing and then their meal showed up. The food looked great and they all eat.

Well Mom and Dad Dannie said are you to coming over to stay. Mom and Dad said sure hun we are going in town first over to Wal-marts. Mom and Dad head out to Wal-Marts for some shopping and lighting of Dads bank account. Max and Dannie headed back to the house and set on the back porch to get some air Dannie kiss and hugged Max for hours.

Adam said it looks like its time to go over to the town meeting. The team loaded up and went over to the town hall. Adam looked out front and said it looks as if all the people in town came to this one. Peter said looks like this is going to be a hard sell. The teams walked in a headed down front. Al said as he came up to the team hi and it looks' like we get a hard after noon on tap.

Al went up to the mike and said ok please everyone be seated. Al said does anyone want to say anything before we start. The crowd said I hear you want to close down hunting season for the rest of the year. Al said we need to clear the woods for Adam and his team to trap and kill the wolfman. The crowd said so what about all the lose of our business from no hunters buying things. Al said haven't we lose a lot as of now the Miller and three out of state hunters what more do we need to lose our kids. The crowd said but we need the money to keep going for the winter. Al said I know it isn't going to be a cake walk but we need time to hunt this thing down.

Well I'm going to turn this meeting over to Adam so he can tell you what's happen right now. Adam walks up to the mike and said hi I'm sorry we are asking so much from you today. We need the woods' clear so we don't have to look over our shoulder to see who's going to shot at use. The wolfman seems the been running a path from the island to the town. We got too as a team to set up in the best place to tack this wolfman down.

Adam said we already had a few close calls at the school yesterday. I would have been crusted if I had to report to another family that their kid was dead. The crowd said is it right that we have two wolfman running around. Adam said yes it seems that way. Adam said they seem to be running with each other but not as a team they seem to be trying to kill each other.

Adam said I would like to put everyone out in the woods and track this thing down, but this is going to be one hard animal to kill. The crowd said why that Adam? Adam said the wolfman seems to have some type of armor plating to his body and if he loses a part he can grow it back. The crowd said do we know where this wolfman came from. Adam said not put we do have some clues and were looking into them now.

The crowd said so what is this thing animal or man? Adam said that's a good question. We shot a finger off the animal in the grave yard and Peters' from the state police put it in the lab. The finger when he both it back had grown about an inch and started to form another hand. The crowd said you mean the finger you have can grow other wolfman if left alone long. Adam said sorry yes It looks that way.

The crowd said so how can you kill something that can grow a new self? Adam said after we bring the animal down we going to have to burn the body until it is all gone. Adam said if there no more question we can take a vote and see how it going to go from here. Al came back to the mike and said I have paper and pencil up here all we need is a yes or no to close the season.

The crowd slowly came forward and cast their votes. After the last of the people wrote down their vote Al counted them. The vote was close but the hunting season was going to stay open. Al said I sorry to report this news hope everyone feels happy with the way they voted. Al said Adam and his team will keep doing what they can to protect use but God help the people now. The crowd said they're not going to hunt the wolfman down. Al said no there are going to do their best to protect you but I'm not sending them back to the woods to get killed. Adam and the team went back to the station and went over the clues again to see if they miss anything.

Dannie and Max were setting on the porch when Dannie's Mom and Dad came out to see them. Mom said I'm so happy for the two of you I could scream. Dad bent over and kissed Dannie and said love you hun. Max said I glad everything went the way it did today. Max said I love Dannie with all my heart and couldn't think how I be without her. Dannie said I'm very happy with you to Max I love you the same. Max got up and hugs her and kisses her.

Mom and Dad said you to want to be alone. We can go somewhere else. Max said no I got to go soon to get ready for work. Mom looked at Dad and said young love isn't it great. Dad slap Mom on the ass and said old love isn't bad . Dannie said ok you two don't make me turn the hose on you. Max said hope we are like that when we get older.

Max said I've got to go and get ready for work. Dannie got up and started to go with Max to the door. Max said good night to Dannie's Mom and Dad .Mom came over and said I happy for you and Dannie and hugged Max. Max hugged Dannie and said I love you very much. Max and Dannie went to the front door an they kissed and hugged. Max said this is getting hard to say good bye to you. Dannie said I know I can't wait to see you again.

They kissed and said I love you. Dannie stood in the doorway and watched as Max drive off. She close the door and went back out to the porch. Mom could see her little girl was missing her Man already. So Mom got up and hug Dannie and said it's going to be ok hun he'll be back. Dannie said I know but I miss him already. Dannie said how did you get over missing Dad when he was gone.

Dad said she curls up with my wallet. The three laughed. Dannie said Dad you're bad. Mom said your Dad is right in a way. I would find the last place your Dad was and lays there I could smell his after shave. Mom said we could go and have supper somewhere to recap the day and think about the week end plans. Dannie said I could make use a few drinks and we could set here for a while and enjoy the sun. Dad said that sound like the best plan of all.

Dad said to Dannie I think you and Max are going to have a long and happy life together. Dannie said thanks Dad that means a lot to me and she hugs him. Dannie looked at her Dad and said but your still number one man on my list Dittied smiled and gave her a big kiss. Mon said it great to see we all care for each other so much. Well Dannie said set down and I'll go get some drink for use. Dannie went into the kitchen and made some drink as she was standing there she looked at her ring and felt warm and loved.

Dannie took the drinks out and give them to her Mom and Dad. But when she got out their Mom and Dad were making out she came out man she said you to get a room. Dad and Mom sat up and said oh back so soon. Dannie just laughs at the two of them. Dannie said try not to melt the ice when you hold them. Mom said any idea where the wedding is going to be and when? Dannie said no we haven't though of it. Dannie sat down and looked at her ring and was happy that she said yes.

Dad said any idea on what for supper tonight. Dannie said you to are staying the night right? Dad said it would be nuts to run all the way back and come back tomorrow. Dannie said great we can think of something to do tonight. Dad said maybe we could go to Max's place for supper and stay there and dance later. Mom said you know that would give use and idea at how good a cook he is. Dannie said I think he's a great cook and he can cook all the time when we are marred.

Dad said can he make a good chilly? Dannie said you would have to try it to believe it. Dad said good maybe I'll order that tonight. Mom said no if your sleeping with me you not. Mon said the last time you made chilly the dogs down the road were running for cover. Dannie said Dad it wasn't that bad was it? Dad said it sure made a lot of gas that night. So we should get ready to go to Max's then Dannie said? Dad said we should have other red chill first.

Adam and the other said I though we had them this time for sure. Adam said it's hard when your from a small town and the money is so hard to come by. Mary said to bad we couldn't find Baxter gold and help the town out with that. Fred said I was thinking the same thing, because I don't need a lot of the money to made things good with me. Mary said we all could take a few million and still have a lot to help the locals. Everyone said good idea if the gold is real. Adam said we should think of the wolfman first then maybe the gold.

Mary said your right Adam one thing at a time. Fred said were do we stand on hunting down the wolfman. Adam said I think our best bet is to trap him in the old pit and began them down there. Peter said I think you're right now all we have to do is not get shot by the locals and the flatlanders in the mean time. Chase said that in its self is going to be a job. Adam said we not going to do any thing until the season is shut down. Devvan said they voted to keep it open and so we aren't going back into the woods until it shut down? Adam said yes I would think as much as I hurt to say it that we should have a few more dead and the local wouldn't have a choice because I will call the state and have he Governor do it for me.

Chase said why don't we do at now before someone else is killed. Adam said because I already try once when the Millers were killed Adam said will we can split up try to do some more of the map. Adam said but would like to put two people in Fred's old tree house to keep and Eyes on the Reed and Reed company. Fred said I can show the persons the road it's about 1/4 of a mile to the tree house. Chase said me and Marry could do the tree house and

Fred and Devvan could do the map work. Adam said ok with me if the others are ok with it. Everyone said no trouble with use.

Adam said take a note book and field glasses to write everything going on. Fred and Devvan can drop you off and radio in every hour so I know everything's ok. Chase said ok, but why not run his four wheel down there? Adam said we don't want to let Reed and Reed to see it under the tree. Chase said ok that's cool. The team loaded up and began their search of the road sides. Devvan drop Mary and chase off and they went in the road that Fred said for the tree house.

Chase found the tree camp and started to climb the tree Marry was right behind him. The tree camp was nice and roomy and they could see up and down both sides of the river down to the river drivers Island. Mary said you can do the first watch and we can switch off every hour. Chase said ok and set down to watch out the window. Chase said for a construction company there seem to not be doing a hell of a lot of work. Chase called Adam and said that they were set up in the tree house, but didn't seem to be anything going on.

Adam's ok just watch and call every hour. Chase looked back to Mary laying there watching down the open hole to the ladder. Chase said what you doing their Mary? Mary said just making sure we don't get any unwelcome guest. Good idea Chase said. Chase said their seems to be a lot of people coming in and out one of the tailor, but not lots of work to being done.

Chase said I can even tell from here that the tool truck hasn't been moves at all for a few days. Adam and Peter were working the river side by the island and headed to town slowly. Devvan and Fred were working the far side of town near the grave yard. About and hour went by and Chase said one of the bridge works just ran into the tailor. Mary said anything happing by the bridge? Chase looked around and could see something in the water by the island. Chase said I think the wolfman is swimming to the main land.

Marry said Adam and Peter that's where they are aren't they. Chase called Adam and said I think the wolfman is heading to shore next to the water front where you are. Wait and load of Reed and Reed trucks are heading out to town to. Chase said I'll call if I spot them near you. Adam said great and turned to Peter and said Chase thinks the wolfman is heading this way and the Reed and Reed people. Peter said good now we can set here and wait to see if the wolfman shows up.

The two set and waited and keep a eyes on all four corners. Adam said I going to tell Chase and Mary to headed out and I will have Devvan and Fred come and get them. Just as he got those works out Chase call him you two get out of there. Adam said why? I can see two Reed and Reed trucks coming your way. Shit the wolfman is almost right behind you on the left and moving fast. Adam said thanks get back to the main road and Devvan will pick you up. Adam set the phone down and said to the left rear and he started the truck and started to roll out.

Just as Adam started to roll the wolfman hit the road about 100 feet behind them. Peter said don't look back and step on it. Adam put the truck to the floor and headed back to town he could see the wolfman was almost on them then Adam makes the turn and hit the tar. The truck took off like a shot. The wolfman hit the tar behind him, but fall and got back up and started at them again. Peter said someone pissed in his corn flake this moving. The little truck was pulling way when to Reed and Reed trucks came by Adam and Peter. Peter looked back and the wolfman headed to the woods like he knew the trucks.

Peter said stop and Adam stopped and pull over. Peter said the wolfman turned and ran into the wood when the Reed and Reed truck went by. Adam said will lets find out who these Reed and Reed man are then?

Peter said you sure you want to do that. Adam said why I couldn't think of a better time to do it. Adam pull back around and headed to the Reed and Reed trucks. The men from Reed and Reed got out with full auto guns. Adam stopped and pull the truck in revere. He hit the gas and got the little truck rolling fast then he pulls the brake an spun the truck around as the Reed and Reed man started to fire. Adam put the truck in gear and hit the gas he could see the Reed and Reed man were too far away to hit any thing. Peter said what the fuck is going on we are the good guys.

Adam got on the phone to Devvan and Fred and said get over to tree house and pick up Mary and Chase and meet use at the station. Mary said to Chase can you see anything? Chase said yes the Reed and Reed people just shot at Adam and Peter. Dam someone just came out of the tailor and he's Mary get the fuck out of the tree house now. Chase was right behind her they hit the ground and Mary said what's going on. Chase said just run back to the main road and don't stop. Chase said some came out with and rockets laugher.

The both headed to the street as they heard something hit the tree house it went up in flames. Mary and Chase make it back to the road. Devvan and Fred pulled up and they jumped in. Devvan said what the hell is going on the tree house just blow up and Adam called of use to pick you up and headed to the station. Mary said the Reed and Reed people open fire on use and Adam and Peter. Fred said what the hell is happen? Adam called Devvan and said get over here now and we need Mary and Chase . Devvan said we got them, but Reed and Reed blow up the tree house. Adam said everyone ok? Devvan said yes but what is up with them? Adam said don't know but we will regroup and hit them at the bridge.

Dannie was getting other drink for everyone and they set to enjoy the last of the good days of fall. Dannie got up and went up stairs to get into her jeans and T-shirt. She sat there looking at her ring and wondering how life would be and how she looks with a Dady. Dannie got a pillow out the bed and put it under her shirt. Dannie stood in front of the full length mirror and played with the looks of the pillow. Mom walk by and stopped because she could see Dannie acting like a Mom.

Mom stood at the door way and looked at Dannie, my little girl isn't little any more and a tear came to he eyes. Dannie turned the saw her Mom crying and went over to hug her. Mom grad her and said you'll make a great Mom hun don't you worry. Dannie said I was just thinking how I would look. Dad came alone and said what you two crying over. Dannie stood back and said so what you think Dad? Dad turned white and passed out Mon said Dannie grad him.

The two grad him and lay him on the floor. Dannie took the pillow out and put it under his head. Dannie and Mom sat down on both sides of Dad and looked at each other and started to laugh. Dannie said this is how Max would take to new to I think. Mom said your Dad and big teddybear at heart . Dad eyes started the open he saw the both of them setting and laughing at him. Dad said your not Dannie? Dannie said I was just trying on the look.

Dad put his hands around the both of them and hugged them. Dad said my Dady will have a Dady some day it's still hard to came to grips with. Mom said all I Feel is a little randy baby be. Dad said dam dvd player and Austin Powers. Dannie pulled the pillow out from up Dad's head and hit her Mom with it your bad you two. But I still love you and they all hugged and got up off the floor.

Mom and Dad got ready to go see Max and have some thing to eat. Dannie was just thinking of Max and How she miss him already. Dannie came down stairs and Mom and Dad were setting in the living room. Dannie said everyone ready to go? Mom and Dad it's time to go and get some thing to eat. Dannie said you're going to love tonight it's fish and chips night. Mom and Dad said what's great they could use a good fish meal for a change.

Dannie said I had it last week the fish and it was great. Dannie, Mom and Dad got in the car and headed for Max's bar and grill. Mom said the town seems to be nice now. Dannie said yes Adam and Chase are back on the police force. That's good Mom said I hear they are good cops. Dannie said some of the best I've ever seen. The three pulls into Max's place and parked out front. Dannie and Mom and Dad went in Dannie said to set up by the bar so she could see Max.

They all set down and Max came over and said nice to see to you guys here and he kissed Dannie. Mom said the service here seems good? Max said what would you like. Dad said a round of beer and your fish and chip dinner. Max said good the fish was better than last week. Dannie said dam I loved last week's fish. The fish man said that the guys got the fish that morning and I believe he was right. So Max said three fish dinner and a round of beers. Dad said is there a live band tonight?

Max got them the beer and said how is every things tonight Dannie? Dannie said I still on cloud nine and can't come down. Max said good I love you so much I still in the clouds . Max went back to the kitchen he came out with the fish dinners and said hope you like the fish? Dannie said I think we will love the fish. Mom and Dad both try the fish it was great. Dannie looked at them and said I can tell the fish is great by the way you two look.

Mom said it's more than great it's the best fish I've ever had. Dad said the same here it's fresh and cooked just right. Dannie said I know it isn't Max a great cook. Dad said we should let him do the barbarqing tomorrow. Dannie said no that's for my number one man to do. Dad smile at her and said thanks hun glad I haven't been replaced. Dannie said I could never replace you Dad.

Max came back to the table is the food good he said? Dannie said everyone loves it. Max said great the guy said it was the best one he seen in a long time. Max said by the way you know your drink the Maine red chill it's the number one mix drink we sell now. Dannie was happy she though it was a good drink not number one. Max said if you think of anymore drinks like that I would love to try them. Dannie said good and she would try to think for some more for him. Max gave Dannie and kiss and went back to the bar. Mom and Dad set back after their meal and enjoy the time they had with the food.

Mom said are we going to stay around for a while or head back home soon. Dannie said I could do both it's up to you two. Dad said I'm fine I just happy setting here with you two. Mom said it's been a long day for me and Dad we could stay awhile and then go back to kick back at the house. Dannie said fine with me.

Adam and Peter got back to the station first so Adam said come help me get the body armorer out. Peter said ok but we need a plan we can't just head in guns shooting we'll get cut down. Fred, Devvan, Chase and Mary came in. Chase said you two ok? Peter said yes we going after the shooters after we put on the body armor. The team suited up and was ready to go. Fred said we got some type of plan. Adam said there's only one way in and out of they and that's the way we will have to go. Fred said they're three ways into the spot. Adam said the main road is the only road in.

Fred said the old dump road is still a good road and it would set use right behind them and catch them off guard. Chase said what old dump road. Fred said you ok the katahdin shadow's motel. Adam said yes what about the dump. Fred said at the end of the parking is a road that runs into the dump then down along the river to the back side of the power station. Devvan said that sounds like a better plan than hit them head on.

Adam said ok it does sound like a better plan. The group went out to the trucks and Fred said to Adam we'll use my truck on this road yours may be to low. Adam, Peter and Fred got in Fred's truck. Chase, Devvan and Mary in the tracking truck. Fred said ok let go and kick some ass I'm sick of my ass getting kicked. Fred drove the Medway and into Katahdin shadow's motel and down to the back of the parking lot. Fred turned left at the end of the lot and went out the parking lot to a little dirt road and they headed down the shore line.

Adam said this must be the old dump he could see cars in the woods and down the side of the hill into the river. Fred said yes people back then didn't care what make it in the river. At the other end of the dump was a road what lead down along the river side you could hear the water move down stream. Fred said you can see the power station from here. Adam ask is this going to put use in the parking lot of Reed and Reed. Fred said yes, but they wouldn't see use coming because it hidden by the sub station.

Fred said as they got to the station want me to pull over next to the sub station and we can get out and cover more area that way. Adam said yes that way we all be able to fire not just one. The team got out and Adam said we are going to split up and move in from two sides. Chase take Mary and Devvan and stay low and go down the side near to station set yourself behind the loader over there remember not to shoot unless you have to, but don't let them get the first shot.

Adam said me Fred and Peter are going around the back side on the left in the woods so keep and eye out for use when it's clear we'll get you in for cover. The team started out Chase and his group move down the right near the station. Adam and the others went up to the left and move throw the woods to have cover. Adam radio Chase do you see any thing moving from where you are. Chase radio back no I don't even see a truck. Adam said it looks as if they're all gone. Adam told Chase to stay hidden until they check things out. Adam, Fred and Peter came out of the woods just before the crow tailor. Adam looked in the window and it was clear. Adam set back and said to the others the place is clear come on up. Chase and the others came up and said ok what's going on here.

Chase said what this shit the place had people and trucks all over the place an hour ago. Adam said the road signs are down to the locals are going across the bridge. Adam tried the lock and the door open. Adam went inside to look at the building not a thing in here at all. But it was clean for setting here for some time. Chase said you can see where the rocket was fired from the back kick moved the dirt. Marry said dam look at the tree house it's a hole in the woods now. Chase said we were lucky to get out when we did.

The team walked up the main road and it's true the sign and every thing were gone. Chase and Fred said we go get the trucks and move them up. So Chase and Fred walk back to the trucks. Chase said Fred so what do you think? Fred said I not sure but seems a lot like Mass. With each turn. Chase said I was thinking the same thing. The two got the trucks and moved them up to the main road. Adam said lets looks around the place to see if we can find a clue. The team slip up and covered the place Chase went down by the shore line where they saw the crow first. Chase said to himself that it seems funny that you could see the island from here on two sides.

Chase said it was the best spot to keep and eye on most of the island. Adam said anything to report guys its seems clear here. Chase said I think we are going to need to check the island closer. Adam said why do you think that Chase? Chase said you can see almost the hole island from here and the Reed and Reed people don't move until they saw the wolfman. Adam said I think you're right their Chase that's all I can think that this place was used for.

Will everyone come up and we are go back to the station. The group got back to the top and was going to start out when Adam looked back at the tailor and said can you see something hang down from under the stairs of the tailor. Peter said it looks like a book. Adam went back over to the tailor and pulled the book free from between the steps. Adam looked and the cover what was a government type seal with classified on the cover.

Adam open the cover and started to read it the papers said it was a classified . It was of the men trying to stop the wolfman program from hurting anyone. Adam started back to the truck and said it looks like we found something after all. Peter said let get back to the station and read it over to see what it is. The team returned to the station and Adam said bring your guns in we got some reading to do. Adam and the others went into the station and Adam said from what I been reading the wolfman isn't alone. He is trying to make a den somewhere.

So Fred's you my be right the white wolf may be his mate. Chase said so if the Reed and Reed people were on our side why did they fire on use? Because they didn't find the den and kill the wolfman and his mate. So where did they come from Adam? From what I've been reading the wolfman is part of a government cover up that made the first ones. Adam said this isn't the first set this is test number eight. Peter said you mean the people who made this thing have tried this on some other places. Adam said you remember James town it looks like one wolfman did all the killing in the town.

But Fred said didn't, they show the people just laying there with not cuts. Adam said have a look at this picture . Dam it's the one they showed on tv without the blood. The wolfman is been busy but this is the first time male and female got lose. Adam said the paper work seems to say that the male is the hunter and the female is away in the den.

Adam said it also said that the male in this test is more man then animal so it could be control better. The male got so smart that he watches the people type in there pass words and got out that way. Dam Adam said the male is wearing some type of armor. Adam said it can be taking down by a AK but you would have to hit it with 20 rounds. Chase said will some good news if that's what you call it. Adam said if the female has kids we could be looking at around nine or more of these things. The town would be in for a lot more fun.

Kevin and Steve came throw the door and said hi their guys what's up. Adam said have an seat boys we got a lot to go over before you go on tonight. Kevin and Steve sat down and started to go over the things that Adam had read already. Adam said the rest can hit the road for the night I'm going to be up tonight reading the rest of the report we can go over it in the morning back here. Everyone have a good night and took off.

Now Adam said to Kevin and Steve the wolfman can be taking down with the AK's but you would have to shot a lot of rounds, but if you tack the 50 calibers you could put it down in one shot. Kevin said I think we will take the bigger guns. Adam said don't be dumb and try to bring it down your self ok. Steve and Kevin got up and went on to the night watch. Adam went over to Annette's to see how things were going and to unwind for the day.

Dannie was having fun with her Mom and Dad when they got up to dance Dannie went over to the bar and got behind to help Max. Max looked at her and gave her a kiss and said I love you. Dannie said the same back at you big man. Dannie said can. I help service some beers? Max said yes I would love that because I can cook for a minute or two. Max kiss her and went to cook. The man at the bar looked at her and said dam your got a man? Dannie said as she showed her ring I got the man. Max came out of the kitchen and Dannie looked at him this is my man she said.

The guys said so is this the beautiful woman Max has been speaking to use about. Max said yes and she is my girl. Dannie kissed him on the chin and said I love you. Max kiss her back and said I love you to hun. Max went by her and service the food he cooked. Then Max came behind the counter as he walked bye Dannie he kiss her again.

Mom and Dad come up to the bar a sat down. Dannie come over and said hi their old people can your use a drink? Mon said do you have pun juice. Dannie said no put have a Maine red chill if that would do. Dad said you think two old people can handle it. Dannie said two Maine red chills it is. Dannie went back to the bar and made the drinks for Mom and Dad.

Max said your parents seems to be having a good thing. Dannie said we all are having a good time. Dannie said I enjoy helping you back here behind the bar. Max said if anyone gives you a hard time back here tell me. Dannie said ok their stud and slap Max on the ass as he walked away. Max turned red and the men on the bar said hay stud want to get me a beer. Dannie looked at Max said I'm sorry. Max looked at her with a big smile. Dad said hay there sweet thing how about other round for me and my woman. Dannie made another drink for her parent and took it over to them here you are big boy.

Dannie said oh by the way gave me your keys I'm drive you two home tonight. Mom said good now we can get drunk. Dannie said you two be good now the last thing I need tonight is you two making out on the way home. Max came and said hello to Dannie's Mom and Dad. Max said you two having a good time. Dad said after a few more of those I will be. Max said you did take they keys didn't you Dannie.Dannie said sure did and I'm driving them home tonight. Max laughs and said good girl and kiss her.

Max went back to the bar to make some more drink and do some work. Dannie said I will be right there to help. Max said take your time and speak to your Mon and Dad. Mom said how is it being behind there? Dannie said it's fun would you like to try. Mom said no just wondering how it was on that side of the bar. Dannie said you sure Mom Max isn't going to mind. Dad looked at Mom and said if you don't you'll be wishing you did all night. Mom ok but I just want to see how it is back there. Dannie said to Max Mom wants to see how it is on this side of the bar. Max said send her over. I'll be happy to show her how to work to bar. Mom got up and went behind the bar and walked over to Max.

Max said running a bar is very much little service beer at home. The people are for the most part good until they get too much in them. So their guys want a bud so I would ask bottle or draft. If he said draft we would get a grass from over here and pour one from the tap. The tap works by pulling it to you and holding the grass like this. Mom said this looks fun can I try. Max said sure here's a glass for you to try. Mom pour the beer like she was born to do it.

Mom went back to Dad and set down and said thank it was fun. Dad said see now you know and you can now going back home with a smile. Dannie came over to Mom and Dad and said do you want something to drink? Dad said sure other round for me and my hot bar keeper. Mom said sure hun and what everyone of these men wants. Dad said so is that your pick up line sweet thing? Mom said pick up or not your going home with me.

Dannie just looked at the two and smiled and shock her head. Dannie went over to Max and kissed him thanks Mom really liked that. Max said anytime she want she can jump back here and help she did really good job.

Adam went over to Annette's place for supper and to see if anything was going on. Adam walks throw the door and Annette said it's about time there. Adam said it's been one hell of a day. Annette said so how's the wolfman hunt going on? Adam looked around just a few locals in the place. Annette said if you are looking for the Reed and Reed Man the take off out for here on a run.

Adam said I don't wonder why they all left town after the gun fire this morning. Annette looked at Adam and what gun fire? Adam said me and Peter were fired on by about four of them this morning and now they are all gone not even a trace. Annette said dam that's up with that .Adam said I can't say here but I have a report back at the apartment that is telling use a lot more about the case then we knew before.

Adam said I don't know what really went on today, but it was some type of eye opener now we can't trust even the locals. Annette so you want me too come over tonight? Adam said sure but we can run over to your place first to get you the cloths we didn't last night. Annette said good so what do you want to eat? Adam said I been wanting a ham club all day. Annette said one ham club and a new coke ok?

Adam said sure I could really use one tonight. Annette went out and made Adam his ham club and returned out front with his coke and meal. Annette said I can lock up around here at nine and we can take my truck over to the house. Adam said this club is good hits the shot today. Annette said you think you'll see any more of the Reed and Reed people in town. I'm not sure but they won't stick out like they did before. Annette said about another ten and we can close for the night.

Adam said will gave me a broom and I will swept up out here for you. Adam swept the floor and around the table's Adam looked down as he was cleaning as to do a good job. Adam saw something on the table leg it was a wire hanging down it was hocked to some type for wireless bug. Adam went into the kitchen Annette was they and he holds his hand over her mouth and spoke low in her eyes. You have a bug under the table out there. Annette said so what do we do with it. Adam said we will close tonight and I will tell you out side.

Adam said so just say everything like you would and we'll close up. Adam returned to the front a swept up his dirt. He said Annette the floor is all clean. Annette said I got to turn the coffee pot and grill off then we can go. Annette came out front and turn off the light's ok, hun let's lock her down and get out of here. Annette and Adam went out the door and Annette lock it. She said ok to speak now.

Adam said yes and they went around the center to Annette's truck. Adam said nice truck their Annette. Annette said thanks it's a rod4 and I like the red color. Annette said it's good on gas to. Adam and Annette got in the truck and headed to Annette's place. Annette said so what you going to do about the bug? Adam said I'm going to remove it in the morning and see how far it can transmit. Adam said so where do you live. I live in a camper tailor at Pine Grove camp ground. Adam said you don't have a house? Annette said I did until the bank took it some years back. I got it because after I close the coffee shop for good I'm going to see the USA on wheels. Adam said is it a big camper. Annette said it's a big one and she needed to get a LTD to run it on the road. Adam said dam can't wait to see this thing.

Annette turns on the Grindstone road and headed out of town. It's a nice ride on the road because it runs alone the river side for 20 miles or better. The river was low but you could hear the water running down the over the rocks. The road had a few spots you could pull over and have a lunch and enjoy the sounds of life rolling by.

Annette pulled into the Pine Grove camp ground and went down the road. From the sign on the road you wouldn't think it was as big as it is, but it's a really nice camping place with the water just running along the end for the place. Annette pulled up in front of a large camper Adam said dam this is nice. Annette said it not much but it's home. Adam and Annette with inside and Adam looked around and said not much this is better than my place.

Annette said thanks' she a nice home. Annette showed Adam the rest of the camper. The bedroom was big and really nice. Annette heard and knock at her camper door. Annette open the door and it was the camp ground owner. Annette said hi what's up tonight James. James said was just checking to see if you where ok haven't seen you around here for a few days. Annette said I was in town at a friend's house we just came out to get some thing and head back in. Adam came to the front and said everything ok hun .James said oh I see you both the law with you hi Adam James said. Adam said hi to James.

Well James said I see your in good hands so I'll let you go then. Annette said thanks to James for keep an eye out for her. James said no trouble your like family around here. James said good night and see you around. Annette said see you around to James. Annette close the door and she got a few things together. Adam said will he seems nice. Annette said yes James and his wife are really nice people. Annette said I'm set you ready to go back into town.

Adam and Annette went to Adam's place . They went in and the book that Adam left on the table was missing. Adam pulled his side arm out and said to Annette while by the door and Adam looked around the rooms. No one around Adam told Annette come in. She said what's wrong Adam? Adam said the report I was telling you about is missing I put it on the table. Adam went back to the door and looked at the lock. Adam could see tool makes from the pick that was use the unlock the bolt.

Annette said that answers one thing they are still around here. Adam said yes now we got to be on guard of them. Adam said have a seat and I will tell you all about the wolfman. So Annette sat on the love seat and Adam told her every thing. Annette said dam your mean we could have little wolfman running around. Adam said it seems so if we don't find the den in time. Annette said you could kill the babies? Annette said remember you said there were more human then animal. Adam said yes but they are still animals that kill humans. Annette said I know but if we killed everything that killed use first we be a lonely animals wouldn't we. Adam said I never looked at it that way. Adam said I don't know about you but I need some sleep. Annette said with a smile me to.

Dannie came down to Mom and Dad and said so how you doing you two? Mom said one more round and I think we will be ready for home. Dannie said ok I'll get them for you and be right back. Dannie made two more Maine red Chills and gave them to Mom and Dad. Dannie said I'm going up and speak to Max tell me when you want to go? Mom said ok Have a good time. Dannie went over to Max said hugged him. He was happy to have her there at his work with him. Max said did you Mom enjoy herself back here? Dannie said yes you made her night.

Dannie after they are done with their drinks I'm going to drive them home ok. Max said sure what time we going to have the barbarQ tomorrow? Dannie said around noon but you can show up any time. Max said I should be their around nine or a little after. Dannie said great and kissed him on the chin. Max said I really enjoyed having you and your Mom and Dad here tonight. Max said you need anything for the barbarQ tomorrow? Dannie said no just my big loving man and his smile.

Max said I can sure help you there and he gave her a big hug. Dannie helped Max for a while and she was having fun. Mom came to the other end of the bar and she gave Max a hug and said thanks for everything tonight, but we need to go sleep it off and be ready for the barbarQ in the morning. Dad told Max that she was going to speak about this all night maybe. Max said glad I could help. Dannie hugs and kissed Max and drove her parents back home.

Dad was right that's all she could speak about was the fun behind the bar. Dannie said look now if we could open a barbarQ bar you both would be happy. Dad looked at Mom Hay you know what doesn't sound like a half bad idea. Dannie said you two sleep on it. Mom and Dad said you know that's a better idea. Dannie said don't make me put you two in different rooms tonight. Mom said no trouble we'll be good tonight. Dannie pulled into the yard and there went into the house. It started to rain it was going to be a cold wet night, but Dannie love the clean smell of the rain.

Dannie Went into the kitchen she got her self some cheese and some wine Dannie said you two want anything before I run up stairs tonight? Mom and Dad said no hun we are ok they hugged Dannie and she went up stair. Good night you two I love you. Mom and Dad said we love you to hun. Dannie sat on her bed looking at her ring and she was really happy and she loved Max so much. Dannie eats her cheese and finishes her wine.

Dannie set the grass and plate on the night stand and got undress to go to bed. She could hear the rain coming down harder and she went to the window to see if it wasn't coming in. Dannie could hear a noise coming from the back porch. Dannie just shock her head and went to bed.

Dannie got under the covers and she could smell Max's sense on one of the pillows' she pull it close and hugs it and slowly go to sleep. Dannie dream were going to be ok tonight so she thought . Dannie dream starts out good she was at the bar helping Max. It was around time for last call. Max yelled out last round and that's when the shit hit the fan. The front door open and the wolfman enters no one seemed to be scared. The wolfman said I'll have a blood Mary? Dannie made the drink and gave it to him. The wolfman took and drink and said there's no blood in this drink. Dannie said maybe it's time you go.

The wolfman said not until I get my blood. The wolfman turned to the man next to him a cut his throat maybe this will help my drink as he held his grass to the blood coming out the man's neck. Dannie couldn't believe that no one was making any plans to stop him . The wolfman stood up and went to the next man. He bit the man's neck and ripped a peace out of his neck the blood shoot around the place as if it was alive. The wolfman said he was sweet and smelled good to.

Dannie was almost frozen in her steps she didn't seem to have any power over the dream. Dannie knows this was only a test she had to call on his power. She looked down at her ring that Max gave her and started to feel the love within it. She moved one step to the wolfman and could see the fear in his eyes. The wolfman backed out and moved to the door. Dannie said this's right wolfman be afraid of love. The wolfman turned an ran. Dannie could move freely now and went after the wolfman. The wolfman stopped at the about five feet away he turned to face Dannie.Dannie said so lets end it now.

The doors open and the other two white wolfs stepped throw and grad the wolfman and made him knee before Dannie.Dannie looked at him and said ready to die again. The wolfman said I can still get you little wolf and he looked at Max. Dannie said die you son of a bitch. Dannie brock his neck and ripped his head off and drop the head and looked back at her Max.

Max seen to be moving as if he didn't see or hear a thing. Dannie looked back to the doors and the wolfman and the two white wolves were gone. Dannie couldn't believe that anything went down. Dannie went back to Max and hugged and kisses him. Max gadded her and set her on the counter and said looks everyone this is the woman of my dreams. Max picked her up and held her as if it was for ever.

Dannie came out of her dream and set up in bed his wanted to stay up and watch tv but know it was only a bad dream. She went to her bathroom to put some water on her face. She looked in the mirror and felt safe when she saw her face. Dannie went back to bed and slowly tried to fall back to sleep. Dannie looked at the clock it was almost 5.30 a.m. she would be getting up soon anyway . Dannie was hoping when she did go down stairs that Mom and Dad were in the house and had cloths on.

Adam wake to the alarm going off it was 6:00 am an Annette was laying there. Adam rounded over and kissed Annette and said time to get up hun. Annette wakes but was sleepy and Adam got up to hit the shower. Annette came in and said Adam you want any thing for breakfast? Adam said no I will get some thing at your place this morning when I remove the bug. Annette pulls her head in the shower you didn't check me for bugs and she smiled. Adam grad her and pulls she in the shower and she didn't have much of a choice. Needless to say she was clean and no bugs. Annette got out and dried off then Adam got out. Will Annette said did I pass the test? Adam said sure did your clean. Annette and Adam got ready to go over to the shop. Adam went down stair to the station and grad the tracker device. Annette said how does this work Adam? Adam said just set the bug in here and the unit will read how far the thing it puts out.

Annette said that's cool like to see how close the assholes are. Adam said ok now when we go in don't say anything until I point at you. Ok Annette said makes me feel like a spy. Adam said we can call double DD .Annette just laughs and said ok sounds good to me. Annette unlocked the door and went in. Adam went over to the bug a removed it and placed it in the tracker. Adam sat down at the counter and said ok Annette I think I will have your big breakfast and some coffee. Annette said ok and got the coffee for Adam.

Annette said I will be back with your food in a few. Adam said it looks like your brother is coming in. Bob said hi to everyone ,but look at Annette funny. Bob knew his sister will that's he could tell something was wrong. Annette grads him by the arm and went into the kitchen and told him. Bob came back out and gave Adam the ok sign. Bob yelled back to Annette sis can I get a big breakfast like Adam's. Annette said ok Bob it will be out in a few.

Annette came out with the two meals and some bacon on the side. Bob said you must have done some good to get bacon.

Annette said sure did and smiled at bob. Bob said I don't need to know. Adam said you got bacon to. Bob said but I'm her brother. Adam said can I get another hot cup of water? Annette said sure you can and got the water. Adam drop the bug in the water and said now we know that they are still in town some where. Annette said so how far are they? Adam said about two miles away . Annette said so what do we do with the bug.

Adam said does your sink have a hog. Annette smiled and said yes. Adam said will go run it throw the hog then. Annette went back in the kitchen and started the hog and poured the cup of water down the sink and it made a hell of a noise. So Bob said the people that shot at you yesterday were bugging this place. Adam said it sure looks like it. Adam said I got to run and will maybe see you for dinner will see. Annette said be careful and don't get hurt.

Adam said good bye and headed out the door. Annette came out and said Adam you forgot something. Adam smile sorry and came back to grad her on the ass. Annette said now that's better. Adam went to the station and Peter and Fred were out front. Adam said hi there guys. Fred said any new things about the wolfman from the paper work you had yesterday? Adam said it was ripped off out of my apartment last night. Peter said by who? Adam said by the same people that have been watching use of the last few weeks.

I also have more news but will tell everyone in side. Adam said ok as they with in side we need the do a search for bugs . Fred said you mean someone been bugging use? Yes Adam said had one this morning at Annette's place down the road. Chase and Devvan and Mary came in and said what's going on. Adam said looking for bugs. Everyone looked around and Chase said Adam came here. Adam came over and looked under the table sure it was the same type as at Annette place.

Adam said we all sure look around when we get home to check for more. Adam put the bug on the floor and step on it. Mary said now were being bug to? Adam said that's not all last night I went out and the paper work on the wolfman was stooling. Dam said Devvan we can't get a break. Adam said the one I got at Annette's place was the same and it has a two mile reach. Adam said so the people that shot at use yesterday are still in town some where.

Chase said great now we got to watch our back for the wolfman and someone else. The plan today is when we are out there looking for the wolfman we need to check all the house around to see if anyone is in them that doesn't look local. Ok lets get things on the road and get this map done tonight. The group went out and started there map work and was trying to get it done before night. Adam told Peter it look's like we are going to have to go back to the island and look harder to find something.

Peter said all the signs seem to point there I just was wondering when we would go back. Adam said I didn't want to say anything to the other but I believe the wolfman is got a den out there. Adam said Annette said some thing to me this morning that I never though about until now. Peter said what's that Adam? Adam said what if the wolfman has had young wolfs by now. Peter said we go have to kill them to. Adam said but they could be mostly human and some wolf. Peter said if you can then I can , it needs to stop here and stop soon before more people are killed.

Adam said it sounds ok when you say it but will it happen when the time comes. Peter said you just have to think for the Millers what would they be like if this thing hadn't killed them. Adam said your right the people first not the wolfs. Adam got a call on his cell phone it was Chase. Chase said you should see this Adam. Chase said I'm on elm street and the old red house on the corner. Adam said I know the one will be there shortly.

Adam told Chase to keep a good watch out for everyone moving. Adam looked at Peter and said looks like Chase has found they're hide out. Adam gave Fred a call to meet them over there. Fred said ok will be there. Adam and Peter got there first and Fred and Devvan showed up .Then Adam went to see what Mary and Chase found. Adam came in first and the rest followed. The main floor was ok. Adam yelled to Chase where are you two. Chase yelled back up stairs. The group started up the stairs and found Chase in one of the rooms. The room had computers and tracking equipment all over the place.

Adam said anything on the computers. Chase said no the computers all have removable hard drives. Adam said it looks like they know you were coming. Adam and the group move around the house and check every room. Mary yelled to Adam from the other room. The team came in to the room and Mary had found a door that open to and small room of guns. The team took the guns and loaded them into the truck. Adam said maybe we can send them a little messenger. Adam said Chase its baseball time. Chase said about time we have some fun. The others said baseball time? Adam went over to the truck and picked out two metal bats from behind the seat. Adam throw one bat to Chase feel like some batting practiced? Chase said oh hell yes.

The two turned to go back to the house and the hole second floor of the house blow up as Fred came running out the front door yelling hit the dirt. Parts of the house blow all over the place and the top of the house was gone . Adam ran up to help Fred and got him down to the street. Adam calls the fire truck and you could hear them coming. Adam said Fred what happen? Fred said you know that box in the back where the guns where?

Will it was set to go out when someone move the gun out of the rack. Adam said so why didn't go off when we all were up there? Fred said it was set on a timer for 15 minutes. Peter said how did you know that? Fred said because it read ten seconds when I saw the clock. Peter said dam we all could he been back up there when it went off. The fire truck showed up and put the fire out. Adam said I think we sure regroup down at the station.

Adam and everyone went back to the station and put all the guns on the table. Adam said why would someone just be watching and wolfman need all this fired power. Peter lets take all the serial numbers and run them though the dater base to see who owns them. Fred said good idea but bet we'll find that they are not on the record at all. So Devvan ran all the number and Fred was right not a one of them turned up as gun that were owned

Adam said so we know these guys want use out of the show but why if we are hunting the same thing. Fred said maybe we aren't hunting the same thing. Adam said what's mean? Fred said maybe the others are waiting for the wolfman to show them where the den is so there can kill all the animals at the same time. Adam said that could be but why don't they work with use? Peter said if you know your government was doing this would you want to clean it up with out anyone knowing.

Adam said yes but we know. Peter said yes and that's why we got to keep a look out. Chase said yes that means every night from now on we should not go home alone. Adam said yes went you go home for the night tonight Fred Chase will set out side until you call them and then head home. Fred said ok I can see that safely is in numbers. Adam said now we got to think of something we need to go back to the island and cover every inch of it. Mary said I was hoping that it wouldn't come to that but all the clues point to the dam place. Chase said so when will we go back to the island? Adam said if it is good tomorrow then we will hit the island.

Dannie got up and looked a the clock Max should be here any time. She put on her sweats a slowly make her way down stair not knowing what she would find. Mom and Dad where sleeping on the pull out and had cloths on she though that was good. Dannie went over to them and could see Mom hair was strange from bring wet from the rain. Dannie though those two are something. Dannie went over and crawled in between them. Mom wake up first she smiled at Dannie and said good morning hun. Dannie round over and hug her and said hi Mom have fun last night as she move her Mom's hair. Mom said my God that was fun. Dannie said please spear me the details. Dad got up and grad Dannie hi there sweet heart. Dannie round over and hug her Dad. Dannie put her fingers in Dad hair and said you two have fun. Dad said slept good if that's what you mean.

Dannie lay down between the two and looked at him. Dad said think my baby is in love and throw the blanket over her and hugged her. Dannie said what do you want for breakfast this morning? Mom said french toast sounds good. Dad said that would be nice for a charge. Dannie said ok I will go start it and you two can get up and come in a few minutes. Dannie looked back as she got up and moved anyway from them to the kitchen hope they get out of bed.

Dannie went into the kitchen and got some eggs out and began to make the french toast. Mom and Dad came in the room and said it smell good hun. Dannie said hope so then she put on a pot of coffee. Mom said so what's on the dinner list for the barbarQ today. Dannie said we are going to have steak and corn and salad. Dad said hope the steaks are the same place as last week end those were some nice. Dannie said yes I got them the same place as I did last week. Mom said good that's a good store to get meat . Dannie said I buy all my meats there.

Dannie said you going to cook the steaks this time? Dad said if Max isn't cooking I will. Dannie said you we be Dad. Dannie handed the french toast over to them and Mom said looks good hun. Dannie said I've got some fruit here to if you want it. Dad said this is good hun what did you do to it? Dannie said just some cinnamon in the eggs why is it good. Dad said very good hun.

Dannie sat down and had her coffee and fruit. Dannie said Max should be around here about ten or so. Dad put his hand on Dannie's hand and looked at her. Dannie said something wrong Dad? Mon said I think he thinks he losing she little girl. Dannie could see water forming in his eyes. Dannie went over and gave Dad a big hug and kiss. Mom said you big softy and came over and hugged them both. Mom said I'm going up to clean up you two going to be all right.

Dannie said yup I know what to do to make Dad happy. Dad said what's that hun. Dannie said follow me big guy. The three of them went up stairs to Dannie's room. Dannie told Dad to get in bed and she went to the closet and pull out a coloring book. Mom laugh said your Dad was saying how he miss making up stories to your old coloring book's. Dad had a big smile. Dannie jump on the bed and pull the cover up over them. Dannie looked up with and little baby girl look at Dad and said read me a story Daddy.

Dad said love to hun and hug her and kiss her on top of the head. Dad started to read her the story once upon a time there was a beautiful young girl her name was Dannie. Dannie hug her Dad and said I love you Daddy. Dannie lay there as Dad made one of his story up.

Mom come out of the shower and said you to having fun. Dad said yes she still my little girl. Dad got up and kissed Dannie and went in to shower. Mom set down you know Dad will don't you hun. He been wondering how much he would see you after you and Max get married. Dannie said about the same as now and some day he'll have grandkids to love to . I think you two will make great grand parents. Mom said thanks hun and I think you and

Max will be great parents. Mom said I'm going to put something on see you in a few. Dad came out and said next and Dannie went into the bathroom.

Dannie couldn't wait for Max to show up and start the barbarQ with them. Dannie got out and got dressed for the day on the porch. She went down and Mom and Dad were out back drinking coffee. Dannie graded of cup and went out on the porch. Dannie said it going too did nice isn't it. Mom said yes and I'm glad for that. The phone rang it was Max. Dannie picks' it up and said hi. Max said hi hun just checking to see if everyone was up and how your doing. Dannie said we are all up and setting on the back porch.

Max said good I'll just walk around the back then and come out there. Dannie said you're here hun? Yup right behind you hun. Dannie turned around and shut off the phone and went down and kisses Max and hugs him. Dad said don't make me turn the water on. Max comes up the steps and said hi to everyone. Max said I hope your not mad Dannie but I got some wine for use and I made a potato salad to I didn't want to come empty handed.

Dannie said you didn't have to, but I would think potato salad we going great with steaks. Max said care to walk me back around and get to food. Dannie said sure show me the way big man. The two went around the corner and Max turned and grads her and gave her a big hug and kiss. Dannie almost got light headed. Max smiles miss you hun. Dannie said I see that and I missed you to hun. Dannie and Max got the food and put it into the house.

Max and Dannie rejoined Mom and Dad out back. Max said so what's been going on today? Dannie said not much just looking forward to you showing up. Dad said will Max do you want to grill or still I do it. Max said I tell you what I will do what I'm good at and you do what your good at. Dad said ok I grill and you make use some drinks. Max said you bet and him and Dannie went into the kitchen to make drinks. Max returns with the drinks and Dannie handled a drink and the steaks to Dad.

Max gave Dannie's Mom her drink and sat down in the lawn chair. Max said we couldn't have ask for a better day for a cook out. Mom said your sure right and it gives use time to get to know everyone better. Max said that's what I was hoping for because I think you two are cool people and I didn't get to know my Mom and Dad. Mom said what happen to them? Dannie said you don't have to tell them if you don't want. Max said it's ok it help me to remember them by. Max said it was summer and the bugs were thick. Mom and Dad went out and it was about 6:00 p.m. in the day. They were going down the road and run into a morse and both were killed on the screen.

Mom said I'm sorry that must hurt to remember. Max said no it help to deal with it better. Dannie got up and gave Max a big hug sorry hun I didn't know. Mom and Dad came over and hugged Max to and said we would be proud to call you your son. Max almost being to cry. Dannie gave him a big hug and said let turns this around to something more cheerful. Max said yes let go get more drinks and make this a real get together. Dad said yes I hear you there. Dannie and Max returned to the kitchen and made up a big bender full for drink and returned to the porch.

Max said anyone for seconds Dad and Mom said over here. Dad said hun you can set the table it going to be steak time soon. Dannie and Mom went in and got the dishes and food. Mom said Max's salad looks really good can wait to try it. Dad said everyone set down the steak are almost done. So Dannie, Mom and Max sat down and got ready to eat. Mom put some of Max's potato salad on her plate and try it. Mom said man hun you got to try this.

Dad said go ahead and put some potato salad in his plate . Dad shut the grill off and said the steaks are cooked. Dad put the steaks in the middle of the table and then sat down to try the salad. Dad said you got too gave me the list of things you put in this Max it is great. Dannie tried the potato salad and just set there and looked as if she was in heaven. Max said did you like it Dannie. Dannie did I'm going to have to smoke after this dinner. Max said good I was hoping you would like it.

Max cut into his meat and said this is a better peace of meat then the last one. Dannie said yup and my Daddy cooked it for me. Mom said Max so how did a man learn to cook so well? Max said my Grandma showed me everything and she was a great cook. Max said could have four or five things going at the same time and everything would come out great. Dannie said my Grandpa was a good cook to right Mom. Dannie said Dad makes' good chilli to. Max said will have to try it some time. Mom said you better call the fire department before you eat. Max said the hotter the better. Dad said see hun I'm not the only one that likes hot food.

Dannie was happy at how good Max and Mom and Dad got along. Dannie said two week ends in a roll and two great meals. Dad said I hear you there kid. Dad pick up his glass and make a toast to good friends and great food.

Adam said so what do we know right now? Adam said we have a wolfman maybe a female and maybe young, We have nuts from the government running use down, shooting and trying to blow use up. Peter said sounds about right. Chase said if the female is in a den we couldn't find anything like that on the island. Mary said yes it seem to be pretty flat. Devvan said but did I see at the base of the island a hill. Adam said yes and that's where our group will end the day. Fred said so what we going to do about the guns. Adam said I though I would put them where I keep the 50 calibers.

Chase said good idea. The phone rang it was the chief of police in Linclon and he wants to speak to you Adam. Adam went to the phone and said hi there. The chief said I think we had a wolfman attack last night my people tell me you are fight one up there. Adam said that's right but I don't think it's going to be the same wolfman because your almost thirty miles away. The chief said that's what I think to but would love for you to look at the crime screen and see if it the same type of animal. Adam said so how many were killed. The chief said seven two adults and five kids. Adam said all at the same place? The chief said yup and all from the same family. Adam said dam will me and Peter from the state police can run down and look the screen over and see how we can help.

The chief said it sure would help thanks. Adam said I'll head down their right now see you at the station about 20 minutes. The chief said great will see you there. Adam hung up the phone and turned to the group and said it looks as if you going to have to run things for a few Chase. That was the chief from Linclon he thinks he has a wolfman down there. Me and Peter are going down to see if we can help out with the screen.

Adam and Peter started out the door and the other got back to mapping the wolfman path. Adam and Peter hit the interstate and Adam put the light on and step down on the truck. Adam said to Peter it was seven people killed in the same place last night. I don't think it was a wolfman because the chief seems to not think it to. Adam and Peter came off the ramp and headed into town. Adam got to the station and got out and went into the build. The chief said hi well this isn't a fun crime screen to work so hope you didn't have breakfast first.

Adam said the last two for ours have been really bad. The chief said will you can follow me over to the screen and have a look for your self. The state crime lab is there right now clean up the mess. Adam and Peter followed the chief over to the place the crime happen. The chief pulled into a small tailor park and the state police crime lab was there and some of the locals. Adam looked at Peter and said it doesn't fit the house is in town and a lot more people around than would be for the wolfman to hit this place. The chief show the two into the build and showed them the two bodies still on the floor.

The two bodies even those they were in pieces all the parts were still there. Adam said are all the bodies like this do they have all the pieces? The chief said yes why? Adam said the wolfman didn't eat anything at all? The chief said no and showed them the foot print. Peter looked at the print and said Adam do you see some thing funny with the print? Adam said do you mean the mark at the back for the print. Peter said yes it looks like a Nikki shoe mark. Adam said I think you're right. The print is funny to it has no skin marks to it. It's just flat.

The chief said that's what we though to so it wasn't a wolfman it was a man trying to be a wolf. The chief said thanks and he had a good idea who did it. Adam said this had to be one sick shit to do this to the kids and woman. Adam said do you know the kids and Mom. The chief said yes the Mom name was Angela and her girls' friend was Kathy, The kids were Cody ,Sirrali , Logan, Keegan and Connor. Adam stop with a look for sick on is face the last name wouldn't be Munson would it. The chief said yes why? Adam said I'm dating their Grandma. The chief said dam I'm sorry I don't know. Adam said has anyone said anything to her about it. The chief said not because we haven't finished here. Adam said maybe I should be the one to tell her then.

The chief said thanks it's hard just to think someone could do this to a family. Adam said I know we had a hard time up in East Millinocket telling the people there. The chief said thanks Adam for coming down and sorry you have to tell Annette this way. Adam said it's not going to fun but it's better from someone she knows then a state cop. The chief said yes I can see that but still not fun. Peter said I hear you there but, Adam I will go with you if you need me? Adam said that would be nice and thanks Peter.

The two went back to the truck and headed back to the station in East Millinocket. Adam came into town and park in front of the coffee shop dam he said this isn't going to be nice. Adam got out the coffee shop had a few locals and Bob Annnette brother there. Adam walked in and turns the open sign to close. Bob said Adam some thing wrong? Adam said yes very wrong. Adam went over to the locals and ask them if they could going and told them a little of what was going on. The locals got up and left.Bob said should I go Adam? Adam said no it's about you to so have a seat while I go get Annette. Adam walked into the kitchen and Annette was cooking. Adam said hi hun will need to have some words with you. Annette looked back and could see Adam eyes were getting wet. Adam said shut down the grill and coffee machine and came with me. Annette said what's wrong Adam? Adam said I want you to set down before I tell you anything. Annette came out front and Bob was still there.

Adam went over and locked the door so no one would bug them. Annette sat beside Bob in the booth. Adam sat down and held Annette's hand. Adam said this isn't good to be easily. Annette said just come out with it and I will deal with it as best we can. Adam said ok me and Peter went down to Linclon this morning and went to a crime screen. Annette Adam said it was Angela and the kids. Someone killed them all Adam broke down and started to cry. Annette face turned white and Bob grads her and held he. Peter said I sorry, but someone tried to make it look like the wolfman did it.

Bob said why would someone do that to kids and a single Mom? Annette couldn't speak she was just to shocked to say anything. Adam got up and got a few glasses and some water, and pulls and chair up next to Annette. Annette said did they find who did it? Adam said there had an idea of who, but didn't give me any names. Annette said I'm going to need a ride home. Bob said I will sis. Adam said I will lock up here for you Annette and clean up a little then go to the station to tell the Man what happen.

Adam said I will be up shortly so could you stay with her for a while Bob. Bob said yes I will be there until you get there. Annette handed the keys over to Adam and hugs him and said thanks. Adam pick her hand up and gave her a kiss see you soon. Bob and Annette went out to Bob's truck and he drove her home. Adam said dam this job sucks some times. Peter said yes it does when this type of thing happens. Peter said if you don't need my help I'll go over to the station and tell everyone what's going on when they come in. Adam said thanks Peter I can get this place cleaned up and go see Annette. See you and the others tomorrow morning before we go to the island. Peter said good night then see you in the morning.

Adam cleaned the grill and the counters off turned the coffee maker off and put the trash out in the dumper. Peter went over to the station to wait for the others. Adam was done and locked the door and went to see Annette.

Dannie said this was about the best day she had out on the porch. Max said it sure is nice out here not at all like town. Dad said that's why I like it out here to the air is so fresh. Mom said that's not true you like the lawn. Dannie said ok you two don't get started on that. Max said anyone for some wine. Mom said if it's half as good as the potato salad then were in for some thing good. Max got up and went in to get the wine Dannie got up and took some of the food in to put it away. Dannie went in and Max was getting some glasses for the wine.

Dannie put the food in the ice box and helped Max out with the glasses. Max poured out the wine and handed it around to everyone. Dad sat back in the chair and said now that's good wine, makes you feel like you stepped on them yourself. Mom said hope you didn't step on them. The wine would smell funny. The group laughed and Dannie said man this is good fine wine and the day slowly fading away.

Max said it will be winter soon the trees are charging now. Dannie said like the snow but don't like to move it. Max said yes it makes everything look clean. Max said maybe we can get a movie in town and watch it tonight. Mom said sounds like a good idea to me. Dannie said sure it sounds good. Dad said not until I've had another glass of this wine. Max filled everyone glasses up and said cheers. Will said Dannie I'm going to pick up out here and put the rest for the food away. Max said I can help you hun.

Dannie said no you and Mom and Dad set here and I'll do it. Max said you sure hun. Dannie got up and kisses Max yes hun I 'm sure. Dannie pick up the table and went in and put things away. Mom said to Max that Dannie and him were going to make a great pear. Max said thanks I hope we have a few grandkids for you to. Dad said good Grandkids I hope so to. Max said will anyone for more wine it's almost gone. Dad said sure and Mom said yes.

Max poured the rest of the bottle into everyone glass and set the bottle on the deck. Dannie came back out and said is everyone happy. Max said couldn't be happier. Max got up and said will we should go see what's in town of movies. Dannie said yes and I'm driving. Dad said we can take the car so we all can ride together . Max said cool I didn't want to drive anyway. The four of them went in the car to the local movie store. It was a small place but had a lot of dvds.

Max and Dannie got out and held hands and walk in. Mom and Dad right behind them. Max was looking over the dvds and said look here a good one it's click. Has anyone seen it and here the 300 heard that was a great movie to. Dad said would like to see that 300 movie to. How about you two Max said? Mom and Dannie said sure love to I've heard good things about it to. Max said ok we can get both that way if one isn't good we can watch the other.

Dannie said do we need popcorn and candy for the movies. Max said it wouldn't be the movie without it. Mom said I like melt balls. Max said I getting sweet treats and Dannie said a payday for me. Dad said you know those sweet treats sound good I'll have some to. Max put everything on the counter and the woman behind the counter rang it all up. Max said we all set don't need anything else anyone. Everyone said ok all set its movie time. The woman put everything in a bag and they went back to Dannie's place.

Adam went back to his place to get a few things and throw them in the truck. Adam headed out to Annette place. The road was quiet and the leaves were falling the truck kicked the leaves up from behind like some type of batman movie. Adam pulled into the camp ground and saw Bob's truck and someone truck. Adam was in plan cloths but could feel some thing was wrong. Adam put his hand gun down the back of his pants just in case something was wrong.

Adam went to the door and Annette came and let them in. Annette looked at Adam and he know something was wrong. Annette said it about time you got here with the money. Adam said sorry I got here with the money as fast as I could. A voice from inside said come on up with your hands in the air. Adam came up inside and could see a man standing in front of Bob as he sat down by the guy on the floor. The man said is that the money?

Adam said yes and stood between the gun man and Annette. The man said set the money down and push it over here and no funny business. Adam said ok as he slowly set the money down on the ground and said you ready? The man said yes push it over now. Adam had his hand on his gun and gave the bag a big kick and it got the man to block it as it came at him. Adam draws his gun and shot the man four times the man drop the gun and stood there getting ready to die.

Annette said he's the one that killed the kids. Adam pulls his gun up and said this one for the kids and shot the man between the eyes and he went down with a dang. Adam said as he was still covering the man Bob get his gun and hand it to me. Bob got up and handed the gun to Adam. Adam said everyone ok. Annette hugs him from behind we are now is he die Adam checked his pulse yes very die. Adam told Bob to go have the camp ground man call Mike and the state police. Bob went by Adam and said thanks and headed out the door to the office.

Adam turned around to Annette and could see she was sad but happy. Adam went over to her and hug her and held her close he said let go out side hun. Adam and Annette went out side and sat at the table. Annette began to cry again she said my kid owe that son for a bitch 800 hundred and he kill them because he didn't get it. Adam said do you know who he is? Annette said I think his name was Boody or something like that.

Adam said do you know why she owe them the money. Annette said yes he sold her some parts for her car. Bob came back and said the cops will be here shortly and Mike to. Adam said to Bob you ok? Bob said yes and that son of a bitch is die thank's. Bob said he was going to kill use after you gave him the money so we can't rat on him. Adam said that's why I kill them first I didn't think he would stop at just killing a few people. Annette said did you have to shot the last shot? Adam said no but between use I wanted to so he wouldn't get out on some lesser charge. Annette said thanks you did the right thing hun. Bob said yes if you didn't finish him I would have. Just for the kids that asshole killed. The state police came rolling in and the first one was Peter. Peter got out and said that's going on here Adam? Adam went over and told Peter about everything that went on.

Peter said you kill them? Adam said yes he die as can be. Peter took a reports from everyone. After taking photos of the screen. Mike got the body in an bag and cleaned up all the blood on the floor. Peter said good night and the cops and Mike went back to town. Annette said this has been one hell of a day. The camp ground owner came over and said maybe you should get a room in town and me and the miss will clean up for you. Annette said you didn't have to do that.

The camp ground owner said yes we do you part of this camp ground and we care for our own. Adam said you should come in town and stay with me and Bob can come over to be with you in the morning. Bob said yes sis your going and we will take care of things here. Annette said ok and gave the camp ground owner a hug and Bob. Bob said see you in the morning sis. Annette said love you Bob. Bob said love you to sis.

Dannie and the others went inside and got ready to watch the dvds. Dannie said anyone use something to drink? Mom and Dad said sure we could use a good drink. Max said a beer if you have one. Dannie said ok I'm going to put the popcorn on to and will be right back. Dannie got the drinks and went back of the popcorn. Dannie gave a small pale to Mom and Dad how were in the chairs and she set beside Max on the couch. Dannie said what's the first movie?

Max said click it is funny from what the newspaper say about it. Dannie curled up beside Max and pull the blanket off the back of the couch and covers them up. The movie started it was like most of Adam's movie he gets to play dumb in it. Dannie finishes her drink and sat it on the table beside Max. Dannie was feeling a little sleepy and hug Max and kisses them. Dannie put her head on Max's chest and watch tv.

She could feel herself falling asleep. Dannie went to sleep and began to dream about the day she was having. Dannie heard a knock at the back door Dannie got up and went to the door. Dannie though it was Pat from next door. Dannie open the door and found out it wasn't Pat it was the wolfman. The wolfman said can You came out a play? Dannie step throw the door way and shut the door behind her. Dannie said what do you want with me. The wolfman said to make you go away and die.

Dannie said well try your best I've killed you before and I will kill you again. The wolfman said don't be too sure of that. The wolfman said then lets go. The wolfman ran off the porch and out to the middle of the field. He turned around to face Dannie. The wolfman said I have my mate with me tonight. Then a beautiful brown wolflady stood up and said yes he got me the fight with him tonight. Dannie said is that all you got? Dannie said go ahead bring it on. The two wolfs charge Dannie and she hit the male and he with rounding off, but the female hit head on and the two hit the ground and started to fight. Dannie said about time someone with a little more skill. Dannie and the female hit again they seem very even in the fight ,but Dannie was still clearly stronger. The male wolf hit her in the side and the two wolves got her down and could hold her there. The female said now how's the better team tonight?

Dannie smiled at them as she saw the two white wolfs come up behind the two for them. The wolfman said for someone about to die you have a funny look about you. Dannie said yup and you and your woman are the ones who are going to die tonight. The female was so mad she pull back and was going to hit Dannie when her arm stopped on the way back. The female looked back as the white wolfs hit her and send her flying across the ground. The wolfman jumped up and went to his mate's side.

The two turned and started the run, but the three white wolves had there way blocked. They stood up and howled as the group and hit them little a Sunday night football team. The two went down and the two white wolfs held their hands behind their backs. The white wolf set the female up on her knees as Dannie came over to her. The female wolf said you may have won now, but soon my team we be strong and we will kill your guys.

Dannie said ok, but now you die. Dannie brock the females neck and the male howled in pain. Dannie pulls the head off the female body. Then she went over to the male and said anything the say before you die. The wolfman said yes your turn we came and I will love every minute of it. A Dannie grads the wolfman's head and broke it off his body. Dannie looked at her sister and said so what do you make of this tonight. Dannie said do you think he mated and had puppies.

The girls said could be but there would be too small to do any harm to use. Dannie said right and we can kill them the same way. The girls said yes and turned to leave. Dannie returned to the back porch and went back inside the house. She walks in the living room and said see the movie is almost over. Dannie wakes up to find she was laying on Max leg and she had her hand on something big.

Dannie looked up at Max and said sorry as she moved her hand. Max smiled and said that's ok hun your Mom and Dad are out cold and been that way for about a half hour. Dannie looked at the two of them and got up. Dannie got a few blankets and cover the two up. Dannie came back over the Max we can go up stair and sleep if you want. Max said I don't have anything to sleep in over here. Dannie said do you have on short. Max said yes I do and I'm wearing and T-shirts . Dannie said if that's ok with you it's ok with me.

Max said it would be if you can keep your hands off something. Dannie smile and said I will be a good girl. So Max and Dannie went up stairs to sleep. Dannie went into the other room to get changed. Max got undress and got into bed. Dannie came out and said hope Mom and Dad sleep ok. Max said they should the chair's look nice and soft. Dannie got into bed and curled up to Max. Dannie said I sorry for having my hand on you a while back. Max said I'm just glad your Mom and Dad were sleeping then. Max said but I did enjoy it. Dannie smiled I could see that. Max hugs her and kisses her love you hun. The two fell asleep and they both were having really good dreams of each other.

Adam knows that Annette would not sleep much tonight because of the day she had already. Adam picked her up and carries her to the bed room. He underdresssed her and got in bed with her and hug her. Annette bring to cry and Adam said let it out and cry hun you need it to start the heeling. Annette said I glad I'm not alone I don't think I could have made it. Adam said I glad I was the one to tell you and could be there for you Annette.

Adam said I couldn't even know what your going throw right now. Annette said I don't think you ready want to. Adam held her close and tried his best to help. Annette said don't think I can sleep right now can we took. Adam said sure it should help you to clear the air. Annette said she just didn't understand why someone could just walk in and kill over a dumb things like money. Adam said you never know what will set someone off.

Adam said I've heard of a lot dumber reason. Annette said I just can believe they're gone just like that. Angela had her bad points but she did all she could for the kids. Adam said could you use a drink right now? Annette said yes along as it was a good strong one. Adam got up and went into the kitchen and made the both of them a good strong drink. Adam handed the drink to Annette a set down on the bed beside her. Annette can we watch some tv.

Adam said yes and handed her the remote. Adam said choose anything I don't care. Annette looked at Adam and could see the hurt in his heart for her. Adam set his drink on the night stand a kissed her. Annette put her drink there to and kissed him back. Annette said Adam make love to me I need to feel loved right now. Adam didn't say a thing he just roll over to her and make love to her. After that the both fell asleep and stayed that way until morning.

Adam arose the next morning feel better but he knows Annette was going the need some time to heel. Adam rolls over and Annette was there awake with a sad look in her eyes. Adam pulls her close and hugs her. Annette started to cry again she held Adam tight. Annette said to Adam when you go to work to be careful I don't need any more love ones getting hurt. Adam said I will Annette and I will be back around five so we can get out of town if you want.

Annette said maybe but we will see. Adam said maybe we should get some thing to eat your brother Bob should be here soon. Adam said your brother Bob is a fine man. Annette said he's the best brother a sister could ever have. Adam said you need anything today call me. Annette said ok but she wasn't going to do much today but put a sign in the coffee shop window.

A knock came at the door Adam got up and opens the door it was Bob. Adam said hi and come in Bob. Annette came out of the bedroom and went over to hug her brother. Adam said I will make a pot of coffee be right back.

Bob told Annette that he call the family last night and everyone is passing the word and were heading up here today. Brother Richard I think took it the hardest he loves you and the kids. Annette started to cry she said I know he would is he coming up to? Bob said yes he coming up with your sister Lill . Good I would love to see him. Adam came out with the coffee for everyone and said I hear your family is coming up good he said maybe will can all go out to eat and get to know each other.

Annette said my sister will pick you apart if that's what you want. Adam said that's ok I can take it. Adam said you going to be with her all day Bob? Bob said yes I'm going to be with her as long as she needs me. Annette stood up and said my two best men and they both love me. Adam said you are the best thing to come into my life in a long time Annette. Annette said thanks to Adam I love you to hun. Adam gave her a kiss and went to take a shower.

Adam feels that he should stay home with Annette today but he's needs to be with the team on the island. Adam got out of the shower and went to his room to get some thing on. Adam came out and Bob and Annette was in the kitchen. Adam walks in and Annettte was cooking breakfast for them all. Adam said you didn't have to do that hun. Annette said cooking makes me feel better. Adam walks over and smells the food it sure smells good and kisses her.

Annette said sat down and I will serve you. Adam said ham hash brown and eggs I 'm not going to have to eat the rest of the day. Annette said breakfast is the most imported meal of the day. Adam said and the best one to. Adam finishes his meal and sat there and drank his coffee. Adam got up a put his plate in the sink and then went over to kiss Annette I will see you later hun get some rest and try to unwind. Bob said I know how to make sis happy and we will started after she has a shower.

Adam kiss and hug Annette and she said be careful hun today. Adam said I will and I will see you later ok. Yup Annette said and Adam went out the door. Annette looked at Bob and said I could be saying good bye for the last time to him. Bob said don't think like that I know police work is hard and you may not make it back some day, but you can't live life that way you got to live for the day.

Annette said ok I can see your point Bob and your right as always. Bob said now go get a shower we need to meet the sisters and brothers. Annette said they're here already. Bob said yup and Richard can't wait to see you. Annette said ok and headed to the shower. Bob called the group to see where they where. They were at the Irving getting some thing to eat and going back to the hotel. Bob said ok me and Annette will be over soon.

Dannie wakes up and could see Max was still sleeping. Dannie was thinking of what her and Mom and Dad could do today. Max moved Dannie said good morning hun. Max said to her good morning I was dreaming of use and what we be like in the future. Dannie said was it good and did I look ok in it to. Max said you looked great for having ten kids. Dannie said ten kids I hope we did more than make kids. Max said yes we went all over the world and skied and had fun. Dannie said it sounds fun but ten kids. Max said I would be happy with just two.

Dannie said me to hun. Dannie said I guess we need to stop thinking about kids for now. Max said that was a good idea he said. Max hugged Dannie and kisses her. What time is it hun Max said. Dannie said around eight or nine why? Max said I've Got to open this week and I do that at ten. Max started to get out of bed and remember things weren't down. Dannie saw them get out of bed and put her head half under the covers. Dannie face was red. Max said I sorry but got to get in the shower. Dannie said don't be sorry.

Max went into the shower and got washes up for work. Dannie lay back in the bed and said dam I hope it isn't that big all the time. Max came out of the shower and got dress for work. Max gave Dannie and big hug and said I will call you later. Dannie said hold on I should go down stairs went you. Max said ok the two went down stairs and Dannie couldn't see Mom or Dad. Max said where are they. Dannie said came with me. Max and Dannie went to the back lawn. Mom and Dad where sound asleep on the back lawn.

Max said dam they love your lawn don't they. Dannie said they just don't know when to stop sometimes. Max and Dannie went back inside Dannie switched the lawn sprinklers on. Max looked at her and said what did you just do? Dannie walk Max to the front door and said Mom and Dad will be in to say good in a few. Just as Dannie said that two people in a blanket came throw the back door. Max started to laugh Dannie you're bad. Max yelled back see you later guys. Max kissed Dannie and went to work.

Mom and Dad came up front and put Dannie in the wet blanket and hug her see hun we have something on this time. Mom said I see Max was here all night. Dannie said yes and we aren't going to have sex until we are married now. Mom said I sorry hun and Dad hug her with a wet smile. Dannie said you two are some thing else. Mom said I not going to be able to look at Max and not laugh now. Dannie said will I'm going to make some coffee would you like some.

Dad said yes but he had to dry off first. Mom said the same I will be back down in a minute hun. Dannie said I'm going to cut up some fruit. Mom and Dad went up stairs and got dress in something drier. Dannie went into the kitchen and made up some breakfast. Dad and Mom came back down and sat at the counter. Dannie said so what do you want to do today Mom?

Dad said lets run throw the Park and have a lunch. Mom said that sounds fun how about you hun.

Dannie said it sounds great to me to Mom. Mom said were should go and take a shower so we can get on the way. Dad said ok and went up stairs to the bathroom. Mom said so you thinking of Max. Dannie said yes with a big smile. Mom said ok what's up? Dannie said we had some took about kids this morning. I want to have about two kids and he said that would be nice. Mom said that's cool so what's wrong with that? Dannie said not a thing and looked at her cup and drank her coffee. Dad came back down and said next.

Mom went to take a shower and Dannie and Dad went out on the back porch to set. Dannie said it's going to be a good day Dad isn't it. Dad said ok what's wrong hun? Dannie said not a thing I was just wondering how you know Mom was the right woman for you? Dad said I know from the time I saw her at she was right for me. Dannie said how did you know. Dad said ok when you see Max do you get all warm and funny inside? Dannie said yes. Dad said did your heart jump and bet went you kiss. Dannie said yes all the time. Dad said this's the same way I feel about your Mom ever day I see her and kiss her.

Dad said hun your in love and you're in deep. Dannie got up and kissed Dad thanks Dad I know you would know the trust. Dad said what are Dad for but to show their kids the way throw life. Mom came out with a cup of coffee and said the shower is free. Dannie got up and went to the bathroom to clean up. Dannie stopped in the bathroom and looked down at her ring and though of Max she because all warm and furry inside she said Dad's right.

Adam was setting at the station the others came in. Good morning Adam said to the team you guys ready for the island today. Chase said I didn't think you would be here after what happen yesterday. Adam said I was thinking the same thing, but I need to get this case over with. Peter said yes this wolfman needs to be killed. Adam and the group got ready to go on the island again. Adam and Peter road together and headed for Patrick's boat rental place.

Adam dove in down to Patrick's and Patrick came out to meet them, Patrick said don't tell me you want to go back to the island. Adam said sure but this time were going over every inch of the island. Patrick said we'll take the big boat again this time. The group loaded the boat up and set off for the island. Patrick said do you want me to drop you in the same place? Adam said no at the top of the island. Patrick said ok. You're the boss. Patrick do you think your going to find the wolfman there today.

Chase said we hope that's all we find. The island was coming into view it didn't look like much from far away but up close it was a good size place. Patrick bought the boat up to the front and set it on a few rocks and use the boat's big motor to keep them there. Patrick said all ashore. The group got off and the same as last time the dogs didn't want anything to do with the island. Patrick no trouble me and the dog we go half way down the island and set in the middle.

Adam said we will call you on the CB if we need you. Patrick said ok see you later. Adam said to the team we are going to walk east and west about six feet apart until we cover all the island. Adam said if anything moves or brakes wind you yelled and the rest of use will join you. Chase said don't worry I get a black fly bit everyone will know. Fred said the last time we need is all of use running ways. Chase said I all set lets do it.

Adam said everyone check guns to make sure they work. Devvan said mind ok. Mary said same here and the others said everything is ok here to. Ok lets head out. The team moved back and forward across the island cover every inch as they walk. About one 1/3 the island was covered when Mary yelled for the guys, they all came running. Mary said it looks like someone was out here this is some type of camp sight. Fred said yes but not used in a very long time. Chase said yes. The tent is all full of holes. Chase looked inside the tent and found a old wine skin that my have been for holding water it was old a had a name on it. Maxwell Fred said can I see that Chase. Chase handed the wine skin to Fred. Fred looked at the name and his eyes began to water. Mary said something wrong Fred? Fred tries to speak but he had a hard time this was my brother's wine skin. Peter said this must be were there send there last night on the island. Fred said yes I think you're right. Adam said I'm sorry about this Fred do you want to go back to the boat an wait.

Fred said no and rolled the wine skin up and put it in his coat. Chase patted Fred on the back you going to be ok big guys. Fred said yes but it just felt little it was yesterday when I heard about it. Adam said it hard sometimes to think of the pass. The group fanned out again and started to search. Adam though to himself that the island was funny smelling like a car with four pine tree air fresher in it. The ground was covered with pine needles and leafs from years' pass. The brush was hard to see throw in same spots but passable.

The team had been on the island for about and hour when there came across the old river drivers grave yard. The team looked around the grave yard for anything the help them find the wolfman. Mary said did the wolfman sleep in here once. Peter said yes but what that got to do with it? Mary said it seems funny a wolfman would find peace in a grave yard. Chase open the little gate and uncovered a small headed marker. That read The graves of the seven unknown river drivers and a small round sign at the base of the stone. Mary said why would there do that when all the yards have headed stones. Mary looked closer and though to her self she had seen that sign somewhere else.

The team started to move again when a cold chill came in the air. Chase can you feel that? The team stopped and grouped up back the back. A voice came in the air so low you could hear it but hard to make out. It was saying leave our island. Adam said can anyone else hear the voice? The team looked at each other and said yes. It makes the hair stand on the back of your neck and an icy chill run up your back. Adam yelled out not this time guys we are going to look this island over form top the bottom. The team closed in a circle and began to move again. The voice seemed to grow softer as they moved away from the grave yard.

Fred said I wonder if this is how my brother died. Adam said ok let get back to work and get this search done. The team had reach the pole line that ran throw the island and the cold chill seen to lift. The team started to feel better. The group was almost done the island and they headed to a small hill that if you looked down you could see a small inlet where the old river driver keep they boasts. The hill wasn't much but did make for a good climb. The team sat at the top of the hill and had lunch.

Adam said I don't understand if the wolfman is coming to this island to sleep where the hell could it be. Devvan said we look the island all over and were could he hid. Mary said their Patrick and the dogs. Adam called Patrick and said how's the fishing? Patrick said you guys almost done. Adam said yup just taking a brake. Ok Patrick said when you want me to come in for you just going to your left to the old boom hock up just down the hill. Adam looked down the hill to the boom hock up it was an old cement landing where the river driver use too tied off the log it was about nine feet long and had big hocks in the top of it. The team started down the hill and Patrick could see they were coming to get picked up. Patrick sure was glad this day on the island was almost over. Adam stood on the old boom hock.

He could see how the ropes the driver use cut the steal hocks. Adam said to himself dam there must had been a lot of wood hocked to this place at one time. Patrick throw the team a rope and Chase pull him into the shore next to the dock. Everyone got on the boat and Adam was the last one he handed his gun to Chase and got on. Patrick started to pull away from the dock and Adam said stops go back in for a second. Patrick said ok. It's your dime.

The team said what's going on Adam? Adam said look at the bottom of the dock it looks as if their a drain hole just below the water line. The boat came back into the dock Adam got a fish pole and put it in the opening it was a round drain that came from the island. Fred you don't think that going to the den do you. Adam said they're only one way to tell. Adam sat on the boat and started to remove his boat and gun belt. He took his shirt off and said hand me the flash light. Fred gave Adam the flash light an he jump in dam he said the water is cold.

Adam took a deep breath and when down into the hole he could see the hole when in about 30 feet in and he could see some light at the other end. Adam came up and said it a drain of some kind I can see same day light about 30 feet in. Peter said you're not think for going in there are you? Adam said they not I can swim that with not trouble. Fred said what if it's the den and that thing is there waiting for you to came up. Adam said good point well I will just go in just half way to get a better look.

Ok Chase said but don't be foolish. Adam said don't worry I'm not that crazy. Adam took other deep breath and went back down he swan half way in and could see that the end did open up into some type of room. Adam came back out and got back on the boat he told Patrick to move away from the dock. The group said will what did you see. Adam said I could see it opened up into a room but that's all. No sign of life. Fred said dam that's a great place to hid that's if he in there. Chase said what about the inferred camera in the back of the car it could show use if theirs a heat sign on the inside of the hill. Adam said dam good idea.

Patrick headed back to the cars. Adam got dress and said dam that's cold. Patrick pulls up to the rental deck and Chase went out to get the Camera. Chase got back on and the group headed back out to the island. Adam said stay about fifth feet out. Adam turned on the camera and it was showing some thing moving within the hill, but not just one it was four or five-heat source. Adam said I think we have the den. Adam told Patrick the head back to his place. Fred said now what do we do how are we going to get in there. Adam said don't know but we can go over this back at the station.

Dannie loaded a lunch and got in the jeep. Mom and Dad said well were all set. Dannie started up the jeep and headed to a little town up north called Pattern. That's where you enter the top side of the park right off a big lake. Mom said it's going to be a good day to look at the leafs and tree that have charge. Dannie went up interstate 95 to Sherman exit and turned left that would take her into Pattern then had would turn left again and headed to the north park gate.

The ride into the park was nice Dannie stopped a few times to look at the area. Dannie stops at one place were you look up at the hill side and see were big rocks the size of house had come down and almost onto the road. Dad said I sure wouldn't want to be around here when the rock slide is moving. Mom said yes they look as if they could really hurt someone. Dannie said will lets go check in and see the park.

The tree line open to a large lake and you could see for miles. Dad and Mom got out and said dam this state is beautiful. Dannie said it sure is. Dannie said as a bird flow over wow and eagle it's sure nice to see them coming back in the wild. Dad said look I think he going to get a fish. The eagle came down to the water and grads a fish at the top of the water. Mom said hun you should have done that good at fishing. Dannie got back in the jeep and they headed to he gate.

The people who run the gates or all really nice people. The gate keeper said just here to look around. Dannie said yes and we will going out the Millinocket side of the park. The gate keeper said have a good day and don't speed. Dannie said thank you and a have great day . Dannie headed into the park the road was nice but could be narrow in some places. Dannie first stop was trout pond camp ground. The place was a big open field where you could put campers or put up a tent.

The place was unreal you could see the tree were charging and the colors were bright. Dad said I think God made heaven right here in Maine how could it get any better. Mom said I hear you they this is a great little state. Dannie said I think we should go to sliding rock for lunch. Dad said great plan. The three got back in the jeep and went down the road. It wasn't long before they saw same wild life. Dannie said look guys that's a morse isn't it. Dad said sure is and a real big one to look at the rack of horns.

Mom it's funny some thing as big as a car can move throw the wood like that. Mom said how long is it to the Millinocket gate? Dannie said it would be about 2.1/2 hours. Ok Dannie said lets get rolling again. There went throw Katahdin stream camp ground and Kinney pond camp ground then came to sliding rock. Sliding rock was made by the river running down over it for years. The water cut a grove in the rocks you could slide down throw to the bottom into the small body of water below.

It was fun in the summer but too cold for this time of year. Hell it's cold of anytime of the year. Dannie said to Mom it's like jumping in a tub full of ice cubes. Dannie bought a blanket of food she had I her jeep. Mom and Dad got to a spot and they went to set on the rock and lesion to the water roll by. Dannie sat the blanket down and they sat down to watch the water flow by. Dannie lay down on the blanket and looked at the sky.

Dannie said this is just the best I wish Max was here with use. Mom and Dad said me to He's a great man. Dannie smiles he sure is and he my man. Dannie had made tuna up and cut some food and put a little wine in spill proof cups for them. Dannie sat back up and made a sandwich and had some fruit and cheese to. Every once and a awhile a car or truck would pass but other than that it was like heaven on earth. Dannie held up her thing of wine and said here's to the man up stairs who make this all for his people to enjoy.

Mom said amen to that hun. Dad said on the way back into town we could stop and say hi to Max if you want. Dannie said sure would like to see him. Dad said cool then we will. Mom said maybe we can stop in town and do some shopping. Dad said she going to make the day be good for her. Dannie laughs I was thinking the same thing . Dad said I sure will be glad when there's one more man on my side.

Mom said don't look now but I think were going to be robbed. Dannie looks at her truck then back at her Mom and said what you taking about. Mom said look down stream and racoon is coming this way. Dannie turned and the racoon was about ten feet away. Dannie got a sandwich and set it out for the racoon. Dad said you sure that's smart? Dannie said I did this all the time when I was younger and never got bit.

Mom said I think they're more. Dannie said yes look three little babies. Dannie said gave me the rest of the food. I will put it out for them. Dad said good I was done any way. Dannie sat the food in front of the Moms' racoon and the baby's they came up to eat. Mom said it's funny watching them eat it's just like meal time at the prison. Dad said it's done look like that. After the Mother was done, she went over to the water to wash up and get some water.

The little ones were right behind her and did the same thing. Dannie and Mon pick up the paper and thing and headed back to the jeep. Dad got up and walked to the jeep and said this is been fun. Dannie drove throw the park and out the Millinocket side of the park. Dannie stopped at the pond that the girl scouts use in the summer month. She remembers there was a small store that sold camping thing. Dannie drove back out to the town of Millinocket and to her and Mom's best thing in the world shopping.

Dannie said to Mom thing sure have charge here. Mom said yes their use the be store open all throw the town, now. It's a little more then an old west ghost town. Dannie pulls into Miller and they get out. Dad went in and headed to the radio shack part of the store where a man could do man thing. Dannie and Mom went to the baby things and were having a field day Dannie loved the kid's things she couldn't wait until her and Max had a baby.

Mom said should we go see Max now or keep shopping for more things. Dannie said it's only around five right now so if we keep shopping we can have supper at Max's place. Mom said cool sounds good to me. Dannie went over to the shoes and was thinking she could use some new sneakers. Dannie tried on a few pears and like the white on red ones. Now we going to have to get a new shirt and pear of pants. Dannie went back over to and other side and looked for shirts.

Mom said I'm done this store is there anything else we can do Dannie. Dannie said where's Dad Mom? Mom said he back in the jeep most likely Taking a nap. Dannie said he doesn't enjoy shopping? Mom said it's ok if he got something that he likes in the store. Dannie said he'll be happy because only one more store left in town to shop that's open today. Mom said oh what's that? Dannie said its Family Dollar store in the old mall. Dannie said lets cash out and go up town then if you're all set here.

Mom said I'm ok with that. Dannie and her Mom went back to the jeep Dad was setting their sleeping. Dannie got her keys out and set off the car alarm. Dad didn't move he just looked at her and said done so fast you two? Dannie said only one more store and we can head over to Max's. Dad said good maybe we can eat supper over there? Mom said good idea hun and her and Dannie laughs. Dannie got in and went up to the Family Dollar store. Dad said ok I'm going to work on my nap while you two shop.

Dannie kiss Dad and said go for it we not going to be long. Mom and Dannie went into the store and looked around. Dannie said this is a good store of people with not a lot of money to spend. Mom said not bad but some things are cheaper at the market. Dannie said they seem to all ways have some thing fun and new in here. Hay Mom here something we could use a Maine flashlight. Dannie held up a peace of wood with a match at one end.

Mom said I bet they got morse shit earring . Dannie laughs wouldn't put it pass them. Good Dannie said they got trash bags good we wouldn't have to stop for them then. Mom said you got everything you need. Dannie said yup a they went to cash out. Dad was laying their looking at them he said the store throw you out dear. Mom said no they had to close they said the truck will be by in the morning. Dad said that's my girl shop till you drop.

Dannie said lets go see Max now I think he making chilli today. Mom said to Dad you eat that your sleeping on the back porch tonight. Dad said is it good and hot? Yup Dannie said make your eyes water. Mom said going in and coming out on him. Dad said chilli is no good if you can't share it with the once you love. Mom said some how gas isn't what their mean. Dannie laughs and Dad said oh is that what wrong with it.

Dannie pulls into Max's and they got out and went in to see Max. Dannie walk throw the door the bar was pretty full so they sat at the bar and said hi to Max. Max said sure nice seeing you here just was thinking about you and kissed Dannie. Dannie said so what's good for the night? Max said the chilli is hotter than hell tonight. Dad look at Mom and she said back porch. Dad said ok sounds good and do you have bread sticks. Max said sure do what do you want Dannie. Dannie said same thing. Mom Dannie said how about you?

Mom said I think I will have the same. Dad looked at her and Dannie said you sure Mom. Yup Mom said and a beer with the meal . Max said ok I shall be right back with the food. Dad said you remember what happen the last time you eat chilli? Mom said yes and I love every minute of it.

Adam and the others unloaded and headed back to the station. Adam pulls into the station and told Peter he was going to check on Annettte be right down after. Adam said the front door should still be unlocked if not

Chase has a key. Peter said ok we will wait of you to come back down before we think of a plan. Adam said ok see you soon. Adam went up the back stairs to his room. Adam went in and there was no one around a note on the table said gone with Bob and will be back tonight love Annette.

Adam said to himself good she with Bob then. Adam grads a sandwich out of the ice box and headed down stairs. Adam walks in and everyone was set with their feet up on something they were in hard though. Peter said that's was fast? Adam said she went somewhere with her brother Bob. Adam said anyone want pizza? Everyone said sure way not. Adam made an order from Rick's place down the road.

Adam said as he pulled out the chock board. Chase said we could float some thing in and blow it up. Adam said good idea but that if this is some local kids in their just partying. Fred said why not use an under water camera and float it in the hole. Peter said that's a great idea that way were know if it's kids or just wolfman and family. Adam said anyone know where we can get a camera and under water gear. Peter said yes at my house I did driving awhile back and still have all the gear.

Good Adam said now we need to try to think if it is the den what next. Mary said we could drill a hole in an gas the animals that way no one will get killed going in for them. Adam said and we could set at the front for the hole and shot anything that comes out. The pizza is here good. I'm hungry Fred said. The pizza man put the pizza's down on the counter and left. Adam said don't you want to get payed. The pizza boy said I did by two men out front who drove off in a blue car. Adam ran out side to see if he could see the person.

The pizza boy come out and said they went up the Millinocket way. The pizza boy said they said too gave you the pizza's and gave me a 50 for a tap. Adam said did they do anything to the pizza? No the boy said but the car there were driving was from the government that's what the plates had on it. Adam said thanks and gave the kid other 20-dollar tap. Kid said thanks call me anytime for pizza. Adam walk back inside and said the guys my had put something on the pizza?

Everyone said what and spit out the pizza in there mouth. Adam laughs and said it's ok but the car the kid said had government plates on it. Devvan said now that's a set of brass balls isn't it. Adam said I would like to kick them in the brass balls just once. Fred said I think just about all of use would like a good shot at them. Adam said not much for use to do here so why don't we shut down for the night and hit the wolfman in the morning. Fred said good plan the wife would like to see me before six tonight.

Adam said Fred tell your wife we are all still planning to come over the see her after this is all over. Fred said good. She ask me about that the other day.

She said you only need to bring yourself because she has everything planned. Adam said sound like a great time. Adam said will guys you all head home and rest we can see what we can get done tomorrow.

Peter said to Adam I have two sets for gear do you want me bring both. Adam said sure I can help you if we go in the den tomorrow. Adam said see you all in the morning. Adam lock up and went up stair to see if Annette was back. Adam walks into the room and Bob and Annette were setting there. Adam went over to Annette and kiss and hugs her. Annette said how's your day today? Adam said good ok we may have found the wolf's den this noon. Annette said was it on the island?

Adam said we found and under hole that goes into some type of den or something. Bob said that wouldn't be off the boom hooks would it? Adam said yes why do you know some thing about it. Bob said yes it an old drinking place for the local kids. Adam said how come I never heard of it. Bob said it wasn't as will know as the others because you had to swim to get to it. Adam said so who made the place. Bob said my dad told me when the river was low the enter was about four feet off the river the river driver make it so they could have a place to warm up and sleep off the river.

Adam said is it big in there. Bob said it's 30feet by 20 feet with ten feet to the roof. Adam said then it could be a den then. Bob said yup it's big and had beds in it the last time I was there. Adam said Bob can you swim in without bring seen. Bob said no because the hole is in the middle of the room. Adam said thanks that going to help use a lot tomorrow when we go back to see if we can see anything in there. Annette said you're not going to swim in there are you Adam. Adam said no we going to put an underwater camera in their tomorrow to see what we can see. Bob said you should be able to see the inside from the hole because the place has four corners.

Adam said great that was a big help. Adam said Annette how's your day go hun. Annette said the first part of the day was hard but I have my family with me. Annette said we went to see the bodies and that was ruff. Adam said I'm sorry and hug her. Another than that the day went ok we went out and had lunch and then came back here. Adam said we don't have to stay here we can go somewhere for supper if you want. Adam said Bob your more then welcome to come with use. Bob said that's ok I'm going to go home and rest for a while. Annette got up and hugged Bob and kisses them and said thanks for bringing around with me today.

Bob said I we see you in the morning sis love you. Adam said good night to Bob. Adam said will there you want to go out or stay here? Annette said I would like to go out, but it may be the far away. Adam said where do you want to go? To the 95er in Howland. Adam said that's just down the road not far at all. Annette said you're sure you been working all day. Adam said no trouble at all. Annette said ok I going to clean up and little.

Adam said I'm going to charge into street cloths. Adam came back out after he charges and the two went out and got into Adam's truck. Adam back out and headed to Howland. Adam said what's so good about the 95er. They seem to have the best fry fish around. Adam said fish good I could use some good fish after all the things I eat. Annette said something wrong with my cooking?

Adam said no I meant all the junk food I eat from time to time. Annette curled up and sat next to Adam. Adam pull his arm around her and held her close. The ride was about 40 miles but went by fast it seen for Adam. Adam pulls off the ramp to the 95er and went down the road to the store. The 95er was a good place for a small town like Howland it gave a good meal at a fear price. Adam and Annette went in a sat in the corner by the window.

The waiter came over and ask if they would like a menu and something to drink. Annette said no I know what I want the fish dinner. Adam said the same for me and milk with my meal. The waiter said I will put your order in and would you like some fresh dinner roll with that meal. Annette said yes thank you and the waiter went to the kitchen. The place was fulled with local people and some flatlanders. The waiter returned with their meals and drinks. The waiter said the fish was fresh this morning so it should still be real good. Adam said thanks and the two started to eat.

Dannie said to Max are you off soon? Max said I've been off for about and hour now I just stuck around because your phone was busy all day. Dannie said you know your phone was busy all day to. Max pulls his cell phone out of his pocket and looked at it then dialed Dannie's number. Max said still busy she said that's funny my phone isn't ringing. Dannie pulls her phone out of her bag. Hay Max said you got the same phone. Dannie said you don't think we may have switched phones.

Max grad his phone and called his number and Dannie's phone rang. They looked at each other now how did we do that. Max laughs and said I though my phone smelled good like you. Dannie laughs we are a set of goof ball aren't we. Max said how's the chilli? Mom said really good better then Dad's. Dad said yes it is better then mind but cooler than mind. Mom said that's why it's better.

Dannie said it was great and ask what Max was going to do tonight. Max said I was thinking of watching a movie with this hot chick I know one out in the country. Dannie said oh is she someone I know as she smile. Max said she setting in your seat. Dannie said too bad I'm going to take you. Max said she a real fighter you sure? Dannie said I'm sure.

Mom and Dad said good we need another nap. Dannie said are you ready to go. Max said yup I can follow you out in the truck. Dannie gave the keys to Dad and said no off roading you two and making out in my truck. Mom said what's the fun in that. Dannie said I will go with you Max. Mom got up and said this could be a fun ride home. Dad said yup fun for her not me. Dad said can I ride with you two. Dannie said sorry no room for you See you back at home.

Dad and Mom went out and Dannie and Max went throw the back door. Dannie and Max got in the truck and followed Mom and Dad home about half way Dannie could see Dad with his head out the window. Dannie started to laugh you had to let her eat your chilli? Max laughs does it gave her gas? Dannie said gas would be good , but she gave off is deadly. Max said that bad wow it's going to be a gas fulled night. Max said Dannie pull into the yard and Dad was outside the truck trying to breath. Dad said sorry hun your truck has a new smell to it.

Dannie said roll down the windows' it going to be good tomorrow anyways. Mom said I do something with a big smile on her face. Max said it can't be that bad is it. Dannie said be my guess and roll down the windows. Max went to the truck and opened the door. The smell hit him like two handfuls of shit slapped in your face. He turned around and said she did that. Dad said it was about a mile back and she had me in tears. Max laughs and said dam where did she learn that from a truck driver.

Dannie said she would make a truck driver proud wouldn't she. Mom stood on the front steps and laughed. Mom said Dannie pull my finger. Max I'll do it and started the going to the house. Dannie said if you do you both we be sleeping on the back porch. Mom said to slow there here it comes, she let off a roar like three trains hit each other at the same time. Max jumped behind Dannie and said did that come out of her. Dannie said Mom I mean it you going to sleep out back. Mom said it ok if I need to do it again I will out side the house.

Max said I hope my chilli doesn't do that to you hun. Dannie said it gives me a little gas but not that bad. The group went in the house throw the cloud of gas. Everyone got inside and Mom said if you need to go to the bath room you better get in there first. So everyone ran up stairs and went to the bath room. Dannie came out and said leave the fan on Mom ,Max, Dad and Dannie went into the den to start the movie. Dannie said anyone use a beer while I'm up Dad said sure and Max said ok. Dannie left the room and went into the kitchen.

She got the beers and went back to the den. Mom was coming down the stair and Dannie said you want a beer Mom. Mom said sure, go in with these ones and I will get me one. Dannie went into the den and handed Dad a beer. Thanks hun did you smell your Mom. No but she should be in here in a few. Dannie sat down next to Max and gave him a beer. Dannie grad the blanket form the back of the couch and put it around her and Max.

Mom came in the room and set on the love next to Dad. Max turned the movie on and set down and kissed Dannie. Max said there something missing Dannie. Dannie put her hand between Max's legs and said this. Max chocked on his beer and said no I think it was popcorn. Max laughs but that was ok to. Dannie smile and kiss Max would you like popcorn hun. Max said no I 'm ok right now hun. Dannie curl up under Max's arm and hug him.

Dannie said look Mom and Dad are sleeping again. Dannie ask Max do you like this movie? Max said no it's kind of slow. Dannie said lets go and set on the porch. Max said ok and the two went out back. Dannie said the air is cool isn't it. Max said yes and held her close to keep her warn. Max said I'll be right back. Max went back into the living to find the two still sleeping Max grads the blanket off the back of the couch and went back out to Dannie. Max came back out and lay down on the lawn chair. Dannie came over and lay on top of Max.

Max put the blanket over the two of them and said now what's better. Dannie hugged Max and could feel the heat from his body yes she said much better. Max and Dannie lay there and kissed and watched the night sky. Dannie said are you sleepy Max? Max said a little but not really.

Dannie said we can go up stairs and watch some tv if you want. Max said ok and before could say other thing Mom and Dad came out the back door in a blanket. Mom said its cold tonight let's stay on the porch in a lawn chair. The night was dark and you couldn't see much. Dannie put her hand over Max's mouth because he was going to say something. Dannie covers the both of their heads up. Mom and Dad got in the lawn chair next to him. Dannie looked to see if they were cover up before she said anything. Dannie said the night air is cold right Mom. Dad and Mom both jumped oh sorry hun we though you to were up stairs.

Dannie said don't get up we were going up there before the nude show starts up. Mom and Dad laugh sorry Max. Max said ok we will see in the morning. Max and Dannie got up and Mom cover they heads. Dannie said don't have to Mom we have something on. Mom and Dad said good night. Dannie said don't make me water the lawn tonight you two. Mom said ok well be good. Dannie said sure you will see you later.

Max and Dannie went up to Dannie's room. Max said are they all ways like that? Dannie said yup they still love each other madly. Max said that sweet if you stop and think about it. Dannie said it is in a gross way. Max and Dannie got in bed and turned on the tv and watched the last show. Max hugs and kisses Dannie until they got sleepy.

Adam said the meal is great your right Annette. Annette said I don't remember when I 've had a bad meal here. The waiter return and ask if they were all set. Adam said I'm set if she is. Annette said I'm ok and the waiter said good I will bring your check. Adam said want to run up the old way Rt. 116 maybe we can see a dear or bear. Annette said yes as long as we don't see any wolfman. Adam said I can hear you there I've just about had too much of the wolfman.

Adam and Annette went out to the counter to pay they check and got back in the truck and headed up old RT 116 the road starts off as dirt and then come back too hot top after a while. Adam drove slowly on the road to look for wild life, not long after they hit the road a small fox was setting in the road ahead of them. Annette said they don't even look wild do they? Adam said no you feel as if you could just get out and pet them.

Adam started to move down the road and about three miles came across some dear in a small field they set and watched them for ten minute and went down the road that would be all that they would see on the ride. Adam and Annette got back to town and went into Adam's room. Annette said she felt sleepy and the two went to bed and went to sleep. Adam could tell Annette was run down from the day. Adam couldn't understand the pain she was feeling. The next few days were going to be hell for her.

Not only saying good bye to her only kid, but five grand kids at the same time. No one should have to go throw that pain. Adam got up and went into the living room to watch the 11.30 p.m. news. The weather was going to be good for tomorrow and no news on anything else so that was good.

Adam said to him self it's about time for the wolfman to do something else he been to quiet the last few days. Adam could feel what cop sense kick in Annette came out of the bed room with Adam's gun and said do you feel that Adam. Adam said he wasn't sure what it was, but he could feel it to. Adam took the gun and Annette follows him around the apartment Adam looked out every window to see if he could see any thing. Adam when into the bed room Annette looked out the window and said is that the wolfman over by McLaughin's Auto.

Adam said where? Annette said look at the car on the far side the white one. Adam said that's sure is and he watching use isn't he. Annette said it sure looks like it. Annette said maybe he knows it was you at the den today. Adam said could be and he knows he gets to it use first before we come after him. Adam said shit hope not that would mean your in danger to. Annette said you have any more guns around here. Adam said yes the boys didn't put up the AK's this noon. Annette said where are they? Adam said in my closet . Annette with over to the closet and got the gun and set them on the bed.

Adam said you know how to use a gun. Annette said brother Bob is a good teacher. Good Adam said two shooters is better than one. Adam said the only way he can get use is throw the front door or the back door off the kitchen. Annette said are those tack strips in the closet to. Adam said yes but there aren't going to do use much good why. Annette said come I will show you something. Annette grads the tack strips and went to the front door and place one about three feet from the door. Adam said great plan he may not have tired, but I think that would make his feet hurt some bad.

Annette said you got it step on that and Mr wolfman will be in real pain. Annette did the same for the back door. Adam said lets set up in the far counter of the living room and while to see what he will do next. Annette and Adam set back in the corner with a clear shot at both doors. Adam said some thing is coming up the front steps and it isn't small. Annette and Adam turn their guns on the front door. Adam said don't shot until he starts in because I want to make sure it's him.

The thing was right outside the door Adam said take off your safety and get ready for some shooting. You could hear the animal breathing on the other side of the door, but the wolfman didn't come in he ran his hand across the door and then when down the back stairs and back on the street and he let out a big howl and took off. Adam said looks like were in the clear for tonight. Annette said good but lets leave the tack stripes down. Adam said ok that way we can get the upper hand.

Annette and Adam returned to the bed room and got into bed to try to sleep. Annette said how long has he been playing game with you? Adam said from the time we tried to trap him in the Millers barn. Annette said do you think you should call Chase a tell him just in case if he heading there? Adam said it couldn't hurt.

Adam got the cell phone and called Chase. Adam said hi is Chase there. Peter said yup and I think he went to bed a while ago. Adam said tell Chase the wolfman was by and he gone now but he was playing his games again. Adam said do You have any tack strip in your car. Peter said yes but why you want to know? You and Devvan pace them in front of the door just so if he comes throw, you can get some time if he steps on them. Dam that would hurt how did you think of that? Annette did Adam said and she can handle a gun to. Peter said she should be on the team.

Adam said I told her that. Adam said don't go out alone he could be close by. Peter said we bring the dogs out to. Ok see you in the morning if you need me call and I will be their as fast as I can. Peter said ok thanks for the heads up on and have a good night. Adam hung up the phone and Annette said they like my idea. Adam said yes and there want you on the team. Adam kiss her and they hug and try to sleep.

Peter and Devvan went out with the dog to the car and truck and got about ten strips. Peter and Devvan got back in side and the dog started to look funny. Peter said going get the other two up and I will set the tack strip. Devvan ran into Chase room and him and Marry was still up Devvan said we got a wolfman out side. Chase and Mary jumped up and got the guns and something on. Devvan returns to help Peter. Peter said I got the doors with strips on them now take some and put them down in front of the windows but don't get to close to them.

Chase and Mary came out and said where is Mr wolfman. Peter said best idea would be by front door. Ok Chase said lets get to the second floor. We can cover the land and there only one way up there. The group got the dogs and with to the second floor and set themselves for a fight. Peter said safety off the dog's look like the thing is close. The front door broke open. Peter said he inside get ready. Then the group heard a blood curling howl and the front door began ripped out its frame. Peter said I think Mr wolfman found the tack strip.

You could hear some thing in pain down stairs. The wolfman headed back out the door with a foot full of nails. The wolfman howled again from a longer ways away. The group with back down stairs and looked at the front door it was hit with so much power the door was in pieces . Peter said that tack strips worked great good thing Adam call use when he did.

Devvan said the wolfman is one hurting wolf tonight look at the blood on the floor he must have step right in the middle of it. Will Chase do you have anything to close the hole with Peter said? Chase said yes in the other room is panel wood and a screw gun. Peter and Devvan got the door close up and said its time for bed. Chase said you can sleep after that? Peter said yes the wolfman wouldn't be dumb to hit use again tonight. Chase said will any ways I think we should move to the second floor the give uses some more protection. Everyone moves to the second floor and they set guard all night.

Dannie was sleeping fine when she started to dream. The dream was ok she and Max were out back on the porch laying in the chair. Max said he had to go to the rest room and got up an went in. Dannie set back in the chair she could hear something like voices in the field. Dannie the voices said will the pain end for use. The voices seen to be getting closer. When will the pain end for use Dannie. Dannie sat up and could see people and bodies crawling to her. The bodies were the ones the wolf kill, but the hunters he didn't kill where there to.

One of the hunters pulls up a gun and shot one of the other hunters in the head brains came out and hit Dannie. The hunter said the wolfman still lives so we can't sleep until he gone. Dannie said I know but how can I help. The hunter said kill them and his family and set use free. Dannie said I've been trying but he will not die. Then just as she said that Tommy's head came rounding across the deck. The head stop at her feet and Tommy had tears in his eyes help me Dannie I 'm in pain stop the hurt. Dannie started to cry I'm trying what do you guys want me to do?

The group said kill the wolfman kill him. Dannie said I will please leave me alone. Then a voice from the other side of the deck said boo how save me, save me got too many to help not any back up sad. Dannie turned to face the voice it was the wolfman. She said you need to stay die so there's people can sleep. The wolfman said will you need to kill me then I guess. Dannie said yes that's a good idea kill you and burn you into steak. The Wolfman said I like my meat red and fresh as he bit into a legs here try some, but watch it the flatlanders will give you gas.

Dannie jumps up from her chair and said its time to die Mr wolfman. The wolfman jumps out the porch and head to the field. Dannie jumps down and follows me across the field. The wolfman turned around and said would like for you to meet my boys. Two half size wolfman came out with their Mom behind them. The wolfman said my family would like the bet you. Dannie said some other time it's time to die and you all are going to die. The wolfman said big words form a lone wolf bitch.

Dannie said not nice to call a woman that and I'm not alone. My two sisters are standing right behind you. The wolfman said ok then four again three sound fair to me. Dannie's two she when after the Mom and Dad and Dannie had the two boys. The boys were fast but not much skill and power. Dannie hit one of the boys and he went down hard. The other came at her and she stepped to one step side and grad him by the head and broke his neck.

The other one she step on his back and broke his neck. Dad wasn't happy As Dannie ripped the heads off his sons and walk over to him. Dannie held him in front of him and said time to going with your sons to hell. Dannie drops the head and ripped the wolfman head off to, the sister kill and took care of the female. The three stood in a circle and howled and then Dannie walks back to her deck and Max was just coming back out. Max said you getting some air? Dannie said something like that and her and Max went back in the house.

Dannie wakes up and Max was just sleeping away. Dannie got up and went to the bathroom and got some water. She came back out and got into bed with Max again. Max wakes up and said everything ok hun. Dannie said sorry didn't mean to wake you up, yes everything great. It was around 4am and the two hugs and kisses and went back to sleep until they had to get up in the morning.

Dannie could feel the warm body of Max and it made his feel warm and safe. Dannie slowly went back to sleep and had good dreams about her and Max. Dannie was sleeping until about 7.30 a.m. she turns over to look at the clock. Then roll back over and hug Max hun she said its 730 a.m. do up open today. Max said yes and his eyes open and he kissed Dannie. Max got out of bed and headed to the shower or at less that the way he was pointing.

Dannie smile may God that thing is big. Dannie was thinking of getting undress and joining him in the shower but said no she had to be good. Dannie got up and went down stair to make Max something for breakfast and see if Mom and Dad were dress and in the house. Dannie found Mom and Dad in the kitchen and making coffee. She walks in get too cold out last night you two.

Mom said we came back in because we wanted some food. Max came down the stairs and walk in the kitchen. Mom face turn red and she said sorry for last night. Dad said I'm not. Mom hit him and said yes you are. Max said this ok it's nice to see two people love each other the way you do. Max said and the way me and Dannie do. Dannie looks at Max and hugs him he so sweet isn't he Mom. Mom said yes he's just like your Dad in a way. Max drank his coffee and Dannie walks him to the door and out to his truck.

Mom and Dad said have a good day Max maybe see you sometime soon. Max said it was great seeing I mean bring here with you two. Dannie said I love you to Max and gave him a big hug. Max said love you to hun do you want me to stop after work tonight? Dannie said no I will be over before you get out and we can have some thing to eat and going up to your place.

Max said good sounds nice and kisses her again. Dannie watches as Max drove off and looks back at Mom and Dad. Mom said good bye Max's poo. Dannie said I bet you were the same way when Dad went to work. Dad said no she had my wallet to sleep with. Mom hit Dad and said you know I missed you when you went. Dad said I know and kiss her. Dannie stood there and said can I come in or you going to replay last night.

Mom said get in here you and lets think about the wedding day? Dannie said you know I was thinking about tomorrow would that did too soon. Mom said good for me how about you Dad. Dad said I'll clear the day. Dannie said we think we would do a summer wedding and have it in the field. That way we can make it a big one. Dad said I think I need a drink.

Adam got up and Annette was still sleeping he moves the guns back to the racks. The time was 8:00 am he got up and went for a shower. Annette heard the water running and got up the watch the news and make coffee. There was a knock at the door and a voice in the hall yelling for Annettte. Annette ran to the door and it was Bob. Annette open the door and Bob said good God Sis what happen last night.

Annette said why you say that? Bob said you been out here? Annette looked out the door and said oh it was just the wolfman last night stop to say hi. Adam came out of the shower and said hi to Bob. Bob said have a little fun last night? Adam said Annette told you about the wolfman? No your hallway said it loud and clear. Adam walks over to the door and looked out at the hall way. Dam I think that guys needs and nail job.

Adam said thanks to your sister he didn't do much. Bob said she shot the thing she's a dam good shot of a woman. Annette said better than big brother. Bob said a lucky shot that's all. Adam said what's that mean Annette? Bob was mad at me the first time we went hunting I shot a dear at a few feet away. Bob said a few feet how about a good hundred yard and one shot.

Adam said you're my new sharp shooter. Adam could hear someone in the hall he headed for the gun then Adam heard Chase voice. Adam went to the door and the team was standing they with dogs and everything. Adam said in a hunting mood today. Chase said as the group came in yup want some wolfman ass after what he did last night to my house. Chase said to Annette thanks for the idea last night the wolfman has sore feet from stepping on the tack strips.

Annette said dam he must be really mad now. Adam said what happen over there last night? Chase said the wolfman came throw the front door and it was blow to bits, but he didn't get in far when he made a bad step. Devvan said he made a hell of a noise the dogs ran for the back of the hall. Mary said he didn't do much but get out of there after. Adam said see Annette your idea to call them helped to.

Annette said I'm just glad I could help. Fred came throw the door and said ok did I miss anything? Adam said no Fred did anything happen at your place last night. Fred said no he didn't hear a thing last night. Adam said where's Peter. Chase said he was going to go home last night but the wolfman had other plans for use he went this morning and said he be back around nine.

Adam said good Patrick isn't open until then. Adam said Chase runs down stair and get one more AK and about five clips. Chase said is Annette and Bob coming with use today. No Adam said but I' m not going to leave them unarmed. Bob said do we get to run over to the shutting range to try them out? Adam said sure Chase bring a few more clips then. Bob looked at Annette and said sounds like fun sis. Annette said sure does' Bob.

Annette said we can shot the old bus to. Adam said make sure to leave some clips for at home use. Annette said we will hun and kiss Adam. Adam said maybe after this is all over I let you shot the 50 calibers. Bob said I would love to try that gun. Annette said now you did it Adam that's going to be all he we say today. Bob said not a thing wrong with enjoying a good gun. Chase came back in and said Peter down stairs now and handed the gun to Bob. Annette said you need a bib brother? Bob said no but maybe a smoke and he laugh.

Adam said you to be care and don't kill any flatlanders today. Annette said we'll try not to and kiss Adam on the chin. You be careful to don't swim with wolfs today. Adam said sure don't want to after last night. Adam and the team with down stair to the station and Peter was checking out his gear. Adam said that's a good idea lets make sure all gear is in working order. The group broke down guns and clean and oil them.

Peter said I got my gear in my car today so we can take the car. Adam said cool with me. Adam said we can bring the dogs in here and leave them so they don't get in the way of the gear.

Devvan said good they wouldn't go on the island anyway. Mary and Devvan went out a bought the dogs in. The group got the guns cleaned and oiled so they loaded up for the day. Adam said went we land over on the island me and Peter will work the den, Devvan, Mary and Chase I want you three on the top of the hill watching out for anything moving. Fred I want you covering me and Peter from the boat. Adam said let's get loaded and rolling. Adam said Fred you can ride with me and Peter. Fred said ok then I'm ready to kill some wolfman.

The team got under way and headed down to Patrick's place. Peter drove throw town and said you know it seems the number of hunters has gone down some. Adam said yes it does and I couldn't be gladder of it. As Peter was pulling into the rental area Adam said stop. Peter said what's up Adam? Adam said that's the car that pull away from the station yesterday. Fred said you sure? Adam said yes it got the same government plates on it the kid told me about.

Adam said Fred get your gun ready. Peter pulls up to the side of the building and Adam and Fred jumps out. Patrick came out of the door and said shit what did I do? Adam said where are the people who own that car Patrick. Patrick said they got the small boat off me and headed down the river that way. Adam said we need the big boat and now. Patrick said no trouble the wife inside with the baby.

Adam said you lock the place up and send her home because there's guys will shot anyone, you don't have to go with use Patrick if you don't want because it could be bad. Patrick said I the best one to drive the boat and I know the river better than you do. Ok Adam said but send your wife home to keep her safe, Patrick said go get loaded a I will lock up around here.

The team loaded the boat and Patrick got his wife and kid in the car and she headed home. Adam said let's go and see what these two are up too. Patrick said there's four of them. Adam said great as they pull away from the deck and headed down stream . Adam told Patrick to pull up behind the old bridge support in the middle of the river so they could look and see what was going on. As they came to the sand pit, Adam could see the small boat over near the island. Patrick stopped the boat behind the support. Adam moves the boat along the side so he could see what was up.

Adam sat down and looked throw his scoop to see what was happen. Adam said it looks like they are floating some thing into the den. Shit Adam said it looks like a bomb. Peter said you're right they're going to blow up the den. Adam said not if I can stop then. Adam said gave me the bull horn. Chase handed to Adam. Adam called out hay you on the island stop what your doing and put your hands in the air. Peter said get back behind the support they going to fire.

Adam grad the support and pulled the boat behind as the gun fire started. Some for the rounds hit the other side and hit the water. Adam said dam I just about had it with people shooting at me. Adam set down at the front of the boat and said when I say move pull the boat just out so I can get a clear shot. Adam said ok slow and Peter move the boat back out Adam could see the boat in his scoop he fired and the shot hit the small boat and ripped it in half.

The Man swam to the shore line and started the shot again. One of the man where trying to do some thing in the water. Peter said what he up to Adam. Chase said it looks like he trying to set off the bomb. Mary said the others are pulling him in to shore. Fred said he got some type of tiger in his hand. Peter said shot him before he sets it off, but he was to slow the man set the bomb off and the island went up in a big bang. Adam pulled the boat back behind the support and said get back everyone. Rocks, cement, dirt came flight from the island. The bomb must have been big. The sky was fulled with dirt and smoke.

Adam pulls the boat back out to see what happen the side of the hill and den with the man was gone not a thing but a big hole in the island. Patrick started the boat and pull it out from behind the support Dam everyone was shocked. Fred said dam those people are nuts aren't there. Peter said no really they know they wouldn't get away and did what there had to do. Adam said Patrick head over to the island.

Patrick turned the boat and went to the island. Adam said pull up to where the den was. Patrick slow down and stop where the den was, but not a thing was left not even a sign of the den. Fred said if the wolfman was in there he dead now. Devvan said did You hear that? Adam said what do you hear Devvan? I could he a howl over on the main land. Fred said yes I heard it to. Adam said so the wolfman wasn't here and those guys kill themselves needlessly.

Than Chase said what's that and was pointing to a cloud of black smoke than a small bang. Patrick said it looks like it from my rental place. Adam said will get use over there so we can see. Patrick turned the boat and said hold on as he ran the boat full out on the way back. Patrick said it looks like the car those guys had was on fire and it was. Patrick pulls into the deck and hook the boat up.

Patrick said dam thank you Adam my wife and kid went home. Adam said I'm just glad they are safe. Adam said the fire department is on it's way. Adam said Patrick you and Devvan stay here and tell the fire department what's going on and the rest of use will go make sure the island isn't burning and check for body part floating. Patrick said if the motor off the little boat is still good grad it f or me. Adam said sure Adam set behind the wheel of the boat.

Fred said dam there people are nuts. Peter said there are crazy then I've ever seen. Adam came around the corner and not any smoke but still some dirt in the air. Adam said Fred, Mary and Chase look over the shore line and both sides of the hill to see if you find any parts laying around and me and Peter will check the water way down stream. Adam said I don't think we will find much but we should look anyway.

Peter said yes that had to be twice the size of the bomb that blow off the second floor of the build at elm street. Adam said yup had to be. He said can even think of how much the people want this wolfman dies that they are willing to die for it. Peter and Adam went down stream and check the shore line and every thing they saw floating in the water around the island no luck no parts. Adam said well lets head back to the others and see if they found anything. Adam pulls up and Mary said you need to see this. Adam got off and hocks the boat up to a tree.

Mary said we didn't find any human part but did some animal parts. Chase showed Adam in one small corner of the old river drivers place was some hair and some blood but no real body parts. Adam said this could be what is left of the wolfman's family. That would set to reason why we hear the howl. Fred said dam we though the wolfman was hard to handle before we going to have to be on guard all the time now. Adam said afraid so think we are going to have to run armed night and day teams.

Peter said last night was just playing games he my be out for blood now. Fred said just wishes we know if it was all the family not just the kids. Adam said hard to tell. The group got back on the boat and head back up stream to Patrick's rental. Adam pulls in with he boat and the fire chief said is the island ok? Adam said the island is off and no bodies. Patrick came to Adam with a pale look on his face he showed Adam a small metal rod. Patrick said it was stuck in the chair my wife was setting in.

Patrick said thank you so much Adam of Making me send my wife and kid home. Adam said no trouble its my job. Adam and the team loaded everything back into the cars and got ready to head back to the station. Adam told Patrick after the fire is out have Linscott hall it off and charge to station. Patrick said sure and went back to his tailor and sat down. Adam and Peter went back to the station house and unloaded the car. The team went in and sat like they had a bad day.

Adam said it looks like we going to have to set guards up in the night from now on because the wolfman is going to be more then just mad at us. Fred said we should put one more in each in the night car to help keep an eye out of the wolfman. Adam said the big problem is we had a good idea where the wolfman was coming and going from but now he could be hiding any where. The group said will lets get to this setting up the night watch and get something to eat.

Adam said how about hot meat ball subs from ricks' Fred said that's sounds like a winning idea. Adam called Rick's an order the food. Fred said I'm going to have to cut himself out on the night watch my wife is all ready worry about me now. Adam said that's ok I wasn't going to ask you to help anyway because you have done so much now. Fred said thanks but I haven't been doing anymore then anyone else.

Dannie said Mom and Dad so are you two heading home or going to stay one more day. Mom and Dad said think we're going to head out soon and get home before the rain start tonight. Oh Dannie said it's going to rain tonight. Mom said the weather channel said for tonight. Dad said so hun what you going to do today? Dannie said I'm going into town and do my nails and have my hair done then my be go on to Max's for supper and wait for him to get done.

Mom said sound like a ok day. Will Dannie said I will let you to have the shower first and I will take my time and clean some things around here and do some dusting. Dannie went into the kitchen and cleaned up the counter and wash the dishes. Dannie open the back door and check to make sure everything was ok and the grill was off. The day seen to be nice and warm but a chill in the air. Dannie said would be good maybe later but she was going to be in town. Dannie came back in and Mom and Dad were just coming down stairs. Mom kiss Dannie and said we enjoy you and Max this week end I think he's a great man. Dad said so do I Max is a good man. Dannie hug and kissed them and walk them out to the car. Mom said we will call you when we get home.

Dannie said thanks you know how I worry about you two. Dad put the bags in the back of the car and Mom and Dad got in and left. Dannie stood there and watches as they went down the road. Dannie went back in the house and got out her dusting supply and turned the radio up and started to dust. Dannie loved loud music while she was dusting or cleaning it made the job fun. Dannie started to dance and dust in the living room and then came out into the front part of the house. Dusting was going good until the phone rang Dannie grads the phone and step off onto the porch.

Crissy said hi they Dannie how your Vacation going. Dannie said how's your honey mood going. Crissy said better than she had plan. Dannie said good. Crissy said are you and Max still seeing each other. Dannie said yes and we are doing great. Crissy said do You remember the old mill in the woods. Dannie said yes loved going up there and playing around. Crissy said me and Allen bought the mill and would like to have you and Max up for Dinner soon.

Dannie said Max would love that and me to. Good said Crissy so how about tomorrow night about 5:30 or so. Dannie said I will ask Max tonight when I go over to see him and will call you at this number and lets you know. Crissy said great hope you can make it. Dannie said I don't see any trouble with that and it will be fun to see the old place. Crissy said well hear from you soon then have a good day Dannie.Dannie said you to Crissy don't do anything I wouldn't do. Crissy laughs sorry we did all them. Dannie laughs and said good day.

Dannie went back inside and started to dance and clean some more. Dannie had the place looking and smelling great in no time. She went up stairs and got into the shower and started to clean her body. The water felt great and she washes up and got out to dry off. Dannie got into a pair of nice shorts and a warm T-shirt. She went around the house to make sure everything was locked and close just in case it did rain later because she was going to be over to Max's. Oh yes she said she needed to get my sweats because she was going to be at Max's tonight.

Dannie went out the door and headed to her jeep she looks at her jeep and said I going to need to stop and wash may truck. Dannie stops into the car wash and wash and rinses her truck. Dannie liked the way the Blue shined went it was clean. Dannie moves the truck to the side of the build and use the vacuum to clean out the inside of the truck then wipe down the windows and the dash. Dannie pulled out of the car wash and headed to get her hair done from Village hair and tanning. Dannie walks in and Pauline said I will be with you I a minute. Dannie like her because she know how to cut her hair. She also came there of tanning when the winter weather was around. Pauline was done with the hair dew she was on and said now how can I help you Dannie?

Dannie said would like to cut all the die ends off and shorting it just a little. Dannie sat down and Pauline began to cut she ask Dannie How everything was going in her life. Dannie said great she is dating Max from Max's place and everything is running smooth. Pauline said Max is a very nice man and very sweet. Dannie said yes he's the best boyfriend she has ever had. Pauline said great I'm glad of you. Dannie said thanks she was real happy to have Max .

Well Pauline said Dannie was that all you need today? Dannie said yup unless you do nails to. Pauline said no just hair and tanning. Dannie pay her an went to the nail place in Millinocket it was Mesue's a nice woman. Dannie sat there as she did her nails and the things she used smell really bad. Dannie then went over the Mill's to pick out some thing hot for Max. She found a red dress that hung to her body really well. She bought the dress and got a set for shoes to match.

Dannie went out with the dress on a headed over to see Max to see what was for dinner and ask about the supper at Crissy's place tomorrow. Dannie park out back and walk into the back door. She came around the corner and half the bar was watching her. Max turned around and said wow Dannie you look hot. Dannie said thanks by the way hun she said you know my boss Crissy don't you? Yes I do Dannie why? She wants use for supper tomorrow night about six. Max said sure sounds' good.

Dannie said I told her you would like it to. Max grad Dannie and gave her a big kiss. Dannie said what of lunch there stub. Max said a white fish with chilli. Dannie said that sounds really good. Dannie said is there a cold beer with that. Max said coming right up. Dannie sat at the end of the bar and just about all the man were watching her. Max came out with the fish and it looked great and smell great . Max came around the bar and said in Dannie's ear if you want you can eat in peace in the office.

Dannie said that's ok I don't mind man looking at me. Max said ok and kisses her. Be right back with your beer hun. Max came back and said did your parent head out? Dannie said yes and they both enjoy you and the week end. Good said Max I had a great week end . Dannie said so you still get off at 4:00 pm Max said yes and you don't have to hang here if you don't want .

Dannie said I think I will go up stair to your place after a while and take a nap. Max said cool with me. So Dannie Max said did, you get your hair cut to hun? Dannie said yes does it look good? Max said yes very nice. Dannie said thanks and kiss Max on the chin. Some of the Men at the bar said kiss Maxy poo can we get some bear ? Max said yes and kisses Dannie and went to service more bears.

Dannie tries the fish with chilli the two things made a great dish. Dannie drank her beer and ate her fish it was great Max sure was a good cook. Dannie finch the beer and fish. Max came back over and Dannie kissed him and said I'm going to run up stair and kick back until you get out. Max said ok and hugs her. Dannie went out the back and up the back stairs to Max's house she went in and closes the door and locks it. She went into Max's bed room and put on the sweats and sat on the bed to watch tv but she fell to sleep and began to dream.

Adam and the team were enjoying their hot meat ball sandwiches. Mary said hope the wolfman's wife and kids aren't still alive. Devvan said why did you say that? Because look how powerful the thing was just on his own, but if he hasn't got anything to live for he going to be harder than hell to bring down. Adam said I never though of it that way but you right Mary. Peter said I was thinking about the same well need to find a place where we can protect owner self and fight back at the same time.

Chase said Adam place is about the best place to make a stand unless we use the up stairs of my place. Chase said but it would leave your back open and Adam's place only has two ways in. Adam said yes but only gave use a small area to fight in. Fred said my place is like fort knocks. Adam said no way to get out and fight. Fred said yup your right.

Will Adam said I can surly hold everyone and me and Annette wouldn't mind. Peter's cell phone rang it was his boss. What's up boss Peter said. The boss said it sounds as if you wolfman hit again. This time in Medwy on the turn pike road. Peter said how may this time. Peter's boss said another four hunters. Ok boss I'm heading over there now. Peter said looks as if the wolfman has hit again. Adam said where this time. In Medway on the turnpike road Adam said yup I know where that is.

The team loaded up and headed to Medway. Adam's phone rang it was Al. Al said we have another wolfman man killing in Medway. Adam said already know heading there now. Al said up the end of the road right field by the lower end. Adam said good Call Mike and I will call you after. Al said good see you later. Adam hangs up the phone and said it at the top of the road on the eight. Adam came to the end of the road someone was standing there with the gate open and said just head down the road to your left and you will see the bodies.

Adam told the guy that he should be in a car or something. The guy said yes could he get a ride down to the truck it was never the bodies. Adam said yes jump in the back of the second car. Adam radio Chase and told them pick up the man. Adam and Peter started down the hill it wasn't long before they came on the screen. Adam said Dam this was the wolfman again. The field of gold was red all over now. Adam got out and get his guns. He walks over to the bodies and said ok Chase get the camera out and started to take photos.

Adam said see if you can find some ids. Fred, Devvan and Mary keep and eye out for our friend. Peter let see if we can find all the body parts and flag them. The hunter said I'm I free to go. Adam said yes but where's your truck.

The man said about a mile down the hill. Adam said let me run you down so we don't have to clean you up next. The man said thanks a this was his last day hunting ever again. Adam yelled to Peter and said he was going to drop this guy off down the road.

Ok Peter said see you in a few. Adam and the hunter headed down the road the truck was there and the man said thanks. Adam said I will let you go first and follow back up. Adam said we should get your statement on what happen. The man said ok then be right with you. The two went back up the road to the others. Mike was coming down the hill and stop in front of the screen. Mike got out and said the wolfman was mad this time wasn't he. Adam said why you say what mike? Mike said just looks at all the flags.

Mary was standing by the far end of the cars when she yelled to Adam. Adam grads his gun and went over. Did you see some thing Mary. Mary said I think I did. Mary said look way down to the end of the field at that big rock. Adam said there does seem to be some thing down there. Adam pulls up his scoop and it was the wolfman standing there crewing on what seemed to be an arm. Adam pulled the safe off and was going too shoot went the wolfman stepped behind the rock.

Adam said good set of eyes Mary it was to wolfman all right. Mary said did it seen he wanted to be seen. Adam said he did that at the last hunters scene but he didn't do the killing. Adam said keep watching let me know if you see them again. Mary said ok. Adam came back and help look for body parts. Peter said it doesn't seem he was very hungry. Adam said he had a meal to go this time. Fred said what do you mean by that? Adam said I just saw them with an arm in his hand. Fred said guess he wanted use to know this was his kill.

Chase all the guns seen to had been fire only ones so they must have been close together when they got hit. Mike started to get the bodies together and see how many parts were missing. Everyone helped but Devvan and Mary who were still watching for anything to move. The rest of the team got all the parts that were left and put them on the road to match then up with the right owner. The bodies were all there but two arms as Adam though.

Mike put them in the body bags as Adam looked of they IDS. Adam found that they were all flatlanders again in this group. Adam said this isn't good eight out of states so far killed. Chase said why kill four for so little food? Maybe like man he kills just for the fun of it Fred said. Adam said to Mary you seen any more of the wolfman. Mary said no not a thing. Will Adam said you and Devvan came on and they will pack up and going. Adam and Peter went over to the truck. Peter was ready to leave when he spotted some thing on Adam truck cover it was a hand. Peter said stop and the group draw their guns.

Adam said what's up Peter? Peter said look on the back of your truck cover. That's when Adam saw the hand. Adam yelled to Mike that he had other part. Mike came over and got he hand and could see were the wolfman walk up and set it there. Fred said sat dam more head games. Adam said he does have a big set of ball and I want to cut them off and feed them to him.

Devvan said the only reason he could get so close is because the dogs are at back at Adams place. Adam said yes we won't make that mistake again. Chase said dam right he could have killed use or about half of use before we could even had see him. Just then a big howl come from back down by the rock and the wolfman went into the woods. Adam said will lets load up and go back to the station to fell out a report. Adam and Peter got in the truck and said man why is he playing game with use. Peter said it could be that he is trying to get use to slip up and he can walk in and kill use with no trouble. Adam pulled in behind the others and everyone with in to the station. Devvan said your got your key Adam? Adam said yes please go get the rest of the team. Mary and Devvan went up stairs to Adams and got the dogs.

Annette and Bob were gone. Devvan and Mary took the dogs out side for some air and food. Then Mary and Devvan went inside with the dogs. Adam said we have come close to getting owner asses kick twice today good things for Patrick. Adam said and now we got the team back together.

They my be small but are a big help to the team. Will Adam said what we going to do about tonight all stay up stairs or all go over to Chase place. Devvan said it would be better to protect the smaller area then all the windows at Chase's. Chase said I don't care we can all crash here to see what will happen the next few nights. Chase said me and Mary will follow Fred home to see he get's there ok.

Then will all can order chinna from the mall up town for supper to night. Adam said ok then lets call it a day for Fred and get them home so we can set up for the night shaft. Mary and Chase follow Fred Home and so he gets back to his wife safe and sound. Mary and Chase Returned from Fred's and set down to rest. Adam said I'm just going to order a bunch of Chinese food and we can eat what we want.

Adam said he was going to run up stairs and would be right back. Mary said if you going to see Annette they weren't there when we left. Adam said thanks that why I was going up to see how she was doing. The Chinese food came and it was nice and this time, the group sat down to eat and shot the shit. Mary said I would think the wolfman foot should be ok in a few days. Adam said I would think so also the way he came back in the past.

So how do you think we and going to trap the wolfman and kill him Devvan said. Adam said I hope we can get him into the pit and block his get away.

Then it would be like shutting fish in a bowl. Adam said I just hope that the woman and kids were die so he don't have too shoot him. Devvan said that was running throw my mind. Peter said no madder how hard it would be we going to have to do it.

Chase said it would be hard but they would grow up to be killers some day. Mary said she was going up stairs to get some sleep she didn't sleep will last night. The group said it sounded like a good idea everyone could use some sleep. Everyone headed upstairs to kick back. Annette and Bob were at and pit at the end of the town that the locals used to line up their guns. Bob looked at Annette and said this is going to be fun.

Annette said sure is we need to let off a little stress. Bob said looks like a few out of state people are lining up guns . Annette and Bob pulled up and got out. Bob and Annette put a few old milk bottles up with water in them about every 20 yards and then four or five out a hundred yards or so. The flatlanders were cleaning there guns when Annette shot the first roll into the far away milk bottle it was a good hit and the bottle blow up. The flatlanders were unpressed by her shooting.

Bob took the next shot a hit the far bottle dead center. Annette said not bad Brother but watch this next one. Annette put the guns on full auto and dump a clip into the next bottle. The flatlanders seen to be a little on edge when she fired. Bob said see the old bus out there watch this Bob dump the clip into the front of the bus and the outer state man got the guns loaded and when. Annette said people don't like bigger guns. Bob said it's to bad it's fun to shot them.

Bod said I'm going to shot the bus one more and headed back out. Annette said sounds fun lets shot at the same time. Bob said sure get set and shot the two put a few new holes throw the bus with the guns. Bob and Annette headed back to Adam place and to clean the guns. Bob said we even made a few flatlanders run. Bob said that's all way a good day when that happens. Bob pull up in front of the build and said it looks like Adam home now.

Annette said hope it means the wolfman is die. Bob said me to it would make the woods a lot safer. Bob and Annette went up stairs to see how things were going. Adam said hi to Bob and Annette and said we needed a brake so we came up here. Annette said cool I could use a nap myself. Adam said we going to all stay here to make it more safe for all. Annette said good it would be Nice to have people around for a charge.

Bob said sis if your going to be ok I think I will head home to see how everything is going. Annette said call me if the family is going out tonight. Bob said sure thing sis I will let you know and kiss her on the chin. Adam said good bye to Bob to and he said did you like to gun? Bob said oh yes we did and it's right on the money as far as shooting. Bob said that's and headed to his car. The day was ok and the crew was falling to sleep. Annette got up and went into Adam's room and lay down went Adam to take a nap.

Dannie was sleeping and She was doing ok in her dream. Her and Max were on a small island and there were alone. Both of them had on very little and what they did have was see throw. Max built a small hut and made a fire in the center of the room. Max was cooking calms and fish. Dannie was getting some sun. The island was fun with it's clear blue water and white sand beach. Max and Dannie had dinner then went in for a swim. The water was warm and you could see throw it a long ways.

After the swim the two came back the beach and lay on some soft sand and began to kiss and hug. The sun was warm and the water would run up over them from time to time. Dannie was getting real turned on and was not going to stop this time when she made love to Max. She got on top of Max and was going to start the love making when the water hit her a she wake up.

Dannie lay there in the bed and said dam just as the fun part was going to start. Dannie sat on the edge for the bed and said how come I can't lose bad dreams like that. Dannie got up and looked around the house for something to make she found same fish and was going to make Max something good for supper. Dannie got out some potatoes and put the fish on the counter she found some lemon and pepper and was going to make lemon pepper fish and braked potato's and some peas.

Dannie put the potatoes on and started to clean house and dust for Max. Dannie still had the dream of the island still in he mind. She turned the radio on and cranked up the music. Dannie was making the house shine. She got the place clean and smelling good in less than an hour. Dannie check the potato and then put the fish in. She put the peas on top of the store on low. Dannie got some plates and candles out and put them on the table and turned down the lights.

The house was spotless and she turned the music down so that she could hear it and waist for Max. Max was coming up the steps because Dannie could hear his big feet. Max came throw the door and Dannie said hi hun have a seat and take a brake. Max looked around and said the house smell great and your cooking. Dannie said yes we are having lemon pepper fish brake potatoes and peas.

Max said it sounds good to me. Dannie said how did work going today. Max said great a lot better now. Max sat in the easy chair and Dannie gave him and beer. Max grad Dannie and gave her a big hug. Dannie went back to the kitchen and got the meal out and sat it on the table. Max got up and came over to the table and sat down. Max said everything looks good even the cook.

Dannie smiles hope its good hun. Max said it should be the lemon pepper is great on fish. Max took some of the fish and try it, it was great Dannie the fish are cooked just right. Max eats the meal and said will that's was great. Max said would you like to go and get an ice cream after supper. Dannie said sure it would be fun. Dannie and Max both cleaned up the plate's and put them in the sink.

Dannie kissed Max and Max hug he back. Max said really to going to Medway of ice cream. Dannie said yes anytime you are hun. Max said I just got to change a I'll be ready. Max went into the room and came back out with a T-shirt and some good looking jeans on. Max open the door and him and Dannie went out on the back porch to watch the sun in the west.

It was a big bright sun with not clouds around. Max and Dannie went down to the truck and got in. Max back out of the drive way and started to the little Chines place of ice cream. Dannie said this was a nice place before they put in the beer. Max said I liked it better when I was a kid and the old man owned it. Dannie said yes he was the best wasn't he.

Max went in and got two ice creams and came back out to the truck. Max said are you in a hurry to get back. Dannie said no why? Max said though we just take a ride up the Grindstone road to check the leaves falling. Dannie said sounds fun can we stop at the rest area to check the water level. Max said sure the ride up to the rest area was ten miles the road ran along the river and made of a nice fun drive.

Dannie said oh we forget to go to Crissy for dinner I'm going to call her and say I'm sorry for missing the dinner .but we can make it of after she gets back to work. Max said dam that's right tell her I'm sorry to hun.

The leaves looked like multicolor butterfly getting ready to leave all at the same time. Max said it's funny you can live here all your life and not really see the beautiful things it has to offer until you slow down. Dannie said so true You miss a lot of things just buy driving to fast or walking by and not seeing things. Max pulls into the rest area and him and Dannie get out to look around. Dannie said the good days for summer are passing fast. Winter will soon be on use. Max said yes winter isn't the best time in Maine I like fall and spring.

Dannie said me to Max fall and spring are the best times of the year. Dannie walks over to the river side and look at the running water. It was a little low for this time of the year. Max came over and hugged Dannie and pick her up and kiss her. Dannie put her arms around Max and kiss him. Max said I would like to have a house right up here and leave the town behind.

Max sat down with Dannie in his arms still on the side of the bank watching the sun go down across the water. Dannie said look Max a deer is on the other side getting some water. Dannie said how can people shoot something so pretty. Max said I don't know I couldn't kill one I know. Dannie lean back and kissed Max and said good because they seen to come up to me without bring scared.

Max and Dannie got up and headed back to town. Dannie curled up under Max's arm and hugs him. Max runs his hand throw she hair and it was soft and smelled sweet. Dannie ask do you want to stop and get a movie for tonight. Or just watch tv. Max said we can get a movie if you want is there anything new out. Dannie said I don't know but we can check to see.

Max turned the truck onto the main road and headed to Mary's Ann Market to see if they had anything new. Dannie and Max went in and to the left to the video area. Max said find anything good. Dannie said no but this one sound funny. Dannie said good we have a movie now some popcorn and we should be good to go. Max said are we forgot anything. Dannie said I'm set you set Max or you want something sweet. Max said I think I'll have a thing of dots those are all ways funny at movie time.

Max and Dannie went back to the bar and went up stairs to Max's place. Dannie went into the bed room with the movies and sat on the bed. Max grad a few beers out of the ice box and came into the room. Dannie said lets watch the movie if it's no good we can turn on the tv. Max said want me to pop your popcorn of you. Dannie said sure hun. Max went into the kitchen and put the popcorn on for five minutes.

Max came back in the room an Dannie was under the covers. Dannie said all I'm missing now is my big man. Max sat the popcorn down and got in beside Dannie. The movie came on it was a funny both Max and Dannie were laughing that the group. Dannie and Max were having a good time and enjoying the popcorn it was nice and fresh. Dannie could see the moon coming up out side and it was going to be a full moon.

Dannie sat the popcorn on the stand next to the bed and turned over and hug and kiss Max. Dannie and Max forgot all about the movie. Dannie said I'm sorry Max but I just want to have you closer. Max said the same we both going to need cool shower aren't we Dannie kisses him again. Max kiss her on the head and said love you hun. Dannie said love you to baby.

Adam and the group got up the make some thing for supper. Annette said we have hamburger patties' and lots for rolls. Annette said Adam do you have any potato I can cut them up for fries. Adam said yes but you don't have to cook for use. Annette said I cook you guys clean. Adam said that's a good deal. So Annette said so only thing missing is a beer an something for after. Adam said me and Peter can walk over to Rick and get something.

Annette said good she watch Adam and Peter starts to walk out the door without their guns. Annette yelled hay were your guns. Peter and Adam both looked at each other and said good call their chief. Devvan and Mary said we going to take the dogs out to hold up. Adam and the group went over to Rick and got beer and some clips. On the way out of the store some local kids were setting out front. Adam said isn't it about time to head in for he night. The kids said the wolfman isn't going to come into town.

Adam said he been here the last few nights. One said just trying to scare use like Mom did. Adam said follow me for a minute want to show you some thing. The boys went with Adam and Peter. Adam said walk up the hall way and look at the walls. The kids said so what's this. Adam said the wolfman's calling card he left it last night. Adam open the door and went in with the food and shut the door.

Peter said your not going to leave him out there are you. Adam said no give them a second and you'll see. A knock came at the door the kids wanted to know if Adam would walk them home. Adam said yes just a minute. Peter said I will go with you Adam and Peter went out with the kids that lived by the old church. The kids said thanks and went into the house. Peter said just another day as a small town cop.

Adam said yes isn't it great.

Peter said it sounds great but you get too close to the people. Adam said that's part of the small cops life. Adam and Peter got back to Adam's place and just in time for hamburger and fry and beer. The night was going good no signs of the wolfman. About nine the group set up guards. Adam said two on the rest sleeping switch every two hours. Adam said I will take the first two anyone else Annette said I'll take the other side.

Adam said Annette your don't have to do this. Annette said that's ok gave use more time to sleep. Adam said keep an eye on the dogs too there seen to know when he's around. Annette said you think he going to show tonight? Adam said you never know because he hasn't anything to lose. Annette said why didn't he hunt down the government people that killed his family? Adam said I couldn't tell you that maybe he did and we don't know about it.

The time was around 6:30 pm the sun was down and the streets were closed. Annette said I see something move in the dark by McLaughlin's auto. Oh she said just a homeless person looking for a bed for the night. Adam said hope he locks the doors. Annette said most of them do. Adam said that can be much of a life moving from town to town not know where your food is coming from. Annette said some chose to live that way. Adam said there goes Kevin down the street Annette said they have been doing a good job.

Adam said yes I have not hear anything bad about them in the last few weeks. The first hour went by fast. Yup Adam said hope for a quiet night tonight. Annette said I sure could use a good nights sleep. Adam said it looks as of Rick going to close soon he throw out his trash. Adam said I like that store but it's a little too small to be much more than it is. Annette said anyone moving over there? Adam said no it quiet over here. Annette said its the same a good night even for a full noon.

The shy was bright and you could see just about every thing the moved. You could tell it was a cold night the wind moved with an almost evil chill to it. Adam felt a chill round up his back. Adam said its eight time to switch watches. Annette this is fun can I stay for the next two hours? Adam said if you not sleepy at all. Annette said no I'm ok until ten or so.

Adam said same here the team could use a little more sleep than they got last night ok you're on. Annette said it same funny that I want to be the one to kill the wolfman and I can understand why? Adam said I can under stand why you would you like to know? Annette said yes show me how good of a cop you are. Ok Adam said you can't help your kid and grandkids from bringing killed and you're mad as hell and you want someone to pay for it, But I rob you of the kill when I shot asshole last night.

Annette was quiet and didn't say a thing because she knows that Adam was right she wanted to be the one to kill the son of bitch. Adam said hun you ok? A voice broke the still it was Peter he said Adam go to her and I 'll watch your post. Adam got up and went into the bed room and found Annette crying in a soft voice. Adam said I'm sorry hun didn't mean to came out with that in this way. Annette said yes I need that I glad that I wasn't going nuts I wanted to kill him and you did rob me of that.

Adam said now you look at it aren't you glad he got what he should have. Yes Annette said to Adam and I glad my man was the one who protected me and my brother. Adam said love will make some people do things they wouldn't do other wise. Annette said I know I wanted to kill him so bad I could feel it deep in my soul. Adam said as he shut the door can I tell you something now that must stay between use. Annette said yes.

I kill that man because I felt the same way I did when I found the one who kill my Mom and Dad. I though if I killed this person some how it would bring back Mom and Dad . The man was unarm and in the woods when I came across him. He ask me not to kill him but I said did you gave Mom and Dad that chose. He said no and I shot the first knee than I shot the second knee. And when I armed at his head I ask did you think at the time you were doing the right thing.

The man said no I never could think it was right. I almost let him go but he tries to pull a knife on me and I said this is for Mom and shot him dead. Annette was still and did say a thing she know that was the same thing she was thinking at the time. Adam open the door and said is everything ok out here Peter? Peter said yes all is will out here. How about you two need someone to broke you? Adam said no me and Annette will stay for the next shift. Ok Peter said I have this place.

You and Annette cover the bed room side and I will let you know when the time is up. Adam went back to the room and left the door open. Annette and Adam set their guns to one side and hug and set in front for the window to watch. Adam said the night seems cold and Annette said no it seems right now. Annette hug and kiss Adam and said did it make you feel better when you did it?

Adam said no Mom and Dad were still die. Annette said you know I feel the same way my kids are still die. Adam said it's only human to think that way Annette. Adam hug her and said the pain we get better with time but you shouldn't block out the good times you have with the kids before this. Annette said that's true I did had a lot for fun and good times with all of them.

Adam said I was glad I could help you same and that it was not you but everyone that though that way. Annette said I think I love you? Adam said I don't have to think I know. Adam sat there watching out the window until 10:00 pm then Annette got Chase and Mary up to take there place. Adam and Annette went to bed with a new understanding of each other and a new love for each other. The night was going good no sign of the wolfman.

Dannie fell to sleep in Max's loving arms and was off to dream land again. Not the dream land for milk and honey. Max was still watching the movie but know Dannie was asleep Max felt happy that Dannie trusted him so much that she would sleep in his arms. Dannie began to dream of the day the two young girls came into the modeling studio. The day was good and Dannie was in the middle of make up when she could feel something wrong.

The three for them went into the studio and Dannie put the music on like last time. The girls started to dance and do a good job when one of them had red coming from the front of her dress. Then the other one looked at her and screamed. The wolfman step up and ran the rest of his hand throw the body of the first girl then said can I cut in and drove his other hand throw the second girl.

Dannie drops the camera that she was using and headed to the stage. She said why did you kill these girls isn't it me you really want. The wolfman said you don't know what I want from you by now then you are dumb. Dannie said you want me as a females don't you. The wolfman howled don't think of yourself as so good looking as to be mind. Dannie said what do you want?

The wolfman said I want your soul and to became the top dog. Dannie said you can't have my soul and you never be top dog. The wolfman throw the two girls at her and said then I will kill you and your father. Dannie said it seems you have done a poor job it so far. The wolfman stepped off the stage and looked at her and said the time isn't over for me and you and I still have a charge to get you.

Dannie said came on big man and try see if you have the nuts in you now. The wolfman made a jump at Dannie and Dannie hit him and knocked him backwards. Dannie said so big man how do you plan on turning me. The wolfman said you'll see little one you'll see.

Dannie was mad a hit the wolfman and knocks him back into the center of the room. Dannie jumped up to face him head on and he was gone. Dannie looked around the stage and he was no where to be found. She could hear a voice in the dark saying all I need is more time little one and you be mind. My die little wolf slut. Dannie yelled came take me now you shit of brains. The wolfman said good your getting weak. Dannie said weak or not I can still kick your ass and kill you.

That's the way I want you come to me with your pain. Dannie could see the wolfman behind the set. Dannie came at the wolfman and he graded her and held by both arms your getting there sweet thing you're almost mind. Dannie said no I love Max and his the only man for me. Dannie could feel here power returning she broke the wolfman hold and throw him into the wall.

The wolfman went right throw the wall and landed in the hall way. Dannie ran out into the hall to see the wolfman run out the front door. Dannie started to run and chase down the wolfman. She came out of the building and didn't see what way the wolfman headed. She looked around and smelled the air she couldn't tell where he was. Dam she though this would be the first time he got away from me.

She started down the Main street heading out of town. She felt that this was the way the wolfman went. Dannie stepped up her pace and started to run. She saw a foot print in the soft sand of the road and began to run faster. Dannie had and idea that he was heading back to the island throw the woods. Dannie said I will run down the road and make it there before him.

Dannie made it to the pit and went down to the old bridge and sat and waited for him to show. It wasn't long and the wolfman hit the water just up stream from her Dannie stood up as the wolfman swim by her and said out for a dip? The wolfman looked up in shock as Dannie came crashing down on him. Dannie graded the wolfman head a ripped it off. Dannie went to the shore went the wolfman head still in her hand. Dannie looked that the face and said home is just a head of you.

Dannie turned the head to the island and gave it a throw you could hear the wolfman's head say some thing as he crash throw the trees on to island. The wolfman said it's still not over. Dannie could hear a voice and feel something around her. It was Max Dannie, Dannie Max said are you ok. Max said you were try to get off the bed in your sleep. Dannie wakes up and said I'm sorry just a bad dream. Max held her and said your safe now hun your man is here.

Dannie hugged and kissed them and said my man is surely here all right. Max said the movie is over would you like to watch the tv or just go to bed. Dannie said I don't care I'm sleepy but if you want to watch tv go right ahead. Max said I'm feeling sleepy to so Max shut off the TV and they lay there and hug and kiss for a while. Max said you know Dannie I would like to do something with you if you want.

Dannie said sure as long as we don't have to get nude and run throw the bar. Max said will not that but it's something I always wanted to try. Ok Dannie said I'm in. Max said grad your pillow and follows me. Max grad two big blankets and his pillow and went out on the Porch.

Max lay down the big blanket and him and Dannie get into it and he put the second one over them. Max and Dannie looked at the shy it was a cold night but heat from them made them warm. Dannie said is this all you wanted to do? Max said we will keep the rest for when we get married. Dannie curls up in Max's warm arms. Dannie looked at the shy and said do you ever wonder if there's anyone out there. Max said bet someone up there is say the same thing. How can we say we are the only thing alive in the world?

Dannie said it nice out is it cold or just me. Max said if your getting cold we can go back in. No Max I just want you to and she put Max's hand on his chest. Max said oh my your real cold sorry we can go in now. Dannie said not cold Max. Max said oh sorry for that then. Dannie said ok. I'm having fun Dannie said did You hear that? Max said what? It sound like a big jet flying over head. Max said it is look there you can see the lights flashing.

Max said maybe we should head in can your feel what it feels like snow. Dannie said I think you're right its is snowing. Dannie and Max got up and got the blanket and the pillows and headed in. Max and Dannie went in the room and sat on the bed with a blanket around them and watch the snow. Max Move down to his pillow and Dannie slide up to him. Dannie curl up to Max and said good night love you hun. Max said as he put his hand on her breast love you to hun then he moves his hand down and hugs her. The two with to sleep with dreams of each other dancing in the back of they heads. The snow stop out side and the night looked white and clean.

Chase and Marry were watching the road of anything that moved. Marry looks out and said Chase it snowing. Chase said I see what, will that's Maine for you sun one minute and Snow the next. Marry said it should be better to track the wolfman in if it makes a few inches. Chase said its midnight should we wake the others Mary said lets do one more hour than get Peter and Devvan up. Chase said ok now one more hour isn't going to hurt. Chase and Mary went for other hour and got up Peter and Devvan. The night was almost over and no signs of the wolfman. About six o'clock now and the dogs seem the be ok.

It was about 7:00 a.m. when Fred came up the stairs. Fred knocked on the dog and Peter came over to let him in. Fred said see you guys had fun last night? Peter said no it was quiet all night. Fred handed Peter an eye and some type of tracker device. Where you find that Fred Peter said? Right here in font of the door. The others were coming out of the bed Adam looked at Peter and said what you got there? Peter said I think the wolfman left use a messenger last night.

Peter turned and handed the eye and tracker to Adam. Dam Adam said now what type of game he want to play. Devvan said Maybe he telling use we need to learn. Peter said he could have just left a note. Mary said so what do we learn to. Adam said maybe this thing. Adam looked the unit over and said no switches how's it work. Fred said twist it see if it's a twist type switch.

Adam grad the device by both end and twisted it and the three lights to came on. Adam move around the room and the lights didn't charge. Adam headed to the back door and one light got faster while the other one got slower. Adam said yup it's some type of tracking device. Now the big question what is it for, tracking use or the wolfman. Chase said maybe the owner of the eye. Adam said the only way we are going to find out is to track the lights. Annette said you guys started with the showers and I will make coffee.

Fred said I will run over to Rick's and grad some donuts. Devvan said hold on Fred we can walk the dogs at the same time. Fred and Devvan and the two dogs went out to ricks'. The sun was just coming up and the air had a chill in it. Fred looked up and said pink shy in morning not good. Devvan said isn't that for sailors? Fred said yes but we're up the river without a motor. Devvan laughs guess you could say that. The group got in the shower and after they got out Annette had coffee for them.

Devvan and the Fred came back in with fresh donuts for all. After everyone was feed and showered Annette said Bob should be here soon so you guys can go if you want. Adam said you sure Annette? Annette said yes as she heard he brother pull up out side. Adam said will lets find what this thing is tracking and where we need to go. Adam kiss Annette and said see you later. Annette said be right here or some place close by.

Adam and the group started out the door as Bob was coming up to see Annette. Good morning Bob Adam said your sis is up and waiting. Bob said good she can be slow sometimes. The team loaded up the trucks and headed for the lights. The first try was to head out of town but the light almost when out so Adam turned around and headed back to town. He went two the other side of town and same thing. Adam said to Peter looks like the thing is still in town.

So Adam went half way in town and started to go up throw town the lights started to flash faster and it seemed they were headed for elm street again. Peter said I think you're right it looks like the same house as before. Adam pulls up out front and the lights were almost solid. The team armed themself and said let go. Adam and Peter lead the group into the house. Adam said what this thing was for we are almost on top of it. Peter moved throw the door first and he saw someone headed sticking throw the wall. Peter said it looks like the wolfman found his friends off guard.

Adam said the lights are almost stopped so what it is should be in that room. Adam and Peter stood on one side of the door and Fred came up to open it. Adam said on one ready go to door open wide and the place looked like the miller's barn. Five men lay die on the floor with arms and legs ripped off. Adam moved into the room and he said looks like we know who the eye was from. One man set in the middle with one eye and it looked like a hole punch throw his rib cage.

Adam use the tracker to find the reason for the lights. On the desk next to the man was a small round metal device that make the lights solid as Adam set the unit next to it. The thing looked like a dime. The group all came into the room. Adam said to make sure not to move anything until we get a charge to go over the seem. Peter said I will go and get the camera and the kit.

Chase Adam said take the other and look around the place. Chase and the others went looking around for any clues. Adam pick up the metal part and looked at it closely. Adam could see the word's satan9 on the front of the plate. Adam looked around and could see the hard drive in one machine was still there. He went over to the screen and turned it on. It seems the man in the chair was trying to clear the hard drive but the wolfman got him before he could start.

Chase and the others came up stairs from the basement and said we need to move out side of here. Adam said why? Fred said the down stairs is set with a bomb and isn't small one. Adam said this machine still has a hard drive in it. Devvan said just grads' it and pulls it out with the handle on the top. Ok Adam said you guys get outside and behind the trucks. Adam handed his gun to Chase. What you going to do Adam Chase said. I'm going to take this hard drive and hope it isn't the switch for the bomb.

The group cleared the house and Adam close his eyes and pull the drive. It came out like a charm and he was still alive. Adam turned to head for the door and he heard a click. He turned to the machine to see a timer come on 20 seconds. Adam made a run for the door as he came throw the front door he yelled get on the other side of the trucks. The team head for the other side and Adam know he wasn't going to make it. He jumps into the back of Devvan's truck and pull himself next to the rail. The house went up like a roman candle and the hold area was fulled with smoke and small parts of the house.

The fire truck were called out and they came out and started to put out the fire. Adam looked at the hard drive he was holding and put it in his inside jacket pocket. Adam said to hi self you must be one hell of a drive to have all this to happen. Adam said lets get clean up back at the station and go over thing from there. Adam the fire chief said now what do you want me to write in this report? Adam said wood stove fire I don't know think of something.

Adam and the team went back to the station the regroup. Adam said now we need someone who can get into this hard drive and tell use what's on it. Fred said I know just the person to do the job. Adam said ok who than Fred? Fred said the woman that knows everything my wife. Peter said she works with computers. Fred said if she can't get into that drive then no one can.

Ok Adam said call her up the ask her if she would do some police things for use. Adam said also ask her what she want's for lunch. The hold crew will be over for lunch and we will cook and clean up while she works on the drive. Fred called his wife and she said yes and she was so happy to meet the team. She said are the dogs were coming, too? Devvan Jean wants to know if the dogs are coming, too? Mary said sure we can bring them.

Fred held the phone away from his ear you could hear her loud a yell. Fred said ok what do you want for dinner? Jean didn't even stop to think fly clams and Maryann's potato salad. Fred said ok see you soon. Fred put the phone in his pocket and said Dam hope she doesn't have a heart attack.

Mary thanks she never see a dog and had one to touch. Devvan said her life must have been lonely. Fred said yes but she not going to let me hear the end for this day for weeks too came.

Dannie could feel the sun in her face and the day warming rays. Dannie sat up in bed and Max slowly came too. Dannie could still see some of the snow from last night hanging from the window. Max looked at the clock 8:00 a.m. wow I sleep well last night how about you Dannie as Max hugs her a kiss her good morning. Dannie said it must have been the fresh air last night because I had a great night last night.

Max said I've got to work until four today then run to Bangor for more beer would you like to come along and we can go out to eat? Dannie curled up to Max's warm body and said yes love to hun. Dannie said what would you want of Breakfast this morning. Max said you know what sounds good on a morning like this French toast and hot coca. Dannie eyes open wide and said your right Max that does sound good.

Dannie got out of bed and Max started to get up behind her. Dannie turned and push him back down on the bed I'm making breakfast and you stay here in bed. Dannie pulls the covers up on Max and kiss him as she got back out of the bed. Max though to himself he was a lucky man too had someone like her to be his wife soon. Dannie came back with breakfast and a kiss for Max. Dannie sat at the edge of the bed and had some French toast with Max.

Max smiles at her and put some butter on her lips and kiss it off. Max was done with the meal and said it was great. Dannie said thanks and you should get up and hit the shower soon do you think. Max got up and headed for the shower. Dannie watches as Max walk across the floor nice ass she was thinking. Dannie lay down on the bed and watch out the window as the days sun warm the parking lot below. Max came out of the shower and said next.

Dannie kiss him as he walks by. Max went into the room and got into some work cloths. Dannie came out a little wait looking like a dream. Max stopped as he saw her dam he said you look great hun. Dannie said with a smile thanks their stud. Max laughed and kissed her. Max said so what your plans for the morning. Dannie said going to wait until noon watch the one movies we rented, then have dinner with this stub of a bar keep.

Then try to pick him up after work and go out with him. Max said lucky man to have a beautiful woman after him. Max and Dannie went down to the bar. Dannie said I got the floor go and get the bar ready Max. Max said ok but you don't have to help if you don't want to. Dannie said get the beer I love helping my man. Max went out to the other room and got a few cases of bar and restock the bar.

Max came back out and watch Dannie swept the floor and though she looked hot. Dannie looked back to see Max looking at her ass. Dannie said hun your not going to get much work done by looking at my ass. Max came back to life oh yes work. Dannie got the floor done and picked up dirt from the floor.

Dannie sat on top of the bar she was thinking for something. Max came back out and said good job hun. Dannie said only the best for my man. Max started to walk by her behind the bar, she put one leg out and stop him then

Max turns to her and kisses her she Throw the other leg around Max and grad him and plant a kiss from hell on him. Max was so special that he couldn't speak. Dannie said just remember this for after we are married. Max said I can stop thinking for it now. Dannie held him and there kiss until it was time to open the doors. Dannie looks up at the clock and said its time to open.

Max handed her the key would you mind open the doors and turn on the open sign. Dannie didn't know why but went she drops off the counter she know why. Dannie hug Max and said I'm sorry hun. Dannie went to the door and open it and turns on the sign. She came back to the counter and Max was starting to be able to move again. Dannie kiss Max and said see you at dinner time. Max kiss her and slap her on the butt on her way out love you hun he said. Dannie turned around and said love you to big man. Dannie went back up stairs and put the movies in that her and Max rented the other night.

Adam said will lets get some food and head over to Fred's place. Fred said good my wife will have a great day today. Adam and the group went down stairs and Adam saw the sea food truck just up the road. Adam said good Peter ride with me, Chase run down to Marry Ann's get some fresh corn and clam mix with one beer. Chase ,Devvan and Mary went to the store.

Adam and Peter went to the clam truck. Adam pulls in and ask the guys how much his clam were. The guy told him and Adam said good gave me 15 lbs. of clams and five of you biggest lobsters. Peter said you hungry Adam? I just want to get something else because everyone isn't into clams. Adam gave Chase a call. Are you still at the store Adam said? Chase said yes get some potato salad about 5 lbs Adam said.

Chase said ok see you over there then. Peter said this is starting to be a good old new England clam's bake. Adam said I just remember something thing. Peter said don't tell me you need butter to. No Adam said you never been at Fred's house have you? Peter said why he live in a pig pen. Adam laughs and said no but your not soon going to forget it and his wife.

Peter said ok Adam tell me now before I have to run of the hills. Adam said ok Fred lives underground. Peter said what you say underground. Adam said yes underground you just wait until you see this place. The team got to the place and everyone had they hands full. Fred came out you guys need help? Fred said my wife is pacing the floor we better get down there.

Fred said by the way dogs in last Jean never see one that she could pet so she a little afraid. Peter said what afraid of a dog? Fred said doesn't worry Peter she will tell you everything. Peter said don't tell me she Jack the ripper kid. Fred and the group stop and laugh their heads off at Peter. Peter said what do you want me to think those dam stories of his.

Fred walks throw the door the others came throw and Peter stood there and said what the hell is this place. A voice from the bottom of the steps said come on down don't be scared. The group move down the stairs as Peter looked all around the place. Jean grads Fred is that the dogs oh may God they are sweet. Mary Jean said what is their names. Mary said Maxy and Pad Jean laughs hope their female. Jean said do they bit.

Devvan said no and laughs but there my lick you to die. Jean said can I pet one of them. Mary said sure just call they're name a say heal and she came right over and set next to you. Jean said Maxy heal the dog came over and sat next to her. Fred said come on hun stop shacking and pet her see I will show you. Fred got down and starts to pet the dog Jean slowly put her hand on the dog and start to feel it's fur. Jean started to cry. Mary said what's wrong Jean?

Fred said she happy she never been this close to a dog before. Jean looked over and pad was just setting their Jean said pad heal. Pad came over to set on the other side of Jean. Jean sat on the ground and hug both dogs the fur is so soft and warm. Fred said you going to be with the dogs I will show the others the kitchen so they can unload. Jean said yes, yes hun.

Fred said follow me you guys and we will up pack the food. Fred walks down the hall and to the right into the kitchen. Peter said dam this is big what you cook for an army . Fred said my grandpa did all this work and left the house and land to me. Oh and as soon as we get back in the other room my woman will tell you about the light and thing it's her home she wouldn't want me to tell the story.

Jean came around throw the door and said Fred right he get the stories out side and I tell the inside trails. Sorry Peter I forgot that you weren't here the last time. My name is Jean and welcome to my home. Peter said is the rest for the house like this? Jean said I think you'll find it better. Oh yes Peter the lights you see, I can't be out in the sun or light that's why we have this type of lighting.

Peter said it was a little dark at first but my eyes have getting use to it. Will we can take a look at the house then Fred can show you the pots and pan. Did you guys get potato salad and lobsters to. Adam said you can smell them? Jean said yes it's from bring in here the air smells the same all the time so when something new comes in it's a enjoy to smell. Will let do the house the first stop is the bathroom.

Jean said this is one of my best places. Jean walked in and said here the best part a water fall shower. Jean turned the water on and it comes out like a wall fall and four light in the water keep changing the color of the water. Next was the toilet. The thing was gold on silver color. The mirror was four feet by eight feet long. The floors look like stone. Jean said will this the first room.

The bedroom was next Jean open the doors to the room and the roof was unreal must be 20 feet up there. The bed looked like two king beds put together. Jean said Mary come here. Jean said push that button there? Mary pushes the bottom and the door in the wall open to two walk in closet. Jean said his and hers. Fred said more like hers and hers. Jean said you would think the bed and floor would be cold, but go ahead and feel them.

Adam put his hand on the floor it was warm but not hot and the bed the same way like someone was in it already. Fred said come over here and I will show you how he did it. The group went to the other side of the room and Fred pick up a set of small stones in the corner. Fred said see the water run under the floor it's warm water that heats the floor and the base of the bed. Peter said if you would have told me this in a story of yours I would say you were full of shit.

Fred and Jean laughs she said that's why it's my story because you don't have to clean off your feet when he done. Jean said this next room my be a little over powering the first time you walk in. Mary said is this the room with the river and pond in it. Jean said yes it is you have a good recall for things? Jean said I send a lot of time in here swimming and enjoying the water fall as I write.

The group came around the corner and Jean very right the hold team said shit this is big and the pond looks fun to swim in. Jean said Fred's best fishing hole to. Fred said can you see the wall fall in the back over there in the corner it make most of this went grandpa found it he left it just as it was. Jean said I'm going to go out in the hall and let Fred show you the water fall. Jean said I will be in the computer room. oh Adam said you may want this to look at Jean while you're there. Adam handed her the hard drive.

Jean started out the door Adam she said how long have you had this drive on your. Adam said sent this morning after the house blow up. Jean said Fred wait a minute Fred on open the water fall. Jean said come here Adam and let me show you something. Adam came over and Jean said you see the side of this drive this part that runs all the way throw? Adam said yes what is it. Jean said its c4 plates.

You mean it a bomb Adam said? Yup sure is this drive was make if someone got it and tried to plug it in it would blow up. Adam said how big of a bomb. Jean said more than you would care to set off in your pocket. Fred said can you disarm this one. Jean said yes and it's a good thing Fred got it to me or a lot of you guys would been die now. Fred said you sure hun your can handle it. Yup seem this same drive on the internet and it gave a step by step disarming blue prints.

So don't come into the computer room until I come for you. Fred said ok hun be careful. Jean went down the hall and you could here the door close. Adam looked at Fred and said you sure she can do this? Fred said she wouldn't be go in there if she couldn't do it. Fred said ok the water fall. Fred pulls the large metal handle and the sun hit the water fall and the light show up the pond. Dam Devvan said this is just to cool.

Fred said if you look at the water you can see fish moving around in it. The pond was as clear as glass. Ok Fred said and close the light back up. Fred said we can go back to the kitchen and get things started for lunch. Adam said you sure we should go with Jean in there. Fred said she ok and she said not to bug her remember. Ok you guys you heard the man lets go get a party goes of Jean so she can eat when she done.

Dannie was feeling great she did all Max's wash and gave the place a good cleaning. The movies were ok but not as fun as watching them without Max. Dannie looked at the clock it was almost time to go down and see Max. She went into the bathroom to freshen up. Dannie was so happy that she almost forgot the time. Dannie put on some clean cloths that she had with her. Dannie went out the front door and down the stairs to see her man.

Max was behind the counter and he was doing ok. Dannie walks up and sat down at the end for the bar. All the man in the bar know her and stayed away because Max was a good man. Max saw Dannie and said what would you like hun? Dannie said something for dinner and a beer and a big kiss from my man. Max said well that sounds good and gave her a big kiss. Some of the men at the bar said Max's poo how come we don't get a kiss.

Max said because you my like it too much. Max said here's your beer hun and do you want the special today? Dannie looked up it was chilli with fish. Dannie said yes hun and a dinner roll with it if I could. Max said ok and went out back to the kitchen to get her food. Dannie looks around the bar a few local and some flatlanders but not really busy. Max comes back from the kitchen with Dannie's meal and said is that all hun. Dannie said I don't see a beer sweet checks. Max said oh ok didn't forgot I was just catch off guard by your beauty.

Dannie smile and said they better be a good kisses with that. Max said right away there hun and got her a draft beer from the tap. Max said here you are and walk around the counter spin her bar stool around and gave her and kiss from hell. Dannie was very special. The guys at the bar started to howl and said way to go Max. Max set Dannie back on the stool and went back behind the bar. Dannie was still in the clouds from the kiss. Max said anything else hun? Dannie said a smoke my help.

Max laugh and said now you know how I felt this morning. Dannie face turned red and she said oh yes I though that was fun. Max said I see you enjoyed it to. Dannie tries to cover up a little until she cold back down. Max went to serve some more beers to the others. Dannie was enjoying her meal when someone comes up behind her and said hun can I get some of that loving to. Max came down and said you better set your drink down and leave right now if you know what's good for you.

Dannie put her hand out to stop Max and said it's ok he drunk. Max said it's never ok to say things like that a woman. Dannie said cool down Max an held him back. The guys said yes Max stay behind the blonde with tits so you don't get hurt. Max grad Dannie and started to move her and she said please do this for me and get a glass of ice. Dannie he drunk you could get hurt Max said. Trust me hun I know how to take care of myself.

Max now get me that glass of ice. Max went behind the counter said you sure hun. Dannie said I'm sure. Max put a glass of ice on the counter. The guy said what's that for. Dannie turns around and said it for you. What's Max sending a woman to fight me? The man looked at Dannie and said come on Daddy want it. The man started to play with his fly.

Dannie set one step closer and gave him a kick that every man and woman in the bar felt. Max just could believe what he just saw. The man went down like a rock hitting his head on the floor. Dannie said Max hun I got some trash for you to take out. One of the man at the bar help Max pick the guy up. Dannie said wait Max. Dannie took the glass of ice and put down the front of the MAN's pants. Dannie said he you are small dick some ice of that two inch thing you call a dick.

The hole bar started clapping and cheering Dannie. Dannie set down at the bar and Max comes back in. Max said remind me to wear a cup if you get Mad at me. Max kiss her and said way to go girl. Dannie said I'm small and weak but I pack a mean kick. A woman came throw the door and up to the bar it was his girl friend. Max she said what did shit head do this time? Max told everything to her and said the new Boucher took care of him. Max points to Dannie setting at the end of the bar. She said that little girl did that.

She walks over to Dannie and said sorry Dannie he a real asshole when he drinks. Max the woman said gave her a beer on me. Dannie said thanks but he coming throw the door again. The woman said guess he needs a second learning. The girl walk over to him at the door and he said coming bitch hell me. The man started the stand and his girlfriend kick him harder than Dannie if that could be done.

The man fell back out the door screaming in pain. She looks at Dannie and said have a good night hun I've got to remove the trash. Dannie said you to and rise the beer to her. Dannie said shit my dinner cold all the men in the bar just turned and drink their beers. Max laughs and said I will get you a hot dish. Dannie said make it snipping sweet thing and she smiled. Max laughs my woman she full of surprises.

Dannie sat down and finishes her dinner. Dannie came behind the bar and said to Max I'm going up to take a short nap to much for a work out this noon. Max grads her and hug her then gave her a kiss sure hun I will see you a little later. Dannie kiss Max and said any more shit you want me to clean. Max said no you do really good hun. Dannie hug Max back and kiss him love you. Max said love you to hun. Dannie went up stairs and crawled into the bed and curl up to Max's pillow.

Adam said she been in their a long time. Fred said yes but she knows what she doing. Adam said we will be ready for dinner in about 15 minutes. Jean came around the counter and said it smell great is it done. Adam said everything came out all right. Jean said yup and someone may need to take this up and let it blow up. Jean pull the c4 out or her lab coat and said it has five minutes to go. Fred said hun let me go throw it out for you.

Fred went up and took the c4 up on top side and throw it anyway from the cars. Mary said dinner is ready lets eat. Jean said take the food the pond room and we can eat at the big table. Adam said so can you get the files off the drive? Jean said yes it may take awhile I 'm running a code program to find the right code to open the files. Fred returned and the group went into the pond room. Devvan said it's so quiet you could fall a sleep fast in here. Jean said that's why all the lawn chairs so you can kick back and chill out. The group set the table and everyone sat to eat.

Jean said the clams are great how you make them. Adam said a little beer in the clam mix. Jean said they are the best I've ever had. Chase said so how long will the code take? Jean said it could be an hour to two days. Chase said dam that's long. Peter said how did you get so good with computers? Jean said I couldn't use them until they came out with the lcd screens the old tube one hurt me to set in front of them. Jean said I read book on programing and how to run them and that's all. Fred said the meal was great but we need one more thing.

Jean said you can get the beer just don't go over board with it. Adam said what so great about beer. Fred said one is all you need for the day. Adam said will lets try this beer, but we got to clean up this mess and the kitchen first. Jean said I will check the drive to see how everything going. Jean got up and the dogs got up to follow her. Mary said girls Jean doesn't need you help. Jean said that's ok I would love to have him with me if that's ok with you two?

Devvan said girls you be good and don't get into anything. Jean said will girls come and I will show you the lab. Jean walk out the door and the two dogs follow her. Fred said you know what this means? Devvan said yup she a dog loving ? Fred said yup and it would make her a good friend while I'm out. Mary said dog are fun to have around and Jean seem to really like Maxy and Pad. Yup Fred said I will have to get her a dog.

The group clean up the kitchen and wash all the dishes and clean the counters. Jean came back to the kitchen and Maxy and Pad right beside her. Jean said you guys are great I never had this many people in here ever. The group said glad we could be here to. Jean said so Fred you going to show them the beer. Fred said yes you going to like this . Jean said to Adam the program has the second letters done so it's going very fast.

Fred said ok back to the lawn chair and the beer. Fred went into the ice box a got one beer for each. Peter said what kind is this? Jean made it for me in the beer room. Fred said but before you drink it, I have to show you how to do it. Adam said pop the can a just down it. Jean said if you did that you wouldn't stand more then three second and pass out. Fred said believe me when she say that I did and wake up 20 minutes later. Dam super beer. Will pop the top and take one little drink very little drink.

Now let it set in your mouth and feel the flavors. Jean said you best go and set down before the beer hits' you. The group started for the pond chairs. Adam said this is the coldest and best beer I've had. The other said so smooth going down. Fred said it stays that way throw the beer. The group sat down and Fred said like some music. Sure Adam said as he could feel the beer take hold. Chase said dam went can we take other drink Fred said anytime you want but do it in small drinks and every ten minutes or so. Peter said wow I can feel the first one. Fred said it save me a lot in beer a year. Adam said I can see why Chase is already passed out. Fred how long will it last. Fred said you can stop drinking it and in 20 minutes you strange and no hang over.

Adam said we shouldn't be drinking anyway we're on duty. Fred said sorry I forgot I was having a good time. Jean said see hun now you got him drunk they can't help other people. Fred laugh and said be right back. Fred came back in with other blue bottle in his hand. Adam said now what you got Fred? Fred said trust me you be as good as old you in one minute. Adam drank a mouth full then the other all but Chase who was all ready out for 15 minute so far.

Mary said I can feel my mind clearing. Adam said dam Fred your should put this on the market. Fred said we can't because like Jean the beer can see sun light. Adam said wow that was cool. Jean said lets go to the lab and see how things are coming. Adam said great idea. Jean said oh what about Chase Adam. Mary said I'll stay here with him until he gets up. Jean said ok but you my want to take the drink away from him before he gets up.

Jean and the others went to her lab. Jean said I call this my toy room because when Fred gone I spend most my time in here. Peter said this is better than most crime labs I've seen. Jean said thanks and she showed them the drive. Jean said its got two letters now sa but it working on the right. Adam said can we type in words while it's doing it. Jean said yes but your need the code to start the program.

Adam said try satan9 see if what mean something. Jean type in the words and the computer stop running the code program and the drive started to run. Jean said good it's the code where did you find that name Adam Jean said? Adam said it was on the tracking device we found in the house before it blow up. Jean looked at Fred with a Mad look I her eyes why didn't you tell me Fred. Fred said hun I didn't want you to worry. Fred hugged her and said I'm sorry.

Jean said we will speak about this after everyone is gone. Adam said the program is coming up. The screen read satan9 and open a set of files. Jean said this looks like a video log. Jean pulled one up and started the clip.

Dannie wakes up and it was ten of four she got up and went to the bathroom to freshen up for Max. Max came though the door and said Dannie I'm home. Dannie said I'll be right out. Dannie came out of the bathroom and Max was looking at her funny. Dannie said what wrong Max is my hair messed up. Max said no just can believe you this noon you showed them who the boss was and then some. Dannie said I hope he all right after that second kick. Max said I don't think he going to forget first one.

Dannie said I'm sorry I don't do things like that I don't know what came over me. Max said you have nothing to be sorry about I was going to kick his ass then throw him out anyway. Max grad her and said Daddy got something for you and kiss her like she old western movie. Max said will I'm going to jump in the shower, cold shower and be right out.

Dannie said take your time hun and I'll be right here. Max went into the shower and to get cleaned up. Someone knocks at the door and Dannie went to see who it was. It was Vicki she was carrying a fruit basket with a bottle of wine in it. Vicki said hi and this just come for you. Dannie said for me who would be sending me this. Vicki said it from someone call sore nuts. Dannie started the laugh. Thank Vicki for bring up to me. So Vicki said who's sore nuts. Dannie said the man the give me shit in the bar this noon. One of the men told me about that but I though he was pulling my leg. Vicki just smiles and said see you later Dannie.

Dannie said ok you have a good day to Vicki. Dannie shut the door and Max came out of the shower. He saw the basket on the table who those for? Dannie said they came for me from Mr sore nuts. Max just started to laugh and said I guess you left a mark on him. Max said open the wine and try it see if it good or not. Max went into the bedroom and got dressed and came back out in the kitchen. Dannie said the wine isn't bad little dry but not bad. Max said let me try it? Dannie gave Max a small glass of wine.

Max drank it and said good like you said and dry be good with fish. Dannie said I was thinking the same thing. Max said are you ready to go to Bangor hun. Dannie said yes if you are hun. Max and Dannie went down stairs to Max's truck and got ready to leave Max said we going to have to stop for the beer first but after that we can do anything you want. Dannie said good and curls up under Max's arm.

Max was in heaven again but this time he had a hand full of Dannie's chest. Dannie looked up and kisses Max make sure your mind is on the road.

Max said yes hun, but it really wasn't. Dannie said maybe you should hug me now hun I think your getting a little turned on. Max pulls his hand out of her shirt and Dannie set up to hug and kiss him. Max said thanks your right I was getting very turned on. Dannie said I know there a big snake in you're short. Max face turn red and Dannie hug him.

Max pulls off the ramp and went to sam's club for his beer. Dannie sat in the truck as Max and one person from the store load the truck. Max then open the door and push a button and Dannie watch the bed cover roll out and cover the load. Max locked a snap at the end of the bed and got back in the truck. Dannie said that's cool I don't know your truck did that? Max said yup would have used it the last time, but we had to big of a load to cover it.

Max said ok what you want to do now? Dannie said I'm a little hungry how about same food? Max said well what would you like to eat? Dannie said anywhere I can get a good steak. Max said I know where you can do that and have a great meal to go with it. Max said the 99 restaurant over by the mall is great food. Dannie said ok let do it then. Max drove over to the restaurant and got a spot up front. Dannie said hun the sign said v.i.p only.

Max said yup we are all ways v.i.p's at Grandpa place. Dannie said your grandpa own this one. Yup the man who took me in after Mom and Dad passed away. Dannie said will I've got to meet this man. Max said I will have to say something before you meet them if they're here they say just want's on they mind so they can be a little hard core. Dannie said well this should be fun then.

Max walked in the door with Dannie and up to the check in. The young lady there said hi Max your grandma and grandpa are working tonight. Max said great can I get a table for two. The family table ok tonight sure Max said. The young lady took the two of them into the dinning area and set them at a beautiful spot in the dinner. Dannie said wow this is all for use. Max said you tell grandpa and grandma I'm here. The lady said sure Max she going to be happy to see you. Max said ok thanks.

The waiter came up to him and ask would you like a menu or wait for grandpa to pick it out for you. Max said we will have the house wine and a menu. Max said don't look now but trouble is on it's way. Dannie looked over her right side and show two grey hair older people were coming their way. Max stood up as Grandma hug him first and gave a small slap you the face and said you haven't been around for a while you know how we miss you.

Max said yes Grandma. I'm sorry I want to tell you something. But before he could speak Grandpa said my my who's this pretty little thing you bring use Max. Max said this is my wife to be Dannie. Grandma said Dannie isn't that a man name, Then Grandma said oh my God she isn't a he in woman cloth. Max said Grandma no her name is Dannie. Grandma said sorry hun , but you never know these days. Dannie was laughing and said that's ok.

Grandpa said stand came hug use you are family now. Grandma said spin for me so I can get a good look at you. Dannie did and Grandma and Grandpa both hug each other and said Max good looking girl. Nice butt and breast make find Great Grandkids for use Grandma said. Max said Grandma don't run her off before we get married. Dannie just laughs and said we were going to start here care to watch?

Grandpa broke out in a big laugh and slap his legs and she is funny to. Grandma's said so can we join you for supper or you want to be alone. Dannie said we would love to have you join use. Good Grandpa said we must open a good bottle of wine. The waiter was standing behind them right away sir be right back. Max said have a seat and you can get to know them. Grandpa said what you hungry for tonight Max?

Max said you think hard and tell me. Grandpa looked at Max and said you look like a good T-bone and some cheese stick. Grandpa said and you Dannie what do you feel like. Dannie said see if you can see what I want? Grandpa said you look like a fruit lover with a wild side for steak I think you should have owner best steak and brake potato and sour cream with cheese on the potato Grandpa said how I do.

Dannie looks at Max and said he's right on the dime isn't he. Grandpa said it come from cooking for so long. The waiter return with the wine and pored each one a glass he said are you ready to order or still I get some bread sticks for you first. Grandpa said take this to the cook and yes on bread stick.

Grandpa gave him and note and the waiter went to the kitchen. Dannie smelled the wine and spin the glass then took a drink. Dannie said this is great what is it? Grandma said from over seas it's about 1500 dollars a glass. Dannie's eyes open wide did you just said 1500 a glass?

Grandpa said yes but your family now you get the best when you come here. Dannie looks at Max and he had a big smile. The waiter returned with the bread sticks and said your meals should be up short. Grandma said so Max how did you meet this pretty lady? Max said she came into the bar to have my chilli. Grandpa said see Max I told you all that cooking would get you something. Dannie smile and laugh Grandma said so do you work Dannie?

Dannie said yes I'm a model in town. Grandpa said yes I know you now oh my God be right back. Grandpa got up and yelled for the bar keeper and said as he was going to the bar area we need to do something. Dannie said is every thing ok did I say sometime wrong? Grandma said no with a laugh you get some picture in the bar that he got to take down. Dannie said not my beer picture? Grandpas came back with a few rolled up picture in his hand sorry hun I'm ok now.

Dannie said you didn't have to do that? Grandma said yes he a little pass the time hun. The waiter came back in a flash sir is everything all right? Grandpa said yes take these and ripped them up and don't opening them. Yes sir right away. Grandma said hun came set before you blow a seal. Max said wait can I see them. The waiter said sir my I let him see them? Grandpa said yes but you don't look.

Yes sir and he hand the pictures to Max and turned around. Max open up the pictures and said wow nice swim suit and roll them back up. Max handed them back to the waiter and said throw them away like Grandpa said and winked at the waiter. The waiter smiled back at Max and said right away sir yes sir ! Dannie hit Max in the side and said in a low voice you're bad.

Grandma saw it to and gave him the one finger point. Grandpa said good now we can enjoy supper. Grandma said yes we can. After a few the waiter returned with the meals and said the picture are gone and put the meals in front forever one. He said here your meals and can I pour you some more wine. Everyone said yes and he poured the wine and said have a good meal. Dannie said he a good waiter isn't he. Max said yes a really good one. Grandpa looked at Grandma and said we need to give him more money. Dannie took a bit of her steak an just sat they with the most happiest smile on her face.

Dannie said this is great meat you did a great job of choice of steak, Can I call you Grandpa? Grandpa said I wouldn't have it any other way glad you like it. Dannie said but how did you know I liked it well done. Grandpa said a man like me knows his meat. Max said yes Grandpa you do and this is one fine meal. Grandma said he good but I'm better. Grandpa said you right hun you are the best. Grandpa said would you like some great ice cream home made?

Dannie said ok tell me what favor I'm see how good you are? Grandpa this is hard you look like a strawberry fan with some nut and a cherry on top. Dannie said man he is good I will have that. Max he a raspberry man with Carmel and nuts. The waiter came back and said did you enjoy your meals. Everyone said yes. Grandpa hand a note to the waiter and said they would like this please. Yes sir right away sir and the waiter went back to the kitchen after the ice cream.

Grandpa said Max and Dannie me and Grandma are going to let you to eat your ice cream alone and you come and say good bye to use in the kitchen before you leave. Max said sure thing Grands. Grandma and Grandpa went back to the kitchen after hug Dannie and Max. The waiter came back out with the ice cream and said do you need anything else forks? Max looked at

Dannie she said I'm ok and Max said I'm fine just check please. The waiter said the meal is on the house.

Ok then thank you. The waiter said have a good night and went back to the kitchen area. Dannie looks at Max not eating his ice cream what's wrong Max. Max said to tell you're the true. I don't like raspberries. Dannie started to laugh I don't like strawberry. Max started to laugh Max said you want to trade? Dannie said yes I like raspberries. Max said I can handle strawberry better. They traded and ate it with one eye on the kitchen door.

Max said so what should leave the waiter? Dannie said we could leave 40 would that be to little. Max said no he going to love seeing use come in the next time. Max said are you set to go? Dannie said yes but we got to go say good bye. Max said hope Grandma doesn't say anything bad. Dannie said why should she I though we got along good. Max said not that way but she said what on her mind some times. Max and Dannie went back to the kitchen and tried to find Grandpa and Grandma. The kitchen worker said they're in the office at the end of the hall.

Max and Dannie went down the hall and Max was ready to knock on the door and he heard some noise coming from the room. Dannie said they are doing it in there are they? Max laughs it sure sounds like it. Max and Dannie stood there for a second then made there way back to the kitchen working just tell Grandpa and Grandma that Max and Dannie said good night. The man said don't tell me there doing it again. Max said sounds like it. Dam the man said I had three and now it four.

Max and Dannie just looked at each other and started to laugh. Max said ok just tell them we have to leave fast. The guys said ok I'll make sure they get it. Max and Dannie were laughing all the way back to the truck. Max said I can't tell how many time I've walks in on those two doing it. Dannie said well they still love it and each other that's got to say a lot for them. Max said your right they do really love each other, but on the job.

Dannie curl up under Max's arm and they went home. Max said this is a good night isn't it. Dannie said sure is maybe we can lay out on the porch tonight. Max said cool that's if you don't mean. Dannie said no I enjoy feeling the heat from you. Dannie said I like your Grandma and Grandpa. Max said I wouldn't be anything today if it wasn't for those two and I know they liked you.

Dannie said your think we should start on the great grandkids for them. Max laugh and said I told you they say what's on their minds. Dannie said you know I like that about them at less they aren't afraid to say what they think. Max said is that the exits all ready wow that when by like a flash. Dannie said good we are almost back to your place.

Adam said my God that looks like the old wolfman from the new reports. A voice started on the firm clip. This is the first Satan the animal, man is part of a DNA test. Over there in the cold room is the northern ice man. It's believed that this ice man was somewhere in the easily born of man. Maybe even the first man to walk the earth. As you can see, the body had seen it better days but he a every close copy for Satan one. The DNA from the ice man and the Satan one are a die on match. They could be twin brothers. The ice man was found in the North woods of Maine in the ice caves.

It seen the ice man walk and then fall to his die in the cave then was frozen. He was found by a few local cave drives looking at the cave for the first time. At the lab here we rebuild the DNA to a form we could use to make the Satan one from. The man was born though a woman we pick from the street that no one would miss her. The mother die after giving birth. The man you see now is about seven years of ago, but all really every unstable we can only feed and check him if we knock him out with gas first. The body is almost all human but has lot of hair.

Someone came into the firm doc the things is out of its cage. Doctor said dam shot it don't let it break free. Dam the doctor said the animal is free. Call the cops and tell him you spotted a wild animal run lose by the down town area. So what do you want me to do with the others Satan two and three. Gas them load everything and lets get out of he now. That were the clip ended. Jean said my God that thing out there is some thing of human. Adam said why would anyone want to bring back some thing from the die.

Peter said because man always wanted to play God. Jean said their eight more file want to watch more. Chase and Mary came throw the lab door and said did we miss anything. Fred said yes the wolfman we are hunting is a prehuman from the pass that they found in the ice cave for Maine a long time ago. Mary said we are hunting a man not animal. Peter said from a long time ago. Jean said we can watch the next one if you want. Adam said I'm still try to under stand the first one.

Adam said will lets run one more then call it a night and come back in the morning if that's ok with you Jean? Jean smiled sure it is. Adam said ok then roll the chip. The next clip started with the same doctor. Will we had to build a new cage unit for two and three because the two males are too strong together. Unlike Satan one two and three are like little kids they can be trailed to do thing but aren't as mean as number one was. We're not sure this is a good thing they would need more anger to make it in the wild. We have planted tracking devices in the man to track him in the wild to see how they would live. We plan on letting two go today then three a few days later.

Day two of number two is been gone the trailing team has watch the thing get fish from the stream and small animals. It seems to have a good time in the wood the animal had stayed out of the towns for now, but we watch him look at the other human from afar. Day ten number three is out and seems to be tracking number two. Two days have pass and two and three have found each other so they do have the skills to find each other. The two seems to be heading north to more wood and game. Day 20 the two come across and wild bear at first it looks as if they my get along with it, but the bear went after number two and badly hurt him three came in a kill the bear.

The bear ended up as food , but number two die and three seems to be lose without the other one almost sad or crying. Number three is heading north and the teams seems to be losing him. Will we know that the man can make it in the wild so we are going the try to make a few more from semen that we got from all three to see if we can make one at would make a good warrior. Jean said they trying to make an army of these men. Fred laugh and said what would there call them hair Joes . Adam said I don't know about that but I bet that's where the bigfoot animal came from. Jean said but why let it go if you don't know how it would do with other human?

Peter said I don't know maybe that's why the Reed and Reed people came in to hunt and kill them. Chase said man and these shit heads are run the country. Mary said it does make you think. Will Adam said it's getting last thing we sure call it a night. Jean said so you be back in the morning Adam or everyone? Adam said everyone will if that's ok. Jean said yes and the dogs to?

Mary said I don't think they let use go without them. Devvan said Jean you know Maxy wouldn't mind stay the night if you want her to. Jean look at Fred can she Fred hun? Fred said sure she can, but we going to need some of her food. Devvan said ok I will run up and get some and be right back. Jean was so happy she started to cry. Mary said Jean you ok? Fred said she happy no sad. Jean said yes more then happy.

Devvan came back with the food he said should be more than she needs until tomorrow .Jean said anything I should know? Mary said you may want to take her out and have her do her thing in and hour then she'll be good for the night. Fred said we can do that it should be dark then. Will Adam said Jean it's been really fun and you are a great person glad I got to now you. Jean hug Adam and the rest and they went out to their truck and went to Adam's for the night. Jean said Fred what do dog like to do. Fred said came and I will show you. Jean said came Maxy and the dog walk with her and Fred to the pond room.

Dannie said as they pull in the bar good we can get some sleep now. Dannie got out of the truck and said to Max need me to help hun. Max said I'm ok will grad a hand cart and be done in a few. Ok I'm going up stair then and go to the rest room. Max kiss Dannie and she went up stairs. Max started to unload the truck. Dannie went to the bath room and got in her night cloths. She couldn't wait until her and Max could go out on the porch to curl up. Max came throw the door and said now I'm all your's now hun. Dannie said good I want to go out on the porch again. Max said well I 'll be right with you hun. Max went into the other room and get his night cloths on and pick up the two pillow and blankets they use last night.

Dannie and Max went out to the porch Dannie said the air is nice tonight not cold. Max said maybe we can sleep some tonight out here. Dannie said maybe we can will see. Max and Dannie put the blanket down and got set to curl up with each other. Max said did you have a good day hun? Dannie said sure did and enjoy Grandpa and Grandma. Max laughs they are a little weird sometimes but mean good. Dannie said it good to see two people so much in love like use.

Max said yes like use and put the covers over Dannie's head and started the kiss her and make out. Dannie was getting really turned on by Max and she could feel Max was feeling the same. Dannie said to herself if he wants me I'm not going to stop him tonight. Max pulls the covers back down and the two lay there looking at the shy Dannie felt nice and warm next to Max.

Max said the shy is nice and clear tonight isn't it? Dannie said yes and the moon is almost full it looks like you could put your hand out and grad it. Dannie said doesn't life feel better when your in love? Max said sure does. It's better a sweeter. Max and Dannie slowly fell asleep on the porch under the night shy.

Max pulls the cover over their heads so they could stay nice and warm. Dannie dreams were ok, but some what funny. Dannie could see that they were on the porch but almost as if they were floating in a stream or on air. The air was cold but fresh Dannie could feel her self having and good time. She could feel the wind pick up and something small and soft hit the blanket it feel like snow, but she couldn't look out to see she could feel the weigh of the snow on the blanket and it feel heavy and was getting heavier by the minute.

Her heart was beating faster and faster then every thing stop, she wakes up and felt cold and a little wet. Dannie pulls down the cover to see it was snow for real and coming down fast. Dannie wake Max and he open his eyes to a snow ball. Max jump up what going on it's snowing. Max and Dannie got up and went back inside.

Max was cool and Dannie was a little wet she run in the bedroom and jump into bed. Dannie said Max get in here I'm cool. Max hops in bed and the two set there rolled up to each others arms trying to get warm. Dannie was shacking so bad Max handle her closer. Max said you should warm up here shortly. Dannie said its was cold but fun and I'm starting to get warmer.

Dannie and Max started to warm and fall back to sleep. Dannie good night would slowly come to an end. Dannie found her self walking in the cold and snow of the north. Dannie made her way into the woods the woods seems to get thicker the more she moved the tree seemed too come to life. Some tree's grad her hands and other her legs the more she tries to fight the stronger the tree held her. The trees pin she to the cold wet snow and then something came out of the tree it was the wolfman.

The wolfman stood over her and said as he knees three inches from her face oh are you happy tonight. Dannie snap at him and said if I could get free you'll be die right now. The wolfman ran his hand down her right side and smell the air and said smell like someone needs something. Dannie said you do anything I'll ripped it off and make you eat it. The wolfman said it looks like you don't have a say.

Then two sets of white feet stood beside the wolfman and said not while we are here, The two grad the wolfman and stood him up. Dannie pulls at the tree and broke there hold on her. She stood up and said to the wolfman so who doing who tonight? The wolfman said you must understand my father is more powerful than your. Dannie said then why is he in hell not heaven right now? The wolfman snapped at her and said because he likes the earth around him.

Dannie howls what earth just a word spoken from my father. The heaven and earth would be no more. The wolfman said then why doesn't he do that? Because he made it all and loves his child. Dannie said I'm not the one you should ask forgiveness it my father. The wolfman said forgive for what not killing you. Dannie said for those word you we die and ripped the headed from the wolfman and laugh.

Dannie though with the die of the wolfman she would wake up from this dream and be safe in Max's arm but no not tonight. A howl came from a far. The wolfman's said so who is left to help sweet little Max. Dannie said you asshole and throw the wolfman head into the tree. Dannie ran as fast as she could to the sound of the howl it was the female and she had Max. Max was in a state of dream and he wasn't able to run speak or yelled just set there and looks at want was going to happen.

Dannie said back away from him and I will give you your man. The female said you didn't kill him and she back away from Max. Dannie said he fine he just needs a new head and the two sisters wolfs throw the body of the wolfman at the female. The body hit her and knock her back and Dannie stepped in between the two and kill the female wolf.

She turns to Max and said I'm sorry hun that you had to be here but I love you and will protect you with my life. Then both Max and Dannie came out of the dream with a jump and were awake looking at each other. Dannie said you have a bad dream hun? Max said yes I guess so don't remember much but you saved me. Dannie said will that's good and hug Max until her went back to sleep. Dannie lay their thinking that her and Max must be mean to be together because their mind were one for a second. Dannie looked at Max and was really happy and hugs him and when back to sleep.

Adam got home and Annette and Bob were there. Annette jumps up and hug Adam. Adam ask her how her day went. Annette said they're going to Barry the kid tomorrow. Adam said what time is this going to happen. Annette said ago 1:00pm tomorrow. Adam said ok I will work until 11:00am then will come back to go with you. Annette said you don't have to do that Adam. Adam said yes I do there your kids and they are important to you then they important to me to.

Annette hugs and kiss Adam thanks yes they sure are important to me. Adam said to everyone will so what about what we saw on the video clips today. Chase said why did the reporters say it was a mix between man and wolf and the tapes say it was just human. Adam said the report could have been from the group working as Reed and Reed and they didn't know. Chase said yup that could be true because that's what we got from the news reports.

Peter said then why's is it killing human and howling? Devvan said it could see use as food not human remember it is human and we look little like white rats maybe to it. Mary said if you remember to the nature AMERICAN use bird and other animal calls to tell each other their location and animal group like wolfs howl to find each other. Annette said this thing isn't a wolfman but human?

Adam said that seems to be it. Annette said what kind of human is it I've never see anything like it. Adam said it could be one of the first humans to walk the earth. Annette said did they find it? Adam said the man was frozen in the ice caves up north and they use its DNA to make this thing. Annette said people can be twisted can't they. Peter said yes but think if you could find what geans to made a man bigger stronger and able to do things today human couldn't it would be worth millions.

Annette said then this thing human or not has to be kill, just thin if this human was some how aloud to live then we could be replaced with it in say 30 years or less. Annette said then we would have taking a grant stand back in time and have to start all over again. Peter said you do put some good points up Annette if it got lose an could hide for years it would very will replace use. Chase said now I've got a lot to look at now that we know its human can we really kill it.

Adam said it's human but kills other humans so that's all I need to know to kill it. Everyone said I guess your right Adam it is a killer and that's that. Adam said let get something to eat and set up watch. Adam said is Rick's pizza ok the work and a few beer sounds good to me. Yup the group said sounds like a plan. Adam order two large pizzas with the works. Annette said did some happen to one of the dogs today?

Devvan said no we left her with Jean and Fred for the night. Annette said you know your going the have the replace her with another puppy don't you. Adam said yes we would have to ask Fred in the Morning. Adam said I think that we will run three hours shaft tonight that way we can get six hours to sleep. Peter said that sounds good I'll take the first watch. Devvan said so will I.

Mary said me and Chase will do second then. Adam said me and Annette will do the three if she still wants to. Annette said yes it's fun to do. Ok then Adam lets go for some pizza and beer. Devvan said I will come got to let pad out to do her thing. Peter and Chase said we will help out to. So the men went to Rick's and the Women stay at the house. Adam said I'm going to call Fred to see how the dog is doing with Jean.

So Adam call hi Fred so is everything ok over there. Fred said more then ok Jean is having a great time with Maxy. Fred said do you know where I can get her a lab puppy like Maxy? Adam said how soon would you want it? Tomorrow said Fred because it's going to be hard for Jean to let Maxy going after tonight. Adam said don't worry we will doing something about that tomorrow. Fred said if it cost anything let me know and I will pay you back.

Adam said ok I will let you know. Adam hung up the phone and said to Peter looks like we need to stop at the pet shop tomorrow . Chase said Fred wants a dog for Jean? Adam said yup he said a lab puppy like Maxy if we could. Chase said Steve's pet store had four female puppies a few days going when I stop in. Good hope he has one tomorrow. We the guys got back to the room and Mary and Annette were setting the kitchen shooting the shit.

Adam said were back and your right again Annette Fred want me see if I can get and puppy for Jean. Annette my friend Steve should have some let me call them. Annette called Steve, Steve said he had on female lab left.

Annette said Adam he has one female lab left. Adam said good I 'll take it in the morning what time he open. Annette said Steve Adam will take the dog and what time you open? Steve said I should be in their around 7:30am maybe sooner just knock on the door and I will open it for him. Annette said thanks see you in the morning then. Annette told Adam 7:30am put may be open sooner if you knock. Great job Annette let dig into some pizza and beer now. The group had its full of pizza Adam said I'm going to turn in now so make yourself at home and see when my watch is on.

Annette said I think I will turn in to see you in the morning. Adam and Annette went into the bedroom and got in bed. Adam said man or not we got to bring it down right Annette. Annette said the same way you did the other man who killed my kids. Adam hug Annette and they made love and went to sleep. Peter and Devvan had the first watch. Devvan said Peter do you think we'll see hair ball tonight. Peter said he kill the others last night who's to say we not next.

The video said they move north maybe now the others are off his back and can't track him they will head north. Peter said it a full moon tonight hope that isn't a bad sign. Devvan said me to I hope he gone. Peter said I wouldn't bet on it. Chase and Mary said see you in guys and went to bed. Peter said it sure getting quiet around here at night could get to like it. Devvan said sometime to quiet. Peter said it sounds like a few wolfman are lose in the bedrooms. Devvan laughs and said humans have sex to release stress.

Peter said the human race is some thing, here we stand at the edge of bring no more and people still want to make love. Devvan said they should make a sport of it world best lover. Devvan said I bet it would be the best watch program on the air. Peter said I see the man that Annette said was living in the car next door is back man I feel for someone like him. Peter said it getting down into the teens at night hope he can some live in that cold. Devvan said people live in all kind of weather.

Will look at the time it's time for Chase and Mary to run the floor. Yup Peter said the time sure runs by fast when you can pass it with someone. Devvan headed to get Mary and chase up. Chase came out with her and said its time to Charge the guards. Peter said only thing was moving out there was the old man that got in the car next door again. Chase and Mary said thanks and have a good night. Chase looked out the window and saw that it was quiet.

You could see a lot that night the moon was in full brightness. Mary said I bet Jean will have a good day today with getting a puppy and things .Chase said some time I feel bad for her not being able to come out in the light, but you look outside tonight and the world so peaceful you sometimes like it that way. Mary said it does seen nice to see it quiet. Mary said it would be nice to set somewhere in a nice warm place and just watch the world rush by. Pad set up and Chase said what is it girl do you hear anything. Mary Chase said I think big an hair out side the door. I'll set to

shot go wake the others. Mary went in the room and got the others. Chase could hear some noise on the wall like nails on a chalk board. Then not a thing the other all came into the room and said what's up Chase? Chase said I don't know the dog started carm down and it seem to have gone again.

Chase said can you hear that? Adam said yes it sounds funny. Will there's only one way to find out is to go out a see what it is. Chase said you nuts? Peter said set yourself to cover the door and I will open it. The group got ready to kill anything in the door way. Peter open the door and it was clear no man animal or anything insight. Adam said Peter when we step out you take right and I will take left. Adam said you ready? Peter said no but lets go.

The two men jump out into the hall way and Adam saw not a thing And spin to help Peter. Peter said it's ok it's just the man from across the street sleeping in the hall. The team started to carm down. Annette said we can't leave him in the hall for the wolfman. The old man said he not going to kill me. Adam said old man who do you know that? Because he said he wouldn't. Adam and Peter looked at each other and said maybe it's the wine speaking to him.

Adam said will old man came in and you can sleep on a warm floor. The old man said thanks' you sure? Peter said he sure came on. The old man got up and came in and said thanks and went over to sleep next to the heat. Adam said will it's almost shift charge so me and Annette will take over, but good job you guys we had a good drill. The group set back down and Chase and Mary went to bed. Peter said I guess I will try to get same more sleep. The old man in the corner was already sound to sleep. Adam looked at the old man then at Annette he said the wolfman said to him that he wouldn't kill him. Annette said look at him would you eat him. Adam laugh and said I see your point. The night went on without a problem.

Dannie wakes up and could see it was just about time to get up. Dannie looked up at Max he was smiling at her good morning Max. Max said it is a good morning with you here. Dannie said do you want anything for breakfast? Max said coffee and the fresh fruit I got the other day. Dannie said my kind of meal. Max said I like my fresh fruit but I don't like cutting it up. Dannie said good I like doing things for my man . Dannie got out of bed and kissed Max she said you coming?

Max said in a few because Mr happy was awake . Dannie grad the covers and pull them off. Dannie said oh my he is up isn't. Max tried to cover up as best he could and got out of bed. Dannie just smiled at Max and said maybe you should take a shower then eat. Max said maybe that's a good idea and headed to the bathroom. Dannie went into the kitchen and got breakfast ready. Max came out of the shower and Dannie said feel better hun?

Max said yup the fruit looks nice hun. Max said so what you going to do today hun? Dannie said not really sure but was going to the car wash a clean my truck and have the oil charge. Max said sounds good maybe if your not doing anything tomorrow you can get my truck 's oil charge for me. Dannie said would love to I like your truck it's sexy. Max said I don't know about sexy but it's a nice ride.

Dannie said so what her name? Max said it was Mary but now I call it Dannie. Dannie said why name it after me? Max smiles its small, good looking and picks a mean kick. Dannie just started laughing and said will a girl has to take care of her self. Max said I know what you mean hun to many shit heads out there.

Will Dannie said I'm jumps in the shower then going down to help you with the opening? Max said ok hun I'm going to clean up around here and drink my coffee. Dannie went to the shower and got wash up. Dannie could smell Max in the bath room and wish he was in the shower with her. Max had a smile on his face think about Dannie in the shower as he drank his coffee. Dannie came out and went into the room and dry her hair and got ready for the day.

Dannie came out and Max gave her a big kiss and they went down stairs to the bar. Dannie said on the way down sun is warm today isn't. Max said yes a good day to do anything you want. Max open the back door and went into the bar. Dannie got the broom and starting swiping the floor. Max came out with beer for the bar and started to clean and stock the beer. Dannie smiles at Max working. Max went back for same hard stuff to full the back of the bar with.

Dannie got done and set on the bar waiting for Max. Max came around the corner and said done you do good work hun. Dannie said I going to hit the road so I can get into Stanley's and get my truck oil done first. Max said ok and gave her a big hug and kiss before she left. Dannie said I will see you for dinner ok hun. Max said yup see you then hun love you. Dannie looked back and said love you to hun and went to her jeep.

Dannie went to Stanley's the works were all there and George was behind the counter. George said good morning to Dannie. Dannie said George can I get my oil charge and grease job done? George said yes Dannie put someone on it now be about 15 minute. Dannie said I'm going over to the Big Apple for some coffee see you in ten. George said ok take your time he said. Dannie walked out the door and every man in the place was watch he cross the road but George.

Dannie walks into the country dinner that was hook to the Big Apple. Dannie could see a lot for the locals eat there and the food was good. The waiter came up to her and ask can I get you something? Dannie said yes a muffin and some coffee, Blueberry muffins if you have one. The waiter said be right back with the muffin and coffee. Dannie sat there watching out the window to see the town slowly came to live. Dannie love the small town ways people never seen to be in a hurry to go away. Dannie did know that the town had gotten smaller then when she was young.

The waiter returned with Dannie muffin and coffee and said will there be anything else? Dannie said no thank you. The waiter said enjoy and have a good day. Dannie could smell the coffee and she cut into her muffin and drank some of her coffee. The muffin was fresh and warm with a little butter on it just the way to start the day. Dannie was thinking of Max and how he was doing right now.

Dannie couldn't wait to get married to Max he was the man. Dannie was done and she got up to pay for the meal. She left five dollars for the waiter he seemed a nice man. Dannie walks back across the road . George was a man of his words he had her truck done and it was waiting in the yard. Dannie walked into the counter area to pay. George said everything on the jeep looked good. Dannie said ok put on my card. Dannie sign the bill and went out to the jeep.

She went home to check her mail and make sure that she had a home. Dannie pulls into the drive way and got the mail out of the box she road on the lawn to the back where she was going to wash her jeep. She got out and went in the house to get the mail inside. Dannie grad her bucket and soap and brush and went out back to the truck. She could see Pat coming across the lawn. Dannie said hi to Pat and said so what's up today their man. Pat said hi and that he and his man were going out of town for a few day he was wondering if she could keep and eye on his place for him.

Dannie said sure Pat when I'm here I will check the mail and bring it over here. Dannie said make sure to put to light on in the house to make it look like someone is still there. Pat said I have them on a timer so it looks that way. Dannie said where you going to Pat? Pat said down state to a wedding.

Dannie said you have a great time then and call when you get back. Pat said thanks and headed back to his house. Dannie washes a clean the inside of her jeep and made it look new. Dannie love thing when there shine so good. She clean up and put the jeep around the front to air out in the nice warm breeze, she said this could be the last day she could get warm sun to sun in so she went up stair to dress down and go out to the back porch to get some sun.

Adam said morning to everyone and the old man. Annette said I have coffee ready and some donuts I got yesterday at the store. Everyone but the old man got up. Adam said sir would you like a donuts and some coffee. The man said yes and thanks you for letting me sleep here last night. Adam said can let a fellow human die in the cold. The old man said thanks for every thing. Chase said hay before you go I got and old small house with gas heat out back if you want you could crash there if you want for the winter.

The old man said thanks I would like that and I could clean and rebuild the place for you if you want. Chase said just don't trash it and I will be fine , the back door is unlocked some came and go as you please. The man old was very happy and thank ever one as he left. Mary said that was a sweet thing to do Chase. Yes Annette said very nice for you. Chase said we got a dog to get and a video to watch so lets do it. Someone knock at the door and jump the shit out of the team it was Bob.

Good morning Bob Annette said. Hi there everyone Bob said. Adam said we are set for the pet shop so let go. Adam kiss Annette and said I will see around 11:30 am or so ok. Annette said yes and kisses and hugs him back thanks. The team got real and loaded up for the pet shop. The group all came into the pet shop and Steve was behind the front counter. Steve said hi to Adam and said I got someone back here that you want he held up a black lab puppy and it was sweet as could be.

Adam said she looks like Maxy and I bet Jean will love her. Chase said here and bag of food for her and a book on how the care for dogs. Mary said I'm getting a little bed for her and some toys. Peter said you got to have a Collor and some walk rope. Devvan said some flea soap and power to. Will little girl I think your going be to in a good home where someone will love you. Steve said is that all guys? Adam said yes and they all loaded up to go over to Fred.

The team all got out and Adam said Mary you go in first with the dog behind your back and we will hide the other things so that we can surprise her. Adam knock on the door and Fred came to open it. Fred said did you get it? Adam show it to him. Fred said will be prepared for water works Jean going to love it. Fred lead the way down and Jean meet them in the live room with Maxy. Jean said I'm going to not like it when Maxy goes but we had real fun last night.

Fred said the two sleep together in the pond room on the grass last night. Adam said will we though you would miss her so we got you something to take her place. Jean said what this Adam? Fred said I got you a dog. Jean was almost in tear when he said that. Where is she is she like Maxy. Will Mary said as she walks around and hands the puppy to Jean how was at this point for setting on the floor hold the puppy and crying. Fred eyes were watering and he bent down and kisses Jean love you.

Jean couldn't speak but Fred know what she was saying. Adam said we got a few thing for you to so you could take care of her. The team sat everything in front of Jean. Jean tried to say thanks but still was unable to. Fred looks at Adam so what do I owe your for everything. Adam said not a thing Jean already paid use all. Fred said thanks she would hug you all but think we going to have to wait a few.

Fred said what's her name? Adam said that's up to you and Jean she your dog. Jean got up with the puppy and hug and kissed all the team. Peter said it gave you a warm feeling inside. Devvan said yes it does as tears run down his face. Jean said in a low voice still try to believe what just happen will let go look at some of those clips. Adam said sure I've been waiting to all night.

The group went into Jean's lab and fired up the computer. Jean said I watch Satan five throw six and the only Charge was that they got a female and the last ones were born deformed didn't even look to be able to do much just set like a lump for clay.

But eight and nine came out to what you are chasing around now and some other thing to you will like. So I will run eight and go show the dog where her bedroom is. Fred said not on my side of the bed. Jean laughs no you can sleep at the foot and smiled. The clip began the same man was their Satan eight has turns out the be a female and in great sharp she seems to be born with every part this time.

The man said satan9 the male is also born with all parts. This is the day we been waiting for now we had a pare to breed. Maybe we can put them together to see if they will get alone. The next clips came on Fred said Jean set them that way so it would run like a movie. The man said the two are getting along great and they're both ten today. The female can speak but she doesn't to use.

The male seems to be getting smarter and smarter as the days go by. But we may

have to breed them and take the kids away to train them the kill. The male will not let the female eat any meat that had a human smell to it. The male seem to be under able to eat human me at all we don't know if that's something he choice or just can't do. The next clip came up and the man said we came in to empty cages this morning from the video tape the male had learn how to open the locks by watching the staff now there, are lost we'll have to kill the two. Adam said dam then why did he or she kill and eat some for the millers.

Fred said just maybe the government man made it look like that so we would hunt and kill the pair. Peter said dam what if the female is the only one who didn't kill man for food the clip said that the male wouldn't let her eat meat the smelled human. Chase said yes and now one of them is a killer and the other isn't. Devvan said we need to look at the big picture here that they aren't from this time they need to be kill to stop the spend for the human or animal what every it is.

Mary said this is all too much to take in right now. Fred said we also miss something this human can think so he could be planning to kill use off so he could live in please. Adam said that's very true look what he did the other night to the guys in the house . Jean came back so what did you think? Adam said we can't thank you for all the work that you did for use. Jean was carrying the puppy you have all ready pay me more then I could have ask for.

Jean said it make you think doesn't it. Peter said sure does and if its is human and has kill then it's no different than if you or I did the killings. Jean said that's what I was telling Fred last night. Jean said but it isn't fair because will made him no God. I think the man who created this human thing should have to face the judgement. Adam said your right Jean this is something that someone should pay for.

Devvan said so Jean did you pick a name for her? Jean said yes and I think it a good match for her. Jean said I'm going to name her Coco. Mary said that is the right name isn't it. Adam said Jean could you burn a copy of this onto cd. Jean said sure but you got to do something with this drive I don't want it here. Adam said sure we can throw it away after we get home. Jean said no you need to erase all clues of it. Chase said a 50-caliber shot should do the trick.

Mary said I got a better idea take it to the steal mill a drop it into the hot metal. Jean said that would do it and it would be gone forever. Jean made a copy and gave it to Adam. She unhooked the drive and gave it to him. Adam handed the drive to Mary and said that will be you're and Devvan job for the day. Fred said we aren't going to need you today so if you want to you can stay here with Jean and Coco.

Fred said good I will but what's going on this noon. Adam said I'm going with Annette to put the kids in the graves. Jean said kiss her and tell her we all love her. Adam said I will she will like that. The group started to leave and Jean said not so fast you guys and girls. Me and Coco have a big hug for you all before you go. Jean hug and kiss all the group even Maxy and Pad.

Jean said thanks' you all for this great puppy. The group went back to the station where everyone did their jobs and Adam went up stairs to Annette. Mary, Chase and Devvan and Peter went back two Chases' house because the new door would be on Chase said. Mary said good let's swing by the steal mill and melt this hard drive.

Dannie was done her truck and clean the inside and wax it. Dannie went in to clean up before she went over to see Max. Dannie went into the bed room and got same thing clean from her closet. Dannie found her geans and white T-shirt she said those would look good together. Dannie went out and got into the truck to go see Max. Dannie was driving to town she could see a large group of people at the grave yard. Dannie said to her self it must be a big one today. The town was slow for a day of hunting not much going on and quiet. Dannie went to Max's and the bar was slow to not many people there. Dannie kiss Max and said hi. Max said here for dinner hun? Dannie said yes and I'm hungry. Dannie said I want a cheeseburger and some onion rings .Max said I guess you are hungry.

Max said would you like a beer to hun? Dannie said no a cold red Maine chill would hit the spot. Max said ok and went back to the kitchen to make Dannie's meal. Dannie looked around and said not many in for this time of day hun. Max said it's the day of Annette kids and bring put in the ground. Oh Dannie said it sad about that hope she doing ok. Max said lucky for her Adam came alone when he did or there be two more today.

Dannie said yes it's dumb all the girl owe him was a few hindered and he kill all them for what. Max came out with the meal and said I will make your drink now hun and get my food and join you to eat. Dannie said cool and took a bit of he burgers this is good meat hun. Dannie said so you get off at four so what you want to do tonight hun. Max said don't know maybe take a short ride and get and ice cream maybe.

Dannie said sounds good maybe if it's not cool we could grad a blanket and cruddy at the beach. Max said sounds fun I think I would like that. Max said did you get your oil charge today? Dannie said yes and George is and good Man. I like George he does good work and his place is growing every year it seems. Max said I see you pull in you did a good job on your truck hun. Dannie said I was told if you take care of things and thing will last a lot longer.

Dannie was done her meal and said how your day been going hun? Max said you see it not much to do but wait until the night picks up. Max said that's one thing you can count on in little towns with not much to do is people drinking to pass the time. Dannie said I know it seem it was that way when I was young to. Dannie said I'm going to run up stair a take a nap for a while. Max said it sounds good wish I could join you hun.

Dannie gave Max a kiss and hug and said I love you Max. Max said I love you to hun will see you in a few. Dannie went out the back and up the stairs to Max's place. She went in and saw the dishes in the sink and said she would do them up so Max wouldn't have to when he got home. Dannie was washing the dish and was thinking if she would still work as a model full time when her and Max got married. Dannie said I would like less hours and still have some money coming in but she had everything payed for and really didn't need to work at all, but it was fun and she enjoy looking good. Dannie turned the TV on and sat on the bed she was a little sleeping but not too bad. Dannie hug Max's pillow and to her surprise fell to sleep.

Adam said to Annette it time to go and help her to the truck Bob was on her other side just incase she needed him. The noon time was bright but the grave yard still seemed lonely. The black car with the kids came down the road as if it was the last thing they would do. Adam, Annette and Bob got out and went to the grave side. Annette could see all the open grave so cold and bark her heart feel sad for the kid not bring able to be in the same graves to keep each other warm. The praise came up to the grave with red roses.

The praise bless each rose in the Name of the Father, son and holy spirit and place one on each coffin. The praise open the Bible and read from it. Psalm 8 O 'lord ,our Lord how majestic your name in all the earth !

You have set your glory above the heavens.

From the lips of children and infants you have ordained praise.

Because of your enemies, to silence the foe and the avenger

When I consider your heavens, the work of your fingers, the moon and the star much you have set in place, what is man that you care for him?

You made him a little lower than the heavenly beings, and crowned him with glory and honor.

You made him rule over the works of your hands; you put everything under his feet: all flocks and herds, and the beasts of the field, the birds of the air, and the fish the sea, all that swim the paths of the seas .O 'Lord ,our Lord, how majestic is your name in all the earth !

After say this all the coffin were lower at the same time Annette couldn't control her sadness any longer. Annette knee on he ground and said dear Lord you take care for my children and my pain. Annette place her hands on her face and cried. Adam kneed down and held her and said let it all out hun. The praise came over and Annette got back up to her feet and hug him and said thanks father.

The praise said keep the children in you heart and your pain let go of you kids are with the father now. The people came by and hugged Annette and said I sorry for your lose. Adam said to Bob too held your sister I will be right back. Adam put a small light on the coffin and said may this light keep you safe in the darkness and gave you hope.

Adam started to cry and went back to Annette side. Annette looked at Adam and kiss him and said thanks for everything. Adam said I feel as if I was part of them now. The group of people left and Annette, Adam and Bob were left there. Adam said would you like some time along with the kids. Annette said that would be nice and kiss Adam and Bob.

The two went over to the car and waited for Annette to say her good byes. Bob said she a strong woman she will make it. Adam said how about you Bob will you be ok? Bob said yes in time the pain we be better.

Annette was an hour with the kids, but Adam would stay there all night if she wanted him to. Annette came back to the car and hug both Adam and Bob thanks she said. The three got back into the truck and headed out of the grave yard. Annette looked back and place her hand on the window with a kiss for her kids. As the tears roll down her face and she started to cry once more.

Adam in his heart could feel her pain, but know that he couldn't help her with it because she needed to take some time to heal. Adam went home with

Annette to get away from town. Bob went home to so he could heal. Annette came in the camper and it was clean from top to bottom. Adam went back to the bed room and made the bed

for her. Annette got into bed Adam held her until she went to sleep. Adam got up and went into the other room and let her be alone with her pain.

Dannie was in a deep sleep about her and Max. The dream seemed sometime after they were marred. Dannie was feeling big, but a good big with child. Max was taking her to the doctors to gave birth. Dannie could feel the baby pushing and the

pains of birth. She seems happy because it was her and Max's first. Max was the real man pacing the floor and at anytime could pass out.

Dannie could feel the pains getting close and the doctor move her into the birthing room. Max sat in a chair beside her turning a pale white and passing out. Dannie said great just her and the doctor some help he was he was busy with try to get the baby. The doctor said here we go I can see the head. Dannie was hurting from the pain. Dannie heard a small cry and the doctor said it's a girl. Dannie was happy and then the doctor said oh my. Dannie said what's wrong as she could feel more pain.

The doctor said here comes number two. Dannie said a second one, as the pain was coming stronger. The doctor said this one is a boy. Dannie said doctor I can feel more pain what wrong. The doctor said the third is on it's way. Dannie almost pass out from this one. The doctor said this one is a girl to. The doctor said as he pick the three up for her to see you have three pretty baby puppies. Dannie screen as the doctor show her the dogs.

She looked over at Max and he had turned into the wolfman. The wolfman said oh my there have the same color fur as me and he howled. Dannie was trying to get away. Dannie got to the floor and start to run. The wolfman said hay hun wait for the kids as the puppies ran after her. Dannie ran down the hall and into the street. Dannie turned in time to see a bus about to ran her down then she wakes with a jump.

Dannie sat up in bed breathing hard and trying to get a grip on things. Dannie said to her self dam that wasn't fun. Dannie got up and went to the bathroom and put some cold water on her face. Dannie looked into the mirror and started to laugh hope my kid are paper trained. Dannie looked at the clock it was almost time for Max to came up so she went and sat on the porch to get air until Max came.

Max came out the back door a few minutes after. Dannie watches him walk around the bottom and back up the steps. Max face turn on when he saw Dannie setting there. Max said hi Dannie did you get a nap. Dannie said and you were in it.

Max said good I like to be in her dreams. Dannie said not this dream and she told him all about it. Max said my God you have some wild dreams.

Dannie laugh and Max smiles will he said feel like Lincoln today. Dannie said yes like to go to Wal -Marts if we could. Max said good I need a few things there. Dannie said maybe they got some puppy supply and the two a laugh. Max said maybe you never know. Max said I'm going to grad a shower then I will be ready to go. Max went into the bathroom and got into the shower. Dannie went into the kitchen to get some thing to drink.

Dannie came back out and sat on the couch until Max was ready to go. Dannie turns on the radio and put the music up high to dance to. Max came out of the bedroom and though he was back at the bar. Dannie smile and said hay their big man how about a kiss. Max said sure their sweet thing and kisses her. Max went into the bedroom and got dress for Lincoln. Max said I ready hun to go.

Dannie said me to baby let hit the town. Max and Dannie went down to the truck and got in. Dannie got next to Max as she always did. Max held her and started for town. Max said lets take the back way it's a nicer ride. Dannie said sure I like the old road. The old rt. 116 was a nice country road with sometime some wild life to look at. Dannie said we must be close to Lincoln I can smell it. Max said it not as bad as it can be today.

Dannie said hope Wal-Marts has some new movies this week. Max pulls in at Wal-Marts and the park lot was full. Dannie and Max went inside and went shopping the word's Dannie love to hear. Max and Dannie went throw the hold store looking for thing to by. Dannie said the cloths here are ok, but don't last. Dannie said you know what's fun is Madden's you never know what your going to fine.

Max said I like that store to let's cash out and go over there. Max got out to the truck and looked up at the sky it looked and smells like snow. Dannie said going to be a cool one today. Max said yup and maybe snow. Dannie said yes it does smell like that doesn't it. Max and Dannie went over to Madden's and it was fun like being in a place that something could jump out at you at anytime.

Max found some great deals on tools and Dannie found the shoe she was really happy. Dannie said this was worth the trip. Max said yes what you say if we hit subways and then back home with an ice cream. Dannie said yes as long as the ice cream was from Gilmore's farm. Max said you got it hun home made ice cream is the best. The two cash out and went to subways. Then over for ice cream on the ride home they went the Interstate it was the fastest way. Dannie said I love this ice cream it's creamy. Max said you don't fine ice cream like this much. Max pulls off the interstate and headed to town Max said do you want to sleep at your place tonight or my place. Dannie said here would be nice we can watch the transformer's movie I got then. Max said yes that would be cool. Max pulls into the drive way and help Dannie in with her things.

Adam set watching TV as Annette sleep he know she my be there for a while so he locks the camper doors and made some coffee. The smell of the coffee got Annette up. Annette came out and she hugged Adam and said the coffee smells good. Adam said I can make you're some thing if you want me to. Annette said no got some fruit in the ice box if you want it. Adam said fresh fruit not bad idea. Adam said you know we don't have any guns with use tonight don't want to charge it and stay here tonight. Annette said it's up to you the rest of the team is at Chase tonight aren't they.

Adam said yes the camper is locked to and it would take a cutter torch to cut the lock open. Annette said it's ok if I was going to die then I'm glad I'm with you. Adam said the same here if I go down fighting then I would want you in it with me to. Annette eats same fruit and had some coffee and sat next to Adam in the chair. The Tv was playing some old movie that they do at this time of they year. Adam said hunting season is almost over and we can get back in the woods the hunter down the human, wolfman or what ever he is.

Annette said maybe if we don't try to hunt him he wouldn't try to kill use. Adam and Annette were setting there and someone knock on the door. Annette said it must be the camp ground owner. Adam said I will get it just in case. Adam when to the door it was the owner and he said too came on in. The owner was with his wife and he was carrying some type of gun. The owner said the campers got together and got you some brandy and a fruit basket.

We were at the grave yard and it was a nice service. Annette said thanks' I though so to. Adam said what kind of gun is that. The owner said it's one of my elephant guns. Adam said you have more then one? Oh yes the owner's wife said the dam things are all over the place in the house. Adam said do you have one we could use tonight? The owner said sure double barrel or single shot. Adam said anything will do. The owner said hun me and Adam we be right back in a minute had a drink with Annette.

Adam and the camp ground owner with back to his place. Adam walks throw the door and his wife was right the man had about 20 of the guns all over the place. He got one that was double barrel and handed it to Adam. Adam said shit this thing is big. The owner said it will help when you shot it that way it not going to kick so bad. Adam said ok I can see your point.

The owner hand Adam a box of shells only six in the box. Adam said you think that going to be all I need. The owner said if you don't kill it the first two shots then the other four aren't going to do you any good. Adam said yup that's true. The two went back to the camper an Annette and the camp ground owner's wife were having a drink. Adam said we are set of tonight.

The owner said to his wife we should be getting back in for the night. His wife said ok and hugged Annette and said see you later hun. Annette said tell every one thanks. The owner said we will have a good night. Adam said well I will Adam locked the door and we should be all set.

Annette said want a drink this is good brandy. Adam said sure and they sat back in the chair and hug each other and drank bandy. The night was peaceful Annette was ok but the pain was still fresh in her eyes. Adam said you want other hun and she said yes just one more. Adam pour another roll and to two went into the bed room area. Adam said it's going be a long time before the pain gets better.

Annette said I'm not sure it will I'm going to have to get a brake from this place for a while. Adam said you wait until this case is over and I will go with you. Annette said I can't leave Bob behind he my best brother. Adam said no we can't we can go all throw the USA and see everything we wanted to see and find a place where we could call home. Annette said that sounds great and yes Adam I will wait for you. The two finished there drinks and when to bed. Adam hug and held Annette until the both of them fell to sleep.

Dannie set her things down and went to the kitchen for some water. Max said I'm going to put the movie in ok? Dannie said yes do you want any thing hun. Max said a beer would be nice hun. Dannie got two beers and headed to the living room. Max was on the couch and had turns on the movie. Max said this is one of those movies you could watch over and over again. Dannie said I know I got one or two like that to. Dannie handed the beer to Max and sat down next to him

The movie was as good as the first time they saw it and both enjoy laying there and being together. Dannie was feeling sleep and Max was almost asleep Dannie said I think it's time for bed hun. Max and Dannie went up to the bedroom. Dannie got in bed and she watches while Max got in bed. Dannie jumps Max and kisses him hard.

Max was happy and lay back in the bed and let Dannie kisses' him. Max and Dannie did some making out then things cooled down and there went to sleep.

Dannie dreams were in the back of her head and she didn't want other dream for puppies she had to think of some thing good before she went to bed so the night would be ok. Dannie dreams wouldn't go good but it gave her a view of the future if she did kill the wolfman. The year she know was around 2030. The human race as we know had charge we some how slipped back in time. The wolfman had lived and his people were the master race now.

The good news was everyone was on the same level no poor no rich. The people were living without cars, houses or anything the humans of the pass need. The people were stronger and hunted to live. Most for the group of people were hunter together. People had hair again and looked some what like wolfman but more man than wolf. Dannie said it's true the human race is in rewind. Dannie didn't know what to do the people were losing the skills that they parent had.

Returning to a more wild animal type of life. The sad thing was no one was growing anything anymore and the food was getting short. The food supply was so low that the groups of people would meet and it was the kill or be eaten. The end time were near. City lied in dust as if the big boom had killed everyone. Dannie was shocked that this would happen to the world her and the two white wolves had failed the world would die because they lose the battle.

Dannie sat on a tall building to see the world below. Was this how man was to be the maker of his own death. Tears ran down Dannie's face as she watches the last two human battle for life. Would man die at there own hands or would humans some how came back from the edge. A white light came a sat next to Dannie the voice in the light said I guess human are no more. Dannie said why father why let him do it. I love them so I let them make there own way.

Now with you I will start life over again and this time woman we rule and man will follow. So Dannie you are with Max and you two have the earth to yourself live long and make me happy this time. With that the light went back to the heavens and Dannie rule the earth as it's new Eve and Max as Adam.

It was true life had come around to live once again. Dannie wakes up and was sad tears came in her eyes and she though man can't die this way not if she could do anything about it. Dannie couldn't fall back to sleep, but he morning was almost here. Max was sleeping good and she curls up and lay next to him. Dannie was almost nuts, what do the dreams mean and how does she fit into him. Was she going to kill this wolfman thing or have some hand in it death.

Adam wakes up and was setting in the kitchen area watching the sun came up. It was going to be a good day and Annette had a lot of thing to do. Annette hope that Bob would go with her and Adam. She know she had to sell the dinner and close shop. Bob would have to close his house up or get someone to rent it. Adam came out and kiss Annette and said thinking this morning?

Annette said yes you still want to go ahead with the plans to leave? Annette said more then ever now she needed a brake. Adam said good because I still want to go if you want me. Annette said it wouldn't be the same Without you. Adam said good we need to head to town so Bob will be able to find use. Annette said let take a shower and go then. Adam said you first I will make coffee and ran the gun back to the camp ground owner. Annette said ok be right out shortly then.

Adam unlocked the door and went to the camp ground owner's house. The owner was up and said hi to Adam. Adam said hi and that he was returning the gun. The owner said he was welcome to use it anytime. Adam said he would have love to shot it once just to see how it kicked. The owner said like someone hitting you in the chest with a hammer. Adam said that sounds like fun to me.

The owner said you have to come by and let me shot the 50 cal. And I let you shot this animal. Adam said it's a deal have to do it some time so. Adam went back to the camper and Annette was just getting out of the shower and Adam said fresh coffee is on. Adam kiss her and went to the shower and got cleaned up. Adam came out and Annette was already and Adam put his cloths on and grad a cup of coffee to go.

The ride to town was a short one and just before town was a two-mile strange run. Annette said look a morse in the road way up there. Adam slowed down, he said that's not a morse it's the wolfman. The wolfman saw Adam had stop and started to run that him, even those he was still a 100 yards away.

Adam said keep and eye on him Annette Wait I turn around. Adam started moving back ward to get away from the wolfman. Then he stopped shit he said the other is still alive to she came up behind use now. Adam said will Annette this is going to be a bad day for someone. Adam put the truck in drive and hit the gas the little truck smoke the tire and start back at the male wolfman. Adam told Annette to put her head down below the windshield. Annette got down your going to hit it. Adam said he giving me no choice.

Adam looks ahead the wolfman was closing fast and Adam was about 55 miles an hour and going. Adam said came on you huge son of a bitch and feel ford power. The wolfman moved aside at the last second and Adam put his hand out the window and gave him the finger chicken shit he said, but Adam only had a few miles before he had to slow to turn so he keeps down on it until he had to slow.

Annette said it ok to came back up hun. Adam said yes the wolfman was chicken. Annette looked back and saw the two wolfs going back into the woods on the river side. Will Adam said I just this leaves no doubt that we got to kill him and the female before they get use. Adam got on the phone to the others and ask if anything went down in town last night. The group said no but we haven't heard from Steve or Kevin.

Adam said will the male and female just tried to kill them so get ready and we will go looking for the boys. Adam hung up and said shit I hope Steve and Kevin are ok. Annette said I hope they are ok to they are good kids. Adam and Annette got to the station and the group was there and ready. Bob said what happen Annette? Annette said I will tell you up stairs when I have a gun in my hands.

Adam kiss her and went up to get his gun Annette and Bob went with him. Adam grad his gun and said now it's war. Annette said keep a cool head he want's you to make a mistake. Adam said we will he isn't going to get me off my game again. Annette kisses Adam and Adam when to find the boys. Adam got back out side and he said we need to watch really good now the wolf's want use die.

Peter said we should go track them the show them we aren't afraid of them. Adam said we need to know what happen to Steve and Kevin first. Adam and the group set out to find the boys die or alive. The first place they went was by the wildness drive road. As Adam turned the counter to came to the road both the boys cars were in the road one rolled over and the other run into the side of the other.

Adam hit the gas and got their as fast as he could he pulled up and saw the two boys in the grass on the side of the road. One of them was still moving. Adam and the others jump out to see how the boys were. Thank God Adam said the boys were alive but looked like there been in a battle. Adam yelled to Chase to call the ambulance. Chase made the call. Adam and Peter were with the boys.

Steve said they can speak they told use if we didn't hunt them any more they wouldn't kill use. Adam said there spoke to you. Then they said so we know they wasn't shitting use they brake our leg like sticks. Adam said at less you're alive. Steve said yup I guess that's good. Adam said that he would make sure the two die for this and that the two boys would have their car repaired.

Steve black out from the pain. Adam looked at the group and said we got to stick together and bring these wolfs down.

Dannie got out of bed and went to make some coffee. She sat on the back porch with the sun hitting her in the face it was cold, but refreshing. She heard Max came down stairs and into the kitchen he came out with a cup of coffee and said good morning hun you sleep ok? Dannie said yes I just got up for some coffee. Max said it smell fresh out here doesn't it. Dannie said this time of year it smell the best out here.

Dannie said do you ever think of how the world we be in 10 to 30 years from now hun. Max said the way things are going now I often wonder if there we be a tomorrow. The USA is heading for a big crash and we will be there to try to pick it up after it's all blown to hell. Dannie said good I'm glad I'm not the only one who thinks that way. Max said I bet there's lot that feel the same way.

Dannie said do you want something to eat before work hun. Max said do you have fruit hun? Dannie said yup I will make some up for use and we can eat it in the kitchen where it's warmer. Max said ok I'm in for that. Max watch Dannie walks into the house he was thinking of how good she looked in sweats. Dannie got out some fruit and had some fresh grapes to she cut the fruit up and put it on a plate for them.

Will Dannie said guess here's to the end of the world. Max smiles only after we get married. Dannie said a long time after we get married. Max said when do you think we should set the date? Dannie said this morning would be nice. Max said it sounds great before we are done coffee I hope that way we can shower together. Dannie said now that sounds like a plan. Max looked at the clock I got to shower so you can get ready .

Dannie said I can go first that way you not going to have to hang around waiting on me. Ok Max said I will clean up down here then get a shower. Dannie kiss Max and went for a shower. Max was thinking he should go up and get in the shower with her. Max cleaned up and went up stair to see if she was out of the shower. Dannie came out and sat on the bed and said your turn stud.

Max smile and went of a shower. Dannie wanted to get back in the shower and send her man to work with a big smile but she said no Max wants to wait. Max came out of the shower he got dress and the two went down stairs and turned off the coffee and headed to Max's place. Dannie was watching the fields on the way the grasses were turning brown. Max pulled into the parking lot and went around back. Dannie and Max went inside to set the bar up for business that day. Dannie clean the floor and Max stock the bar when they were done. Max said back and made out with Dannie.

Dannie said lets open the door and start the day. Max when to the door and Dannie jump on his back and he carry her to the doors. Max spun her around and pin her again the wall. Max said I love you and we need to set a date so today when you out a about think of a time and place. Dannie said lets getting married then have a wedding down the road. Max said it's a good idea, but your Mom and Dad will get mad. We can tell him the date and just go on with the plans.

Dannie said I think we need to do something soon before we both go mad. Max said if you want sure maybe is week end we can try to do it I mean get married. Max said I know cold showers aren't helping anymore. Dannie kiss them and said sure let go for it. Max said good we need to do it soon. Dannie said yes we do need to do it soon.

Max open the door and the cool air felt good. Dannie hugs him and said do you want me to take the truck in for an oil change? Max said could you. It would help me out big time. Dannie said sure would love to. Max gave her his key and said thank hun and kiss her. Dannie said I should head down there be for he gets busy. Max said ok I love you hun and see about noon maybe. Dannie said sure hun and kisses him. Dannie went out back and got in Max's truck and started it she let the motor warm up. She had to pull the seat up and play with the mirror than she put it in gear and went to Stanley's.

Adam got the boys to a safe place and had the cars turned up right and toed to Linscott's auto to have the body work done on the car and repainted. Adam said we should go and tell the boy's father now so he doesn't learn it second hand. Adam calls the boy's father and tell them everything. Adam said now we go to war. Peter said we need some how to track the animal. Chase said what about the tracking device in the female wolf. Fred said you know that could work if we can get the right radio wave.

Devvan said do we find that? Mary said if we could find just a peace of the tracker we could see if they're a radio wave number on it. Adam said let go then it's about time we start play the game. The team went back to the old burn down house and start to look for the tracking unit. Adam and Peter went into what was left of the basement and looked for anything. The rest of the team fan out and look the grounds over.

You could see people looking out the windows hoping the house wasn't going to blow up again. Fred said Peter right behind you on the other side for the desk. Adam move the desk an found a broken tracker. Well Adam said this isn't going to help use much. Fred said throw it here Adam. Adam handed the tracker to Fred. Fred looked it over and said most of the parts are here I bet Jean could make one for these thing.

Adam said she sure helped use the last time let see. The team loaded up and started to Fred home. Adam said to Peter we need somewhere to get them out in the open to hunt them down. Peter said you remember once we done those two we still have the white one to deal with. Adam said shit were going to be up to our asses in wolf shit or human whatever the fuck it is.

The team got to Fred's house and unloaded and went down to see Jean. Fred came throw the door and said hun I'm home and I got a few friends. Jean came to the living room with Coco fast on her heals. Jean said no not other hard drive? Adam said no and handed the tracker to her. Oh Jean said a homing device. Jean said I can fit it, but I can sure make a new one with the part in the lab. Jean said but didn't you have the tracking device with you the last time that came from the wolfman? Adam said yes, but we were hoping that the female still had hers.

Mary said I see Coco is getting alone good down here. Jean said yes she my best friend. Jean said bye the way were's Maxy and Pad? Devvan said they are in the truck. Jean said is that smart with the wolfman thing running around hunting you. Mary, Devvan and Chase went back to the truck and got the dogs. Adam said will it takes a while to get this done Jean. Jean said about an hour maybe a little more. Fred you and the others can kick back and enjoy the pond room until I'm done. Fred said good then he stopped did you hear that? Peter said it's sounded like gun fire. Adam said it was ,we must have trouble up top. The three men grads their guns and started run for the door. Fred yelled to Jean to shot the door behind them.

Dannie went to Stanley's and pull up with Max's truck. Dannie walks in and George was behind the counter. Dannie ask George if she could get Max's truck in for an oil charge and grease job. George said you're lucky we can but it in right now if you want? Dannie said great then she went to set down in the seats in the front window. The man in the service bay came out to get the keys and got in the truck and put it in the bay. Dannie watched as he charge the oil and check the truck over. The man did a great job at looking at all the levels of oil.

He moved it back out and checked the oil level one more time to make sure it was set. Dannie said to herself 15 minutes not bad. George said your truck is done Dannie. Dannie got up and pay George and said that was fast. George said he a good man on the oil charging bay. Dannie walks out and looks at the truck and saw it needed a good cleaning. Dannie said I hope Max doesn't care.

Dannie when home the day was still nice and warm. Dannie pull Max's truck up to the back porch so she could wash and clean the truck. Dannie started with the inside and cleaned window up the seats a wash the dash and made it shine. Then when she was happy with that, she washes the truck down and it shined like new she thought she would wax it for him to, but she had to run over and check Pat's house for him.

Dannie went out front of Pat's house to pick up the mail and look the house over to make sure everything was locked. Dannie came to the back door and it open she said will Pat must have forgot to lock it. Dannie open the door and yelled hello anyone here. No one yelled back to her. She walks inside and set the mail on the table. Dannie turned to go and saw something in the kitchen as she was going out. Dannie picked it up and it was a jar of sex jell. Dannie sat it on the counter and wash her hands she said I don't want to know where that's been.

Dannie locked the back and went back to waxing Max's truck. Dannie said I hope Max like Mother's wax it cost a good price and it shines like glass. Dannie got the wax on and use her cordless buffer to shine it. Dannie was really happy the truck was really bright and it was clean. Dannie went back into the house and washed up and put thing away. Dannie put on some clean geans and a warm shirt.

Dannie got back in the truck and headed back over to the bar. She came into town and stop at her job to check the mail and see if everything was all right. Dannie went throw the mail and found a post card from Crissy it read have a great time here it's fun to be in love. Signed love Crissy PS by the way I'm going to be gone for other week so have other week off with pay. Dannie said to herself getting sex must have made her happy. Dannie was getting use to the time off she said to herself this could be a good thing. Dannie got back in the truck and headed to the bar. She was happy now one more week and no work.

Dannie pull Max's truck up out back where he always parks it. Dannie tries to set the mirrors an seat back where they were. Dannie got out and she saw Max's standing their looking at her. Max said good job girl. I like the shine. Dannie said its Mother's wax it does a great job. Dannie throw the keys to Max and said she is clean as a baby's bottom in the inside to. Max came down and hug and kiss her did you get the oil done to? Dannie said yup all good and ready to go.

Max said will I made something good for lunch today hope you're hungry. Dannie said you know I'm hungry. Max said will I hope you like Mexican food . Dannie said if it's hot I will. Max said have a seat and I will get you a beer and your food. Max came out with a bowl and it had a large taco salad in it. Dannie smile Max you must stop reading my mind I love taco salad. Dannie put her fork in it and took a bit she could feel the hot in the salad.

Dannie said Max this is great is this going to be on the new menu. Max said I will give it a week and see how many I sell. Dannie said I hope you sell a lot because this is really good. Max said thank and went to sever some other customer. Dannie ate her food and sat and watch people in the bar. She saw an older pear of people setting there enjoy a beer and a kiss. Dannie was setting there and head a loud bang like it was far away but really strong.

Max looked at her and said what the hell was that. Dannie said it sounded like something blow up. Dannie when to the back door and all the way across the field in the foot hills see could see smoke coming up. Max walks out did you see anything Dannie. Dannie said yes over there in the hills. Max said hope it wasn't other still. Dannie said people still run those things around here. Max said oh yes but you wouldn't catch me drinking it. Max and Dannie returned the bar.

Dannie said Max can I get other beer this taco salad is great. Max said sure and poured her other. Max said here you are hun enjoy. Max watch Dannie ate and waited on a customer until she was done. Max said so what you going to do for the rest of the day. Dannie said going to see if I can find out how to get married that's if you still want to then have a wedding later. Max said yes I still want to.

Ok Dannie said I'm going to find out how to do it. Max gave her a kiss and Dannie went out to the jeep to go back into town and to the town office to see what she have to do. Dannie walks into the East Millinocket town office and said to the lady behind the window what she needed to do to get married. The lady said the two of you came in fill out a licence and fine a justice of the peace and one person to stand up for you and that's all. Dannie said wow is that all cool she said and went back to report to Max. Max saw Dannie come in the back and set at the bar.

Adam ran as fast as he could to reach the top side Peter and Fred on his heals. Adam stops when he saw Mary in the hole shooting at the truck area. Adam said what's going on? The wolf are trying to get to Chase and Devvan Mary said. Adam said where are there? In the back cage with the dog's Mary said. Adam looked and could hear the two trying to get the cage open, but he could only see the feet on of the animals. Adam said Mary let me see your gun. Adam took the gun and arm at the foot and shot hit the animal and pissing it out.

The two wolfs stopped what they were doing and ran down the line for cars out for sign of Adam. The four came out and set up guard for the others. Than a loud bang and a loud howl as if something was really hurt. Peter knock on the side of the truck hay you can come out now. Chase yelled back can't the door lock. Mary went around open the door. Devvan and the two dogs came out first than Chase.

Adam said dam you smell funny. Chase said don't even go there. Fred said came over here you guys now. The others move around the counter the see one of the wolfman laying at the end of the field. Adam said lets going it the charge we needed. Peter said slow Adam the other one can't be too far away. The group slowly move into area where the wolf was laying , but he wasn't going any where without legs.

Fred said the bomb I throw over there must had not gone off until he stepped on it. Careful he still moving the wolfman turned over and looked at the group. In a voice of pain and madden he said you got to kill use we can control the hungry for human flesh. Adam said where the other one he said she isn't going to be fun hunting because she will hunt you and kill you when your off your guard. Adam said will see about that shit head. And she carrying my child so she will not stop at anything to kill you.

Chase said it me shot him and be done with his mouth. I'm glad it's over run from the others and the white wolfs you set on me is getting old kill me now you poor example for humans. Adam said the white wolfs aren't from use. The wolfman laughs then have fun trying to kill him. Mary said let me see your gun Chase said why? Mary said I'm sick of his shit.

Adam said anything else to say before you die? The wolfman said I'll save a seat in hell for you and laughs and started to claw at him. Adam draws up and shot the wolfman in the head and the head was gone in a bang of blood and parts. Just after that you could hear a low howl maybe a mile away from the female as she know the male was die. Fred said we need some gas to burn the body with. Chase said I have a can on the back for the car I'll get it.

Chase and Mary and Devvan went to the car for the gas. Adam poured it all over the body and ran a small trail back two the group. He lit it and watches the fire burn the body of the wolfman. Mary said one down and one and a half to go. Adam said if the white wolf isn't part of these two them what really is she. Peter said the one million-dollar question. The body seem to burn with the flames of hell it was got in a short time.

Fred said I'm going to tell Jean so she doesn't worry. Ok said Adam we will be there in a few. Fred walks back down into the house and told Jean everything about what happen. After Jean charmed down and she cried I though you were hurt. Fred said know he had to stop working with the group and be with his wife. Fred hug Jean and said don't worry hun I will be here with you until this thing over from now on. Jean said now they're going to need your skill at tracking this female. Fred said your sure hun. Yes I'm sure dear.

Fred hugs her and they went back to see what Jean could do with the tracker. Adam and the others came back down and shot the front door and went out back to see Jean. Jean was happy to see all the guys and dogs alive. Adam said how we doing? Jean said good almost have a blue print set to make one, there she said now to check and see how may things I'm going to need. Jean went over to her part's den and looked throw her parts. Good Jean said I got parts of three of them.

Peter said why three? Jean said so you all can trap her in from three sides. Adam said we need a good mind like you're in the police force. Chase said we need food so why don't we get some thing and cook it while she works on the units. Jean said good idea. Adam said ok now what to eat? Mary said we could order from the Chinese place down the road. Jean said I've never tried that type of food I'm in. Adam said ok lets order and go get the food and let Jean work.

Devvan called in the order and the team went as a group to the place remembering the warning from the male wolfman. The group went after the food and return to the pond room and the big table to eat. Jean came out and said me and Coco smell some thing good out here. Peter said I think the night shift is going the get harry. Mary said why do you think that? Peter said night is the best time to get use off guard. Devvan said yes but the dark is just as bad for her as it for use. Fred said it doesn't have to be with night scopes and night vision glasses. Adam said your not saying we hunt her at night?

Fred said why not if she has a tracker on her we could throw her off by not letting her rest. Adam said as crazy as it sounds it would work keep her on her toes and run her down. Mary said I know what your saying, but isn't that going to run use down also. Adam said yes but if we work in groups of three we can sleep some and the others run her that night. Chase said what about the ones sleeping what going to keep her from killing the ones sleeping. Fred said if the ones' sleep were in some place safe it would work. Fred said and I bet Jean would love having you guys around day and night. Adam said maybe just maybe this will work. Jean said I don't know about these things but it sounds little a plan to me. Jean said by the way this food is unreal I've never had anything like it

Dannie said all we need to do is get a licence and a justice of the peace and one person as a witness. Max said that cool so do you think we should still do it or wait. Dannie said I think we should do it. Max said cool will when do we do it. Dannie said soon I hope. Max said we can think it over tonight and make your minds up in the morning.

Dannie said cool I think we can do that and come up with a good plan. Dannie said she was going up to the room for a nap and wait for you. Max gave her a big kiss and said see you in a few. Dannie said sure will hun and went out the back door and up the steps to Max's room. Dannie went in and get into bed thinking of the day and she would soon be Max's wife. Dannie though man its going to be fun now we can do it anywhere we feel like it.

Dannie curl up to Max's pillow and fell to sleep with a big smile on her face. She started to dream the door open and she went down the stairs to the parking lot. Dannie was faced with a group of people that were all in peace's blood was all over the place and a die wolf in the center. The wolf turned over and said I didn't kill you ,but my woman will make sure you never have the charge to have children. Dannie said your die why don't you think I can't kill her to? The wolfman said because she carrying my baby and I know you not a killer of kids or are you .

I will do as my father want's of me. Your father the wolf said is a lesser God then mind. Dannie laughs so he tell you this, your father is an old fool. The wolfman said we'll see about that . The wolfman said you have to kill her first before she kills your friends and family. Dannie said she isn't going to have the change to do it I'm going to rip her heart out before she can get to them. The wolfman said is that the sound of someone dead right now.

Dannie could her a voice of someone in pain it seems to be coming from the north. Dannie started to run for the sound and the wolfman said don't be to slow hun . Dannie made it to where the sound was and she saw Max on the ground and the female wolf standing over him. The female said I don't have a man any more so I'm going to take this one. Dannie said after you kill me first. The female wolf said I'm going to enjoy that too much.

The female charge Dannie an she hit hard and the two fell to the ground. Dannie said will about time someone with a little power came into this fight. Dannie got up and back handed the female and she went throw the air and hit a tree. The female wolf said not bad. The female wolf charge again and hit Dannie harder. The two roll down a small hill a into a road way. Dannie got to her feet and saw a large truck coming for the female wolf. Dannie laughs at her because she didn't see it coming. Dannie looks at her and said its time for you to get the next ride out of here.

The female wolf turned just to catch the truck slamming into her and the truck and the female with over the side of the hill and hit the ground so hard that the truck blow up and burned. Something came rolling down the road and stop at Dannie feet it was the baby of the females. Dannie pick it up and it looked at her, the child said Mom . Dannie said no and he snaps at her. Dannie said Mommy went that way and throw the baby into the burning truck. The baby gave out a scream of something being cooked alive.

Dannie knee to the ground and said father did I do the right thing with the little one. The two other white wolves came and pick Dannie up and said yes hun you did the right thing he cannot live if man is to be. Dannie said but that doesn't seems right he didn't have a charge to do anything . The two white wolfs said yes and he not going to kill anyone one now to. Dannie turn and went back up the hill to find Max . Max was setting there and said you did your father proud. Max said if man is to live we have to protect him from himself. Dannie wakes up and was starting to understand her dream some what better. Dannie heard the door open it was Max. Max said you get any sleep hun. Dannie smiles yup and I'm ready to get you she jumps up and jump into Max's arm. Dannie said I do if you do? Max said I do and we will.

Jean returned to the lab to work on the trackers. Coco was right behind her and she said came girls if you want to visit. The dogs got up and went to the lab with her and Jean started to work on the tracking units. Jean got one of the unit done and turn it on it started to beep. Jean got up and went to the group Jean came around the corner with the dogs. Jean said I think well have something up on top side again. If I read this right she about two miles and closing. Adam said great job Jean the tables had turned But why is she coming back here? Chase said I think she wants to kill some of use.

Jean said that would be my guess to. Jean said I will start on the other two and you guys can check to see what she up to. Adam said let roll she could be near in a few minutes. Fred said ok but lock the door when we leave Jean just in case she gets by use. Jean said get going she not far away now and take this with you. Peter said great now The edge is on our side for a change. The team went up to see if they could see what she was up to. Adam was the first one out and the unit was almost sold red. Adam said set up a circle and get ready for a fight.

The beeps when sold safety off she here somewhere over there. The group heard a howl that make their skin claw. A loud female male voice saying you will all die for this. Adam said over where we burned her male. Open fire we may be lucky and hit her. The team open fire in the area they heard the voice come from. The tracker started to beep again and the light showed she was moving away from them. Devvan said that felt good for a charge shooting and not bring shot at.

The lights slow became slower and slower. Adam said I think we got our point across. Chase said I hope she knows we got the upper hand now. Fred said we my had the upper hand now, but she running on revenge witch makes her more powerful then before. The light stop beeping and the team started back down and Adam said shit Annette and Bob are at my place. The team loaded up and headed to Adam's place. As the team enter town the lights started to beep again.

Adam said she headed for town all right. Adam turned on his light and step on it the other did the same. Adam pulls in the station just in time the see the female enter the stairs of his home. Adam jumps out and opens the door he started up the step as a hail of gun fire came from his room. Adam and the other couldn't get near. The lights started to slow again he know the female must have got out the back way. Adam yelled up Annette are you ok? Annette yelled back yes. Adam said we are all here so don't shot guys. Annette said ok I think she went down the back stairs. Adam and the others got up and went in to see Annette and Bob.

Annette set her gun down and hug Adam. Annette said if we hadn't heard the siren we would have been toast. Adam said so your ok then good I was hoping we get here first. Annette said how you know she was coming here. Adam said Jean make use a tracker for the wolf. Fred said lets get what we need and head back to the house. Devvan said yes let get this war rolling. Annette said I want in no wolf try to take me out and I stand by and do shit. Bob said if a sis is in harms way then I'm in to. Adam said lets roll then and the group headed back to Fred's place. The team got back to Fred and unload and went in.

Jean said I see we have two new people. Adam said yes this is Annette my girlfriend and her bother Bob. Jean said welcome and I will need to show you around. Annette and Bob said it would be great to see the hold house. Jean show them around and Coco was right with him every step. Jean came back and said the other two trackers are ready to roll let kick some ass !

Fred looks at her and said hun you getting into this Jean said I guess. Adam said now we got two more people on the team we can put two cars with tracker in them and one here at base. Jean said this is going to be base cool she said. Adam said I think tonight we will began to keep the asshole up all day long running. Mary and Chase you we be in one car and Bob and Devvan in the other. In the morning we will put me and Annette and Fred and Peter. We will keep working in 12 hour shift until she make a mistake and we kill her.

Dannie said ok now we got to think of a time that we are going to get married for real. Max said I was thinking Christmas day. Dannie said you know what would be a great idea wouldn't it. Max said yes what greater gift to each other than each other. Dannie said do we gift rip each other.

Max said anything You want hun. Dannie said we can get the licence after work today if you want to. Max said it fine with me were, do we get it? Dannie said at the town office. Cool Max said I think we will do that. Dannie said you should almost be done here aren't you. Max said yes just got to clean in the kitchen a little then I'll be ready to go. Dannie said good can I help you with the cleaning. Max said yes if you like doing dishes.

Dannie yes lets get them done and went back into the kitchen to help. Dannie said this is the first time I've been out here the place is almost spotless. Max said you have to keep it this way or you get closed for food. Dannie started to clean the dishes and Max worked on the grill it looks really clean after he got done. Dannie said you must do a lot of dishes in a day times. Max said it can be a mess sometime and hard to keep on top of.

Dannie said will you do a great job at keep it clean. Max said thanks hun it's nice some times to have someone know you do good work. Dannie said will I'm done how you doing huns. Max said same here will lets going check out this license. Dannie and Max got into the truck and headed to th town office. Max got out and Dannie came with him to the office. Max looked at the women behind the counter and said we are here to get a marriage license.

The women said sure I need your and her driver license of an id and we can fill out the form for you. The women with back and got the paper work out and started to type. Max looked at Dannie and smiles I can't believe were doing it Max said. Dannie hugs him and said it's just the laws to make it illegal we still need a justice of the peace to marry use. Max said are you getting all light headed and a warm feeling inside. Dannie said yes and a scare feeling to what if Mom and Dad fine out. Max said we should be able to keep it from them until we really get married.

Dannie said I sure hope so will she coming back. The women handed back they Id's and said it well be this feed that the bottom and you to sign it and your on your way. Max gave her the money and sign his name and then Dannie sign hers the woman said good luck with you marriage you to. Dannie and Max said thanks and went back to the truck. Dannie looked at the license and gave Max a big kiss. Max and Dannie were very happy.

Max said now to find a justice of the peace. Dannie said we could go back to your place and look in the yellow pages for one. Max said ok lets do it. Dannie and Max headed back to the bar and went up stairs to Max 's place. Max grads the phone book and looked in the yellow pages for justices. Max got to the pages and was reading throw the list of names most we in Lincoln. Max looked at one name and said well I'll be dammed. Dannie said what wrong Max is there no one in the book. Max said yup a lot of them in here and one name you may know . Dannie said well tell me Max how is it? Max smiled, Vicki is a justice of the peace. Dannie said no the Vicki that works for you. Max said yup the every same one.

Dannie said do you think she would marry use. Max said why not and he got up and said lets find out. Max and Dannie went down stairs and Vicki was behind the bar. Dannie went over to her and ask if she was a justices of the peace still. Vicki said yes I'm still one. Dannie said then can I ask you something? Vicki said sure as she drinks some water. Dannie said marry me and Max . Vicki face was shock and she spit out her water and started to jump and hug the both of them . Max said does this mean yes? Vicki still jumping around hug, the two said yes you big baby.

Vicki said ok then when do you want this to happen? Max looks at Dannie and said well as soon as we can. Vicki said how about tomorrow night after we close the bar. Max looked at Dannie and she said yes and Max said ok. Vicki said you have someone to stand up for you? Max said no we haven't asked anyone. Vicki said that's ok I will get you someone. Max said great thanks Vicki and hugs her and Dannie did to. The two went back up stairs and set on the bed. Dannie said tomorrow night cool you going to near a good suit my man. Max said and you need a dress hun. Dannie said dam we need wedding bands. Max said we can hit the road and get to Linclon and get them the same place as we did your ring. Dannie said th ones in Millinocket were good . Max said even better let go the to went up to Millinocket and got the weddings that they saw in Ferland's . Max said these are real nice ones aren't they. Dannie said just right she kiss Max and they went back to Max's place . They got out and went up stairs.

Dannie said I got a good white dress that I can use Max said I got a black suit that stills fit to. The two curled up on the bed hugging and kissing. Both still on cloud nine. Max pulled her close and said this is the happiest I've every been. Dannie said me to hun. So what we still going throw with the real one at Christmas? Max said you bet and we could going anywhere you want for the honey moon.

Adam said will lets get the plan together and start it. Ok Mary, Chase, Bob Devvan you will take the front 12 hours and work in groups of two if one picks her up call the other and team up the run her. Here is a tracker for the both of you and you should have one AK and 50 cal. In both cars too gave you max fire power. Bob said I want the 50 cal now I hope I see her.

Adam said not gun fire in town unless she in the clear. After your shift is over we all meet up top to charge out and tell what happen that shifts. Will good luck you guys and happy hunting. The group all went up as the others loaded up and put one dog in each car as a warning. The group headed off to hunt down the wolf female and keep her up all night. Adam and the others returned to Fred's home and set up in the pond room to sleep.

Jean said I hope this works and we get her trap in a few days. Adam said thanks to you we maybe able to kill her without her killing use first. Fred said yes I told you she was smart Will Jean said have a good night and see you in the morning . Good night the team said as they all got into the army beds Fred had set up . Annette said hope they do ok tonight . Adam said I don't see why they shouldn't .

Devvan and Bob went to the east end of town and started to run a back a fore to pick up a sign . Mary and Chase went to the west side and worked there way in . Bob said will it looks as if we have a bit the tracker was just lighting up . Devvan said I'll call the others and then try to fine her . Devvan got Chase on the phone he said we got a light and that we are down by the boat landing in Medway .

Chase said ok me and Mary well be there don't try to take her on alone. Devvan said yup will call if the light get stronger. Bob said well it seems as if she isn't going anyway she could be sleeping or just killed something and eating. Devvan looked at Maxy and she was ok with things to. Devvan said Maxy is cool with the spot to see would be going nuts right now if she was close to use.

Devvan looked back up the hill a set of lights were coming down the road, Devvan said that must be Mary and Chase. The two got out as the car pulled up. Chase said we just got a light when we hit the top of the hill. Devvan said she isn't moving right now so she sleeping or feeding. Mary said I bet she on the island tonight. Chase said how the hell we going to run her if we can get her off he island. Bob looked funny will I can help if you stop by the house before we go over there.

Chase said will we got to get her up and Bob is part of the team now. Ok Bob said lets go to the house and do this thing. Bob got to his house it was on their way to the island. Bob went in the house and came out with a rocket launcher and three rockets. Chase looked at Bob and said where you get this? Bob said at a yard sale and laugh. Chase said yard my ass. Ok lets hit the old farm road an it well take use to the base for the island keep radios on and report any charges .

The group went down the road and turned on the old farm road and headed down the road to the island as they got closer the signal got stronger. Marry must be right it looks and if she on th island right now Devvan said. Bob said we can now wake her up and get her moving tonight. The group pull up the old bridge landing and set to shot Bob's toy.

Bob said now when I shot this thing no one is to be behind me ok. Mary said whys that Bob. Bob said you'll see once the thing goes off. Chase said shot the thing at the center and top we don't want to bring down the power lines on the island. Bob armed for the center and said fire in the hole. A flame came out the back and the dirt and grass were burned. The rocket hit the island about ten feet in and the hole island was shacking . Mary said I see what you mean now Bob.

Chase said if we need to shot other one I want to try it. Bob said no trouble. The team looked at the tracker and she was on the move. Bob said it looks like she headed to the top end for the island. Chase said ok let shot other one that the top and drive her off the island. Bob handed the launcher to Chase. Chase said ok let clear some trees and arm for the top of the island. He fired the rocket and it hit just where he wanted to. Chase gave out a cowboy yell and said man I need one of these.

The team show that the hit worked she was headed off the island the far side of town. Bob said she on the run now. Chase said will let keep her on her toes tonight. The team all got back into the cars and went to rt. 116 across the singing bridge. Devvan hit the bridge first and the bridge play its song dam that does sound like a song. Bob said yup that where it got its name.

The team got to the interstate over pass and the signal got stronger and stronger. The groups stop to see if there could see her anywhere. Dam said Mary. The signal is strong she should be near. Just then a big truck roll across the interstate over pass blow it's horn as if to get some thing to move out of his way. Devvan said there she is and point to the bridge . She is a smart shit she crossing above use. Chase said let go then she could be in the deep woods before we get to the other side.

The team headed for the other side and be the time there got over there she had made it the woods behind the Irving station. Bob called on the radio maybe we can get her before she crosses the Grindstone road. Chase ok head at way and we will be right behind you. The team flip around and headed to the road. One there they sat at the end for the road and watch the signal from the trackers. Mary said dam it's almost time to switch off and we having so much luck.

Devvan radio she heading this way and she came out f the wood about a hundred yard up the road. The team jump out and open fire on her she hit the woods on the other side and was headed away from them now. Chase said she going to hit the river and the woods on the other side by the boat landing it looks like we need to head in and charge over. Bob said shit and we are just began. Chase said I know but we need to keep fresh so that we can run her down. Devvan said ok I guess.

The team headed back to base and to report in the Adam and the others. The group got their Adam and the others were just coming up from the house. Adam said ok did you she her tonight. Bob laugh yup she up and running. Chase said yes true to the wolf alarm clock, he open the trunk to show the others . Adam said what the hell did you do with that thing. Chase said we waked her up and drove her off the island with it. Where did you get it Adam said? Chase looked at Bob and said in a yard sale and smiled. Annette said I seen it in that yard sale before and she smiles at Bob to. Ok Adam said as long as the island isn't on fire we should be ok.

Dannie said lets try to get some sleep I can't see how but lets try. Max was happy and he couldn't wait until tomorrow night. Dannie felt the same way. Dannie curl up to Max and hug him. Dannie said you know we can watch TV if you want. Max said ok and turned the set on it was the movie channel and King Kong was on. Dannie said this is a good movie want to watch it. Max said sure he enjoy the movie the first time he saw it to. Dannie turned over and kissed Max and Max hug her. Max said are you happy hun. Dannie said yes and I hope you are to? Max said I never been this happy before. Dannie said good and rolls back over and Max pulls her in close.

Dannie lay their watching TV and Max was about to fall to sleep. Max said the movie was nice but he was sleepy and lay his head down and hug Dannie and kiss her. Dannie said I feel sleepy , but I'm going to watch the rest of the show. The movie only had about a half hour but she watches it. Dannie could hear that Max was sleeping she turned the TV off and turns over to curl up beside him.

Dannie slowly fell to sleep she began her dream like always good, but then became a little weird. Dannie and Max were about to have they first child. Max was happy and filming the event with his video cam. Dannie was in hard labor and calling Max almost every thing but a man. Dannie could feel the baby coming out with every push. The doctor said you almost have it the baby is coming soon. Then it was over the baby came out with the last push Dannie was wiped out but want to she the baby. The doctor said as the baby started to cry.

You have a baby girl and she ok. Dannie was happy and Max was crying his first child. The doctor handed the baby up to Dannie and Dannie had tears in her eyes she beautiful isn't she Max. Max said just like her Mom. Dannie said would you like to hold her Max. Max set down the video cam and picked up the baby. Max said she got your eyes and your teeth. Dannie said Max babies don't have teeth. Just then the baby grad Max and bit into his throat and the two went down on the floor. The baby was ripping apart Max's neck.

Dannie tries to get up but her legs were still hocked in and she could move. The baby ripped Max's throat out and he was die. The baby was making its way back up the bed and Dannie could move. The baby sat at the foot of the bed Dannie looking at her setting there. The baby was blue and cold she said Mommy I'm cold. Dannie said came to me and I will warm you hun. The baby said no want to go home. Dannie said you your home hun.

The baby started the crawl to Dannie then Dannie could feel the baby try to crawl back inside her. Dannie yelled for the doctor but no one was coming. The baby was pushing her way back into her and Dannie could feel the pain. The baby got about half way in and Dannie could feel her getting back in the spot she started. Dannie was screaming and no one was coming. Then Dannie could hear a small voice Mommy I'm back hug me. The baby ripped her two little arm throw her Mommy check and hug her.

Dannie wakes up all sweaty and breathing hard Max was still sleeping it was about seven that moving. Dannie got out of bed and made a pot of coffee. Dannie was still shacking by the dream but it was only a dream she though. Will at less she hoped? Dannie sat back in the chair with her feet up and was drinking coffee when Max came out of the bedroom. Dannie said good morning hun You sleep good. Max said no had a bad dream but don't remember it.

Dannie said same here and I got up to make use some coffee. Max said good so you still happy that we going to get married tonight. Dannie said yes and I can wait until we get back here after. Max almost spit his coffee out and his face turned red. Dannie said you got to check and see if the suit still fits. Max ok and went to the room and looked for his suit. Max got into to suit and walk out to show Dannie. Max said it still fits me and I think I look good in it. Dannie said think you do I think your really nice looking in it.

Max don't you think you should get ready for work. Dannie said gave me those pants and shirt and I'll press them for you. Max said ok and went back into the bed room and got ready for work. He came back out and set the suit in the chair. Dannie and Max went down to the bar to get it ready. Dannie did the floor and set on the bar while Max fill the bar. Dannie kiss Max and said she had to go iron his pants and get her dress ready for tonight. Max said ok and kisses her and said see you later.

Dannie went back up stairs to do Max's pants and take a shower so see could go after her dress. Dannie got the pants and shirt looking real sharp and put them on a hunger. Dannie got in the shower and wash up she was thinking of her and Max tonight and getting turned on but she got a gripe and wash up . Dannie got out and dried off and went down to her jeep. Dannie went out the drive and could see that Max already had a few people show up to the bar.

Adam and Annette went out in the same car with pad. Fred said Peter in the other with Maxy. Adam called on the radio and said I we check by the boat rental. Peter head to the other end of town and start there. Peter called back we are on the way. Adam went out of town and headed to the boat place and he pulls in and Patrick said hi. Adam said you see any thing around here Patrick.

Patrick said no I 've been here and not a thing has happen. Adam said ok keep your eyes open for any thing and call me if it happens. Patrick said ok see you later. Peter and Fred got to the other side of town and not and thing the tracker was quiet. Peter said you think her move on? Fred said I don't think so she wants use real bad. Peter said I guess you're right we did mess up her man.

Fred said it looks like someone is moving the light on the tracker just lit. Peter called Adam on the CB and said she at the far end of town and moving again. Adam said we will head that way now get your self to and opening so you can see her coming. Peter said we already there setting between the two water ponds up here. Peter called she moving my way we got two lights.

Adam said shit and hit the gas a turned on the lights. Adam calls we are on the way should be there shortly. Peter said good she getting closer. The two men got out and set to shot at the female the signal was getting faster. Fred said she should be here soon then and big crash in the woods about 50 yards in. Peter said the lights are staying the same. Then some more crashing it sounds like she in a fight with some thing Fred said.

Peter could hear because for the siren Peter got on the radio and told Adam to shut the siren off. Adam turned it off and Peter heard other crash. Fred said you think we should check it. Peter said not until Adam is here and all four of use can check it. Adam rolls up and him and Annette got out. Peter said we have heard crashing around in the woods over there, but no signs of her but the light started to fade and Adam said lets going see if we can see her on the field over there.

The team move over to the field and could see stream coming from something. Adam moved closer and said it looks like breakfast gave her a fight. Annette said she that big to bring down a full-grown morse. Adam said oh yes and she eats some of it too not a lot so we know she hungrily. Adam said if she had food then she may need to rest. The road just up there goes about 30 miles in we may be lucky and she could be moving on the road.

Adam said follow me and we will see if she up there. The team went up the road and turned on the dirt road. Adam was watching the road for tracks because he know if she was going this way she would have to hit the road to get around the pond. Annette said she been here. Her tracks are run along the road side. Adam radio back we found some tracks. Peter said yup we see them . Fred said the lights are working we must be getting closer to her. Peter radio ahead we have lights. Adam called back same here.

Adam said see seemed to be head up to the old rail road crossing on the Grindstone road. Annette said she can move fast. Adam said she very fast. Annette said will the government made a powerful human or broth one back . Adam said yes but like all human we don't like to be told what to do. Annette said yup she female also. Adam laughs yup wouldn't want to be around when that time for the month comes. Annette laughs and said could be bad.

The lights started get stronger and stronger Adam called back looks like we are on the right trail. Peter said it looks like your right. Adam said there's a big field up here. We may be able to see her from there. The field open up and as Adam hit the top of a little hill. Annette said stop I think that's her over there. Adam said good eyes It's her. The female was over a mile and half in front of them.

Adam stopped and the group got out and Adam tries a shot off at her missing by only a few feet, but she know they were after her. Annette said let me see the gun Adam. Adam said you sure woman. Annette said yes and tried a shot off at the female it hit a tree right next to the female and she picked up the pace and get in the woods. Adam said dam woman she going to be mad at you now. Annette said bring it on bitch Mommy got a big one now. Adam said ok lets get turned around a head for Grindstone. Fred said it looks like she headed for the old train crossing up there.

Adam said I think you're right and we need to keep her run all day if we can. The team got turned around and started back down the road to town. Fred said to Peter no sleep and little food the female is going to be some mad. Peter said yup but it may also give use a brake because she could slip up and make a mistake. Fred said hope she doesn't take it out on some poor family. Peter said we can only pray she doesn't.

Dannie got home and went to find her dress and see if she needed anything to go with it. Dannie picked out all her things and tried them on so she could look her best. Dannie said now that's the right set up and I'm going to look really nice. The phone rang. It was Dannie's mom she was checking in to see what was going on. Dannie said not much and how is Dad and you doing? Mom said Dad is cooking same chilli and my eyes are water from the smell. Dannie said I wish I was there to have some with you. Mom said I 'm not eating it and he going to be sleeping in the love seat tonight. Dannie laughs Mom you love Dad right?

Mom said well yes hun Love them with all my heart why would you ask. Dannie said will I was wounding how you know he was the one? Mom said it was love at first sight. Mom said the kind of love you feel all warm and safe in. Dannie said it's that way with Max . Mom said then you to should get married or are you all ready. Dannie said no Mom but we have been thinking of it, then having a real wedding for Christmas. Mom said go for it then me and your Dad did. Dannie said you couldn't wait to get marred.

Mom said ok kido I know you to will when is it? Dannie said tonight at the bar when it closes. Mom said ok we will be there and I will tell your Dad on the way. Mom you sure he isn't going to be mad I love my Dad and don't want to hurt him. Mom said if he missing it he would be so good bye and see you soon. Dannie said love you Mom. Mom said love you to and just then another voice came on love you to hun. Dad Dannie said where are you? Dad said in the kitchen I heard your Mom go quiet after I heard marred and picked the phone up.

Dannie said you're not mad are you? Dad said no but we got to run if we going to get there see you love you hun. Mom said see you later hun. Dannie said love you two see you. Dannie sat down the phone a cried she was so happy now Mom and Dad where going to be there. Dannie said to herself can't say anything to Max. Dannie jumps up and got everything she was going to need for tonight.

Dannie said I've got to go get Pat's mail and check his house. Dannie went out the back door and went over to Pat's place she check the door and it was locked. And she went around front for the mail. She open the box and got the mail and went back to her place for lunch. Dannie couldn't think she sat down and was so happy she hug herself and got a beer and some cheese out of the ice box.

Dannie went out side to get some fresh air and eat something. She was thinking she should call Max and tells him about Mom and Dad coming to the wedding tonight. Then Dannie said he did do that thing with the ring so maybe I will just get him back bye having them show up tonight. Dannie said no she was going to get Max and that was that.

Dannie was thinking she should try the dress on to see if it still fit her. Dannie went up stairs and got into the dress it was great she looked hot in it and Max was going to love the dress. She dance around I the dress for a few then got back out of it. Dannie was still a little hungry so she went down and got some fruit and other beer. Now all she had to do is wait for the night to come.

Adam and the others turned onto the Grindstone road and head out the old rail road crossing. Annette said all this time the thing could have been walking right throw my yard and I didn't know it. Adam said right now she is most likely looking for some place to sleep for awhile. Adam and Annette went pass the Pine Grove camp ground and Adam had a light on his tracker.

Peter called Adam are you getting any lights? Adam called back yes. She must be crossing the river and in the wood on the other side by now. Peter said I think and Fred done to that she may hit the interstate and hide in the deep woods on that side. Adam said I'm not should if she would, but will see when we hit the bridge in a few. Adam slowed down and pulls over under the bridge. The team got out and went on top to look for tracks. Adam said she went throw here you can see tracks in the soft sand.

Adam said you know guys I'm not sure were to going from here I'm out of my town so I can't illegally do anything, but Peter is state and he can run up around and hopefully cut her off. Fred said she could be just setting and waiting for use to split up too . Adam said that crossed my mind to Fred. Will team what should we do now. Annette said we could set at the rest area down the road to see if she makes any moves from here. Peter said I think maybe that would be to best plan. The group got back in the car and went to the rest area to speak.

Adam pulls into the rest area the group got out and sat at the table with a tracker close by. Fred said she seems to be setting still maybe just getting her wind back. Adam said it good to a point we need to speak about something anywhere. Peter said if it about the baby if she has it before we kill her I'm not shooting it I could bring myself to do it. Fred said we can't gave it to the government they would just make more of them. Annette said what if she knows where the tracker is on her and cuts it out and is just waiting for the time and place to trap use. Dam Adam said we are just over thinking it aren't we.

Adam said I though we said this human thing can't be aloud to live. Fred said yes but how can we play God and say she needs to die or not. Annette said God or not isn't the trouble here it's a human that shouldn't be alive. Peter said yes what if we don't get her and she has other kids and then in a few years they start killing out small towns, say 30 years they replace humans as we know. Adam said I know this but if we walk away now and drop owner guard she kill use one by one. Annette said we need to get this under control she may not have the kid before we kill her and will be done with it.

Adam said I think she made a choice the light just went out she move to sleep or is head back to town. Fred said me and Peter can hit the interstate and head back down and you to could move down this road. Adam said ok but anyone gets anything call first we need to be strong to get her down. Peter said I sure not going it alone. Fred said try that didn't work. We let get moving and see what happens. The team move out of the rest area and headed different ways. Adam said I sure hope this is the right choice. Annette said yes I'm sure it is Adam.

Fred and Peter got on the interstate and headed to Medway but wasn't having any luck at all. Fred said she must have double back to sleep hope Adam is lucky. Annette said can We stop to check my mail before we go down the road. Adam said sure and we can take a short brake . Good Annette said I was feeling like I need to eat something.

Adam and Annette pulled into the camp ground and went into her camper. Annette looks in the ice box and got out some meat and bread. Would you like a soda Adam Annette said? Adam said sure Any thing we do. Adam set back to eat and to drink some soda. Annette said should We have the guns and tracker here. Adam said shit dam I'm dumb sometimes. Adam got up and started out the door to get the gun. He made it to the trailer door and he could see the female just out side.

Adam lock the door and said shit and back up the stairs. Annette know there was some thing wrong she said she out side isn't she. Adam said yes and she doesn't look happy. Annette got her cell phone out and called the camp ground owner. She told him that she was in the camper and the wolf female was out side and they didn't have the gun inside to shot her. The camp ground owner said don't worry I'll be right over with the elephant gun.

Annette said thanks and hung up the phone, Annette said back up is close by. Adam said good I think she know where we are now. The female started to move to the trailer and Annette saw two men came out with large gun. One man yelled at the female and she turn to see where it was coming from she saw the gun and turned to run. The two men ran up to the woods where she went in and unload on her, but missed her.

Adam jumps out and gets his gun and went over to the two men. Adam said looks like she gone for now. Adam looked where the two shot and there had cut two good size tree right off. Adam said thanks a few more second and we would be wolf food. The camp ground owner said no trouble I enjoy shooting my toys. Annette came out and lock the camper and the to got back in the truck and headed back up the road. Adam said we got the be more careful she almost had use that time.

Annette said yes she is really smart and we can't let your guard down like that again. Adam said she almost out of range again. Adam said we can head back to town and see what Fred and Peter saw. Annette said ok now We are armed again. Adam was thinking to himself man that was close this female is really good and is able to get the jump on use so dam fast.

Adam said she must have been a great hunting back in her time she seems to know where thing are moving and how to stock them. Annette said my father was part Indian he seemed to be able to hunt by the smell of the air.

Adam said where did we go wrong or did we just make thing too easy for use self to hunt and kill was just faded out. Annette said to be honest with you she should live and be able to make a family. Adam said why would you say that? Annette looks at the path we are on now that would one more person or thing hurt that wants man die we can't seen to keep the kids of today from killing everyone.

Adam said we are on a slow boat to hell aren't we. Adam and Annette got to the end of the road and Fred and Peter were setting there. Will be you see anything Fred Adam said. Peter said no did you guys see her. Annette said she almost handed use a world of pain. Adam told the two what went down with the female. Fred said she is a smart little lady isn't she.

Dannie heard a knock on the door it had to be Mom and Dad. Dannie ran to the door to open it and it was them. Mom and Dad came throw the door and Dannie hugs them both. Mom said so what do we need to help you with. Dannie said everything is set. Mom said we got to be able to do something for you hun. Dannie said Dad can do something for me. Dad said you don't have to ask hun I would be happy too gave you away.

Mom said now do you have something new, something old, something borrowed, something blue, and your can't see Max until you are to be married tonight.

Dannie stops I didn't think of those things and why can I see Max until the wedding. Mon. said its bad luck for the two of you to see each other before the wedding. Dad said will hun it's about five now so let just go back to the country dinner and get some thing to eat. Dannie said ok We could do that. Dad said good I will drive so you to can plans.

Dad hug Dannie and said my little is getting married I can't believe it. Dannie, Mom and Dad went to the dinner and it was slow for that time of day. Mom and Dad sat on one side and Dannie sat on the other side. The waiter came up and ask would you like something to drink. Mom and Dad said coffee and Dannie wanted a diet anything. The waiter said the special are on the board up front and I will be right back with your drinks.

Dad so how do you feel hun about the getting marred thing? Dannie said I hope I doing the right thing but it feel right and I love Max. Mom said hun I know the day we went to the bar with you that you would marry Max. Dannie said I hope you're right and the wedding going out good tonight. Dad said hun it should I think your doing the right thing.

Dannie said thanks I feel much better now about the hold thing. So Dad said are you to going somewhere after the wedding tonight. Dannie said we hadn't though about it we though we would spend the night at Max's and then do something the next day. Dad said good start on my grandkids as so as you can. Dannie face turn red and she said Dad we are going to have kids but not right tonight.

Mom said ok. I'm going to have the fried chicken and the brake potato what you to going to have. Dannie said the same as you and Dad said the beans a ham steak. Dad said as the waiter returned with the drinks do you know where your going to live. Dannie said Max likes my place and we could rent his place out to make him more money. Dad said you sure you're my kid your Mom would have rented for more money she could spend. Mom hit Dad and said you love it when I spend money to hun.

Mom said we are ready the order and she told the waiter what she wanted. He said good. It should only be a few minutes for your meals. The waiter returns to the kitchen and places the order. Dad said to Dannie I bet Max is in the same sharp you are right now maybe worst. Mom said he worst like you were hun. Dannie said he's most likely pacing around the floor right now getting cold feet.

Dannie said he should be out for work right now I should call him. Dad said he could be wondering why you're not there. Dannie got up and went out side and called Max. Max said hi and he was setting down in the chair when she called. Max said I though you be here by now hun. Dannie said you know it's bad lucky to see to bride before the wedding. Max said yup but I need someone to keep me on the track and carm me back down so I don't go nuts walking the floor.

Dannie said I will send the right man for the job over to you after he eats his supper. Max said who would that be? Dannie said my Daddy he been throw this before. Max said they know and they aren't mad? Dannie said Mom said if we did going throw with it and they found out they would be mad. Max I'm feeling a little better now that was one of the things I feel bad about.

We Dannie said you set back and he will be there in a few and you two can hang out before the wedding. Max said thanks hun I love you and can't wait to see you tonight. Dannie said I love you to and can't wait until tonight to. Dannie hung up the phone and went back in the food was on the table. Dannie said Dad I got a job for you after Supper. Dad said don't tell me Max is pacing the floor . Dannie said yup he need someone there to hung out with and took to so he can cool down .

Adam and the others said it was just about time for the other to start we should get back and work on a game plan for tomorrow . Fred said that sound good to me. The group went back to Fred's place to join up with the others and tell them what happen today . Chase said I know she was smart but I though we were smarter. Adam said we let she get close and she did .

Chase said ok she may be back on the island by now if she didn't stay in the woods on grindstone to sleep. Adam said we good lucky you guys and keep together tonight. Mary said we can run her like we did last night if she on the island again. Bob looked at Annettte your get some sleep sis and think for how the kill that thing in the morning. Annette said you be safe Bob don't be dumb.

The two groups switched off and Chase and his group went out to run the female. Adam and the others went down to rest. Chase and the others headed for the island to see if she was there but no lucky. Bob said she must be still up the Grindstone road so the group headed up that way. Mary said if she up here then she had same rest and will be ready to fight tonight.

Chase went pass the camp ground and he started to get a light he called back to Devvan and said are you getting any thing. Devvan said yup just got a light she must still be up here. Chase came up to the rail road crossing dam she already on the other side headed to town. Chase said we could run down to the Medway rest area and she if she came across there to get to the island.

Devvan said why does she keep going back to the island. Bob said it's simple she almost ready to gave birth. Devvan said I sure hope not she will be twice the danger. Bob said you hit that on the head she will be hell to bring down. The group got back to town and headed to te rest area. They got out of the cars to let the dogs do they thing and eat some thing.

Mary said the girls have been run day and night at the end of this they will need a brake. Devvan said yes they will and so will we. Mary said I hear you there I going on a long holiday. Chase said think we all need a long brake after. Just then a light showed on the tracker. Ok guy looks like we have her coming this way. Bob said it looks as if she want to go back to the island.

The lights were getting more and more. She isn't too far away now. Then the lights stayed the same Chase said see must see or smell use here. Bob said she will most likely move around use then came at use head on. Devvan said she should she my get lucky with the dark on her side. To Many if it was just two here but four is a little more then she wants to fight now Bob said. Mary said the lights are fading now she must be around use now. Chase said think you're right.

Chase said it's going over to the old farm road and see if she on the island again. The team loaded up and drove over to the island side and the tracker seemed to say she was on the island. Mary said we going to try to get her moving with the rocket thing again. Bob got the unit out of the trunk and said so where should we shot tonight. Chase said drop one about the center first to see if that gets her up.

Bob loaded a rocket in and set for the shot. Then he said fire in the hold and he shot at the island it hit almost die center for the island the blast shock the island, but the wolf didn't move. Mary said it seems she at the base of the island tonight. Bob said I don't want to shot down there because of the power lines. Devvan said dam she knows that to I bet. Bob said I can try a little closer but not too much more.

Chase go ahead you got two more rockets she may thinking we are getting closer. Bob loaded again and said fire in the hold and shot the next round. The second shot hit closer to the lines then Bob would have cared for. The female didn't move she was still. The female wasn't really on the island because she know it wasn't safe . She spend the night on the shore close to the island . Chase said it's going to be a long night I think. Mary said she going the be there unless we get a boat and go after her. Devvan said maybe tomorrow night we will have to do that.

The tracker was still the same Chase said ok put the car next to each other and we can round down the windows. The group set the car so they could see the island. Mary said we should have two watch and two sleep. Chase said that was may plan to. Chase said ok how wants to sleep and how wants to watch. Devvan said ok me and Bob can watch the first five then you two the next five.

Chase said ok went me now if she ever move a tree get use up right away. Bob said you bet we will. Devvan and Bob sat out on the hood so that they wouldn't fall to sleep. The nights were getting cold but not too bad. Devvan said I wonder if she having the kid tonight. Bob said a hell of a time to do that he said, she on the run and could be killed anytime.

Bob said I'm not sure but if she human her baby would need lots of care until it could fend for its self. Devvan said maybe children back then didn't need that type of help and could kill and eat from day one. Bob said we are tacking about a human not an animal here. Devvan said she so strong and power compared to use as humans they could it be the same for the baby of this human.

Bob said I never though of it that way but you may be right. That would make sense she could leave the child on the island and run use all day then feed her kid at night. Devvan said I think while she runs one group around the other should check the island and see if she had the baby. Chase got up sounds like what's a good idea but where do we put the baby so she can't get it back. Devvan said lock the baby in down to Fred place she never be able to get in there.

Dannie's Dad went to see Max he walks in and Max looked as if he was ready to jump up and run a ten-mile race. Max said Dad oh can I call you that now. Dad said if you didn't I would be mad. Dad said ok were got to get you charmed down. Max said you must know how I feel you marred her Mom. Dad said I sure do and this is what helped for me. Dad said you got any beer? Max said yes but I don't want to get drunk. Dad said we aren't just a buzz to help you settle down some. Max said ok I can go for that.

Max got the beer and the two sat down and started to speak. Dad said you have the same trouble I did went I got marred. Max said it does seem a little dumb to get so up tie over this isn't it. Dad said hell no you want every thing to go off with a bang. Max said as long as it doesn't blow up in my face. Dad said I bet Dannie is going throw just about the same thing right now. Max said you think so? Dad said I know so. Max said we got two hours before the bar closes and the wedding starts. Dad said good other beer and some sports should help the time to pass.

Dannie said I hope poor Max is doing ok. Mom said if I know your Dad he got the big all charmed down. Dannie said I sure hope so wouldn't want him to back out at the last second. Mom laughs that man love so bad he would never do that. Dannie said that's not all I'm worry about? Mom said ok then what is it? Dannie said it's hard to say this to someone it his will you know? Mom said you think he short in the pants? Dannie said dam no if any thing very big in the pants.

Mom said ok so what wrong with that? Dannie said what if I can't keep him happy as far as sex goes. Mom laughed again and said the first time your father drop his pants I took I was going to die when he stuck me with that thing. Dannie said your saying Dad is large . Mom said hun large is just little compared to your Dad. Dannie face turned red and she said I'm not sure I wanted to hear that. Mom said it's ok I not going to say anything about it to him. Dannie said I sure hope not I can't face him thinking he knows.

Mom said so is he really big or just big, big. Dannie said I think it's at less ten soft. Mom said that good than you not going to have any trouble with that I hope. Dannie said what if it gets big than I can hold. Just get on top and do what you can with it. Mom said I need a drink all this sex suff is making me miss your Dad. Mom Dannie said I think we should have a few and stop this took. Mom said yes I know you do all right just release. Dannie got a few beers for the both of them and they went out to the porch of some cold air.

Vicki said ok you guy get the ribbon up and who's got the cake? The guys said the cake is out back and we need a ladder to put the ribbons up with. Ok Vicki said ladder is around the counter by the office and who in charge of sweeping? Vicki went out to the kitchen to look at the cake the guys did a hell of a good job for man. The cake had three level and was white with rose trim. And had a bride and groom on top. The rose color made up about three dozen red rose all over the cake. Vicki's went back out front and ask how made the cake. The guys said the wife did is it ok? Vicki said more then ok it great.

Vicki said the lights are next and I will give you all a free beer on me. One man said is that after the wedding Vicki? Vicki said only if you aren't marred. Dam Vciki said to herself I may get a man out of this thing after all. Vicki said has anyone been looking out for the two to show up. The guys said yup a look out at both ends. Vicki said good guys. It's looking good.

Vicki went down throw her list and said everything was going as plan. Vicki said great everything is set now all I need is two more people. Vicki said ok guys have a set and I'll get your beers. The guys had a set and drank their beers it was now about 12.30 a.m. Vicki said they should be here now.

Max and Dad were up stair putting on their suits Max said do I look ok Dad? Dad said you look sharp young man. Max said thanks I needed that. Will I'm going to meet you down stair I'm going to put my cloths in the car? Max said ok he was going to head down now to. Vicki's back door look out came in Max is on his way down. Vicki said good keep him in the back of the kitchen until we get Dannie in the office.

Dannie and her Mom were all set to go and got in Dannie's jeep. Dannie drove into town and she could feel butterflies. Mom said we almost their my little girl is going to be some wife tonight. Dannie said now you and Dad will have a son now. Dannie pulls in up front and Vicki's looks out came in she here. Vicki said ok that when she comes in take her to the office. Dannie walks in and was send to the office. Max and Dad were still in the back of the kitchen.

Vicki said for Max and Dannie Dad to be both out now. Vicki placed Max in his spot and Dad went back to bring Dannie out to Max. Dad got back and saw Dannie and she hug him. Dannie said is Max ok Dad? Dad said he ok and ready to see his wife. Dad said hun you look great and Max is going to be a luck man. Dad said you ready hun as he put his arm out for her.

The two slowly walks out the door and over to Max. Max looked as if he could pass out at anytime. Dannie took Max's arm and said love you hun take a deep breath and release you'll feel better. Vicki said we are here tonight to jeon this man and woman in the holy bond of marriage. Vicki said with their bands of gold life for Dannie and Max start a new. Not life as two but live as one in sprit, mind and body. Should no man came between the two that God had jeon. Dannie do you take Max to be your husband too die do you part. Dannie said as the tears around down her face I do with all my heart.

Max do you take Dannie to be your wife to protect and love her to die do you part. Max said I do with all my heart. Vicki said you my kiss the bride. Max and Dannie kissed and the guys in the bar throw up hand fulls for popcorn to cheer the wedding. Vicki said now you are marred so how do you feel. Max said happy then he ever been. Dannie said she could dance the night away. Vicki said your going to have to wait until the cake is cut. Dannie said there's a cake to cool. Vicki told the guys to roll the cake out so Dannie and Max could see it. Max said dam that a nice cake who made it. Dannie said I like that cake to it really nice. Vicki said the wife of the guys here got together to make it for you. Max said will tell the wife thanks it's great. Dannie cut the cake and feed it to Max. Then Max did the same thing but wipe it on her face. Mom and Dad were happy they had a son now.

Dannie and Max had a few drinks and danced a while and then headed up stair. Dannie said to Mom and Dad you can have the house to yourself tonight. The two kissed her and hug Max welcome to the family. Max carried Dannie throw the door way and sat her on the bed. Max said he need to go to the bathroom and be right back. Dannie kiss him and said ok love you. Max went into the bathroom and was going to come out nude, but Dannie had the same idea. Dannie got nude and set on the bed. Max came back in and they both started to laugh will Max said we are have on the same suits, Dannie said yes and it looks good on you.

Max could believe the body he was looking at it was unreal. He got into bed and held her as the kiss and felt the heat from each other. Dannie though to herself this was going to be a great night. Dannie turned over and turns off the lights and to two will you know and made love for hours.

Chase said to Marry this wolf or human is smart, isn't she? Marry said yes she a female are that's why. Chase said yup, but having the kid is that going to make her more likely to move on or too became more hard to handle. Mary said it could be a little bit of both she going to fight hard now she protecting her kid until she know he or she going to be safe.

Mary said if she had this kid I wouldn't want to be on the team that goes after it. Chase said same here. She would be really pissed at them. Mary looks at her watch and it was about 4:00 a.m. and she said by the time we get back to Fred's and tell what happen tonight to the others we be off shift. Chase said yes as he wakes up Devvan and Bob. The team headed back to the base to speak to Adam and the other. Chase and the others pull into Fred's and got out the dogs to let get some food and water. Devvan said me and the girls will stay up while you speak to the others. Chase said keep and eye on your tracker if it shows one light get down here right away. Devvan said ok I will do that be down as soon as the dog are done away.

Chase, Mary and Bod went down to speak to Adam. Adam said where are the others? Devvan top side feeding the dogs and letting them do there thing. Adam said what happen last night. Chase said not much she made it to the island and stayed there all night. Bob said we even tried the rockets on her and she sat there. Adam said I think she my have giving birth last night I was hoping we could run her down before this happen.

Chase said I think you're right Adam now we going to have a handful of a human's to deal with. Adam said it's going to be fun to try to deal with her now. Mary said we wanted to stay in two groups and one try to run her and the other try to see if they could find her baby. Adam said sound good but where we going to keep the baby that she can't get at it. Fred said there only one place I know and that's here. Adam said yes but that's going to put you and Jean in real danger then. Jean said isn't that bring part of the team then.

Adam said yes but this could be very danger if we don't protect you and Coco. Jean said I know it not safe but if it helps use to trap her then how could it be wrong. Jean said that I don't want to job of having to kill the baby it would be hard to do. Adam said we wouldn't let you do that. Fred said it would be a way to get her in the open so we could kill her. Chase said it may not be a cake walk to get the kid we would have to dart it maybe. Adam said why dart it? Chase said this could unlike a human baby as we see it the things could be up and moving around by now.

Peter said yes we are dealing with different race of humans. One of the lights on Adam's tracker went off will it looks as if we going to find out soon. Devvan and the dog came throw the door and shut it and locked it. Fred said it looks like the war is coming to use. Adam bring it on I'm ready for a fight. The female hit the front door and shock the door. Fred said it looks like I should set the other door in place before she ripped that one down.

Fred switch the door to close and it locks it in place. Jean said only one thing wrong with this. Adam said o k what? Jean said she on that side of the door and we are here. Adam said yup it looks like we are going to have to set here until she gives up. Will that fight went her way now Mary said? Well Jean said we got lots of food and water she hasn't. Adam said good let go kick back and let her bet the door until she happy. Jean said sounds like a good plan.

The female was still beating the door as if she wanted this thing to end now. Peter said she sounds really mad. The beating stopped but the female stayed outside the door. Every once in a while you could hear her howl to let them know she was still there. Fred said Jean You still have the small cam in the hall out a side. Jean said yup I'll get the laptop and bring it up.

Jean went to the lab and got her laptop she came back out and said it looks as if she crying. Adam said do You have audio? Jean said here we go. You could hear the crying of the female over the laptop. The group all look at each other as to say she was crying. She put her head up and howled. Then she got up to hit the door again. The female fell back and seem to pass out.

Jean said something is wrong with her really wrong. Adam said you think she dying? Mary said I think she having trouble gave birth. Jean said we got to help her. Fred looked at her you nuts hun? Jean said she human like me and you. Adam said a human that tried to kill use from time to time. Jean said yes because we are hunting her. Chase said we can't stand here and not do something can we speak to hear? Fred said the door has a intercom. The group move to the door and Adam push the button and said can you hear me. A very soft voice came over the laptop yes. The female said my babies need your help. Adam said how can we trust you to help you.

Adam looked at the other's dam now what do we do? Mary said we try to help that's what any human would do. Adam but what if we help and she kills use after. Coco came to the door and start to dig at it and cry. Jean said I can't stand it open the door and see what we can do. Besides you can cover her and if she does anything kill her. Adam push to button again and said we are goes to help, but one wrong move and we will shot you. The female said ok please help the kids .

Adam said dam not in my wildest dream did I think we would be doing this. The group started to open the door and the female was still down. She said please help my kids. Fred said can you move any? The female said if you can help me. Fred and Bob with to help the female by lifting her under both arms. The group move her slow to the lab. Jean said lay her down on the bed here. The female was in hard labor. Jean said do You have a name? The female said my male call me Hope. Will Hope Jean said I'm going to have to look at you to see what's going on? Bye the way my name is Jean. Jean the female said ok please help. Jean said as she looked the female over will here the trouble the baby is coming out the wrong way. Hope I can help but your going have to true me. Hope said ok do what you can.

Dannie and Max made love most of the night. Dannie wakes up and she didn't remember dreaming at all maybe the sex was what was doing it. Max wakes up and he looks at her did you sleep good. Dannie said little a rock and how about you hun. Max said I felt great and I did sleep really good. Dannie crawls up and kissed Max. Dannie said feel like a fast one before work and she smiled. Max said sure do and the two started to make love again.

After they were done Max said, I need a smoke and laugh. Dannie said I think I need the pack and laugh with him. Max got up and said I'm going to take a shower now. Dannie said save room for me and Max said ok. Max went to the shower and after a few Dannie went in and said is everything clean? Max said I think so. Dannie said let me see and she steps in the shower with Max. The Two got out of the shower and went to dress. Max said I going down stair now hun are you coming, too. Dannie said yes be right there. Max and Dannie went to the bar and Dannie started to sweep the floor and Max did his same thing stocking the bar.

The light and thing were still up form last night and the cake was almost gone. Max said it looks like someone hold a patty last night. Dannie said he think the pretty went all night. Max said and it still going. Dannie said I know I still feel it. Max said what you going to do today hun. Dannie said then go home the see Mom and Dad. Max said to say hi to Mom and Dad for me. Dannie said that must seem funny to call them Mom and Dad. Max said yes but it make me happy to use those word again. Dannie said I'm done here do you need some help? Max said maybe if you could pick the rest of the cake up. And clean the top of the bar it would be a big help.

Dannie went over to the cake and pick it up and put it some small Packard so if anyone want some more they could. Max said we need to think of a place to go for two weeks . Dannie said any place warm and we can swim. Dannie said we need to do something nice for Vicki. Max said yes we need to give her a small vacation. Dannie said I can look same things up and see what would fit the bill. Dannie said I'm done now you could eat off the bar. Max smiles said sounds good to me. Dannie came over and Max was done with his work and the two went back to the office to get the cash draw.

Max comes into the office and Vicki and a man were sleeping on the love seat. Max stopped and said looks like some else got lucky last night. Dannie said good thing They use the blanket. Max went over and got the cash draw and went back out and shut the door so they could sleep longer. Dannie kiss Max looks as love is in the air. Max said I should make some coffee just in case she needs it when she gets up. Dannie said as her and Max went to open the door think I need some sleep. Max said it would have been nice to sleep in tonight with you hun. Max unlocked the door and it was a nice day out.

Dannie said ok I'm going back up stairs and sleep love you hun. Max grad she and hug her and kissed her hard. Dannie said you keep it up and we going to have to wake Vicki so we can use the couch. Max smile and said I love you hun see around noon for dinner. Dannie said yes I will bring Mom and Dad. Max said great and kisses her as she went out. Dannie went up stair as she got out the back door she started to walk a little funny. Dannie know it was all the sex and she would get over it soon she hoped. Dannie went in and got into bed and curl up to Max's pillow.

Dannie went to sleep and start to dream. This time she was going to face the hardest fight of her life. Dannie sat up in bed the white wolfs said you must coming with use sister the last fight we be soon. Dannie got up and went with the white wolfs. The three went down the back stairs and then into the woods behind the bar. Three with down a trail where they come to and opening the female wolf was they giving birth.

Dannie said will we can kill her and be done with the mess why do we have to wait. A voice from inside and around the three said because only at a full moon can you be strong and able to do away with the female. Remember Dannie my child if this female and her baby's live life we charge for mankind forever. Dannie said I'm ready and walk up to the female how was holding her kids.

The female said you are here to kill use? Dannie said I have to you know this don't you? The female said yes I do, but please kill me first as I don't have to see them die. Dannie said ok. The female handed the baby's to the two white wolfs. Dannie walks over to the female and broke her neck and ripped her head off. The head said thank you. The white wolfs handed the first of the two children to Dannie see looks at him and said they look human. Dannie said why do they have to die. The white wolfs said to save man from them self.

Dannie looks up but father they don't even have names . The voice said when the two were first born back a long time ago the name were Adam and Eve. Dannie looked at little Adam and said I'm sorry but I have to do this. Dannie broke the neck on the baby and lay it beside his Mother's body. Then the last baby was handed to Dannie and she looks at eve and started to cry as she broke her neck and place her beside her Mom. The voice said you did the right thing Dannie and the man how did this have to pay for it with their lives. The voice said I'm proud of you and in three days it will be all over.

Dannie wakes up with tears still in her eyes she was sad that she had to kill someone so young, but it was all a dream or was it. Dannie got up and went to get a beer out of the ice box. It was around 10.30 a.m. now and she drank the beer and went to see what he Mom and Dad were up to. Dannie pulled in her drive way and went in. Dannie yelled Mom, Dad where are you Dad yelled we are out side . Dannie started to the back door and said to herself are they dressed or not. Dannie came to the door and said you got cloths on you guys. Mom said yup we do hun and she walks out the door and they were drinking coffee and setting on the chairs.

Mom said well how did last night going? Dannie said all I'm going to say is it was great. Mom said good so what you doing today? Going to think of where to go for a few weeks and look for some thing for Vicki. Mom said Vicki was that the one that married you last night. Dannie said yes she sleeping in Max's office right now with some man. Dad said looks like everyone got some last night. Dannie said Dad I don't want to hear about it. Beside you two have plans for dinner. Dannie said I though we would go to the bar and have dinner with Max before you go. Dad said ok sure we can do that today. Mom said sounds great to me to hun.

Jean said Fred go get towels and blanket to rap the babies in. Adam get some warm water and wash cloths. Ok Devvan and Mary think you can help me. Mary said what you want me to do. Jean said you and Devvan are going to hold her legs up as I work went the baby. Ok Devvan said I think I can do it. The two got on each side of the female and held her legs open and up. Jean said Hope this isn't going to be fun I have to push the baby back in and turn it. Hope said ok go for it. Jean put her hand around the leg and push the baby back in Hope could feel the pain and did a low howl.

Jean said were almost they good the baby turned. Hope looks as if she was going to pass out. Jean said you can push again Hope and Hope pushed and the first baby come out. Jean wash the baby up and it started to cry. Hope Jeans said you have a baby boy. Hope said thanks Jean and said the other is on it's way. Jean rap the boy up and hand it the hope. The second one was coming out right. Jean said good she almost out one more push and Hope push and the second one came out. Jean cleaned her up and she bring to cry and Hope was happy. Jean said you have a baby girl. Jean said you can put her legs down now I can clean her up from here.

Jean handed the other baby to Hope to. Hope smiled my man was wrong some human still have hearts. Jean said I will fit the cords after I clean you up and charge your bed. Adam said as he got closer to, the baby's they look human even have the same feet as use. Hope said yes and these a reason for it. Chase still stun by the hold thing said ok what is it. Because this is the first two human born. Chase said right you telling me we are looking at Adam and eve. Hope said yes and I a few days we will be kill to protect the human race. Adam said how we not going to do this? The white wolfs will do the job. Peter said their more then one white wolfs? Hope said yes three all together. Devvan said why three days from now. Because of the full moon the one that kills use we be at full power.

Adam said we can keep you here and protect you from them. Hope smile wish it was that easy. Mary said yes we stopped you all this time and we can shoot them if they get close. Hope said you can kill something that doesn't live. Fred said what's that you say they are dead. Hope said no they are spirt wolves. Jean said you mean from God. Hope said yes from God he needs to restore the crack in time. Jean said ok hun you're all clean and the cords are fitted.

Peter said ok what do we do from here. Hope said you done a lot already you let me hold the kids until they came for use. Chase said I was just thinking what if the human thing about use coming from ape is wrong. What if we came from the sea on four legs then two like hope then like Adam and Eve we became what we are today. Hope said so you do under stand then the group look at her and said you saying we were wolfman to at one time. Hope said that's what the science told use back in the lab. That's why we are part human and part wolf. Dam Fred said this is too much to handle all at once.

Jean said hope do you need some water or some thing to eat. Hope said yes if it not to mush trouble. Adam said we were all wrong about you two. Hope said no you were right if we live we would have tried to kill all of you in the end. Jean said what would you like Hope. Hope said for once in my life I would like to eat something human oh. I mean human food. The group said dam I though we were in trouble. Hope said I gave you my word that I will not harm you at all. Adam said then we still do the same ok guys guns on safety and put them away.

Hope said you people are a lot different then any humans we crossed so far. Jean said I know what will fit the bill for food Fred come with me. Jean and Fred went to the other room and ordered food. Jean said this is one of the humans most love food. Fred will be back with him soon. Wood you like water or some thing else to drink. Chase said can we see the babies? Hope said yes they are sleeping but they are ok to hand around. Hope handed Eve to Chase he looked at her and said she beautiful. Hope said what is this beautiful thing you said. Chase said is mean She is really good looking. Oh Hope said see is beautiful then.

The group got to hold all the kids and handed them back to Hope. Think of the story Fred could make up from all this suff today. Jeans laughs he is something isn't he.

Fred called I'm back send Adam and Peter up the help bring the food down. Peter said what did he get the store. Adam and Peter went up and saw it was pizza Adam laughs I was thinking the same thing. Adam said you did get some beer to. Fred said yes what's pizza without beer. Peter said great now we going to have a drunk wolfwoman.

Adam and the other got back and Hope said it smells really good. Jean said let me put the baby on the bed next to you so you can have a peace. Hope said I'm so hungry I

could eat a horse. The group laughs I bet you could. Hope tried the pizza and said that this is great. Jean said its pizza and yes it is really good. Hope said what kind of animal does this pizza look like? The hole group broke out in a loud laugh. Hope said did I say some thing wrong. Jean said no pizza is made from bread meat and onion and cheese and sauce not a animal. Hope smile and laugh to. Hope said I've never felt this good around humans.

What is that thing you drinking Adam Hope said? Adam said it's called a beer. Can I try it Jean said as long as you do drink a lot of them? Hope said ok She smelled the beer it smell funny like mud. Adam said it is a lot better to drink. Hope drink it and said it is good but funny going down. She drinks the rest for the beer in one drink. Mary said slow down There you could get sick by drinking it to fast.

Hope said can I have more pizza. Jean said eat all You got it all for you. Hope said that's nice of you. Just don't drink too much to fast. She said is it because it makes you feel funny. Yes Devvan said but if you drink too much you get sick.

Dannie said ok let's head over to see Max and see how he doing now. Dannie , Mom and Dad headed off and went to town . Dad said nice around here again that hunting season is over. Dannie said yes and not many hurt this year. Mom said did the cop's kill that wolfman thing? Dannie said I don't really know Because I haven't been watching too new much. Dannie pulls into the bar and went out back. Dannie went in with Mom and Dad and Max was behind the bar. Max saw Dannie and came over to see them. Max said hi to everyone and kiss Dannie.

Dannie said hi and sat at the bar. Mom and Dad sat down beside her and said hi also. Max said would you like a drink. Dannie said a beer would do. Mom and Dad beer ok with them to son. Max smiles yes Mom. Max said tonight blue plate is pork loin with grave and brake potato and corn. Dannie said that sounds really good tonight I will take that. Mom and Dad said same for use to. Max said good three pork dinners coming up. Max went back to the kitchen after getting the beers for them.

Mom said seems to be a little busy today here. Dannie looks around and said yup it is today. Vicki came around the corner and said dam it's morning already. She looks as if had been a long night. Dannie said sleep good. Vicki smiles too good it's noon . Then the man she was with came out and said maybe I should go to work tonight. Vicki kisses them and he went out the front door. Dannie said so what's this ones name Vicki Dannie said? Vicki laughs you know I never asked. Dannie looked at her and said too much to drink last night.

Vicki said yup and headed out throw the back to her car. Max came back out and said was that Vicki just then. Dannie said yes she looked like a train wreck. Max said hope she can do her job alright tonight. Max said I'll be right back with your meals. Max went in and came back out with the food. Max said here we are would you like any sour cream with this. Mom said yes that would make the potato. Dannie and Dad said sure. Max said be right back. Dannie said the food smells great.

Dad said Max should open a dinner and just cook food. Dannie said he would do good at it wouldn't he. Mom said yes as she bit into the pork lion it was great. Dannie said dam It is great. Dad said and it's and big peace for meat to. Dannie almost laughs, but her face turn red . Dad said what it is a big meal. Mom said Dannie was thinking of other meat. Dad look at Dannie then at Mom you didn't say anything about you know? No hun it Max we were speaking about. Dad said just what I want to hear other man with big meat troubles.

Dannie said ok I'm trying to eat here. Max came out with the sour cream and said how's that food. The three said it is great. Max said good the meat from Mary Ann Market. Dannie said I never had pork from there but I will now. Max said will you guys enjoy and I will be back soon. Max returned and waited on the guys at the bar. Dannie said this is really great dam Max is a good cook. Mom said good we can set back and watch him and your Dad cook while we drink.

Dad said ok with me. Man are better cooks away. Mom hit Dad and said I never hear you say any thing wrong about my food. Dad said no you're a good cook hun I love your food. Dannie said I think you cooking is good to Mom. Mom said good then lets have another beer. Dannie said I will get it for you. Dannie got down and went behind the bar and over to Max. Max's kiss her and said something wrong hun? Dannie said no just get a few more beers is that ok hun. Max said sure. The boss wife aren't you. Dannie said I'm sure am the one.

Dannie got the beers for them and sat back down and finch her meal. Dannie turned around I her chair and drank her beer. Max came back and said ok you guys ready for some thing special? Mom said sure. Max went out back and came out with three warm apple pies with ice cream on them. Dannie said I love apples. Mom said dam it looks' good Max did you make it. Max said no it was here from the other night no one got it out.

Adam said to Hope I see you like the pizza. Hope said yes is good and this beer thing not too bad. Mary said what do the kids eat Hope? Hope said yes we got to save pizza and beer for the kids. Jean said pizza no beer. Hope said why it's makes you funny feeling. Devvan said it's because human don't feed kid beer and thing like that. Oh Hope said I didn't know.

Peter said why did your man kill the people in the house? Hope said they were the one how gave use life. He want to thank them for that. Dam remind me to stay on your good side. Hope said the people should had not made use at all. Adam said I understand that but why Tommy and his Mom and Dad. Hope said the male did kill those humans but the ones that made use made a gean would drive use the kill humans.

Adam said so you didn't kill anyone other than the people how made you. Hope said yes that right. Then why all the attack on use. Will it was because we though you were like the others but now I see different? Coco came into the room and went up to the female. She looks at it and said Jean is this your baby. Jean started to laugh sorry it's Coco my pet. Hope said what a pet? Fred said a pet is an animal that is keep by human.

Ok Hope said so you keep food as pets. The hold group started in laughing. Adam no we don't eat our pets. Hope said what good are they then? Jean said as friends someone to pass the time away with. Hope said you Humans are funny. Adam said there's no way to stop the white wolfs from killing you guys. Not Hope said you must understand that we were here once and now this is your time.

I just glad to have time with the babies. Hope said thanks for that time I have with them. Adam said glad we could help you. Hope pick up Coco and look at her she said she licking me she like me. Jean said I guess she thinks you are one of use. Hope said nice pet. Hope said why do those to big pets hide. Mary said because there are afraid of you may be. Oh funny I'm not afraid of them.

One of the baby began to wake up it was Adam Hope pick him up and look at him like a loving Mom would. She said you hungry little man Hope pick up some pizza and said try this it good. The babies smell it and began to eat it. Hope said he like this pizza thing. The group said dam able to eat food just after bring born. Hope said your babies don't eat at first. Jean said no they drink milk for the first few months. Hope said what's milk? Jean said it's what a female has coming from her breast.

Oh so that what this thing are for as she looks at her breast. Adam said to Hope you do have some type of armor don't you. Hope said what's armor? The scale like things all over you. Oh Hope said I got hair to but you don't. The baby was done the pizza and get a loud burp. Everyone laughs guess he likes pizza. Adam said dam we got the think of a way to help you. Hope said sorry but the science said the white one couldn't be stop be man.

Devvan said we could look the wolfs up on the internet see if someone out there has a clue how to stop them. Adam said that's not a bad plan . Jean said I have wireless network down here I can work on mind and if you have laptop go get them and we can all try together to find something. Devvan said me and Mary have laptops in the truck. Peter said I have one also in my car. The three got up the going and Hope said wait you need your guns. Peter said way because some thing is up on top side .

Devvan said is the white wolfs Hope? Hope said no it's the last to people how gave me life and four others. Adam said dam they must have tracked her. Adam grad his tracker and turned it on he went over to Hope and ran it down he body. The tracker went solid on the bottom of her right foot. Jean got a knife Adam said. Yes Jean said here it is. Adam said Hope this is going to hurt a little. Hope said go for it. Adam cut the tracker out of he feet. Fred said ok now what? Adam said got a bottle small one we do. How about a pill bottle with screw on cap. Great Adam said Fred you sure the river run strange out of here.

Fred said yes comes out on the other side for the road why. Adam send did you ever play send a letter in a bottle. Throw the tracker in the river and see if they will fall for it then we can get top side and hit them with their backs turned. Adam and the others ran to the pond room and threw the bottle in the river it went like a shot. Adam turned his unit on and said it's working it moving down stream. Jean came in Hope said the cars are moving off to the road. Adam said get your gun this may not last long.

Jean said to Fred be careful hun. Fred's kiss her and said I will. Adam said Fred you, Annette, and Bob are staying here to protect everyone. The others got their gun and headed top side . Close the door behind use Adam said. Annette said be careful to Adam. Adam said let go guys. The group got up stairs and set on both side of the driveway in the grass until the car returned.

Dannie the food use great hun and the pie to it now was around 8:00pm. Max said to Dannie are you going back with your Mom and Dad to the house? Dannie said aren't you going to get anytime off tonight? Max said Vicki is out back and will be here soon. So I'm off here in a few. Dannie said good we can stay here or go look for something for Vicki in Linclon. Max said that sounds good to me Linclon it is. Vicki came out and said hi to everyone. Everyone said hi back. Vicki said thanks' Max for letting me came in later. Max said that's ok you didn't look to hot this morning.

Max said will guys off to Lincoln we go. Mom said me and Dad are going back to the house you young kids go out tonight. Dannie said ok but you old people can come to. Dad said old people we just try to bet you home. Dannie said save a spot on the lawn. Mom smiled ok We keep it warm for you. Dad and Mom said good night an see you later. Dannie and Max went out to his truck out back. Dannie said do you know if she needs some thing. Max said she want to take time off and go somewhere, but she can afford it.

Dannie said she doesn't make good money? Max said she make more the all the other, but she seems not to have any money all the time. Dannie said ok so are we going to send her somewhere or just get her thing nice. Well Max said her tv is broken maybe we could get her a flat screen tv. Dannie said sounds good just remember we need all the little things she needs to run from the cable. Max said it's about ten now so where we going to find a store open tonight. Dannie said Wal-Marts and Madden's are on Christmas hours.

Max said great then let check Wal-Marts then if we don't find one there then we can go to Madden's and look around. Max and Dannie hit the interstate on the way down to Lincoln and the time when by fast. They pulled into Wal-Marts and went in to look around the park lot had a few people in it for this time of year. Max said to Dannie they away have good deals on tv and things at this time of year. Max said here a 32-inch flat screen. Dannie said too manly and not very pretty. Ok Max said let's look at the once that are over there. Dannie came around the side and said that's the one a 35 inch flat screens with a nice look to too soft and girly.

Max said you think she need a matching pare of shoe for it and smile at Dannie. Dannie said oh Max don't be nutty shoes no put and hand bag maybe. Max just laughs at her ok so this tv then. Max went around to get the other thing she needed to hook up the tv to cable. Then Dannie had one of the people help her to get the tv on a cart and move it to the front to cash out. Great Dannie said hope she likes it.

Max said I bet she loves it. Max payed for it and then put in the back of the truck. Max switch the cover to cover so it would be safe. Will Dannie said think we should see if Wing-Wong is open I think they run until 11:00 p.m. tonight. Max said sound good could eat something right now. Max and Dannie went over to Wing-Wong to have something to eat. The place was filled for a night like tonight. Max and Dannie sat down and order a Pu-Pu for two it was great with the beer. Dannie loves the food there.

After the meal the two headed the old way back home. Dannie said so we going to run this over to Vicki tv or gave it to her in the morning. Max said we could drop it off at the bar to her and then go up stairs for the night so Mom and Dad can have time to himself. Dannie said ok It works for me. Max said I was thinking we don't need two places to live so I was thinking of moving my things to your house and renting out mind to gave use some mad money.

Dannie said no your moving your thing into owner house we are married remember. Max said yup your right hun we are. Dannie curl up under Max's arm and said the night looks like rain. Max said it was going to be heavy shower tonight. Max said the new bridge in Medway should look nice once it's in. Dannie said yes you can see up and down the river with no trouble.

Max pulls into the parking lot of the bar and back up to the deck. Max said I will go get the hand truck and be right back. Dannie looked around and said to her self this place could use a little weeding. Max came back out and loaded the tv on the hand truck. Dannie went in and told Max to going in the office and she would send Vicki back to see the tv. Max said make it sound like we are letting her go. Dannie said your mean but it does sound fun.

Dannie went out front and said hi to Vicki. Vicki said hi where's Max? Dannie said he out in the office and wants to speak to you. Vicki said shit what did I do wrong this time. Dannie said I don't know he seem very mad. Vicki went to the office and Max was setting behind the desk. Vicki said hi to Max and he said have a seat Vicki. Max said I was going over thing around here and wanted too say your doing a good job. Vicki said thanks I hope I still working here tomorrow? Max said me and Dannie had a long to took about and we said we think you should get some thing for to show who we care for you and what you did last night.

Vicki said with a smile so it's good not mad? Will Max said sure is turns around and look at your new tv set? Vicki looked back and said my God that's a nice set it a flat screen to wow. She jumped up and hugged Max thanks. Max said Dannie pick it out she said it looked girly. Now I need a hand bag to go with it. Max started to laugh that's the same thing Dannie said. Vicki hug Max again and then said so Dannie was in on this plan.

I'm going to have to get your two back for this you know. Max said ok and got up and Vicki and Max went out front. Vicki walks up to Dannie and said thank and hug her then said you know I'm going to get you two back for this. Dannie said you do know it was all his plan don't you. Max said a around of beer on the house. The customers said cool. Dannie said he wanted to get shoes to go with it. Vicki said Spock like a true man then. I told him a new hand bag. Dannie laugh yup see I told you. Dannie hugged Vicki and said glad you like it. Vicki said thanks to you two I can watch tv tonight. Max and Dannie was happy with the way thing went headed up to Max's room. It was now about 12:00 p.m.. Dannie and M ax got into bed and made love. Two too went to sleep in each other arm.

Adam said dam these guys can be that dumb are they. Just then a car pull in the drive with another right behind it. They got about 50 feet from the team an stopped. Then out of now where the three white wolfs showed up and hit the cars rolling them over the wolf's attack the cars and Adam try to pull the tiger of the gun but not a thing would happen. The wolf's kill all the man and stood there looking at Adam and the other in the grass. One said to Peter two days and we come for her. Then the three turned and left.

Adam said shit I though we were going to be lunching meat there. Mary said I'm still pissing in my shorts. Chase said why didn't they kill use. Devvan said maybe Because we aren't the ones how made the animals. Will we got to call Mike and have him come over and get the bodies? Adam made the call and Mike said he be right over to do it. Chase said I'm going back down and tell the other what happen.

Chase when back down and told the other what went on. Hope said the white wolfs say anything about me. Chase said yes sorry they said two more days and they would come for you. Hope said ok thanks and she went back with Jean to the kids. Mike show up and said what the hell happen here. More wolfs Adam said. They were white ones this time. Mike said white wolfs you didn't shot them. Adam said both times the guns wouldn't fire.

Mike said it sounds like the old Indian tail my grand Dad use to tell me. Mike said these man must had done something really bad to be kill by sprit wolfs. Peter said sprit wolfs what this about? Mike said my grand Dad was a Penobscot Indian he would tell a lot of story of the old. Mike said help me with these men and I will tell you the trial. Adam said ok and him and Peter got into the suits and help Mike. One of the men was old and had to use a wheel chair. Devvan said you don't think this man is the one from the newspaper do you. Adam said he sure looks the right ago.

Mike said that's funny not Ids on anyone. Adam said I'm not surprise. The last one was loaded in and Mike said will now the story. It' s been a while but here it is. It was of an Indian woman that had dream of bring a wolf that hunted for the great spirt in the shy. She would hunt the people and animals that some how make the soul of the earth mother sad. She would dream a few nights or weeks then go into battle again the bark ones. She couldn't stop until the earth mother was happy again.

Adam said can These wolves be stopped any way. No my grand said it was their job and it wouldn't stop until it was over. Mike said maybe this group was the reason the white wolfs came. Adam said no it for the female she gave birth. Mike said how would you know this? Adam said the female told use this. Mike said you been into Fred beer Adam. Adam said no she down stairs with her baby right now. Mike said your shitting me? No Peter said she down there. Mike said can I see her? Adam said yes but you can't say anything to anyone. Mike said sure you know me. Adam I will keep it quiet. Ok then follow me and don't do anything fast. Mike said ok and the two went down stairs to the female.

Hope could smell someone different coming. Jean came out and said she told me someone else was coming down with you. Adam walks in and ask if someone could meet she. She said yes but why does you sound of death. Mike said it's Because I put the people in the ground that die around here . Hope said ok you my came out. Mike walked around the corner and said my God there did make a human no wonder the white wolfs kill them. Hope said and they will be back for me and the kids. Mike said sorry I can't help.

Hope said that's ok I know it must be done. Mike said thanks for letting me came down I got to get the bodies back to town and fit them to be burned. Hope said did one of them have a wheel chair. Mike said yes why? Hope said good the night mare is die with him. Adam said is this the one how started all this. Yes he the one how made all of use now he die the pain we Stops I can die happy now. Jean said we going to try to keep that form happen if we can. Mike said you can't stop the spirt wolfs. There are from the great spirt.

Mike said will got to go and Adam and Mike went back to the car. The other said will we can go back down stairs with the laptops now an see what we can do. The group when back down stairs and start to look around the web to see if they could find anything about the white wolfs. Devvan said I got something here it's off the Penobscot Indian web page. Devvan said it said just about the same thing as Mike said. Devvan said the order to stop the white wolfs yo need to right the wrong that made them come in the first place or to kill the person the sprit wolfs are using to make them real.

Hope said I can't do that it wouldn't be right to kill someone how did really have anything to do with this. Adam said your more human then some of use. Jean said she right but it be say if we kill Hope and the Kids the white wolf would go away. Jean said it doesn't seem fair Because Hope did ask to be here. Fred said so what if the night the white wolfs are to show up we drug Hope and the kids to make them look die. Marry said so the trouble is we have to kill them or the white wolfs will. Hope said I can ask you to do this but I would feel better to die with friends.

Fred said Jean is there a way to make this as painless as we can for her and the kids. Jean said yes we can use the same thing that vets use to put the pet down with. Jean said it would put them to sleep first them stop they heats. Hope said where do we get this drug. Jean said Mike should have it on hand we could ask him to do it. Hope said good then we you do this for me and the kids. Jean said it's going to be hard but it's better then be kill the other way. Hope said ok then let make the best of it and stop think about it. Chase said she right lets make her last day fun.

Chase said who about a claim and lobster bake. Mary said sounds great ok with me. Hope said I don't know but if it's as good as the pizza and beer I like the idea. Fred said you guys know what time it is now. Adam said no and looks at his watch dam 12:30 am. Devvan said ok then we can do that in the morning how about ice cream. Peter said maybe we should ask Jean first before we just do something. Jean said I'm cool with it we can all move into pond room and sleep they're tonight.

The group moved into the pond room Jean bought a few blankets so the baby wouldn't have to sleep on the grass. Hope and the baby's curl up on the blanket and Jean put a blanket over Hope. The other though it was a dam shame that she had to die for something she didn't do. Annette and Adam curls up in the grass the place was warm and it did take long before everyone was sound a sleep. The group even forgot about the ice cream.

Dannie was hoping her dreams would be for something good but how good can it be if you have to kill a child. Dannie start in an open field this one she didn't know. All the people that were killed were there asking her to end there pain soon. Dannie said she would help and do what she could the stop the pain. The bodies held up two babies and said kill them and set use free to go home to God. Dannie said is this the only way to free you. The bodies said yes the wolf's children and their Mom must die.

Dannie was walking over to the babies and looking at them she said you don't know how much this is going the hurt me. She break the necks of the two babies and set down on the ground and howl and cried. A voice came to her be strong little one the time is almost here. Dannie said father do the little ones have to die. The voice said yes children they do I have shown you what we happen to the human race if this animal is aloud to live. Dannie said this is that will happen or my happen. Will my child the voice said the human race will no longer move on the face of earth every again? Dannie said ok that I must do it father then you will be done. Thank you Dannie two more nights is the full moon the voice said and it will be all over then.

Why the full moon father why then Dannie said? Because you and Max's love will be the strongest. Dannie said ok father then it shall be. Good my child go on be happy for it's a good thing you do. Dannie was standing there with the two babies at her feet and said I wish this would have never happen. Just then the female wolf showed up you kill my babies you bitch . Dannie said it has to be so I shall have to kill you.

The female said only if you can get me first the female turned and ran. Dannie headed out after her and the two seen to be running for the island. Why do we keep going back to the island ? The female jumped in the water and swam for the island. Dannie jumps in to the water and headed after her. The two got out and ran to the grave yard area. The female turned and faced Dannie ok now we fight. Dannie said why here why this place? The female said your father didn't tell why this place was so special.

No why is it so special? The female said close your eyes and when you open them you will see why it's is the place I choice to die. Dannie close her eyes and open them again the island was charge into a beautiful garden, but not just and a beautiful garden. Dannie was standing in the middle for the garden of Eden. And the tree of life was right beside her. Dannie said so this is where the fall of man took place. The female said yes that's why no one lives here and that's why I choice to die here. Dannie said is it true is this where we started from.

The voice said yes my children's life started here and man fell from grace here. In the end times man will return the be judged here. The female said now you can kill me that you know the trust that is to came. The female knee and Dannie broke her neck and ripped her head off. She place the body under the tree of life and said going and be judged. Dannie wakes up and set up in bed Max eyes open and said is there something wrong hun? Dannie said no Max just a dream.

Max set up and hug her and she lay back down and rounded up to Max. Max slipped off to sleep again but Dannie lay there think about the dream. Dannie was wandering what it all means how was her and Max's love going to get strong in two days and was this the bring of the end of man. Dannie slowly fell back to sleep but the dream was still fresh in her head.

Adam got up and Annette and some of the others were already up. Hope and the babies seem to be resting good. Adam got up and went out the kitchen the woman were cooking a big breakfast for everyone. Adam walks in and kisses Annette you guys have been busy this morning. Annette said we wanted to make should Hope and the babies were feed. Adam said good She was still sleeping when I left. Coco came around the corner. Jean said hi their hun You sleep good. You like the new little ones Jean bent down and picked her up.

Adam said look I think she has friends the two babies were nude and following Coco. The girls said were your mommy this morning. Hope started to make soft and little howling noises, the babies heard her and heard back the pond room. Mom was up and the girls bought in the food for Hope and the kids. Hope said as the two babies came to her you two hungry. Jean said we make some thing for you and the babies to try. Wow Hope said it smells good. Jean and the women sat down the help Hope feed the kids. Mary laugh Eve can really eat good and Adam seems to love bacon. Hope said there where hungry little ones aren't they.

Annette said Hope you should eat to you need something to keep up with these two. Hope looked at every thing and said I don't know where to start. Jean said try some eggs they are fresh this morning. The bacon is nice to if Adam leaves you some. The others got up and watched as the three had food. Adam told the men theses coffee on in the kitchen. Hope smell the air is that like the beer I had. Adam said not put it is good and it helps to wake you up. Adam said try a drink but it hot so don't drink it fast. Hope smell the steam from the cup and tried the coffee and handed the cup back to Adam. Hope said will that's some thing I don't like. Adam laughs It does have a kick to it. Hope said you human eat some funny things. Fred said will if we going to make a meal for dinner then we need to do some shopping. Adam said ok me and you can go an the others cans stay here to see if they can find anything on the internet. Jean said stop and ask Mike about the drugs . Adam said ok and him and Fred headed out the door to Adam's tuck.

Adam said we going to have to stop at the bank so I can get some money. Fred said ok and the two stop at the credit union and Adam went in to get some money. Fred said as Adam got back it that the fish man just went throw. Adam said great then lets hit him first then. Adam turned around and headed to where the fish man set up. Adam pulls in and the man was just about to set up when he saw the two. He said hi to Fred and Adam and said looks like a fast day today.

Adam said could be how many clams do you have? The man said 100 lbs. And soft shell lobster. Adam said we take the clams and 10 lobsters if you have him. The man said yup would you like a thing else. Adam said no and payed the man. Fred said you want me to pay for some for this? Adam said no you can get the beer and butter for the clams. Fred said good and they went to the store and Fred got two case for beer and some real butter for the calm.

Adam said wow all we got to do is to stop at Mike's and ask him about the drugs. Fred said it's sad we have to do it this way I like Hope and he kids. Adam said yes but if we can't find a way to stop the white wolfs it better this way. Fred said you're right. Adam stop at Mike and went into speak to him. Mike said he had more then they would nice to do the job. Mike said this is good I was hoping to see the female and speak to her again. Adam said stop by tonight she would welcome seeing you again.

Dannie got up and Max was still sleeping she round over and kiss him . Max open his eyes and said good moving hun. Dannie set up and said I will be right back hun she got up and went to the bathroom. She had a bad feeling and she throw up. Max heard her and said you ok hun. Dannie said yup as her throw up again. Max was thinking I hope she has morning sickness. Dannie came back out and said will I think we need to go get a test. Max said you think so wow he jumped out of bed like a school kids.

Max hug Dannie and said do you want me to run out for one while you rest. Dannie said ok and Max got his pants and shirt on and kisses Dannie and almost ran all the way to his truck. Dannie said I hope its is he would be so disappoint if it wasn't that . Dannie lay back on the bed and though of how good of a Mom she would make. Then it hit her the dream said she would be her strongest in two days. Dannie said how strong it would be if she was. Because the most powerful love was when a man and a woman were going too gave birth. Dannie smiled it got to be true then. Max came back throw the door and gave the test to her.

Dannie said ok as she read the test and went in the other room to do it. It was about ten minutes and she came back out and said will Dad your kids can swim. Max was jumping around like a nut yelling I'm a Dad and kissing Dannie and hugging her. Dannie said I know what we can do she got on the bed and got the phone. Max said you calling your Mom and Dad to tell him? Dannie said yes. Max said I'm going to run down stairs and learn on the other phone. Dannie said ok. Max ran down and pick up as Dannie was saying hi to her Mom.

Dannie said Max has something to say to you and Dad. Mom yell to Dad and he came to the phone the both were listening ok Mom said we're both here. Max said do you want to tell them hun. Dannie said no go for it. Max said ok you are going to be grand parents. The phone went quiet Mom started to yell and Dad will it took it laying down. Dannie said ok Mom and is Dad ok. Mom was laughing and yelling yup he out like a light. Dannie said is he ok. Mom said yes he fell into his chair. Max said I'm sorry I didn't think he would react like that. Mom said that's ok he did that the last time he heard about a baby.

Mom said I'm happy for the two of you and I will call you back after I hose your Dad down. Dannie said love you Mom. Mom said we love you two hun and you to Max. Max said thank and he hung up he phone and ran back up stair and grad Dannie and kisses her. Max was in another world with this new. Dannie said you happy with the news hun. Max said yes, yes, yes And hug her again. Dannie said good I'm glad for use to. Max said I'm going to take a shower care to jeon me. Dannie said the baby shower isn't for a while. Dannie said race you there and the two went to the shower.

Adam and Fred returned to Fred's house and called the group out to help with The food. Adam went out back with the drugs and told jean and Hope how they worked. Adam looked at the kids on the floor playing with Coco and said dam this isn't fair. Hope said but Adam you and Jean and the others gave me a charge to enjoy my children. Now anything that happens now is joy as I see it. Adam got up and kisses

Hope on the forehead and said you would make a great human. Hope eyes water thank you Adam, Hope said Jean your right he is a nice man.

Adam went back to help the others with getting things ready for Hope and the kids pretty. Fred said to the girls if you want to go back and be with Hope and the kids use guys can handle the food. Annette said sure and Mary said what would be nice. Peter said yes the women's should be together at a time like this. Annette and Mary with back and the kid were sleeping on the grass with Coco curled up beside them. Adam said it only one more full day and Hope and the kids will be die. Peter said I'm trying not to think of it so can we took about some thing else.

Fred said I could get the book on the Baxter gold and show you. Chase said that would be a better thing to work on. Adam said we can do that but let do this thing for Hope. So did we find anything more about the white wolfs that we could use. Peter said no we found only what we know that Mike said about them. Devvan said we can get the food ready now and put it in the warmer to keep it hot. Coco came around the corner and right behind her was Adam and Eve. The ladies were right behind them. Devvan sat on the floor and said you two getting hungry are you.

Jean said I think they just want to look around. Fred said where's Hope and the others. Hope is in the pond and Mary and Annette are with her. Peter said how's she doing Jean. Jean said good knowing she and the kids only have one more night. Fred said but she's ok with it those? Jean said yes she enjoying the time they have left. The babies and Coca head for the living room. The babies like watching the fish throw the floor. Jean though it was funny how there try to get them.

Jean said come, Coco let's go see mom and what she doing. The four of them went back to the pond room and Hope was drying off. The kids came over to mom and wanted to her to pick them up. She bent down pick up all three of them Coco to. Hope said you having fun with the kids little one. Jean said she really likes the kids. Hope said it seems they know what each other is thinking. Annette said it could be true I remember my Dad saying we were able to speak to all animals at one time but we lose it after we fell from Gods grace. Hope said do I smell something good cooking. Jean said yes the men will be done with it soon and we can eat out here and have fun.

Dannie and Max got out of the shower and Max got ready for work. Dannie got dress so she could go in town to she her doctor. Max said you got plans for dinner today? Dannie said no if I can get out of the doctor on time we can eat together. Max said great and hug Dannie and kisses her. Max said I got to run so see you later hun I love you. Dannie said see you at noon. Dannie walks out with Max to his truck and there kiss and Dannie said be careful to day Dady. Max smiles You do the same Mommy. Dannie watches as Max drove out and she went to her truck and got in and headed to town.

The day was great Dannie was a Mom and Max was the Dad. Dannie when up to the town of Millinocket her doctor's office was next to the car dealer at the edge of town. Dannie pulls into the white birch mental building and parked out back. Dannie walks in and checked in with the nurse. The nurse ask Dannie if she could help her . Dannie said yes I think I'm going to be a Mom. The nurse said so you need a test to find out if you are or not . Dannie said yes and I hope it's yes.

The nurse said we can fit you in about a half hour if you want to wait. Dannie said yes I will have a seat and wait. The nurse handed Dannie a hand full for paper work to fill off and a clips board and pen. Dannie sat down in the waiting room and started to fill out the paper work. Dannie looked at the paper work and said dam they want too know just about every thing they can about you. Dannie spend 20 minutes fill out the paper work then she returned it to the nurse. The nurse said have a seat and the doctor should be with you shortly.

Dannie sat down and watches the birds in the feeders out side she enjoyed see the different type of birds. The sun was warm coming throw the window and Dannie almost fell to sleep. The nurse came out and said to Dannie the doctor will see you now. Dannie got up and went with the nurse to see the doctor. The doctor said please have a seat Dannie. Dannie sat on the table and the doctor said so you going to be a Mom will great I will test you to make sure .

The doctor made her get undress and put on a robe. The doctor gave her the test and said she could put her cloths back on and an wait for the test the be done. Dannie got dress and sat on the table. It was about ten minutes and the doctor came back and said will you're right your going the be a Mom Dannie. Dannie smiled at her and said Max is going to be so happy. The doctor said great to many young woman cross my door not want to be a Moms. Dannie said no I want this baby and Max does to. Good the doctor said will you are all set just see the nurse and she will tell what you need to know.

Dannie was happy she hug the doctor and said thanks. Dannie went out front the n and the nurse handed she some paper work on how to have a heathy baby. Dannie said good bye and went to her jeep. Dannie was going to run right back to see Max and tell him but said she had to stop somewhere first. Dannie drove out and went to the Dollar store. She got a female and male out fit and pay for them. Dannie got back into her jeep and headed to tell Max the good news. Dannie got back to the bar and went in and sat at the end until Max looked up and saw her.

Adam came back with a big plate full of fried clams. Hope said what are these things Jean? Jean picked one up and said There called fried calms. Hope said smell good and she picked one up and put it in her mouth. Hope face said it all. She loved the things. The kids came over and had same to the kids loved them. Mary said it's funny to see new born's eating real food. Peter came in with a few lobsters. Hope looks at them and said how you eat this thing? Peter said watch me and I will show you. Hope watch Peter brakes the lobster up and eat the meat from the thing.

Hope said I think I can do it and got water in her face the group started to laugh. Hope looked at them and said is that the way it should work. Chase said you can't eat lobster without getting it on you. Hope tries the meat it was sweet and very different to her. Devvan said so Hope do you like sea food. Hope said yes this is good. Fred said for supper tonight the girl are going to cook hamburger and ringing rings. Bob said the kids can really put the food away can't they. Hope said we keep eating like this we will get big. The kids were done and went over and curled up next to Coco how was sleeping in the grass.

Hope said I hope Coco is going to be ok when me and the kids are gone she sure like the kids. Jean said I was thinking the same thing we may have to get other dog for her to play with. Fred said we will see how she does than if she needs a friend we will get one. Hope said wow I'm full I can't eat any more I think the kids have a good idea. The group cleaned up the food and all came back in and Hope and the kids were sounded to sleep. Jean turned and hugged Fred she said it's sad that tomorrow night is the last night we will see them.

The hold group could feel for her but couldn't do anything to stop what was going to happen. Adam said lets let them rest and came back when they are awake to enjoy the time we had with them. Annette said yes what's true we can't help them but we sure can make it fun for them the last days. Adam said Annette feel like making a cheese cake for the group for tonight meal. Annette said a bet Hope will go nuts over it. Adam said me and you can go get what we need and began it back. Peter said you know we haven't even taken a picture of Hope and the kids.

Jean said I have a camera and we can take picture tonight when everyone is here. Fred said cool will we going to need hamburger and onion. Adam said me and Annette can get that when were out for the cheese cake things. Chase said you think we should get a few beers for Hope. Jean said I don't like it but why not she should enjoy herself. Adam said ok will we will see you in a few. Adam and Annette when to the local store and got the food they need for the meal that night. At the check out the cashier said you cooking for an army. Adam said not just a wolfman and the two laughs.

Max headed down to Dannie and said is it a baby. Dannie said with a big smile and show the outfits to Max you going to be a Daddy. Max was so happy he started to yell and grads Dannie and hugs her. Max said a round of drink on the house the bar was cheering for Max and Dannie. Dannie said so I'm going to run up and call Mom and Dad and tell them ok. Max said sure will be up in an hour or so. Max hug Dannie and kiss her and said I love you. Dannie said I love you to Max. Dannie went up stairs to use the phone to call her Mom and Dad.

Dannie call Mom and Dad to tell him the good news. Dad said hi and Dannie said hi grandpa. Dad said hi hun me and Mom are so happy for you and Max. Dannie said thanks Dad. Dad said so how did Max take the news? Max did better than I though he would he jumped and yelled he was a Daddy all morning. Dad said great and your Mom wants to speak to you love you hun. Dannie said love you to Dad. Mom got on and said so it's true I'm a grandma. Dannie said yup the doctor said it's a baby.

Mom said so what you want boy or girl? Dannie said I would be happy with both. Mom said that's good I didn't care myself as long as you were ok. Dannie said I feel the same way can't wait to start buying thing for the baby. Mom said we will have to take the gust room and make it into a baby room. Dannie said yup just as soon as we know if it's a boy or girl. Mom said I'm so happy for you. Dannie said I'm going to take a nap so see you maybe this week end if Max has some time off love you Mom. Mom said love you to hun and tell Max good job and kiss him.

Dannie hung up the phone and feel really sleepy and went in for a nap. Dannie fell to sleep every fast she could help it. Her dream started back on the island with her two sisters wolfs. A light show in the center of them and a voice came from the light. My children this is the last night before we have to do our job. You done great so far but tomorrow night is the real test you need to be strong. The female and two kids have to die if not the world of man we come crashing down around them.

The voice said Dannie you are at your strongest tomorrow the child you carry will make you unstoppable. The voice said you will name her baby Kaci a name of great women. Dannie said it's a girl thanks you father for that. Now children you stand on the place were mankind started it fitting that the that you see the way this place looked before the fall of man. The island charge before their eyes to and beautiful garden and the shy was so clear. Dannie said is that the tree of life father. The voice said yes Dannie and when man is free from sin again he will eat from the tree and know all there is the know.

The voice said I have plans to start mans judgement soon so he knows I love him. Dannie said thank you father for all you have done. The voice said go and sleep for tomorrow man lives or dies. The light without an Dannie could feel herself floating in the air back to Max's home. Max came in and kiss Dannie and said I love you sleepy head. Dannie open her eyes and said her name is going to be Kaci. Max said how do you know it's a girl. Dannie said a voice told me. Max said dreaming again hun and kisses her and lay down beside her.

Adam and Annette returned from the store and unloaded the food. Annette comes throw the door and said are the kids up. Mary said no her and the kids are sleeping still. Adam put the food in the kitchen and Annette started her cheese cake. Jean came out to see how everything was going she said to Adam we need to speak. Adam said sure and kissed Annette and said he be right back. Adam and Jean went to the lab. Adam said ok Jean what's wrong? Jean said I can't give the kids the spot to kill them. Adam said we need someone to. Jean said I can't do it.

Adam said I will if you show me how to do it. Adam didn't know Hope was awake and could hear what they were saying she know that it was up to her the kill hear and the kids she wouldn't want one of her new friends to have to live with it. Jean showed Adam how to give the shots and Adam said dam this is going to be hard. Jean said I know that's why I can't do it. Ok then Jean when the time comes I will do it. Hope know she couldn't let Adam do it.

Jean and Adam returned to the others to see if Hope and the babies were awake. Everyone sat on the lawn and had fun with the kids. Jean said where

Fred? Fred said I'm back he came throw the door carrying a book. Jean said if you going to look at the old book for those dumb gold coins set here and enjoy the kids to. Hope said what is gold? Fred said gold is a metal that man look for that's worth a lot of money. Hope looked fun money now what that? Fred laugh money is what the people of the earth use to get thing like food and cloths.

Hope said you don't hunt to eat? Fred said no we hunt for the fun of it now. Adam and Annette had getting done with the cheese cake and came into the pond room to see Hope and the kids. Adam looked at Fred and said is that the coin book. Fred said yes we were going to look at it. Adam and the other sat down with Hope and the kids. Mary was looking just lightly at the book as the men looked at the pages, but she was more with watching Coco and the kid's play. Fred took out the coin from his pocket and place it where it came out from in the book.

Mary looked at the coin again. Said oh my God ! Fred said what Mary do you know some thing. Mary said the coins I know where they are. Everyone looks at her and said how do you know that? Mary said let me see the book and coin. Mary turns to the page of the island Mary looked and start to smile. Well Adam said you want to tell use. Mary turned the book around and the team was looking at a shot of the island from the sky. The team said so it the island. Jean eyes open your right Mary the coins are on the island. Now the others said ok out with it. Jean said go for it Mary. Mary said why is it the only picture in the book is shows a view from the shy. Fred said because someone want you to look at the island. Mary but why she said. Annette said Medway it an Indian name for where to river meet.

The Team said yes the clue were two limbs meet. Mary said yes the two rivers are branches for a river in the middle is the island and at their feet is the graves of the river drivers. Adam said yes but where at their feet. Mary said under the foot stone that has the seal on it and she turned the coin around this seal. Fred said my God your right Mary it's been right in front of me all this time. Chase said now. All we have to do is see if it is still there then. Fred said it's been there all this time it can wait one more day then. Fred said this is Hope and the kids time.

Dannie said how was your day hun? Max said great now that Daddy's home and hugs Dannie. Max said you want to go to Lincoln for supper tonight. Dannie said can. We go to china light. Max sad yup never been there, but will try it out to see what it's like. Dannie said it's good I have had a lot of food from that place. Max said ok then I will hit the shower and get ready. Dannie had other plans' she grad Max as he was trying to get up and pull him back down and make love to him. Max was happy and made love to her then got up after and when into the shower.

Max came out and Dannie said she was out on the porch. Max said you ok hun she said yup I'm just getting some air. Max said I'm all set you want to go now. Dannie said yup lets do it. Dannie and Max when down to the truck and got in to went to Lincoln. Max was pulling out of the drive way and Dannie's Mom and Dad were pulling in. Max stop and round down the window and said we going to get some thing to eat care to come. Mom said yup but we will have to take my car. Max back around the building and got out with Dannie.

Mom and Dad got out the hug Dannie and Max. Dannie said so you to are really happy then Mom said yes. Max said good. Her name is going to be Kaci. Dad said you know it's a girl how you are only a few days in. Dannie said I heard it in a dream. Dad looked at Mom she your kid all right. Dannie said why you say that Dad? Dad said your Mom said the same thing when we know of you. Mom smile so let's go and eat. Max Dad said you can drive I don't feel like it.

Max got into drive and headed out to Lincoln. The ride down Mom was thinking about how they could redo the guest room for the baby. Mom said to Dannie think for what to do with the baby's room. Dannie said not sure but going to have a while to think about it. Dad said so where we going for food? Dannie said to china light. Dad said good. I wanted to try that place. Mom said I hear it's good. Max pulls off the ramp and headed to town. Dannie said as they pull into the town this would be a nice town if it wasn't for the smell.

Max said the mills keep these little towns up and running. Dannie said I know but it just would be better. Max said yes as he pulls into china light. The group went in and sat down to eat. Dannie said I want a Pu-Pu planter. Max said make it for two. Mom and Dad said make it for five and we will share it with you. Max said five Dad said yes it will give use left overs. Dad look at Dannie and you could see tears in his eyes. Dannie said you ok Dad? Dad said yes just my baby going to have a baby. Mom hug him You old softy you are just like Max.

The waiter came up and Max said we will have a Pu-Pu planter for five and three beers and a soda for my wife. Dannie said that's right can't drink now. She said I will have a coke please. The waiter went out and returned with the drinks and said your order will be up soon. The waiters' bought out the food and there sat and tried to think how to paint the baby's room. Max said a light yellow with and power blue trim. Dannie stopped and said I can see that and I think it would look great. Mom said you know I think your right hun. Dannie said are you two staying for a day or two.

Adam said will we know where the gold is now lets find the food. Annette said I can do the onion ring how wants to do the hamburger. Fred said we can round the barbarQ out and cook them right out here. Mary said I can help with the onion rings if you need it. Annette said sure it would be nice. Chase Said Hope would you like a beer. Hope said yes you mean the stuff that makes your head funny. Yup that the stuff Chase said. Jean said don't let her drink too much now you guys. Chase got some beers for group. Fred got the barbarQ out and started it.

Annette and Mary went in and got the onion rings going. Peter said so how are we going too told when we need to do things tomorrow night. Hope said it has to been done before midnight when the moon is at its highest point. Adam went out to get the hamburger and help Fred with the cooking. Chase and Devvan got up and went out the got plates and things for the table. Hope looked at Peter and said after tomorrow night you guys burn owner bodies can you do something for me Peter? Peter said sure what that? Take the rest for use and put it back on the island.

Peter said yes it would be my honor to do so. Hope said thanks and she was going to miss all of them. Jean said can You tell me why you guys choice the island when everyone else stay away from it. Hope said you do know what the island is. Jean said is it some thing different about that one island? Hope started to laugh a little. I will tell you but we will wait until we all set down. Jean said dam I can't wait to hear this. Fred turned around the meat is done. Peter said I will check on the others to see how they are doing. Peter went out into the kitchen and everyone was ready to headed back to the pond room.

The group sat every thing on the table and showed Hope how to fit a hamburger in a bun and eat it. Will hope Fred said you going to tell the story. Hope said there not much to say but that the island is where man started his life. The group looked at her and said how do you know this. When you go to the island, close your eyes then open them and you will see what I mean. Jean said it does make sense God did say that man wouldn't live in the garden until the day of judgement. Chase said I think I need another beer. The group was quiet and didn't real know what to believe. This story Hope said is true in a few days you we know.

Jean said I can't go there to see it that's to bad. Fred said we can always go at night to the island. Hope said no never do that. Devvan said why Hope? The dead ones run the island at night and will kill everyone oh try to sleep there. Jean said why didn't you get hurt by them. Because we away left for the main land before the hour their walk the land. Bob said so shooting the rocket on the island wasn't what make you leave. Hope said no the man were about to walk. Fred this is better then your stories every could be. Fred said you got me there, but now I can tell this ones .

The group cleaned up and set near the pond until Annette said oh you know we didn't have cheese cake. Hope said chesses cake. Annette said came and I will show you. The group got up and went into the kitchen and said as she pulls it out of the ice box. This is cheese cake Hope and Annette gave everyone a slice. Hope put a small peace in her mouth and said this is good can I have more then this. Annette said sure Hope and put a big slice on her plate. The group returned to the pond room and Hope let the kids try some of it. The kids loved it and that make Annette really happy to see children enjoying her cooking again. After the food and dishes were put away the group called it a night and crashed in the pond room.

Mom said sure we were going to help you set up the baby room to if that's ok with Max. Max said sure we all can do something with it. Will Dad said the food was great but I'm getting sleepy now are we going back to the house after here? Max said yes after we stop for ice cream. Mom said that sounds like a plan. The group payed for their food and went for ice cream. Dannie drove on the way home and Dad was sleepy he fell to sleep on the way back.

Dannie drove into the drive and got out and open Dad's door he wakes up and said wow he must have been sleepy. The group went into the house and Mom and Dannie went out to the back porch. Max and Dad went into see what was on the tv. The night was bright the moon almost full. You could feel a cool chill in the air. Mom said hun we are very happy for you two and hope you to have a long life together. Dannie said if its as good as you're then I think we will do good. Mom and Dannie hugs and went back to see the men.

Dad was out cold and Max was will on his way to. Mom said look the two kids are almost to sleep. Dannie said I will help you get Dad to the pull out if you need to. Mom said just put a blanket on him and I will get him there after. Mom said you better get Max up stairs before he falls to sleep. Dannie came around to the couch and kissed Max come on sleepy and we will go up stairs. Max got up and said good night to Mom and went with Dannie up stairs.

Dannie sat Max on the bed and strip him nude now hun get in bed and I will be right back. Dannie went into the bathroom to do her teeth and then back out and got undress and got in bed with Max. Max seemed too came back to life as he felt Dannie's nude warm body on his. Dannie make love to Max and they fell to sleep. Dannie was happy one more night for the dreams and she should be free to dream about Max and her.

Dannie felt herself on the island once again but this time it was different she feel something evil around her. The smell for ash and sulfur as if hell was on earth. A man with a hood came to her and said you will fight her tomorrow night. Dannie said yes but who are you the face couldn't be seen but it looked like fire and hot metal. I'm her father and she is my child. Came fight with me and we can rule the world. Dannie said I don't need to rule the world it's for my father to do. The man said your father is not here why is he chicken. Dannie said he fares no man.

The man laugh I'm no man I'm he how walk the dark of hell. Dannie said then go back to hell because you will see your child there soon. The man said don't be sure because human are protecting her as we speak. Dannie said then they will have to die just as the once how made her did. Then Dannie said that shows how weak she is and you are. An light came down from heaven and a voice with the light said be gone Satan for she is working for me and she will kill the other as I told her to. The man turned into flares and went into the ground. The voice in the light said you did good Dannie now going and rest for the fight tomorrow. The light went and Dannie was back in her room with Max.

Hope got up and part of the group was up and some were still sleeping. Hope looked at her children laying there round up with Coco and felt sad. Hope know it was he last day and she was in a way happy the running was over, but not at the cost for her kids and her life. Mary and Jean where up and was going into the kitchen to get coffee and food started. Hope got up and went in the pond for a swim until the babies got up. Hope like the feel of the cold water and it made she feel free if only for awhile.

Jean and Mary were in the kitchen and Annette and Adam came in. Adam said need any help with breakfast. Jean said yes you can watch the bacon and Annette can help with the French toast if she wants. The food was ready in no time the group move the food to the pond room. Hope was out of the pond and the others where all awake. Hope said it smell good. Hope sat on the ground next to the table on order to feed the kids. Hope said the food is good the kids love it. Fred said I'm just glad we could make their time here good. Hope said I can't thank you for all you people have done.

Hope said I only wish I could die on the island. Adam said if you want that we could set it up for you. Hope said you already done too much for me now. Jean said I wouldn't be able to go because of the sun. Hope said if you went at night you could be hurt or kill by the die that walk the island. Peter said we could show her how to use to drugs and put her on the island before dark. Chase said sure It wouldn't be any trouble at all. Mary said in the morning we could go and take care of the bodies. Hope said you would do this for me and the kids. The team said sure you want to die that way it's you free will to. Hope said I don't want you to help me, but I don't want you to have to live with having to do it.

Jean said we understand and if you want it after lunch this noon then we'll see to it. Hope said ok then Jean can you show me how to do this drug thing and will it hurt. Jean said no it will put you to sleep then after a wait stop your heart. Hope said it sound ok then. Jean said I will show you a little later right now let enjoy the time we have together. Devvan said should the babies and Coco be so close to the water. Hope said the babies should be able to swim, but can Coco? Jean said I don't know so Jean and Hope with over to the water to make should they didn't get hurt.

The team got up and clean the food and dish's up and returned to watch to kids play in the water with Coco. Bob said in my wildest dream would I every seen any thing like this. Annette said yes it is really a once in a life time thing. Coco got out of the water and shock out. The babies follow her and Jean dried them off. Jean said to Hope we can go into the lab and I can show you how to use the drug and the others can watch the kids for you. So Jean and Hope went to the lab. Jean said it's really not that hard the do you stick the needle in the arm a little ways and push on the back here and it put the drug in your system. Hope said we you set the drug up in the needles for me. Jean said yes and I will put them in a small case to so they don't get broken. Hope hug Jean and Jean hug her back it will be over in just a few after the shots are in. Hope said thanks Jean. Jean said it's ok and the two went back to the pond room.

Dannie wakes up she was feeling a little sick but not bad, she could stop thinking of what was going to happen tonight and if she could kill the kids for real. Will she said that's up to tonight so she put in the back of her mind? She could feel Max warm body. She move up and got closer to him. She runs her hand across Max's chest and could feel the heat. Dannie was getting turned on and Max started to get up. Dannie put her hand on Max's third leg and started to play. Max's eyes opened and said good morning hun. Max round over and kiss her and they made love for an hour. Dannie said after that she was going to see how they could do in the baby's room today.

Max said good he want to see the size of the room and see how the paint would look to. Dannie said we not going to paint today are we. Max said no we need to clean the walls off and fit all the little holes first. Max said do You have a place for the bed in the room. Dannie said I have a storage unit out on the side of the house we can put it in with the other things. Max said we got to think of getting my thing over here to so we can rent my place. Dannie said will we be bring all it here? Max said no the dresser and chairs and things like that I will leave there just cloth and paper work. Ok Dannie said lets get a shower and go down for coffee.

Max said the shower seems to be in use right now. Dannie sat up and said yup your right so let's make out some more. Max said you don't have to ask me twice. Dannie and Max made out until the shower was open. Max and Dannie got their shower and headed down to see Mom and Dad and the coffee pot. Mom said hi you two didn't think you be up so soon. Dannie said we sleep good and we want to check out the baby's room this morning before Max when to work. Max said the coffee is good this morning. Dad said thanks I made it.

Dannie grads a fruit and went to the spare room. Max was right behind he with Mom and Dad. Dannie open the door and said wow I haven't been I have for a long time the room seems bigger then it was. Max said this is going to make a great kids room. Mom said you could leave the bed in here and just work around it. Dannie said it's going into storage unit next to the house. Max said may I do the painting and you guys do the fitting it up. Dannie said you sure you want to the colors you want are good, but can you do a good job with the painting.

Max said trust me. The paint job will take you by surprise. Mom look at Dannie and Dannie said ok it's all you're to paint. Dad said a man can be soft and caring if he needs to. Mom said oh no Dannie the men are going too soft on use. Max said I can start after work tonight fill the holes and getting the walls tape off. Dannie said ok big man you got to get moving to work Dannie kisses him and they went out to his truck, but open the door and remember the car was the only thing here. Dannie yelled Dad your going to have too given Max a ride to work. Dad said ok and came down and told Dannie don't move any thing big I can do it when I get back. Dannie gave them both and kisses and said ok.

Dad gave Max a ride into the bar and Max said thanks and went into the bar. Dad returned to town the pick thing up for Max like tape and thing to get the room ready for paint.

Adam said speaking of lunch what do we get your for the meal Hope? Hope said the pizza thing would be nice again. Chase said we could have Rick's bring it out and have Hope get the door. Fred said we don't want to make him shit his pants. The group laughed and sat there watching the kids play with the dog. Jean said maybe we should make the pizza order and it should be here bout 11:00 Am? Peter said I will call it in and go get it. Annette said this real bits big time why should we gave up on our friend when we can fight. Adam said the guns are no good again something that isn't real.

Hope said don't worry your self it's will come to an end with your help or not and I don't want to see any more friends hurt . Annette said I'm Sorry Hope but it just to me it seems to be another scentless killer. The group said yes it does but your know if it doesn't happen man kind will die out. Bob said we made her why not take want we made and let it do its thing. Annette said does mankind ready think it safe after she die. Annette said who's to say some nut down the road isn't going to do the same thing over again. Adam said I hear you but God does have the final plan for use and he trying to right mans mistakes. Hope said it sounds like you people are mad at the other humans.

Hope said it's hard to understand how man made it this far. Chase said see someone from the outside know we are as dumb as mud.

Peter said I'm going to run out for the food now should be right back soon. Peter went out to his car and headed to town. He was going to the store to get a cake for Hope and the kids. Peter said they will never have a birthday so we can give them one and wish them afar well. The group had stop and sat back to watch the kids before they went. Peter stop at store and had the Names of Hope, Adam and Eve put on the cake. Then he went to get the pizza's. Peter wasn't a soft hearted man the spoke of but he cried over the lose of someone life. Peter returned and ran the pizza's down and said he left something in the car he would be right back. Peter went back up to the car for the cake.

Peter walked in and said happy birthday you three. Hope said what's a birthday? Peter said one a year humans have cake and ice cream to say there are one year older. I got this because we all make a good friend in you and the kids and I want to show you we do real care for one another. Hope's eye water and she cried, I don't know what to say Peter. Peter said look around as everyone was crying to you don't have to Hope. Jean said dam Peter that was nice of you. Hope said is this writing on the cake? Adam said yes it said as he pointed to the words. Happy birthday Hope, Adam and Eve. Hope pick the kids up and said look kids your name are on it.

The group sat the cake on the table and began to eat the pizza. The kids love the meal. Then after the pizza Jean cut the cut and gave two slices to the kids they made a mess. The group laugh at them trying to eat it. Hope said they are some thing aren't they. Bob said just like when Annette had her first cake. Annette said it does bring back some fun time.

Dannie said ok Mom lets brake down the bed and maybe the two stands. We can leave the big dresser for the baby because it's unpainted. Dad got back and said ok what needs to go and what needs to stay. Dannie said bed first and the two night stands. Then we can remove all the pictures and put everything in the center of the room for Max. Dad moved the bed and the stands down to the storage out back then helped move the big thing to the center. Mom and Dannie remove every thing off the walls and pull all the nails out.

Dannie said what time is it I getting hungry? Dad said about 11:00 now. Dannie said lets go see Max and get something to eat I need to go get my truck away. Dad said ok with me. Mom said the same. Dannie and her Mom and Dad went t see Max. Dannie had her Dad pull up out back near her truck. The three went inside to see what was going on. Max was behind the bar and the place was busy of a day like today.

Dannie said what's up today Max? Max kiss Dannie and said don't know everyone is just coming out to enjoy them self. Dannie said so what's good for lunch hun. Max said I made a new dish do you like chicken fingers? Dannie said will yes don't what so good about them. Max said your see and said did your Mom and Dad want to try them to. Mom and Dad looked at each other and said sure. Max said have a seat and I will be right out with them. Dannie sat at the bar and Mom and Dad sat next to her.

Max returns after a few with the new dish. Dannie said it smell good and looked good. Mom cut into hers and a smile came over her face. Max said it looks like one person likes it. Dad said make that two how did you do it? Dannie said hands up all three like the chicken so how you do it hun? Max said I use crackers cheese and eggs and made a dry mix with the cheese and crackers. Max said I put the chicken in the eggs then rolled it in the dry mix then fried it in olive oil.

Dannie said hun. You can put this on the menu I like it. Max kiss Dannie and said thanks hun. Mom said we got everything off the walls and move all the thing she want to keep in the center so you could work on the room at anytime. Max said thanks. Dad said I got you a wall knife and some wall filler to. Good Max said I don't have worry about getting to the hard ware store after work then. Max said I'm going to make you something so be right back. Max came down with Maine cold red chills for them. Dannie looks at him and said you know I can't drink hun. Max said you can this one no alcohol. Dannie takes a drink and said not bad thanks hun.

Max said I ask Vicki if she would want to rent the apartment of mind she said yes. Dannie said I hope you're not charging her too much. Max said 450 a month heats free. Dannie said that a good price. Max said I though we put it into an account for Kaci went she grows up. Dannie said that's a great idea hun. Mom and Dad that sure is a great plan Max. Dannie said me ,Dad and Mom will get boxes at the stores so you can pack this week end. Max said thanks hun and kisses her. They will see you at home tonight hun and kiss him. The three headed to the store for boxes.

Hope could feel it was time to get ready to leave and said will guys you think we should get ready now. The group said ok but you could see they weren't liking it. Adam said ok. We got to do this not for use but for Hope. Mary said lets clean up before we go. Jean said no I need something to keep me busy. Ok Mary said you sure? Jean said yes I'm sure. Adam pulled Fred to the side you will be staying here with Jean she going to need you. Fred said thanks Adam I think she going to have a hard time because Coco is so in love with the kids.

Adam said let go up top and let Jean and the kids say by to Jean and Fred and Coco. Adam kiss Jean and said be strong and we will be back to see you after this is all done. Jean and Hope look at each other Jean said I wish there was some another way. Hope said there isn't and I glad you gave me the time with the kids. Jean said will you take care of them even after she knows what was too came next. Hope eyes water as she kissed Jean and Fred and little Coco. Jean said I will never forget you and the kids. Hope said thanks glad we got to know you to. Hope turned to leave and Fred hugs her and kiss the kids. Hope said good by my friends and thanks for making me and the kids feel human.

Jean started to cry as Hope and the kids walk throw the door for the last time. Hope made it out to the cars and was sad. Peter said hope you and the kids can ride with me. Hope said you don't want me to hide in the back for one of the trucks. Peter said hell No you are a friend now. Hope felt loved Peter gave her a ride to Patrick's boat rental place. Peter pull in and Patrick was in the office. Adam walks in and said we need the boat so we can drop someone on the island. Patrick got up and looked out the window and said shit is that the wolfman.

Adam said no it his mate and the his two kids. Patrick gave the keys to Adam and said you can drive this time. Adam said she isn't mean. Patrick said I better off not leaving here. Adam said ok and loaded the boat for the ride over to the island. The group pull away from the deck and headed down stream to the island. Chase said it not the same is it now that it someone you know. Mary said no and tried to be strong. The group came to the island and hock the boat to a tree so everyone could get off. Hope said I don't know what to say it's been a great few days with you people.

Hope hugs everyone and said will it's time I will see you on the other side . Adam said you don't think we are going to let you die along do you. Hope said you sure you want it this way you guys. Mary said we wouldn't have it any other way. The group went to the spot where Hope was happy. It was the field where she enjoys playing in when she was here.

Hope sat down with the kids and said I guess little ones it's time. Mary said will can help by giving all three for you the drug at he same time if you want. Hope said could you please. Adam, Mary and Chase took the needle and got ready to do it. Adam looks at Hope we all care very much for you and the kids so we will be here until the end. Hope said thanks as the group gave them all the drugs. Adam and Annette held Hope's hand as she slipped away to sleep.

The group sat down the cry and feel bad for Hope and the kids. Adam got the gas and put it on them so that he could make sure that it was done right. Adam lit the fire and Hope and the kids were gone in no time. Bob stopped to think how unfair it was to kill something that shouldn't have been there at all. Chase said lets see if Mary was right about the gold. Peter said it couldn't hurt now Hope would have wanted use to.

The group went to the grave yard and they could feel a chill in the air. Mary looks down see I told you the stone had that mark on it . Peter got down and pulled the small mark up . There was a little black box under the stone . Peter picked it up and handed it to Mary. Peter was replacing the stone when the group heard a voice leave owner island . The group could feel chills run down there backs and a pick poll landed in the middle of the grave yard . Adam said time to leave the group ran back to the boat and left the island . They returned to Fred's to let him open the box . The group was floored when it open to show the 199 others coins . Fred said this is all of owner and we all we get a share of it .

Dannie and Mom and Dad got the boxs and went back to Dannie's house. Dannie went into the house and said you know I feel sleepy right now I think I will get a nap. Mom said me to. Dad said I could use one two. The three went to bed for a nap. Dannie started to dream she could see her self on the island with a fire burning before her. She looked close at it. The Fire it was hope and the kids.

A voice came from up in the clouds so it done little one. The voice said you didn't have to fight her the humans and her did what was needed to bring the side back to equal. Dannie said was this really needed to make it right. The voice said yes little one it was. The voice said now you are free to dream about life now your job for me is done. Dannie said thank you fahter I will do as you say. The night went black and Dannie found her self back home safe and sound.

Dannie was happy she didn't have to kill the kids for real. Max came into the dream and there layed on the sand of some shore and hug. Max said I glad you did your fathers will and kiss her . Dannie could see the sun dropping down and the night slowly work it's way in. Dannie said now life is right and man can go on but for how long will this last.

Five years later Dannie had her kid and Named it Kaci now she getting ready for the second one. Max is still running the bar and Dannie is working part time as a model. Adam, Annette and Bob went off to see all the states, but returned after three years. Adam ran for town manager and won hands down Annette reopen her dinner and Bob will he still cames to see her every day.

Chase and Mary got married and run the police force as husband and wife. Devvan is now the night watch for the town. The dogs are still part for the team and work night and days. Peter worked for the state and retired and is fishing now. Just about everyone else is doing the same thing. The three white wolfs were Dannie , her Mom and her boss Crissy.

The team split the gold up and came away with about ten millions a pease and the rest with to help local poor. Will I wish I could say this was a happy ending, but remeber the finger from the wolfman will it grew and made its way back to the island? Where it went into the soft dirt. The island has a way of making thing started over. The hand grow into a new human and this time look like a man. The hand came out of the ground as the man came to life to start the hell all over again. The end or is it.A person wakes into Dannie's room she looks at Dannie laying there. Dannie knows it's her Mommy . Kaci Dannie's real Mom bents over and picks her up from the crab . Kaci said hi little girl you sleep good last night . I wish I knew what you were dreaming Dannie . Then again maybe not . So the next time your baby sleep maybe she will be dreaming up a book . Dreams can came true and kill you . The end

From the mind of the Sandman.

Written by Allen Daigle